W9-AYW-384

STINKING RICH

STINKING RICH

BY
ROB BRUNET

Down & Out Books
3959 Van Dyke Rd, Ste. 265
Lutz, FL 33558
www.DownAndOutBooks.com

This is a work of fiction. Names, characters, places, and events are either the product of the author's imagination or are used fictitiously. Any similarity to real persons, living or dead, events, or locales is coincidental and not intended by the author.

The author is represented by MacGregor Literary, Inc.

Cover art and design by JT Lindroos

ISBN: 1937-4957-7-9

ISBN-13: 978-1-937495-77-0

For Maria

O God, make me good, but not yet.

—Evelyn Waugh
Brideshead Revisited

ONE

Danny Grant couldn't afford to lose twelve hundred bucks at blackjack, but he did anyway. When he and his pal Lester Freeden had each played their last dollar, drowning themselves in Jack and Cokes while they were at it, they got bounced out of the Great Horned Owl Charity Casino. The towering Ojibwa doing the honors wore a nametag Danny couldn't read.

"What's that say? Eddie? Ettie?" he asked, trying hard to focus.

"Effie," said the bouncer. He yanked Danny off his feet with one hand and dumped him in a planter.

"What kinda name is that?" Lester asked.

"Big Effin' Indian," he answered. "Mister B-F-I to you. Drive straight and slow off the reserve or I'll show you how I earned it."

Danny stood up, teetered a moment, his head cocked to one side until its off-center weight nearly toppled him back into the yucca. Stone-faced, the bouncer said, "You really don't want to know."

Lester nudged Danny's elbow and they stumbled past row after row of seniors' tour buses in the blazing white light of the late night parking lot. When they reached his car, he looked back at the casino. BFI was still watching them.

"You wanna drive my car?" he asked, leaning on Lester's shoulder for balance.

"Sure thing, Danny-ol'-buddy-ol'-pal. I got your back. Least I can do for you." Lester flashed a grin, exposing an extra wide gap where he'd lost two teeth in a bar fight gone bad. "You lean back and relax while I drive us on home. Just call me Jeeves. You must be some tired, sir. Lotta work losing all that dough."

Danny closed his eyes and pretended to snooze until they pulled in at Lester's place, a nineteen-foot trailer perched in a clearing on a plot of land his uncle owned. They pounded back three beers each, listening to Whitesnake and cursing the casino. Danny said he figured the Indians made more money renting colored chips to white gamblers than the settlers had *ever* made trading beads for beaver pelts.

Every two weeks on pay day, Lester would get a lift to the casino from whomever he could. Anything to avoid putting gas in his own car. The man was an incorrigible sponge, but he came by it honestly, born into dirt poor dysfunction. When Danny let him mooch drinks or bum a ride, it was kind of like giving to charity, with the middleman cut out. Besides, this particular Friday, Danny'd had a grand plan to turn twelve hundred bucks into ten thousand at the tables. It hadn't worked out that way.

"Damn Indians are rigging the frigging thing," he said.

"The only person I know who ever wins anything is Terry."

"Terry Miner? That jerk lies his ass off. If he was winning at the casino, you think he'd be holed up in that piece a crap trailer?"

"The hell's wrong with livin' in a trailer?" Lester asked, spreading his arms wide.

"It's not that. Terry's trailer is a shithole is all. Never mind he's just babysittin' the damn thing."

"Ain't you the Queen of Sheba. Think you're somethin' special just 'cause your house has a basement? It's your *mother's* house, numbnuts. Leastways, Terry don't live with his *mommy*."

"Lay off, Lester. You're drunk. Gimme a smoke."

"Get your own cigarette, numbnuts."

And Danny did. He staggered out the trailer to grab a pack of cigarettes from a fresh carton on the dashboard. Lester had left the keys in the ignition, so when Danny opened the car door, the bell chimed. That woke Lester's dog. He perked his ears where he lay under the trailer and started to growl. Danny knew the dog well. Its mangy fur was a mishmash of orangey brown, black, and grey and, as mutts go, it wasn't terribly bright. It had bitten Lester more than once, but the guy kept it around to make sure people stayed away from his trailer. Not that there was much to steal, even when you counted the things Lester had stolen himself.

Scared shitless his shin would be used as a chewy bone by the wacko dog, Danny grabbed the whole carton of Players Special Blend, Kings, and scurried back to the trailer.

"Down boy. Good dog. Lester, Shooter's growling here..."

"Shooter," said Lester, "back off."

Danny pulled the door shut behind him. "I thought you were supposed to keep that stupid mutt of yours chained. The cops said so after he ran those kids halfway to town."

"Yeah, yeah. But he's a guard dog. A boner fide Rottweiler. Mostly anyways. Maybe a bit of wolf in him, according to the guy I bought him off."

"All the more reason to tie him up."

"What good's a guard dog on a chain?"

"Someday they're gonna haul him off and put a bullet in his head. He's seriously messed up. Snarly and everything."

"He ain't no fuckin' Poodle, for sure. But there ain't nobody gonna take him away. I hook him up when I go out. Long enough he can get to the end of the driveway but not so's he wraps round the trees. He listens good, long as I yell. And he's afraid of my big stick. Gimme a smoke, will ya?" And Danny did.

Three beers later, Lester asked the question Danny didn't want to answer: "Where in hell did you come up with that wad of cash tonight?"

"It wasn't much. Just a couple hundred," he lied. "Borrowed most of it from my old lady." Another lie, even if the payday was supposed to be all about her.

"Bullshit. You had over five hundred in chips. I saw."

"Well, yeah, I was winning early on, y'know." That, at least, was true.

"Uh-uh. No way you won that much, numbnuts. I was there."

"So maybe I started with a little more. I dunno. Who the fuck cares? It's all gone now." God's honest truth—hurt like hell.

"Yeah, it's all gone. And you don't seem none too pissed about it neither. You ain't been working in four, five months and unemployment don't pay shit to a guy like you. Where'd you git that money, Dan?"

"I'm telling you, it was just a few bucks. I got lucky is all."

"Lucky, my ass. You walked in there with a wad bigger'n I've ever seen. That's some gig you got, ain't it? Terry said somethin' about a job he got you."

"I ain't got no job. I got the employment insurance and my mom pays me for chores and stuff."

"Buuulll-shit. Don't you go takin' me for a fool."

Danny staggered to his feet and said it was time to leave.

Lester said, "I know you got that dough somewhere, mister-I-don't-cry-about-losin'-nearly-a-thousand-bucks. And it ain't from your mother."

"Getting late. I'm kinda drunk and I still gotta drive home."

"Gimme a break. Your mother's place is barely two miles from here. You could drive it blind."

"And I have. More'n once. But I gotta go. Maybe we can go to the casino again the next time you get paid, eh?"

Danny opened the door and stepped out quietly, so as not to disturb the dog. Halfway to his car, he reached in his pocket for a cigarette.

"Shit," he said, remembering the carton he'd left on the table. He doubled back, but Shooter stirred, snorted, and got to his feet.

"Lester. Your freaking dog again." Danny didn't dare move closer. Shooter had taken a position between him and the door, growling louder and sniffing at the air as if Danny's fear were tantalizing as a rib steak.

"So? Just get in your car," said Lester. "He can't bite through the door, numbnuts."

"Yeah, but I need my smokes. Carton's on the table. Throw it to me, would ya?"

"Nah, I'm kinda too tired to get up, Dannyboy."

"C'mon. Just throw me the smokes."

"Come get 'em yourself." Lester sniggered. Shooter growled, stepping closer.

Danny started to sweat, his stomach clenching. "Tell your fucking dog to back off."

"Good boy, Shooter. Good doggie. Nice guard doggie-woggie. Oh, geez, you left me your lighter, too. What a pal. What a nice rich pal. Kinda guy drops a thousand bucks on blackjack and doesn't give a damn. I sure am a lucky guy to have a friend like you, eh? Whaddya think, Shooter?"

The dog barked. Twice. Loudly.

Danny backed away, then stumbled. He turned and ran the rest of the way to the car. Shooter ran after him, leaping and snapping those hungry jaws. Danny felt a tug at his elbow as he jumped in and slammed the door on Shooter's head. Saliva flung from angry pink and black gums as the dog struggled to yank itself free. Danny released the pressure and the dog pulled back then flung itself at the driver side window. Was the deranged mutt trying to bite the side mirror?

Danny started the car, gunned the engine twice and leaned hard on the horn to piss off Lester. He floored it in reverse down the driveway, peeled his tires, and watched in the rearview mirror as Shooter chased him half a mile up the road.

Next morning, Danny rolled a cold can of Coke back and forth across his forehead. His mother had laid a plate of eggs and toast on the table before darting to her shift at The Boathouse.

"Nice to see you here this morning, hon," she said. "She must be something special, making you slink off days at a time for, what is it, four months now? When are you going to bring her home so I can check her out?"

Guilt twisted Danny's gut. Couldn't his mother be just a little less enthusiastic about his make-believe sweetheart? He should never have dreamt up that part about her studying at Queen's to become an engineer or something. Fact was, Danny hadn't had anything like a real girlfriend since he was sixteen years old. Even then, he was pretty sure nine consecutive nights in a tent with his neighbor's cousin from Montreal didn't count as a relationship. But it was something.

Danny's mother pecked him on the forehead and said, "There's lasagna, but it's for Ernie. Please don't eat more than a slice or two."

He opened the fridge and lifted the foil to peek at the golden-brown melted mozzarella, unable to resist dipping a finger in his mother's sauce. "Want me to drop it over?" he asked. "That'd be sweet," she said. "If you need a little cash, there's some on my dresser. Heavy tippers last night." As she leaned in to give him a hug, Danny heard a rattle in her chest. Much as she fought the cough, it took hold, and she hacked her way out the door.

Her goodbye hung in the air, heavy with the scent of Opium, the late night perfume she seemed able to carry all hours of the day. Wandering into her bedroom, he shifted the can to the back of his neck where it was still cold enough to do some good. He leafed through the stack of fives and tens on her dresser. Nearly two hundred bucks. In the five years since dropping out of high school, he had struggled to get his act together and bring home more than a few dollars for rent now and then. Meanwhile, his mom slogged for tips, wasting away year after year of her life getting her ass pinched in local roadhouses, and all she had to show for it was an aggravated case of asthma. She'd long quit smoking herself and Danny always took his outside. Just about the only decent thing he did, he figured.

He counted out eighty bucks. Enough for a fresh carton of cigarettes. There was already food for the week at the farmhouse where he'd been living while his mom thought he was with the Queen's girl. Half tank of gas in the car. And he'd get the next envelope stuffed with cash in a day or two. This time, he wouldn't blow it.

Turning to leave, he came face-to-face with the picture of his mother tossing him naked into the air, standing waist deep in brilliant blue lake water. She'd made a poster of it for him on his fifth birthday and moved it into her own room when he outgrew it in his.

"Fuck it," he said, throwing the money back on her dresser and opening the Coke. He guzzled it, stomped out of the house, and went to take back his carton of Players Special Blend. Kings.

TWO

Perko Ratwick stood at the kitchen counter in the Libidos' clubhouse and cracked two eggs into a mug of beer. He splashed in some Tabasco sauce and drank the mixture in one long gulp.

"Can't see why you wants to use them Nasty Nancies for protection, Perk," said Mongoose. He reached over Perko's head to pull a jar of marmalade off the shelf. Even at ten o'clock on a hot August morning, both men wore heavy black leather jackets with identical patches on the back. The patches said "Libidos" in ornate lettering, under which was embroidery that looked like a penis riding a chopper, a testicle on either side of the fork. The hairs in particular looked realistic.

"The gang's name is Nancy's Nasties, Mongoose. And you know the drill as well as I do. I use Libidos muscle, this becomes a hometown operation. I have to give up half my twenty percent. This is my gig, my sale, my points, and my call. And I say, *back off.*"

Besides, thought Perko, he wasn't about to have Marty "Mongoose" Muldoon or any other fellow gang member steal the show when the deal went down. He'd put in nearly fifteen years trying to make Road Captain, and nobody but nobody was going to ruin his big moment.

"Alls I'm saying, Perks, is those pussies from Nancy's crew won't have your back the way we does. What kind of heavies got names like Bernard and Frederick, anyways?" He slathered marmalade on half a chocolate muffin and tucked it in his mouth with two fingers.

"I could care less what their names are, *Mongoose.* They're only charging me five hundred bucks each for the night."

"You best be hoping they's worth more than what they's charging you is alls I can say." The chocolate crumbs that didn't spray into Perko's face got caught up in Mongoose's three-day beard. "And what about the farmer? You think some punk ass kid's gonna keep his mouth shut if ever the cops get at him?"

"The cops can grill him all they want, far as I care," Perko answered, wiping his face and taking half a step backward. "He's never met anyone but Frederick, and only once at that. I give him all my instructions over the phone and I use a voice distorter when I do it. The shithead doesn't know a thing except he has to get the hell off the property when I drop off his weekly pay packet."

Mongoose scratched his red-orange stubble and smelled his fingertips. His nose wrinkled. He licked off a few crumbs and wiped his hand on Perko's shoulder. "I hope you's right for your own sake. You screw this up and you'll be wishing *you* wore a picture of your granny on your back." Mongoose turned and tramped out of the kitchen.

Perko's stomach roiled. He raised his arm to shoulder height, about to give Mongoose a cheap shot face mash into the door jamb. At the last second, he dropped his hand to his side, fingers limp.

It wasn't so much Mongoose's put-down that made his skin crawl; it was his implied threat. Everyone knew gang promotion worked in one direction only. If you were kicked out of the Libidos, you knew too much to be demoted to a lower tier gang. When you lost your patch, you lost your jacket, your face, your teeth, your hands, and your balls along with it.

Much as he needed a smoke, Danny decided to deliver the lasagna to Ernie before heading back to Lester's. He could bum a cigarette off the old man and make sure Lester was gone for the day by the time he showed up.

Ernst McCann lived in an axe-hewn log cabin high on a hill over Pigeon Lake. The view out his living room window would have been worth a million bucks to some clown from the city. Except they'd like as not build a three-story "country home" and cut down sixty or seventy trees to show it off. The view didn't matter one whit to Ernie McCann: he was all but blind, able to make out swathes of color and movement but no detail. To him, the green of the trees was at least as interesting as the blue of the lake. That, and the pines and cedars smelled nicer than grass.

The man was on his hands and knees in his garden when Danny pulled up. He said, "Still driving that beater, I hear," when Danny killed the engine.

"Mom sent lasagna. Got a smoke?"

"On the picnic table. Heard you pull in, thought maybe you'd treat me to a tailor made."

"Ran out." Danny pulled a pinch of Drum tobacco from the old man's pouch and dropped it into a paper. He stretched the shreds, fluffing them between thumbs and index fingers and rolled it the right amount of tight. Sparking a light, he took a puff and walked the cigarette over to where Ernie had sat himself on a cut sixteen-inch log. Heading back to the table to roll another cigarette for himself, he said, "Garden's looking good. You'll have a nice haul of tomatoes in a couple weeks."

"It'll take three. Haven't had much sun this summer."

The two men smoked in silence for a while. Then Ernie said, "Your mother tells me you applied for a fork lift course. Offered by the government?"

"Didn't get in," Danny lied. "They only took ten guys. I must've been number eleven."

"Don't worry. Something will come along. Always does. You still got the unemployment check coming in?"

"Yep."

"Well, that's something, anyways," Ernie said.

Danny knew from his mother that Ernie lived on disability, on account of his blindness. They'd been friends forever, since before he was born, and she helped him out now and then with a meal or some grocery shopping. In return, Ernie gave them basket-loads of cucumbers, tomatoes, carrots, and garlic; just about every other thing you could grow. How the old man managed it—barely able to see like that—forever amazed him. He and his mom would come by at harvest time to help out some, but otherwise Ernie worked the plot alone, guiding the heavy work with steel wires run for that purpose, and weeding by feel on his hands and knees.

"How's her cough?" Ernie asked, meaning his mom.

"Worse." Danny told him how the doctor had said winters were going to get harder on her each year. "Just wish I could earn enough to send her south. Maybe even move there." He saw Ernie stifle a grimace. "'Course that'll never happen," he said, wondering who'd be around to help the old man if he and his mom were gone. He wished he could let him know about the pile of dough he was making and how it was going to change everything. He wished he could tell him there was more to life than collecting a government hand-out, and how he'd finally hit it big. He wished he could talk—to anyone really—instead of lying all the time.

He asked, "Anything you need done? Before I take off, I mean."

Ernie thought a moment and said, "There's a bag of lime needs carrying from the shed over to the kybo. I can handle it, but if you don't mind..."

Danny lugged the twenty pound sack across the yard and dumped it into the barrel inside the outhouse. He couldn't understand why Ernie insisted on living so completely off the grid. A little running water could go a long way to making life simpler. He put it down to stubbornness. He gave Ernie a tap on the shoulder and said goodbye, pausing only to grab a baseball bat he'd noticed in the shed. He didn't like the idea of facing Shooter empty-handed.

By the time he pulled into Lester's yard, it was just after noon and he knew he could count on his pal being gone fishing with his cousin. It was a manly ritual boys learned from their dads, a weekly reward for hard work shirking whatever job they were pretending to hold down at the time. A perfect way to avoid the missus and the yapping kids. Until the kids were old enough to fish and the cycle began again.

Lester had no missus and no kids he could name, but his cousin had got himself a wife named Mary Lou and three brats under eight; Lester went along for moral support. Since his friend would be off somewhere on a fourteen-foot aluminum boat with a two-four in the cooler and worms in a cardboard box, Danny figured it would be easy to let himself into the trailer and take back his carton of smokes.

The yellow-fanged Rottweiler crawled out from under the trailer before Danny had even stopped the engine, taking up a position between the car and the front door. Danny got out and walked toward the dog, slapping the bat loudly into his left palm as he advanced. Maybe he ought to have borrowed Ernie's shotgun instead.

Shooter backed up, tail down, a tuft of long black bristles standing up on the back of his short thick neck. He was growling but didn't try to stop Danny from going up the steps. The door's lock wasn't quite as flimsy as the rest of the trailer and it didn't give way to Danny's pull. As he leaned his knee into the wall for leverage and yanked harder, car tires crunched on the gravel behind him. He turned to see Lester's hand-me-down Ford drive into the clearing.

"Shit."

Lester stepped out of the car with a grin.

"Hey, Dannyboy. How's it hangin'?"

With his master's arrival, Shooter straightened up, stopped cringing, and started creeping back toward Danny, snarling loud now.

"Hey, Lester, uh, what are you doing here? I thought you'd be fishing."

"Mary Lou told my cuz she'd cut him a new one if he didn't finish cleanin' out the basement for some garage sale she wants to have tomorrow. But, hey, Danny, nice of you to drop by and...what's with the baseball bat? D'you..." And then Lester started to put two and two together.

"I want my smokes, Lester."

"Screw you and your smokes, numbnuts. What are you doin' at my door?"

Danny was still standing on the trailer step, turned halfway around. He looked from Lester to the dog and back. Shooter's lips were peeled in a snarl, showing off his pink and black gums and hungry-looking teeth. Danny slapped the bat into his hand but it no longer seemed to have any effect on the dog. He was sweating hard. Shooter lowered his shoulders into a crunch and moved forward.

"Tell him to back off, Lester," Danny said, thinking his voice sounded a little squeaky. "Back him off or I'll hit him."

"Bullshit, Danny. He'll bite your balls clean off before you touch him. Shooter, go. GO."

The dog leapt forward. Danny jumped. His right foot caught on the bottom step and he fell onto his back, right leg up in the air, presenting a tempting target for the dog. Shooter snapped and missed. Danny kicked him in the head. The dog yelped and jumped back, then prepared to attack again. What was it his mother always said about dogs? About not letting them know he was afraid? How could he *not* be afraid, lying there, waiting for Shooter to rip his calf open?

"Call him off, Lester. He's gonna tear a chunk outta my leg."

"Like I care, Dannyboy. He's just doin' his job."

"I swear, that mutt puts his teeth into me, I'm going straight to the cops. No fucking SPCA nice guys. They'll put a bullet in your damn dog."

That gave Lester pause. "Shooter," he said. "Down, boy. Back down."

Lester lunged forward and grabbed at the plastic-covered clothes line attached to Shooter's collar. The dog escaped his reach and leaned into Danny. Danny flung his leg to the right and swung the bat as hard as he could from his prone position. His palms were sweaty and the bat flew from his hands. It shot like a rocket over Shooter's head and struck Lester right between the eyes. He fell like a bag of rocks on top of his dog, giving Danny enough time to jump to his feet.

Before the dog could get loose, Danny sprinted to his car and jumped in. He slammed the door behind him, and realized he'd wet his jeans. Whimpering, he watched for five minutes as the dog leapt at the car over and over. Somehow, Shooter managed to get his teeth into the side mirror. He tore it off.

The Rottweiler seemed to feel wrenching the mirror from the car made his point. He stopped lunging and barking. Still growling, he moved off a few feet and lay down in the shadow cast by Lester's car, doing his best to gnaw on the mirror's chrome arm.

Lester hadn't moved.

Danny rolled his window down a couple of inches and yelled at him.

"Lester. Moron. Get up. Think I'm coming out with your freaking dog?"

Lester lay still. Danny honked the horn. No movement.

Danny started the car and drove slowly to where Lester lay. He looked at the pool of blood around his head. Lester's eyes stared at the space under Danny's car. Danny could swear he was grinning. The bat had crushed his nose flat, and all his teeth showed, tongue peeking out the gap. Pebbles and pine needles pressed into his cheek. Sticking halfway out of his shirt pocket was a pack of Players Special Blend. Kings.

THREE

Perko gunned the ATV out of the forest and into the barnyard. He dismounted with a groan. As wide and cushy as the three-wheeler's seat was, nothing could make the ride through the bush comfortable. He hated the backwoods trail, but it was critical he never be seen entering the farm's front gate. He maintained complete arm's length insulation from the grow operation that was, in every way, his baby.

The day before, he had called the punk farmer and told him, "Time to go buy beer and groceries. Get the fuck out. Don't be back before dark." He checked the spot between the ancient pickup on collapsed tires and the rusted out baler. No car. The punk was a good listener.

The farm looked like every other halfway-abandoned homestead in central Ontario. For nearly two decades, the owner had let the land run to scrub after many lifetimes of careful pasturing. No self-respecting cow would be caught navigating the stone, rubble, and low-lying juniper. A handful of poplar trees and some spruce had taken hold but no hardwood yet, except in the woodlot and even *it* was overrun by brambles and saplings around the edges. Before Perko's operation had moved in, nobody at all had lived at the farm for at least three years. The hayfields lay across the road and had long been rented to a nearby farmer. Perko knew the geezer must have noticed the recent tenant in the front farm house, but he didn't worry. In the no-smoke-no-fire book of rural etiquette, he counted on him and every other neighbor to respect the "Mean Dog" sign he had tacked to the front gate. Farmers could be every bit as nosy as they were helpful. The flipside was that people in the country knew how to mind their own business as long as nothing too loud or funny-smelling was going on.

14

Perko's tenancy was a strictly cash deal, struck with the eighty-seven-year-old owner. The widow nearly choked on her teeth when he paid eight months' rent up front. She still had enough gumption to ask for a damage deposit which Perko was convinced she immediately blew at the Great Horned Owl Charity Casino. They ran a shuttle four times a day to and from the retirement villa.

The barn was easily a hundred twenty years old. It leaned slightly to one side, but the long grey timbers looked as solid as rock from a distance. It was tucked conveniently behind the farmhouse and further screened by a spur of the woodlot.

Perko headed around back to a bright aluminum garage door wide enough to accommodate a tractor. He unlocked the padlock and rattled the length of old chain through the door's handles. Inside he was greeted by a press of air so thick with organic dust he could feel it on his teeth. A shiver of anticipation ran down his spine as he spread his arms wide and beamed at his masterpiece.

The tumble-down barn's cavernous interior was all twenty-first century. Thirty-mil black plastic lined the inside walls. Styrofoam insulation was glued and tacked to the plastic. Scaffolding erected right up to the roof created four floors where once there had been two. A mosaic of chrome, wire, white and black plastic tubing and hoses ran in every direction, all of it shimmering under a metal halide dawn. Each level had aisles of hydroponic basins, filled with slow-flowing nutrient-enriched water that bathed the roots of row upon row of pungent marijuana plants.

The man-made central nervous system created the ideal growing environment for some of the most potent cannabis the world had ever known. And it was all his.

That his creation looked like a massive fire hazard wasn't lost on Perko, but the smoke his operation was intended to produce would be far sweeter than the toxic mess that would occur should the barn itself ever burn. He had overseen the installation himself, using the Libidos' regular crew of off-duty city and hydro workers—the region's best experts on bypassing power meter monitoring. He paid the men cash and fed them beer and pizza during the overnight build-out sessions. It took less than a week to complete the installation. Perko himself cloned cuttings from two other Libido grow ops.

He used Frederick, one of Nancy's Nasties, to hire a guy to babysit the plants for the sixteen weeks until harvest time. Frederick's great-great-aunt had been the Nasties' matriarch, Nancy Nickerson, a gin-swilling grandmother of six hardcore repeat convicts who ran the original show. The two remaining grandsons were in walkers by now and what was left of the gang had fallen on rough times. Still, it was critical there be no connection between Perko and his pot farmer so that if the place ever got busted, the punk couldn't rat anyone out.

The plants had grown quickly, the Himalayan Gold outperforming the Texada Timewarp, and both crops starting to flower in just under two months. Once a week, he called the resident farmer from a pay phone and told him to leave the property: "Payday. Time to get lost." Week by week, the plants matured, and he walked the aisles like a botanist, pausing here and there to crumble a leaf between his fingers and smell its sweet spice.

Today, things were looking different. A back corner had been sealed off with a black plastic curtain behind which the mother plant cuttings for the next crop were rooting in their little trays, nearly ready to be transplanted. The black curtain served to block out ambient light, ensuring the babies received exactly twenty hours of artificial daylight—no more, no less— from the overhanging light racks. The punk farmer was doing his job well, not that it would ever occur to Perko to tell him as much.

Stacked near the tractor door were dozens of bales of dried pot, each wrapped in burlap and plastic, and weighing in at twenty-five pounds. Perko drew a deep breath, eyes gleaming, and admired his first harvest.

On the other side of the door, he noticed a charred empty oil drum stuffed with odds and sods of plastic and framing materials. It looked like farm boy was using his noggin and doing the barrel burn indoors rather than sending a thick black smoke signal up from the yard. He'd have to tell him to check the HVAC filters to make sure they weren't getting clogged.

Done inspecting the barn, Perko walked over to the house to leave an envelope containing sixty twenty-dollar bills on the kitchen table. On the envelope he scrawled a note: "Tuesday night, make yourself scarce. The Boss." Then he underlined "Boss" because it made him feel good.

On previous visits, he had nosed around the house a bit to get a sense of his employee's at-home behavior, looking for evidence of parties, or girlfriends, or anyone other than the farmer himself. Visitors were strictly forbidden. Based on his snooping, Perko was satisfied that the only company enjoyed by his charge was a lizard that occupied one of the rooms on the second floor. It had to weigh nearly twenty pounds. Perko made another mental note to find out just how big lizards could grow—he didn't want to wind up ambushed by a dragon.

Today, he noticed a few bags of dried bud, more than his farmer could possibly smoke on his own. Clearly, the guy was selling a little on the side. Perko shrugged. Selling factory leavings *was* against the rules, but he was willing to let it slide. When you were growing over a million dollars' worth of marijuana and some poor sod was fool enough to shoulder the personal risk of incarceration, it was best not to quibble when he sold a little plant waste. If the punk got busted dealing, he had nothing to gain by confessing to running a factory-scale pot farm, never mind the fact that he didn't have a clue *who* he actually worked for.

Riding back into the bush on his ATV, Perko smiled with pride at the elegance of the operation. He'd learned a hell of a lot with the Libidos. They were so smart, he figured they ought to be running the whole damn country.

FOUR

After killing Lester Freeden with a baseball bat to the face, Danny drove straight to the farmhouse. To think. To be alone and think.

He'd killed a man.

A friend, if he could call Lester that. It was an accident. There was that. Maybe he should tell the cops. Danny actually turned around toward town twice, thinking that's what he'd do. But tell them what? That Lester had it coming? That he ought to have given him back his smokes?

Danny pulled to side of the road and puked until his heaves were dry.

He didn't like his odds explaining to a couple cops that he'd whacked Lester in the head with a baseball bat because he was afraid of his dog. Could he even be sure it was Shooter he was aiming for? Or that he cared Lester was dead? He just didn't like the fact it was him had done the killing. Lester, stupid asshole, couldn't even die without fucking things up.

At the farm, he stepped out of his car to open the gate. He waved absentmindedly to the farmer doing whatever it was needed doing in the hayfield across the road. Despite having watched the old man for hours on end, Danny had never spoken to him; nor did he intend to. Lonely as he was, he knew better than to get close to the locals.

The farmhouse stood squarely between the barn and the road. Danny had seen a thousand lookalikes all over the Kawarthas, moving with his mother every time another landlord gave them the boot. It had a front door dead center between two identical windows: one each for the living and dining rooms. Its front porch was big enough to hold two weatherworn chairs on one side and a rocking loveseat on the other. The lone arched window on the second floor was still intact but its glass panes were cloudy with age. The hundred twenty-year-old building was in bad need of a paint job, bare wood exposed on most boards.

Danny let himself into the kitchen at the back of the house and spotted the envelope left on the table by his biker boss. His gut wrenched at the reminder of how he had blown the whack of cash the night before at blackjack. It plummeted to new depths as his synapses jumped from the casino to Lester's trailer to his cold dead eyes staring up at him, blood oozing from his crushed nose. He knew full well his mother would hate the idea that the money with which he planned to give her a better life came from criminal activity—even though he was pretty sure growing pot was low on her personal totem pole of crime. But murder? With a bat? Even if attempted *dog*slaughter would be a better name for it, how the hell could he explain that one to her?

He clomped through the darkened front room devoid of furniture and made his way upstairs. In the first of two bedrooms, a futon lay on the floor with a sleeping bag and a pillow. Danny kept an ancient TV/VCR/DVD player beside the bed, but he preferred to use the television in the kitchen downstairs where the hacked satellite hookup meant he could watch pretty much anything pretty much any time.

The second upstairs bedroom was home to Danny's pet iguana. With a body as big as a tomcat and a tail just over three feet long, Iggy projected an aura of entitlement well-suited to a being whose ancestors predated Danny's by like a hundred million years. He ate green bananas voraciously and shat non-stop. As a rule, Danny kept the second bedroom locked and would visit the iguana every so often to smoke a joint. When it came to combating the deep sense of boredom, isolation, and sheer paranoia at being on guard at a grow op, watching the lizard utterly ignore him was fascinating to the committed stoner.

That Saturday afternoon, with Lester Freeden's frozen face stuck in his mind, Danny sat on the overstuffed armchair in the iguana's bedroom and rolled up a doublewide doobie.

"Iggy, my friend," he said, lighting the joint and taking a deep haul, "you are one lucky lizard. Nice and safe and all the bananas you can eat."

Perched on the windowsill, the iguana turned its head slowly, its gaze sliding past Danny then back again, as if to say, *Feed me one more banana, pothead, and I'll bite off your little finger while you sleep.*

"You can't get near me while I sleep because I always close your door," Danny said.

I'm patient. I'll wait you out. Or have you forgotten that I can sit here for three hours without moving, my eyes open, frozen in space, while you fry your brain one joint at a time?

Cold dead eyes, thought Danny. Like Lester's. Staring right past him. Or through him, like he didn't matter at all.

The chair was in the middle of the room, facing the window. Danny sat and smoked and stared over the lizard's back at the world outside. The warped glass bent his view of the farmer across the road heaving basketball-sized rocks into the shovel of a front-end loader. It was as though the fieldstones grew and ripened under the winter snow so they could be harvested every spring, Danny thought. After a hundred twenty years of farming, you'd think the stones would stop surfacing. A loose rock wall at least five feet wide and three feet tall edged every farm field in the Kawarthas. Each stone had been sifted from the earth so it wouldn't bend a farmer's plough or damage his harvesting equipment.

"That farmer is working just as hard as his father and his grandfather and his great-grandfather before him," Danny told the iguana. "The equipment gets better, but the farms keep getting bigger. The only way he'll ever reap his reward is if he stops farming and sells the place to someone crazy enough to work as hard as he does."

And just what would you know about rewards? You're living in a rundown farmhouse, waiting for the cops to come along and bust you for a crop of skunk weed that isn't even your own. Or, better yet, maybe they'll arrest you for murder, you moron.

"I'm no murderer. It was an accident. Stupid bugger didn't have to sic his dog on me like that. It wasn't my fault the baseball bat flew out of my hands." For a moment, Danny puzzled over how the iguana knew he'd killed Lester. Then he snorted a laugh, remembering the iguana couldn't even really talk.

That's right, Danny. Don't believe I can talk and, while you're at it, why don't you pretend the cops will never find the corpse.

Iggy was right. Danny was scared out of his wits at what would happen when someone found Lester's body. And find it they would. Lester had more enemies than friends and no one was all that likely to show up at his trailer looking for him. But a body was a body and before long, someone had to find it. When that happened, Danny would be on the short list of people who ever had anything to do with Lester.

One of the first places they'll canvas will be the casino. Dozens of people saw you two together the night before Lester ate dirt.

"Oh, man, you are so right, Iggy. What am I gonna do?"

Bury him. Bury him in the woods.

"I can't bury him. The ground is as full of stones as that field across the road. Can you imagine the mess of rocks I'd stir up trying to put him six feet under?"

Six inches, six feet. What's the difference? Just drag him far enough into the bush to hide the smell a while and let the critters get at him. Cover him with a bunch of leaves and a bit of dirt. The worms will take care of the rest. Snow will be here before you know it. In the spring, Lester will thaw out and be pecked clean.

"I dunno, Iggy. Sounds too easy. Someone will find the bones, at least, and then they'll know someone killed him for sure, and they'll come looking for me."

So, sink him.

"Huh?"

You heard me. Sink him. In the water. Take him for a short ride that'll last forever. Tie a bag of rocks to his feet and throw him overboard into the lake. Let him lie there with the legendary schooner. Maybe he'll become The Ghost of Big Bald Narrows or something.

"Yeah, you're right. I can throw him in where it's like forty feet deep and no one will ever find him. I can use chain and nylon rope, too. Wrap him real tight so that even if his bones come loose, they won't, er, come loose. Do bones float, Iggy?"

Naw. Bones sink. No need to worry, they'll just lie there on the bottom.

Danny thought this was starting to sound like a plan. He went downstairs to the kitchen to get himself a cold beer and another banana for the iguana. Two minutes later, he was back in Iggy's room, sweating and shaking. He tossed the banana at the lizard and said, "Oh man, oh man, Iggy. Someone's going to find Lester for sure. Someone's gonna snag Lester's eyeball on a fishing lure...in his skull, I mean, when all the flesh is off it and his brain's been eaten by some huge carp...and one of them fishermen is gonna hook it and pull it up out of the lake and..."

You're probably right. It'll be like, "I got one, yeah, I got one, man, this is one heavy mother, naw it's just weeds, man, it's dragging like a boot."

Danny's hands shook as he brought the beer can to his lips. In his mind's eye he saw Lester's skull, a shiny orange lure stuck in one empty eye socket.

"So, it's the bush, then," he said after a while.

Uh huh. And what about the dog?

"Shooter? What about him?"

His master is dead and the dog doesn't particularly like you already.

"So, what am I supposed to do?"

Deal with him.

"How?"

Do I have to tell you everything?

Danny felt blood rush to his head. He couldn't believe he was being upbraided by a four-and-a-half-foot bug-eater. He imagined Iggy skewered and roasting over a fire surrounded by stoned teenagers on a beach somewhere in...

Ingrate! Here I am, coaching you out of this mess, and all you can think of is turning me into midnight kebabs. Deal with your own problems, numbnuts. Iggy turned his head away and gnawed on the banana.

Danny's heart was pounding so hard he thought he could hear the ocean in his ears. Iggy had just called him *numbnuts*. Lester always called him numbnuts. Lester called everyone numbnuts. It was a Lester word. Could Iggy be in cahoots with Lester? Could Lester's ghost have inhabited Iggy's scaly carcass? Was there nobody he could trust? Trembling, he stood up and turned to leave the room.

You need some help. Someone to deal with the dog, while you deal with Lester's body.

Without turning to face the iguana, Danny said, "Who the hell is gonna help me dump a body? Who do I know that's stupid enough to get involved with something like this?"

Besides Lester.

"No one's as stupid as Lester."

Right. But he's dead.

"Terry, then. Terry Miner." Danny walked out of the room. On the way down the stairs, he struggled to figure out whose plan had just been hatched—his or the iguana's. He stopped in front of a faded mirror in the front hall: still Danny, but with Lester's glassy eyes now. He was sure he heard the iguana laughing at him from the bedroom.

Perko counted six under his breath as Frederick skipped a stone, creating barely perceptible ripples on the wavelets lapping onto the shores of Big Bald Lake.

"There. Me, I win," Frederick grinned.

"Bullshit. That was five skips. Same as me," Perko answered, grunting at the gut pressure as he bent over to pick up another stone.

"Five? No way, tabarouette. Dat was six. Not five."

"The last one was more like a tumble. We throw again. Still double or nothing."

Frederick scowled and kicked at the ground to dislodge another piece of shale. Perko's stomach made it hard to reach the ground but Frederick had an even harder time. Thin as he was, his head-to-toe brown leather get-up was so tight, it looked sprayed on. The cow-hide squeaked when he moved. "So what we do Tuesday night," he said, "we meet those New York guys with their crew some place first?"

"Yeah. At that Mexican joint outside of town." Perko found a stone he liked and flicked it across the water. "—three, four, five, six, and seven. Who the hell puts a Mexican restaurant and hotel on Highway fucking Seven in the middle of nowhere anyway?"

"You meaning Helena's Hellhole? Dat one?"

"That's the one."

"Aw, merde. Bernard, he can't stand the spicy food. He say it makes his hair go straight. He's gonna be pissed off that guy."

"You just tell your fucking partner to keep his mouth shut. This ain't no dinner party. It's a meet. Business to discuss, details we gotta work out, and then we head over to the farm. He can go to Tim fucking Hortons with his five hundred when it's over, far as I care."

Frederick threw a stone. "Five. Merde. That's eighty bucks I owe you. We go again."

"Naw, forget it," Perko said. "That's enough for me. So I owe you five hundred minus eighty." He took a wad of bills out of his pocket and peeled off four twenties before handing the rest to Frederick. "You get the other five when the delivery's done."

"Right. Boss." Frederick took the cash without counting it and squeezed it into the front pocket of his brown leather pants. "The New York guys—the Skeletons—who they using for local crew here?"

"A couple of guys, brothers I think, from Nicaragua. They say they're refugees or something."

"Them guys were supposed to get deported like three years ago?"

"Yeah, those ones. Seems they keep appealing, finding excuses to stay in Canada. The Skeletons like 'em because they don't mind running back and forth across the border. Nothing to lose, I guess. They get caught, 'least they won't be sent home."

Frederick grunted. "And how much we moving?"

"Three hundred kilos. Dried, baled, ready to go. Shouldn't take more'n five minutes to get the shit loaded."

"Three hundred? Dat's a lot of cash."

"Yeah, well, it was almost a load of guns," Perko said. "The Skeletons wanted to offset half the load against hardware they moved last month."

"Dat's a lot of guns."

"No kidding. Nearly lost the deal when they found out this wasn't a full-on Libidos gig. That I'm running it solo. They said they're doing mostly guns for green when they take shipment from Toronto, Cornwall, even Montreal now. The urban bangers can't get enough metal."

"So, what did you do?"

"I told 'em out here muscle means muscle. We need to off someone, a hunting rifle works plenty good. We don't gotta hide our guns in our pants."

"They went for dat?"

"No."

"So what?"

"I cut the price."

"Oh."

"And promised to take them bear hunting."

FIVE

Danny found Terry Miner lounging outside his borrowed trailer in the park on the shore of Rice Lake. Covered in rust, the sixteen-footer perched off-level between concrete blocks and tree stumps. It dipped a full foot lengthwise and at least six inches across its width, as if to ensure the water would drain out when it rained. A green aluminum awning hung off one side, providing shade to two folding lawn chairs.

"What's cookin', Danny? Welcome to my waterfront paradise." Terry gestured to the unoccupied chair. Danny sat down and the canvas sagged almost to the ground. He pulled an empty beer can from the cup holder on the chair's arm. "Sorry, pal, this here's the last brewski," Terry said, looking pointedly at the can in his own hand. "Unless you brought some," he added, eyebrows raised.

Danny looked out over the waterfront facing Terry's trailer, a carpet of bull rushes running more than three hundred feet offshore. "Nope, I didn't bring beer," he said, "but I've got a half pound bag of pot that's all yours if you can help me out for a couple hours."

Terry whistled through his teeth. "A half pound of that Kawartha Kash Krop? The kush that could a been mine? Correction, *should* a been mine. Man, you must be looking for some kind of help to come askin' me."

"You're the one who blew it."

That past April, Danny had run into Terry at the unemployment office. It was one of those spring days when the sun announced summer coming, even as the brown mounds of sand-crusted ice clung like glaciers in north-facing ditches. Always the scrounger, Terry was there to pick up his check to avoid it being mailed to the apartment he was hanging at back then. "Check comes in?" he'd said. "My roommates are all up my ass to chip in on groceries, pay the rent and stuff. Money's all gone before I can make it to the beer store."

They'd cashed Terry's check at the Money Mart and spent the afternoon shooting tequila in the darkened City Lights Tavern on Water Street. Danny told Terry how he was going to get his forklift license and get a decent job, way more than minimum wage. Terry said after tequila they should hit a patio somewhere to check out springtime hotties. He watched the baseball game while Danny explained how his mom needed to live south, skip winters, because of how sick she was getting. Terry said, "Now, baseball players, *they* got real jobs. How hard can it be?"

Danny said hanging around a bar getting pissed in the afternoon didn't seem like a solid career strategy. Terry said, "Met a guy here last night told me he'd set me up. Real good gig." When the guy showed, Danny cracked wise about his head-to-toe brown leather outfit. Tight pants and a tighter motorcycle jacket.

"You want I cut your balls off with a rusty knife?" Leather Man had said.

"No, I—"

They'd switched to mezcal because, according to Leather Man, "The tequila is for, 'ow you say, wimps." Halfway through the second tray of fifteen shooters, Terry crumpled to a heap under the table and threw up all over the newcomer's shiny brown boots. And just like that, Danny got the job tending the grow op.

Clearly, all these months later, Terry was still pissed. "Like you never puked on tequila," he said. He stared straight at Danny, took a long gulp of beer, and smacked his lips.

"Never barfed at a job interview," Danny said. "You want the half pound or not?"

"What do I gotta do?" Terry took off his sunglasses and wiped them with the front of his T-shirt.

Danny told him the whole story, starting with Lester's curiosity about his extra cash, right up to the part where Lester was lying out front of his trailer, guarded by Shooter the villain mutt.

"Are you sure he's dead?" Terry asked.

"Has to be. The baseball bat hit him straight on—shoved his nose right up between his eyeballs."

"I ain't never seen a dead guy before, so you know, how can you be sure?"

"Well, he wasn't moving," Danny said, "and his eyes were open and cold and dead-like. Can't get that look outta my head."

"There's this guy I used to work with looked just like that every Monday morning. Looked *twice* as dead after a *long* weekend."

"This is no joke. Lester's dead and I need your help burying him."

"I dunno." Terry paused to suck the last of the beer out of the can before crushing it and dropping it to the ground. He turned to Danny and said, "I kinda like the idea of seeing a dead guy for once, but that dog sounds nasty, and I'm just kinda chilling here by the lake and all. I think I'll pass."

A dented fourteen-foot aluminum boat rested upside down next to a rock-ringed fire pit; Danny couldn't imagine how the boat could make its way through the forest of weeds to open water and it looked as though no one had tried for quite a few years.

"How'd you find this joint anyway, Terry?"

"Buddy o' mine. I think it's his sister's place. She's letting him use it 'cause she got tired of him surfing her couch. He's got a new ol' lady with an apartment in town and said I could stay here long as I cut the grass."

Danny kicked at the dirt in front of his lawn chair. "Pretty easy gig."

Terry snorted. "You're not kidding. Besides, I owe my roommates in town about six hundred bucks. We had a couple parties, you know, the usual. I figure if I just hang out here on the beach for a few months, they'll forget all about it."

"They know where you are?"

"You think I'm stupid?"

Danny turned to look straight at him and smiled. "So whatcha doin' for the next couple of hours Mister I-don't-wanna-be-found?"

"Aw shit, gimme a break. Can't you bury the fucking guy yourself?"

"And deprive you of this once in a lifetime opportunity to see a real live dead guy?"

Terry sunk his chin into his chest. "A kilo of pot, did ya say?"

"Half a pound, Terry. And mostly tops."

"Make it a pound."

"Half a pound now. Half when he's buried."

"Alright. I'm in. I knew today was gonna get weird soon as I saw you drive up."

An hour later, Danny and Terry pulled up in front of Lester Freeden's trailer. The door to Lester's car hung open just as he had left it the day before and his body lay on its back halfway to the trailer. Hunched over his head and shoulders was Shooter, his mouth bloody and frothing. He snarled and crouched as if getting ready to spring at the new arrivals.

Without speaking, the two men got out of the car. Danny popped the trunk and took out two long-handled spades, handing one to Terry. Danny smacked his on the hard packed gravel as the two men crept toward Shooter. The dog drew his ears down, snuffled a bit, and looked from Danny to Terry to the shovels they both carried. When the two men were slightly more than a shovel's length away, the dog stood up and slunk over to the trailer, dragging a bloody arm along with him. The arm had been gnawed clean out of its socket. When Danny and Terry looked down at what was left of Lester's body, they saw the right side of his face was chewed off as well.

"Look dead enough to you, Terry?" Danny croaked, a lump the size of a grapefruit forming in his chest.

Terry stumbled backward and collided with the front of the dead man's car. He leaned onto it with both arms spread wide and upchucked all over the hood. Wiping his face on his sleeve, Terry said, "Mother of Hell. You're gonna owe me a fuck of a lot more than a bag of dope for this. What the *hell* went down here?"

"Looks like Lester's wacko dog has got hungry is what's went down. C'mon. You gotta help me drag the body into the woods so I can bury it." Danny grabbed Lester's right leg and started to pull. He gagged at the stink, tasting the bile rise in his throat, and swatted his hand at the flies that rose up around him. From where he lay under the trailer, Shooter growled. It came out more like a moan as he gnawed on Lester's humerus.

When Danny had dragged the body to the edge of the clearing, Shooter leapt out from under the trailer, thundered across the thirty feet of gravel, and lunged at him, jaws open. Danny barely managed to jump out of the dog's way. The Rottweiler's head snapped back at the end of his lead. He yelped as the collar bit into his neck. He collapsed to the ground beside Lester's remains, licked his snout, and took a bite out of the fleshy underside of Lester's thigh.

"Damn you, Terry, get over here and give me a hand!" Danny slammed his shovel into the ground less than two feet from where Shooter crouched. The dog looked up at him without turning his head, snorted dismissively, and went right on chewing.

"What about we dig the hole first eh, Danny?" Terry cut a wide berth around the dog, and walked about fifty feet into the bush. "How about over here?"

Danny shrugged his shoulders and followed him to a spot between the tree trunks where there was enough room for a grave. They both began digging. Under its decomposing blanket of leaves, the top soil was light and spongy. Stones started appearing immediately, spread as liberally through the pungent loam as chocolate chips in a two-dollar cookie.

"Pile the rocks on the side, Dan, and we can make a cross or something after we're done."

"We won't be making no cross, Terry. The idea is to hide the damn thing, not advertise it."

"Oh yeah. Got it."

They scraped and shoveled and pried rocks out of the earth for what seemed like an hour. Apart from the occasional curse, the two men worked in silence. The hole was barely a foot deep, and they had piled up at least sixty rocks, when Terry said, "Looks deep enough to me. Whaddya say?"

"Another couple of inches. I want to make sure he doesn't get dug right back up by Shooter or some bear or something."

"Alright, another few minutes then, but I'm getting tired. And I really don't see the difference between one foot and six when it comes to burying. Dead is dead and a hole is a hole. He ain't coming back out regardless, is all I'm saying."

Seven rocks later, Danny set down his shovel. He took his cigarettes from his pocket, offering one to Terry, who took it and pulled out a pack of matches to light them both. "So what are we going to do with these rocks?" Terry asked.

"I been thinking maybe we should bury the dog with them. Kind of like a decoy. If anyone comes looking for Lester, they'll find the mutt's grave mounded with rocks and figure Lester buried him and went off to mourn or something."

"Uh huh. Just one problem."

"What's that?" Danny asked.

"The dog ain't dead."

"He will be, soon enough. We can't leave him here alive."

"Kill the dog? Man, you are one heartless bastard."

"Way I figure," Danny answered, "we'll be doing him a favor. He'll starve here alone. Either that or he'll chew right through that lead of his and come over here and dig Lester back up after we're gone."

"He can't chew that. It's a clothes line, for Christ's sake. Vinyl-covered steel cable."

"He bit the mirror off my car yesterday."

"Huh?" Terry looked over at where Shooter lay guarding his master's carcass. Shooter seemed to grin back. Terry coughed, his breath ripe with vomit.

Danny waved a hand in front of his face. "And besides, dead dogs don't bark. We don't need him drawing attention over here."

"So how we gonna kill the pooch?"

"Lester's got rat poison in his trailer. Had problems with squirrels getting in. If you can keep Shooter busy, I'll bust in and get it."

"Then what? You want me to go buy some hamburger?"

Danny looked at Terry, then over at Lester's body. Shooter growled. "I don't think we need to go shopping for meat."

SIX

Perko threw himself backwards onto the bed and tugged at a pair of black leather chaps, left leg first, then the right, then the left again. Grunting, he heaved himself into a sitting position and rubbed his exposed belly where it billowed out between his T-shirt and the top of his jeans. No one had told him being a badass outlaw would mean wearing a uniform. To make matters worse, Shelley was home, and Perko knew his old lady would have something to say about his leather leggings. She was sexy as hell in a tough, curvy kind of way, well out his league in the looks department, and she constantly reminded Perko he was lucky to have her.

As often as she let him, he slept at her apartment. It beat couch-surfing at the clubhouse. He kept the chaps and a small assortment of clothes here, along with the few possessions that mattered to him: a couple of knives with carved wooden handles, a silver goblet he had stolen during a teen-aged robbery, and a book of quotations by Mahatma Gandhi. Perko didn't get much of what Gandhi was about, but he liked the way he talked. He'd even cut a picture of him out of *Life* magazine and stuck it on the wall next to Shelley's full-length dressing mirror. On it, he had inked: "Hate the sin, love the sinner."

He read the quote again now as he stood in front of that mirror and checked out his full-on gang regalia. He was proudest of his patch: a black leather jacket with the gang's insignia emblazoned on the back. The honor was closely held and only bestowed on members who had proven themselves loyal to the core. Legend had it no one got their patch without at least one murder to their name. The gang kept that legend alive to boost the intimidation factor critical to their enterprise. In reality, members got patched for all kinds of reasons. Sometimes, they simply needed to beef up numbers after an aggressive round of busts. Then there were more sinister deals like the one Mongoose struck. He'd threatened to make one of the gang's leaders eat a pool cue if he didn't support his candidacy. The pool cue in question was halfway up the guy's ass when the two men reached their agreement.

Hate the sin, love the sinner. Gandhi would have made a good dad. The kind of dad who showed up at baseball games and helped with science projects. Not like Perko's father, a bitter man who spent half his life regretting he'd sired three kids and the other half pretending he hadn't. During his rare appearances at home, he griped incessantly about how hard he worked to keep food on the table. Nothing Perko did ever pleased the man and long before he reached high school, he had learned it was best to avoid him whenever possible.

If Perko's old man had been more than semi-literate, his motto might have been "Hate the sin, *belt* the sinner."

Perko Ratwick hadn't set out to be a biker. No more than he'd considered being a doctor, an engineer, or a carpenter. If anything, as a teenager, he'd thought of himself as an entrepreneur. While most of the kids went to parties to get drunk and smoke dope, Perko sold the dope and charged ten bucks to drive people to the beer store.

At the end of his Junior year, his old man gave him a particularly bad pounding for bringing home a report card with five F's and only one C. Perko left home, dropped out of school, and started running errands for the Libidos for food money. He was a quick learner. In no time, they taught him how to strut, how to intimidate the weak, and how to grab more than his share. For their part, the cops who rousted him ingrained disrespect for authority and convinced him that, compared to his father, he had nothing whatsoever to fear from the law. Soon enough, he got invited to sleep on the floor at the Libidos clubhouse. He never looked back.

Apart from the obvious attraction of a lifestyle committed to partying, Perko glommed onto the incredibly useful tips and tricks of the trade. Like when an old-timer named Hawk told him how to deal with Taser-wielding police. "Soon as you see the little snake come out, run at the nearest cop. Doesn't matter which one. Just as long as you sink your teeth into him before you get zapped. That way, he'll get the charge, same as you."

On his nineteenth birthday, Perko Ratwick got patched: the youngest ever Libido. A real up and comer. "You'll never amount to nothing," his father had always told him. Perko wondered what the old man would think if he could see him now, a dozen years later, standing in front of Shelley's mirror, dressed to kill, and about to do a deal worth nearly a million bucks. "Hate the sin, love the sinner," he murmured.

He studied his thick thighs and the way they made the fringes stand out, almost erect, at the sides. He considered taking them off, but he would be riding the three-wheeler through the woods tonight and he really didn't want to shred his jeans on stray branches along the dark trail.

The finishing touch was his favorite pair of Centiagues, Central American cowboy boots with slope-backed heels designed to be useful when the wearer wanted to take a siesta on a city sidewalk. You could squat down against a building, kick back on your heels and snore contentedly. Perko liked the boots for the clicking sound they made when we walked on polished tile floors. He had added the metal heel covers himself.

Ready to go, Perko swaggered into the living room, swung his arms wide, impresario-style, and asked Shelley, "What do you think?"

Busy on the phone, she put her hand over the receiver mouthpiece. "You look like a jellyfish," she said. "What are those stringy things growing on your pants?"

"Fringes," said Perko, "and for your information, these are chaps, not pants."

"Chaps? Are you hanging out with those Nasty Nancies again?"

Perko ignored the jab. "Don't wait up," he said. He gave her a kiss and clicked his way out of the apartment. As the door closed behind him, he could hear Shelley giggling into the phone: "And he's wearing those funny boots with the slanted silver heels, too. I tell you, gang fashion has come a long way, baby..."

* * *

Sitting in his rent-free trailer at Rice Lake, Terry Miner popped a Coors Light and poured it onto a bowl of Cheerios. The door squeaked open and banged shut behind a squat man decked out in a dirty undershirt and red sweatpants.

"C'mon in, why don't ya? Grab a seat," Terry said pushing a folding chair toward his visitor with his bare foot.

"Didn't mean to interrupt your breakfast. Want me to come back?" Chest hair spilled out of every opening of the man's undershirt.

"Naw, not a problem, pal. What can I do you for?"

"I hear you got some wicked weed for sale. Figured I'd check it out. No need to head into town if my neighbor's in the biz, if you know what I mean."

"Sure. What do you need? A quarter?"

"That sounds about right."

Terry stuck his hand between the cushions of the bench beside him and pulled out a twist of plastic wrap no bigger than his little finger. He flipped it across the table. His guest fished a handful of fives and tens from somewhere inside the sweatpants and laid the crumpled bills in front of Terry's bowl of cereal. "Thanks, man," the guy said, and shuffled out.

Terry drew a deep breath, puffed out his chest, and grinned as the door banged shut behind his latest customer. Word had gotten around the trailer park pretty quick that he had amazing skunk weed for sale. For two days now, there had been a steady stream of familiar-looking total strangers at his door. He had the cash to buy beer and smokes and had even gotten laid by the lady down the lane who'd sent her husband packing for being "a good-for-nothing sponge."

Not since his aborted college ball career had he enjoyed this much fame, but his sense of entitlement was deeply engrained. As a football star, his grades had been fixed, chicks were all over him (usually just to make other boys jealous), and he really only had to perform on the field for about ten weeks each year. When he didn't make the third-year cut, Terry had spent one winter and the following spring working in a warehouse earning two dollars above minimum wage before deciding petty thievery would be a better vocation. Thing was, even B & E's took too much effort. He was much better cut out for this drug dealing thing.

Based on his rough calculations, he figured he could easily make two, maybe three thousand dollars and still have enough smoke to last him clear through to New Year's.

Munching his Cheerios and beer, he got to thinking: if he was able to make that much in the trailer park, he could probably sell the dope for even more money at a couple of taverns he knew in Toronto. Getting there posed a bit of a problem, though. He couldn't very well ask Danny—he'd be pissed if he knew Terry was doing anything other than smoking his brains out with the stolen dope—and he didn't know anyone in the park well enough to borrow their wheels.

His thoughts kept drifting back to Lester's car, recalling the set of keys he'd spotted hanging on a hook by the door inside the dead man's trailer. It would be more like borrowing than stealing, he figured, since Lester was dead and had no further use for the thing. When it had served its purpose, he could sell the car to a chop shop. The car was hardly new, but it was bound to fetch a few hundred dollars for parts. It was kind of like recycling. A good deed all round.

His mind made up, he threw half a pound of pot into a small gym bag and begged a ride back toward Peterborough from a neighbor who was headed that way. Walking the last three miles to Lester's impromptu cemetery, he thought about the last thing Danny had said to him when they'd buried Lester two days before. "The Boss man left me another one of his notes," Danny had explained. "'Make like the invisible man', he says. 'Beat it. Get lost.' Just who the hell does he think he is?"

"Uh, a gangster?" Terry had cracked.

"Yeah, yeah, whatever. If the guy's so tough, he wouldn't be afraid to show his face at the farm. Sounds like a wiener over the phone, too. Here I am, growing him a million bucks worth of weed...more than that, I'm sure...and he treats me like some kind of yokel he can just order around like the hired help. I deserve better."

"Better than a thousand bucks a week, Danny? I'll take it, if you're fed up. My damn job anyway."

The more he thought about it, the more his blood boiled. It was Danny who *really* had it easy. Sure, the guy had a way of making it sound like back-breaking work, what with the watering, the trimming, the harvesting, and all, but he was *growing pot*, for Chrissakes. Terry couldn't help feeling he'd been ripped off somehow. Danny sure as hell owed him more than just one pound of green.

The sun was lighting the top of the trees by the time Terry stepped into the clearing where they had done the deed. The air was thick with sparkling summer dust. His knees trembled at the sight of the creamy white maggots writhing on the darkened patch of driveway where Lester had lain. His eyes traced the drag marks they had forgotten to sweep away and when his gaze reached the tell-tale hump of freshly-turned leaves, the Cheerios did a somersault in his stomach. He was glad there was no one around to see him vomit one more time, leaning on Lester's car. Sweating heavily, he steered clear of the pile of stones that marked Shooter's grave and made his way to the trailer. He reached in, grabbed the keys off the hook inside, and stumbled back to the car.

The blood had drained from his head and when he flopped into the driver's seat, he thought his heart was going to pound its way right out of his chest. He threw his bag of pot into the back and drove away as fast as he could without even stopping to see what else he could steal.

SEVEN

Danny snapped into a sitting position, his brain sloshing loose in his head. No question: the screen door slam had not been part of his dream; someone was downstairs in the kitchen.

"Fuck. Fuck fuck fuck fuck fuck fuck FUCK."

It was still light outside, but he couldn't be sure what day it was. The note he had found after burying Lester said to get lost, spend Tuesday night away. Clear enough, but was it already the day after tomorrow? He was sure at least one day had gone by, but was less certain tomorrow was yesterday. Danny had done his best to stay stoned out of his gourd since Lester's burial. Maybe that hadn't been such a good idea.

He listened for voices: nothing. Okay, so maybe there was only one guy. *Big fucking difference*, he thought. *I'm not supposed to be here.*

He looked out the window at the side yard. No car. No motorcycle. Nobody outside. He listened again. Someone heavy tramped up the stairs. No weapon in the room. The TV/VCR/DVD unit was too big to throw. Eyes bugging out his skull, he grabbed a half-empty glass of orange juice and whipped it at the door just as it swung open. He missed. The glass smashed into the wall beside the hulk of a man who filled the doorframe.

Danny choked. "Skeritt!"

"That's one hell of a welcome, Young Mr. Grant."

"Oh, fuck am I glad it's you."

"Really. And how exactly would you greet me if you weren't so bloody glad?"

"Sorry, man. I just...I didn't...hey, do you know what day it is?"

The man scratched his matted grey-brown beard with a bear-paw of a hand and said, "Now, *there's* an interesting question.

Are you going to offer me a cup of tea? Or do you expect me to lick that there—what is it, cat piss?—off the floor?"

Ten minutes later, the two men sat at the kitchen table downstairs. Skeritt's bush-ready attire was the same year-round: heavy plaid hunting jacket with upper and lower pockets and a fleece-lined collar, and grimy green pants with even more pockets, most of them bulging. As a young boy, Danny had often marveled at the things he could find in Skeritt's pockets whenever the crusty old loner wandered in from the woods for a little home cooking. A quick search could be rewarded with anything from spotted mushroom caps to a bulky Swiss Army knife with enough tools to fascinate him for hours.

Sitting in the grow op kitchen, Danny wasn't all that curious what surprises Skeritt's pants might hold until one of his pockets moved. The old man reached a gnarled fist down his thigh, dragged out a chipmunk by its tail, and tossed it to the floor. "So that's where you got to," he said.

Danny asked, "How the hell did you find me?"

"You didn't exactly make it difficult. Folks are saying that barn out back glows in the dark. You may think the farmers around here are stupid just because they don't talk much. Me, I've never been convinced talk was a good indicator of brains."

"People know what's going on here? Shit. How long can it be until the cops find out?"

"I'll tell you this much: when the cops *do* find out, it won't be from a farmer. The police are 'government,' which pretty much makes them the enemy. Besides, a crop is a crop. Most of your neighbors are probably envious, even if they'd never take the kind of risk you and your buddies are taking."

Danny watched the old man pour honey in his tea until the cup nearly overflowed. He said, "I don't get why you came looking for me."

"I wasn't. Not 'til a big fucking Indian told me you were waving a wad around the casino. Thought maybe I should look in on you."

"You mean the tree-sized bastard who threw me out a few nights ago?" Danny started to sweat. Iggy had been right about how many people had seen him and Lester together.

"That's right. Big Fucker's a friend of mine. Let's me play a little blackjack when I get the itch."

Danny asked, "You gonna tell Mom about this?"

Skeritt snorted and sipped his tea.

Danny's mom had always done her best to provide, moving from town to country and back again. Her one-time lover had split for a job out west before she even knew she was pregnant.

"You look a little like him. Same bones," she had told Danny more than once. "I wish I could tell you more but we were like two sheets to the wind, passing in the night, as the saying goes. I mean, he was a good-looking guy and I'm sure we could've got along well enough if we'd tried, but I wasn't thinking that way then. A party was a party, and I was just a party girl. You came along, gave my life meaning, some purpose, a reason to be home on the weekends, and all that was terrific, but I never really felt the need to have a man around— besides you."

Danny couldn't feel abandoned by a father who never knew he existed. Besides, his mother did all the good things a father was supposed to do, and none of the bad. She signed Danny up for hockey and never missed a game while he played three whole seasons in second hand skates before deciding team sports were not his thing. She taught him how to wield an axe to chop a little wood and made sure to take him camping at least twice a year.

"Car camping is for city folk, Danny," she told him. "If I want to sit on a lawn chair under the stars and listen to the radio by an open fire, I'll do it in the back yard. Not in some compound crammed full of people afraid of the dark."

Their favorite place to camp was an island in the middle of Pike Lake. Danny's mom said it used to be Indian land. "But then this was all Indian land once upon a time, wasn't it?" It was close to twenty acres in size, well-treed, and had a commanding view of the lake from a couple of granite-faced cliffs. The First Nations crew harbored fishing boats, canoes, and barges in its natural deepwater cove whenever they converged on the island for "spiritual festivities."

Around the campfire at night, often accompanied by Skeritt or one or two other close friends, they could easily feel they were in deep bush. Apart from an occasional satellite or airplane that marred the night sky, the only proof civilization existed was a white haze that clung to the southwestern sky where Toronto lay a hundred miles away.

Those were the best nights of Danny's life. Sharing hot chocolate and ghost stories, watching the bottle of brandy get passed back and forth, and crawling into a tent to fall asleep to the sound of crickets and the rustling of small animals in the underbrush.

Even when things were bad, even when he messed up big time as boys sometimes will, those nights and weekends on the island were a safe haven for Danny. More often than not, it was Skeritt who would take him aside and share a little adult philosophy, which often amounted to something like: "It won't matter twenty years from now, Danny. Just buckle down and get past it." Whether *it* was failing math again, or getting caught stealing a few beers from behind the counter at a local diner.

Through it all, Skeritt had been the strongest male presence in his life. And here he was again, drinking tea in the farmhouse kitchen, looking at Danny with clear blue eyes that made him feel small and transparent.

"Listen, Danny," the old man was saying, "I promised your mother to look out for you and I always will, but what you actually *do* while I am looking out for you is your own damn business. This *particular* business is a stupid one that can only end in trouble."

It was like a lot of conversations they had had before. Skeritt claimed to be nonjudgmental, yet he had pretty strong views about almost everything. And he could always be trusted to share them.

"Just what the hell do you think these guys are going to do with you when you're done here, Danny?"

"I haven't really thought about it."

"Maybe you should. Way I figure, they'll pretty much have to get rid of you, won't they. You know too much."

"What do I know? Some guy in a bar gave me this address to show up at. Since then, all I get is notes on the kitchen table and some fucked-up voice on the phone."

"Good luck explaining that to the cops."

"So what are you saying? I should leave? Run and hide...is that it?"

"How should I know? All I've got is an opinion. And opinions are interesting, but they're ultimately irrelevant, don't you think?" Skeritt pulled a match stick from his pocket, split it lengthwise with his thumbnail, and began to pick his teeth. Danny stared at him and thought: *At least the damn iguana says what's on its mind.*

"Listen, kid," Skeritt went on after a few moments, "the way I see it, you've got a good gig right now. Like most good gigs, it's going to have to end sooner or later. What you're doing is illegal. The cops may not the brightest lights in these parts. But they're going to find out about this here plantation one way or another. You don't want to be here when that happens. You also don't want to be here when whoever is in charge shows up to collect his dope, or his dough, or however the hell it works. The boss man of this kind of setup is not cute and cuddly, I can tell you that. But take off and hide? I don't know, Danny, it ain't as easy as it sounds. And I'm speaking from experience." Skeritt examined the matchstick which had become frayed in his mouth. He spat out a few splinters of wood, threw the matchstick to the floor and pulled out a fresh one. "Got any food?"

"I think there's some peanut butter in the cupboard."

"Perfect."

Danny prepared a sandwich, slathering it extra thick the way he knew Skeritt liked.

"You've got to have a plan," Skeritt said, "a safe place to go. An out. You can't just start running and hope to find safety. It doesn't work that way."

"I guess I'd just hole up at my mom's."

Skeritt munched the peanut butter sandwich. When he finally spoke, his voice had gravel in it. "You really do think right out loud, don't you? I mean, the stuff that comes out of your mouth hasn't been pre-processed, has it? It just sort of runs out over your tongue into the air and then you hear it for the first time, just like whoever it is you are talking to."

"Uh, yeah, I guess so..."

"Well, if that particular idea had ever suffered the benefit of thought, it might have occurred to you that your mother's is the first place people will look for you. And if it's the cops, it'll be immediate, and if it's some gangbangers, it'll be ugly."

"Oh."

"Any other questions before you shut up and listen?"

"Just one. Are you ever going to tell me why you give a shit, Skeritt?"

"Are you ever going to ask?"

"I think I just did."

Skeritt looked at Danny like he had appeared out of thin air. He wrinkled his forehead and nodded silently.

"Okay. Fair is fair," he said. "If I'm dogging you, you might as well know why. Nothing much can be done about things that happened terribly long ago, anyway." He chewed the last of the sandwich and washed it down with a gulp of tea. "You already know I worked with your mother at The Boathouse."

"She's been picking up a few shifts there again. She's always telling me what a happening place it used to be—nothing like the dive it is now."

"Right. Well, that wasn't the first place we worked together. In fact, I was only ever at The Boathouse for a few months. The place where we first met each other was Patterson's. Before you were even born."

"Patterson's? What's that? Some other bar?"

"No. Patterson had a sawmill operation, started by his grandfather actually. I have no idea what the elder Patterson was like, but Menlo Patterson was better known as Patterson the Prick."

"Tough boss?"

"'Tough' is not the word, and tough alone would not have been a problem. Those were rough days for forestry. Interest rates were through the roof and crews were getting laid off all over the place. In the early eighties, steel and wood in Canada were pretty much wiped out. Anyone who could keep a sawmill in operation had to be tough as nails, and Menlo Patterson was no exception. In his case, however, he was also a capital 'P' prick."

While Skeritt talked, Danny had rolled a joint and he offered it to the old man to light. He paused his story to put the joint into his mouth and wet the paper. He did it with ceremony, almost reverence. His tongue pushed out of his mouth more than an inch and he allowed the joint to kind of loll about on it before closing his upper lip and pulling it out uniformly damp. His grizzled face seemed to settle, his cheeks sagging a bit as he turned the joint around and lit it with another safety match from his pocket.

Not for the first time, Danny felt embarrassed, shallow, and more than a little foolish faced with the raw independence of this mountain of a man. He'd outlived thousands of his peers fighting a tropical war he didn't believe in before running north to Canada rather than risk a second tour in Vietnam. He'd traded the jungle for a forest—one with fewer people and less hospitable weather patterns.

"You see," Skeritt said, expelling a thick lungful of smoke, "they laid more than a dozen safety infraction notices on the Prick's sawmill. At least three different inspectors from the Ministry of Labor. Even thirty years ago, you couldn't buy those inspectors off with a case of scotch. The Prick ran a real slipshod operation—guys losing a finger here, an earlobe there, all kinds of cuts, crushes, fractures—by rights, Patterson's ought to have been shut down. But he was a good ole boy. Pals with three longtime local small-town mayors, all of whom wanted the jobs to stay put.

"No one could ever pin anything on him. If someone dared complain out loud, they always seemed to get in a big fight with some crazy out-of-towner drifting through the local watering hole."

"What do you mean?" Danny asked, handing the joint back to Skeritt. "He'd have people beat up?"

"Beat up. Run out of town. Have their houses broken into so many times they couldn't get insurance. Nobody could ever prove it was The Prick causing their troubles, but everyone knew. The smart thing to do was keep your mouth shut if you needed your job. And around these parts thirty-odd years ago, unless you were a farmer growing your own food, there was no guarantee you and your family wouldn't go hungry from one season to the next."

"What does any of this have to do with my mother?"

"I'm getting to that. Roll another joint would you?" Skeritt coughed, spat on the kitchen floor, and said, "Oh, sorry, I forgot we're indoors." He wiped up the spit with the bottom of his shin-high moccasin. "Got these booties from a Nishnabe fellow last week. Not bad, eh?

"Now, where was I? Oh yeah, so Prick Patterson's been paying off the local politicos or kissing whoever's ass it takes to keep this sawmill from the nineteen-forties running full steam into 1983. I'm working there. So's your mom and a bunch of other hippies. Plus a handful of Indians from the Reserve. Not one of us knew our asses from our elbows when it comes to safety. June thirtieth, a fire started on Number Three Saw. It was six o'clock and no one should have been working at all, what with it being Canada Day the next day. Folks had already shut down just after five, but the Prick sent a crew back in and wouldn't let anyone leave until they completed a last minute order he'd received.

"Probably somebody threw a cigarette on the floor and didn't stamp it out. No one ever enforced the no-smoking rules and the sawdust was never cleaned up right.

"Someone pulled out the fire hose and opened the valve, but the water pump had been broken for months. I was in the front office where your mother worked. She dialed the fire department, but the Prick storms out of his office and tells her to hang up. Says they'll just lay another fine on us. Tells us to put it out ourselves.

"I couldn't believe my ears, but my training in 'Nam wouldn't let me stand still and watch, so I ran across the yard and did what I could. We all did. Someone got a bucket brigade going and they dragged another hose across from the garage. The mill was thick with smoke and people from inside were stumbling out coughing up their guts. Only some of them weren't coming out at all. I wet my T-shirt and put it over my face. Went in myself. I pulled one guy out and went back in for another. That's when the whole place just blew. Sawdust is like gunpowder when it is dry. It was like a fuel-air bomb went off in there. This guy comes running toward me, holding his face in his hands. Knocked me over. Screaming. 'I CAN'T SEE!'"

Skeritt's shout blew Danny to the floor, kicked back as he was on two legs of the kitchen chair. Ignoring his backwards tumble, the older man went on with his story, his voice more somber now. "I carried the bugger out on my back—all two hundred twenty pounds of him—and we collapsed together outside in the yard. There was no more going back in. The mill was an inferno." He paused to take a sip of tea. "Seven people burned alive that day. We stood there listening to their screams. Much as we could hear over the fire."

Danny swallowed dry.

Skeritt said, "And the Prick? He fucked off pronto. Later on, he collected the insurance money, blew one helluva wad on one helluva party all winter down in Florida."

"I don't get it," said Danny. "Why wouldn't my mother have told me about this?"

"She was made to shut up about it. We all were. We were just a bunch of dumbfuck workers who'd caused a fire that killed seven of our friends. The Prick paid for a plaque at city hall commemorating their heroism. He only misspelled two of their names. After a while, most people drifted away to jobs in other places, got on with their lives. The guy I carried out was Ernie McCann. He ended up pretty much blind, as you know. Even then, we had a hell of a time getting any kind of compensation for him. The Prick figured he could just wait him out and he would disappear into the woodwork. I nearly gave up the fight myself, especially when Patterson tried to pin the explosion on me, saying it was some kind of protest. Said I had become all anti-establishment after being carted off to fight in Vietnam and all that. If it wasn't for your mother's help, pointing the way to some of the safety violations we could actually prove, there's no way Ernie or the families of any of the dead and injured workers would have got a damn thing.

"Far as your mother, she was told she'd never get another office job in town. That's how she wound up waitressing. Patterson paid out maybe a hundred grand in a settlement which meant most people got about zero but at least we could feel we sort of won somehow.

"I gave up on the whole damn shooting match. I drifted a bit from job to job and moved further and further out of town until finally I was living out in the bush. I've been there deep nearly twenty years now. Apart from Ernie, your mom, and a handful of folk who give me a meal when I drift by and shoot the shit, no one knows or cares whether I exist and, for me, that's just about perfect."

The two men sat quietly for a few moments. It was Danny who broke the silence. "My mom told me Ernie lost his eyesight in an industrial accident, that he didn't like to speak about it. I never thought about it much."

"Like I said, we all buried it pretty deep. Your mom deeper than most. If it weren't for you coming along three or four years after the fire, she might have jumped a bus out west, or put on a back pack and tramped Europe or something. Instead, she just kept her head screwed on straight and did her best to raise you, Danny.

"Ernie, what with losing his vision, got a little extra money from the government and a big enough disability settlement to put a down payment on that cabin of his. He's got it mortgaged so far out, he'll never see the end of it, and the taxes he owes are worth almost as much as the land, but no one on council will touch him 'cause there's still people with guilt on 'em. I have my social security checks mailed to his place and sign them over to him. He buys me the few supplies I can't do without—some canned milk, coffee, and peanut butter. I pick them up now and then. He's always there at the cabin, anyways."

"Mom still takes him out shopping sometimes—once a month or so," Danny said. "She used to bring him over to our house for dinner and she'd give me a hard time about it if I skipped out. He's an alright guy. Used to get me a toy car or a little Lego kit or something for my birthday. I took him a lasagna just the other day."

"Yeah, the three of us sort of take care of each other. Been doing it twenty years. Not about to stop now, neither."

"So is that why you're here?" Danny asked.

"Well, I'm not just here for the dope, if that's what you mean. Spark up another one, would you?"

Danny picked up a bud and crumbled it onto the table in front of him. As he cleaned out the twiggy bits, his fingertips sticky, Skeritt said, "You asked my opinion, so here it is. If thing's ever go bad—and I mean stinking bad—here's the plan: I want you to head straight to Ernie's place."

"Uh huh, then what?"

"Then what what? Just tell Ernie you need help. He's part Indian. They got this thing about taking care of their own."

"Part Indian? Ernie? I never knew that. How much?"

"Who cares how much? Some. Part. Indian is Indian." Skeritt pulled his bushy eyebrows low over his eyes. "Just get your hide over to Ernie's place if you're in trouble. You can trust him. And you don't have to tell him anything you don't want to. That's up to you. Just let him know you want to see me and he'll get word to me. Won't take long at all. We'll figure stuff out after that."

"That's it? That's your big plan? 'We'll figure stuff out?'"

"It's been working for me, so far..."

"It's *working* for you? Damn, Skeritt, you're a bush-dwelling hermit. You eat small animals you catch with your bare hands. You look like a fucking Sasquatch and smell like day-old fish. How in hell do you sit there and say, 'It's working for me?'"

Skeritt blew his nose onto his sleeve and wiped his moustache with the palm of his hand.

"Dannyboy, I don't think you've been listening to a word I said. There ain't no one you can trust except your family and the people you make your family. You're fortunate to have a couple of people besides your mom who care about you. What you do with that is your own damn business."

Skeritt took the jay Danny offered him and sucked the smoke deep into his lungs. When he exhaled, the cloud of smoke was large enough to engulf them both.

"Now bag me a couple ounces of that sweet weed and I'll be on my way. Throw in some papers, would you?" Skeritt looked out the window at the slanting early evening sun. "By the way, you were wondering which day it is? Far as I can tell, it's the day after yesterday."

EIGHT

Terry got maybe five miles down the road in Lester's car before the engine sputtered, coughed, and died. Out of gas. He checked the trunk and sure enough, Lester carried an empty two-gallon gas can and a siphoning hose. Terry moved the pot from the back seat to the trunk, took the can, and trudged toward the next town.

As cars passed him, he stuck out his thumb in a halfhearted attempt to hitch a ride, without even bothering to face the traffic. As luck would have it though, the third car did pull over. It was a cop.

"Where you headed? Getting some gas for your car?" the cop asked with a smile. His mirrored sunglasses reflected the setting sun.

"Huh? Uh, no sir, officer. I'm just heading home, is all. Yep. Gonna go have a barbeque, need a little gas to light her up." Terry gave a wave good-bye and kept walking.

The car pulled alongside again. The cop was still smiling, his forehead furrowed. "There was a Taurus on the shoulder about a mile or so back. The engine was still warm. Dried puke, it looked like, all over the hood."

Terry blinked and tried to swallow, his throat dry and a bit gritty.

The cop said, "And now here's you walking along with a gas can. You sure that wasn't your car? Been drinking maybe?"

"Oh, no, officer. I don't own no car. Like I said, I'm just on my way home now."

"Where's home, son?"

"Rice Lake."

"Really. Well, you're going to be some hungry by the time you get there, now aren't you. That's got to be twenty miles from here."

"Oh, I walk fast, y'know. Besides, it's gonna be a big barbeque. Yep. For sure."

"Uh huh," the cop made a show of snapping gum between his smiling teeth.

Terry grinned widely, and began to twirl the gas can on two fingers in his best attempt at appearing nonchalant.

The cop asked, "Gonna have a bunch of friends at your big barbeque?"

"Yes, I mean, no! I'm not going to have the barbeque at my place, you see. Heh heh. No sir, I mean, er, officer. I'm just heading to my pal's place. Y'know..."

A puzzled look replaced the cop's smile. He pushed his sunglasses up onto his forehead, and stopped the car. He walked around to where Terry was standing at the side of the road, kicking his right toe into the dirt.

"Whaddya say we go back and have a look at that car about a mile back?"

"I really should be getting going, I think. I got a long walk ahead of me."

"Oh, heck, it won't take long at all and, hey, for as long as I hold you up, I'll drive you that far home after, alright?"

"Well, uh, I dunno. I guess it's alright," Terry was starting to wish he'd said the car was his. Still, he figured as long as the cop didn't frisk him and find the keys to Lester's car in his pocket, he should be able to talk his way out of things. He grinned and stepped toward the passenger door.

"You can sit in the back," said the cop. He closed the door on Terry and walked around to the driver's side.

The cop spun the car through a tight U-turn, throwing up gravel and dust and accelerated quickly back down the road. Pulling up behind Lester's Taurus, the officer typed the license plate into the dashboard computer.

"Well, will you look at that. I guess this isn't your car after all. You said you live in Rice Lake. This here car belongs to a Mr. Lester Freeden. And Mr. Freeden lives just a little ways back this very road."

Not any more, he doesn't, Terry thought.

"Why don't I just go take a look," the cop said.

Through the back seat grill, Terry watched him circle the car once then use a Slim Jim to open the driver door and pop the trunk. He started to sweat and wondered whether he might puke again. When the officer turned around with the gym bag in his hands, he knew the answer. He was toast. The bile rose in his throat and he fought hard to push it back down. He almost succeeded but for a hot shot that backed up into his sinus cavity and came out his nose. Terry wiped his face on his shirt, shaking uncontrollably.

Beaming, the cop thrust his face in the driver's side window and said, "Look at what I found: a nice big bag of pot. 'Major Quantity' is what we call this. Now, I wonder why Mr. Freeden would leave his car at the side of the road with Major Quantity in it just a few minutes from his home. Can you think of why he'd do that?"

"I, uh, I don't even know Mr. Freeden, sir. Can we just go now? Uh, sir."

"Sure, sure. Just wait a second while I throw this in *my* trunk and then we'll take a little drive over to Mr. Freeden's house and see what he has to say about all this. You won't mind, will you? That way I'll know you didn't, ah, take this poor man's car *and* his dope."

"Uh, geez, I mean. Shit. Officer, it ain't me you're after, sir."

"It isn't? After? What do you mean, *after?*"

"Listen, I just took the car, and, and, I mean, I was doing a favor, y'know. And, like, oh man, oh man. I had nothing to do with any of this. Uh, listen, you think that's Major Quantity in that there bag? How 'bout if I can tell you where there is one helluva a lot of pot. Like a total factory scene."

"Well, now, that sounds more interesting than anything else you've said. What say we try this over from the beginning." The cop got back into the front seat and said, "I'm Officer Ainsley. What's your name, son?"

Aunt Helena's Mexican Restaurant and Motel had been chosen for the meet by Enrique and Arnoldo, the Nicaraguan brothers who formed the Skeleton's local crew. This was just one more part of biker gang elegance that struck pride in

Perko's soul. The New York Skeleton gang had the privilege of picking a locale where they could feel safe and everyone could relax. They'd run over the details for the planned exchange of money for drugs—with the money, but no drugs, present at the meeting. It had been hard as hell for him to negotiate a real cash deal this big. After the discount and paying the Libidos their share, he'd have little to show for his crop. But every snaking inch of his gut told him this was a night he'd remember forever—one that would launch him from also-ran to one of the heaviest members of the Libidos Motorcycle Club.

There really was an Aunt Helena, and Enrique and Arnoldo called her that, though she was neither a blood relative of the Nicaraguans nor, for that matter, Mexican. She was a third-generation Italian Canadian whose family hailed from southern France. She made a mean chili, served a meaner margarita, and could be counted on for discretion. She had hung the "Private Party" sign on the front door, only too happy to close the restaurant and accept a hefty tip from a couple of her favorite boys.

Two of the eight attached motel units served as Aunt Helena's permanent residence. The other rooms were open to the general public, but apart from nooners and the occasional late-night guest, drive-by business was slow. More often than not, people staying at the motel were regulars seeking anonymity, access to hearty food, and twenty-four seven bar service. Enrique and Arnoldo had spent more than a few extended weekends in Aunt Helena's complete care when the rigors of gang life proved hard to endure. Tonight, the "No Vacancy" neon burned brightly and Perko knew for sure there would be at least another half dozen Skeletons hanging in the rooms—muscle in case Perko and his crew tried to take the money and run.

Before letting them into the restaurant, Enrique patted down Perko and both Nancy's Nasties, Frederick and Bernard. He didn't seem to know what to make of Bernard's basketball-sized afro. He tried running his fingers through it but they got caught and Bernard slapped him. Finally, he made the biker bend over and shake his head hard to prove it concealed no weapons.

A big round table for seven was decked out with a shot glass at each place, two open bottles of tequila, a few dishes of lemon wedges, and extra shakers of salt. Aunt Helena poured the first round herself and joined in the toast.

"Here's to duty free marijuana!" Perko bellowed. He threw back the tequila and bit hard into the lemon. The other men followed suit with a course of, "Salud!" and "Santé!" Aunt Helena said, "Bon appétit," and a waiter carried in heaping plates of nachos, hot peppers, and guacamole.

The restaurant walls were painted alternate ochre and a luminous blue. Sombreros hung here and there, some on the walls or on rough dark posts that looked like barn beams. A few were even tacked into the ceiling. The brightly colored paper lanterns strung across the dining room on an electrical cord were hung so low Perko had to duck. Two chubby guitar players played non-stop. One had a droopy blond moustache. The other was dark enough to be Mexican but sang with a Russian accent. They wandered around the restaurant, as though it were full of romantic diners. By the time they started their third tune, Perko was ready to make them eat their damn guitars.

"I'll ride in first," he spewed between mouthfuls of food. "I'm coming in from the back on a three-wheeler." He leaned into a second platter of Mount Saint Helena's Nachos, so named because they resembled a mini-volcano, the mound of nachos piled nearly six inches high, rivers of extra spicy salsa running like lava over a thick layer of molten cheese.

"I'll pre-count the money here and then Frederick is going to ride with you and the dough to make sure you don't fuck with it. I'll count it again on site. Cash and crop won't be at the same place same time for more than six or seven minutes. Ten tops."

"Hey, how come Frederick he get to go with the money?" Bernard asked.

"*Tais-toi*, Bernard," Frederick told the other Nasty in a low voice. "You have to drive over the car, okay." Bernard sniffed and Perko looked away, rolling his eyes.

The senior bikers hammered out the details. Bernard would arrive second, accompanied by Enrique. They would open the gate for the Skeletons, who would be right behind them in a pair of rented cube vans. Perko and Frederick would take three of the Skeleton crew inside the barn, while Bernard and one of the Nicaraguans would wait outside, acting as lookouts until the exchange was complete. The bales would be loaded onto the vans and driven east to a safe house in Akwesasne. From there, moving the pot across the border would be routine. The reserve straddled both the provincial and international borders, with no less than six territorial police forces tripping over each other. It was a smuggler's nirvana, favored by every known criminal organization in the world, and more than a few freelancers.

From the start, the Skeletons had refused to give their names. "Just call us Number One and Number Two," said the first one.

"Which number are you?" Perko asked between bites.

"Doesn't much matter, does it?"

Like Perko, the numbered Skeleton wore a black leather jacket with extra thick elbow pads and a pair of jeans held up by an oversized belt buckle. The Skeleton's buckle was a simple skull which he loosened by one notch as he scooped a nacho full of guacamole. Perko tried to adjust his own buckle, a convoluted affair loosely fashioned after a pair of double-D breasts, but found it jammed. He tugged at it with both hands until he realized the Skeletons were smirking at his efforts. With a burp, he asked, "Who're you gonna leave on watch?"

"I don't much care," said Number One or Two. "They can decide between themselves. It ain't like we're going to let either one of them carry the money."

As if on cue, Bernard whined, "Why me I get stuck outside? Again, heh?"

Perko groaned and shot a glance at Frederick who said, "Someone he has to keep the lookout *pour la police, non? C'est toi*, Bernard. You've got the best eyes and the ears, too."

Bernard swore under his breath and stabbed at his chicken enchilada with his fork. "It's the same thing every time. Always, you get the good action and me, I hang around, waiting. Somebody he needs to get his knees cracked, you wear the boots and me I drive the car. We go roll some kid for his stash, you dig around his pockets, while me? I hold the knife. We make a delivery, you carry the bag and I hold the *esti de* door open for you. The Libidos, they want we pick someone up..."

Turning in his chair, Perko raised his well-heeled foot fifteen inches off the ground and slammed it down on Bernard's sneaker-clad toes. Bernard screamed, the Skeletons guffawed, and the Nicaraguans snickered. Aunt Helena popped her head out from the kitchen, smiled widely when she saw everything was okay, and disappeared again.

The darker guitarist began strumming a mariachi-inspired version of *You Can't Always Get What You Want.* Perko prayed he wouldn't sing it. He wondered where the blond guitarist with the moustache had made off to and wished his partner would follow him.

He plowed into a heaping skillet of mixed chicken and beef fajitas. He loved the whole idea of roll-your-own food. Ignoring a warning from Arnoldo, he poured on the green hot sauce and chowed down. His mouth on fire, he quenched it with Aunt Helena's home-made draft beer, interspersing shots of tequila served up with more lemon and salt.

The guitarist had started to sing after all. He wasn't half bad.

Arnoldo and Enrique decided on a knife-throwing contest to determine which one of them would accompany Bernard on lookout duty. They each grabbed a steak knife and Enrique counted off fifteen paces from a sombrero hanging on the door to the men's room. "You shoot *primero, hermano,*" he told his brother. Arnoldo's knife landed dead center. It was thrown with such force that it twanged when it struck the wooden door, the tip buried a good inch.

Grooving on his solo, the dark-haired singer belted out the chorus.

"Cucaracha!" Enrique snorted. "I'm going to spleet your knife right out the *puerta!*" and he wound up to throw the knife as if he were pitching in the World Series. At that moment Perko heard a toilet flush and turned his head to see the bathroom door swing open, pulled from the inside by the blond guitarist. Enrique tried to check his pitch mid-swing, but a knife is no baseball and it flew out of his fingers, spinning end-over-end at sombrero height at the startled face of the second guitarist.

Darkie hit the top note. His voice cracked as he strummed with full arm arcs. Blondie recoiled without fully understanding what was happening. He turned his head and the knife sliced down the right side of his face, neatly shaving one half of his moustache and leaving a thin pink line in its place. A few drops of blood immediately appeared and the knife clattered harmlessly against the tiled wall behind the de-whiskered man.

"*Hola*! Another round of tequila! *Dobles para los musicos*!" shouted Arnoldo, slapping congratulations on his brother's back. "You choose, *hermano. Dentro o fuera*!"

With Lester in the ground, and Shooter the villain dog stone dead and buried under a pile of rocks after eating Lester's strychnine-laced left foot, Danny felt entitled to feel relief. Instead, Skeritt's visit had left him dead tired and angry.

"I'm looking pretty good, here," he said out loud to Iggy, rolling one last joint before leaving the farmhouse for the night. Iggy stared off into space, resolutely uncommunicative or sound asleep—Danny couldn't tell the difference. "I got two more months of unemployment, a cool grand a week cash, and all the dope I can smoke. I'm due ten thou bonus from the first harvest any day now and this new crop will be good for ten thousand more in three months' time. Skeritt is a worrywart is all."

Sure, and you know he won't tell your mom and burst her bubble, now she thinks you're driving a forklift and earning an honest living.

"Leave my mom outta this, you prehistoric rat. I'm going to do her proud. Gonna make sure she's never going to have to worry again about havin' enough money to keep the house or for food or for medicine or nothing."

And she won't need to wonder where you are anymore. You'll be rotting in a jail cell.

"Not a chance, banana breath. I buried the body just like you said and the longer it stays that way, the less chance there is they'll ever tie it to me. I took back my carton of smokes and everything. Anyway, I'm outta here. Gonna sleep at home tonight. Make breakfast for Mom in the morning." As he shifted his weight out of the lumpy chair, Danny felt a nip on the inside of his elbow. He flicked his hand at it, but the creature bit even harder. "Goddamn ants!"

He stumbled into the hall and across to the bathroom where he kept the ant poison. Ants and mice were a constant in the farmhouse, especially in the iguana's room. He had mousetraps set pretty much everywhere. Iggy had quickly learned to avoid them. A part of Danny's daily routine—on the days he remembered—was patrolling the house, refilling traps with peanut butter, and emptying his dead prey into a plastic bag. He figured he had dropped no fewer than a hundred fifty mice onto the compost heap behind the barn.

Before learning that Iggy preferred bananas, Danny had hoped the iguana would hunt the mice, like a cat. Instead, from what he could tell, the lizard viewed the mice as furry accomplices in some kind of wildlife bid to drive the resident human batty. Between the mice, their turds, and the ants—turds with legs, as far as Danny was concerned—the farmhouse was a creeping zoo.

In the bathroom, Danny opened the closet door and reached to the top shelf to grab the ant poison. He froze. Wrapped around the Ant-B-Gon bottle was a patchy brown tail that looked eerily like Iggy dressed up for a party. Slowly, Danny pulled his hand away and stared at the snake. It was brown with grey blocks, or grey with brown blocks. The thing had to be four feet long and was more than inch in diameter in the middle. Its tiny head was coiled back and it held Danny's eyes in its own; suddenly, it struck out and barely missed Danny's hand. At the same instant, a mouse trap snapped shut on the snake's tail. With a flurry of snake skin, the Massasauga Rattler did its best to shake the trap free. Danny slammed the door and jammed a towel under it.

He collapsed in his chair back in the front room.

"Sonofabitch," he fumed. "I might as well be living in the bush with Skeritt for all the damn creatures in this place!" And he rolled up one massive fatty to calm his nerves.

NINE

Roaring through the night on his Harley, Perko felt his guts ready to explode. He shouldn't have had the third serving of refried black beans, but the gooey cheese topping had been too much to resist. The last mile to where he kept his three-wheeler hidden in the forest, the gravel road was rutted like corrugated cardboard. Despite slowing down, he felt like he was tied to an off-level washing machine in the spin cycle. Before ditching the bike for the ATV, he bent double at the side of the road to get more blood into his head.

A few minutes later, bouncing through the forest, he finally gave in to intestinal revolt: it was time to do what bears do in the woods. He stopped, found a fallen tree limb to squat over, and fought to undo his belt buckle. Then he remembered his leather leggings. His stomach did somersaults as he struggled with the extra straps. In the pitch dark, it felt as though the chaps' belt was somehow hooked through the loops on his jeans, and the more he tried to pull it loose, the tighter the noose around his belly became. Finally, he belched loudly and simultaneously farted. His stomach pain vanished and he felt light as a balloon. He lit a cigarette and wiped the sweat from his forehead. He figured he could last until the farmhouse where he'd be able to see what was going on around his waist. Not to mention he'd rather use a real toilet.

Clambering back onto the three-wheeled ATV, he rode the rest of the way to the farm as fast as he could, gulping cold autumn air in an effort to clear his head and calm his stomach.

When he emerged from the trees on the ATV, the first thing he saw was a rust bucket Sunfire parked beside the old pickup. For a moment, he thought maybe he'd spent longer than he thought sweating over his pants in the middle of the forest. Maybe Bernard and the Nicaraguan had beat him to the farm. But wasn't Bernard driving a cherry red Miata with the roof down? His lousy punk pot farmer must have ignored the note telling him to clear out. Silhouetted against a light in a second floor window, Perko saw the idiot's lizard, sitting stock still, staring down at him.

Leaving the key in the ignition of the three-wheeler, he stomped across the yard toward the house, not sure what he was going to do to the disobedient punk but certain it was going to hurt. At the open barn door, he smelled smoke—dark acrid smoke, like something manmade was burning: the stupid farmer was doing a barrel burn tonight of all nights. Turning on his heel to head into the barn, he heard a car drive up the gravel road and slow down at the gate. Perko froze, his gut clenched. Bernard had arrived with Enrico-or-whatever-the-fuck. That meant the Skeletons would be there in a minute or two.

His mind bounced among the moron in the farmhouse, the toilet that awaited him, the smoke coming from his barn, and the arrival of the money at the front gate. The money won out when Bernard honked the horn and Perko heard the Nicaraguan swear at him in Spanish. Looking up at the window, Perko saw the lizard still sitting there. Maybe the punk had taken off without his car. If he had, someone must have picked him up—also against the rules. Perko would make him pay either way.

Bernard honked again, longer this time, and then began to swear: "Tabarnak! Who you punch da head, you grease monkey. Owww! Perko, open the gate, hurry you."

"You've got a fucking key, Bernard," Perko hissed, turning his back on the barn and striding over.

"I think the key it is Frederick he take it from you at the restaurant." He honked one more time and Perko noticed a light turn on in a yard a quarter mile down the road.

"Lay off the fucking horn, shit-for-brains," Perko shouted. Fishing his own key from his pocket, he unlocked the gate and swung it open. He heel-kicked Bernard's driver's side headlight. It smashed with a puff of smoke. The stench of burning wire filled his already-singed nostrils and he felt adrenaline rush from his thighs through his chest, neck, and head until it felt like his ears were on fire.

He rounded the car and pulled open Bernard's door with his left hand while he grabbed the man's hair with his right, pulled him out of his seat, and threw him screaming to the ground. With Bernard's foot off the brake, the car rolled forward slowly. Enrique reached over and grabbed the steering wheel, but before he could make his way across to take full control, the car had lumbered through the gate, scraping its right side along the steel post that held the gate's hinges. The gate itself clanged back against the car and Bernard's squeals turned to a whimper and a sob.

"Aw tabarnak, why you do dat? I just ask you open the gate."

With a swift kick to the man's thigh, Perko started to walk back toward the farmhouse, his knees wobbling. At that moment, he heard the roar of the twin cube vans. The sweat running down his back turned ice cold, and he felt his gut start to roil all over again. He waved the vans into the yard.

"Bernard! Get out of the way, you stupid wimp. Want me to pull what's left of your hair off a your scalp?"

Perko walked down the driveway to where Enrique had managed to stop the car near the barn. When he got there, Perko leaned himself against the warm fender, trying to gain control of his tequila-soaked brain. He needed a toilet bad and couldn't see how he could last another ten minutes. He wasn't about to go into the house to face the farmer now that the deal was going down. If they came face-to-face, he'd have no choice but to kill the shithead—not part of the plan for his big night.

The vans pulled to a halt and Skeletons Number One and Two piled out along with Frederick and Arnoldo. They joined Perko and the others beside the car.

"Frederick," Perko said, his voice a dry croak, "you take Bernard inside with you. I'm staying out here on watch." He paused to wipe sweat from his forehead with his sleeve. He pointed a finger at the Nasty. "You pull this off right, I'll talk to Hawk. You'll be a made guy." He grimaced and clutched his stomach with both hands. "Either one of you screws this deal..." His voice trailed off. He bent double and made a bow-legged dash around the car toward the trees.

The last thing he heard was Enrique saying, "Holy mother of Dios, what ees that smell?"

And Arnoldo's answer: "That, *hermano*, would be Mount Santa Helena. She is erupting all over again."

Terry had misjudged how excited the cop would be when he told him about the grow op. Somehow, he'd imagined Officer Ainsley would lose interest after driving up and down a few dozen back roads. Instead, the cop kept asking him to repeat the vague description he'd assembled from scraps of conversation with Danny. At one point, when they stopped at the side of the road so Terry could take a leak, he'd suggested they call it a day. He could just walk the rest of the way home. Maybe they could go looking again tomorrow or something. After that, the cop got a little meaner, and he made a radio call with the Plexiglas pulled tight so Terry couldn't hear.

Twenty minutes later, they pulled into a farm that Terry was sure couldn't be right. Instead of a darkened yard, there were two white rental cube vans with lights on and engines running. He and Officer Ainsley watched two men walk out of the barn, each carrying what looked like small hay bales on their shoulders. They carried them to the back of one of the vans. The men spotted the cruiser in the yard and shouted at someone out of sight inside the barn. The next thing Terry knew, the cruiser was filled with the sound of a siren and the yard was bathed in swirling blue and red light. The vans sped past the cruiser as the cop radioed for assistance. He jumped out of the car and chased two men who were running after the vans.

That's when Terry noticed the two other cars in the farmyard: a sporty red convertible and Danny's Bondo-special. His heart skipped a beat. Squealing on the grow op had seemed like a decent way out since Danny was supposed to be at his mother's place, anyways. Cop gets a big score, Terry gets off on stealing a dead man's car, and Danny could always find another job. Riding in the back of the cruiser, Terry had even mused about the likelihood of earning a medal—something about community service or something. He'd like that.

It didn't look like things were turning out quite the way he'd imagined.

Two men were pushed into the back seat alongside Terry, arguing in Spanish. They reeked of smoke—some of it good. He grinned at them sheepishly and said, "Hey, you guys friends of Danny?"

Two more men ran from the barn and wrestled each other. They were bathed in flickering light. It was too far to see for sure and the night was inky black with no moon, but it looked like smoke was pouring out the barn roof.

Officer Ainsley fired his pistol into the air and chased the men down the driveway. At the sound of the gun, Terry's throat filled with bile and there was a warm sensation between his thighs. One of the two men near the barn fell to his knees and surrendered. The cop pushed him, whimpering, back to the cruiser. The second man ran off into the bush.

Bright orange fingers licked up the barn walls, then disappeared, only to reappear a few feet away, rippling up and down the hundred-year-old structure.

When the fourth man was jammed into the back seat of the cop car, the two Latinos complained loudly, each struggling to retain his view of the spectacle outside the cruiser. The smaller one ended up on top of Terry. Terry closed his eyes and counted to twenty, praying he'd be anywhere else in the world when he reopened them. He peeked. He wasn't. He closed his eyes and prayed some more. At least the guy on his lap didn't appear to notice Terry had pissed himself.

Officer Ainsley pulled the handheld for his radio out the car window. Leaning on the door, he said, "10-35. 10-35. What the hell is taking you guys so long?"

"What's the matter, Ainsley? What's the rush?"

"Something was going down when I got here. I've got three bad guys, at least three more have escaped. Two driving, one on foot. We've got a burning barn to boot. There goes our freaking evidence."

"Roger. What happened? I thought you said this was supposed to be some loner tending a pot garden in the country."

"Roger that. Something was going down, like I said. Looked like a delivery. Put out an alert for two white cube vans, no markings. Headed south toward 41. They cleared the area as I arrived. Wait, shit! There goes another rat!"

Terry listened to what sounded like a motorcycle being started. He opened his eyes and strained to see into the yard. Then the officer fired his gun again and Terry screwed his eyes shut tighter than ever.

"What's going on?" the radio crackled. *"You okay?"*

"Yeah, just a warning shot. Lotta good it did. Someone else just got out of here on an ATV. Headed into the bush, north or maybe west."

"Hold on, Ainsley. You'll have back-up any minute now."

In a few minutes, more cop cars started showing up along with a fire truck and, eventually, an ambulance. The yard was lit up like a carnival. Police swarmed all over the house and firemen pulled hoses toward the barn. Flashlights scanned the yard and the edge of the brush.

Marveling at the scene, Terry gave up on prayer and joined his seatmates in their back row view of the festivities. Decidedly, the firemen were the coolest part.

Passed out in his chair, the fatty extinguished and still propped between his forefingers, Danny woke from stupor. Something was poking him in the face. The iguana gripped a banana in its teeth, trying to shove it into Danny's mouth.

Time to get up, Sleeping Beauty. Things are going down that you don't wanna miss.

Disoriented, Danny lurched to the window in time to see a police cruiser pull into the yard. It sat silent for a moment or two and then lit up like a Christmas tree. Its siren began to wail full force. Seconds later, two cube vans roared from behind the house, drove past the cruiser, and sped southward along the dirt road. One of the doors on the second van hung open and a bale of pot bounced out onto the gravel. Two men ran after the trucks, one of them tackled by the police officer who leapt out of the cruiser, gun drawn. The second man immediately threw his hands in the air and lay face down on the ground.

Danny rushed to the side window and saw two more men gesticulating wildly. One of them repeatedly bashed the other over the head with a large leather satchel. Finally, the other guy grabbed hold of the bag and it became a tug of war, which the second guy lost when he was kicked in the crotch. He sank to his knees and the first man turned toward the forest. He ran straight into a parked three-wheeler and flipped over the big front wheel. The satchel's handle snagged on the ATV's steering column and the man stood up and yanked on it. Danny watched as the man looked up the driveway toward where the cop was and saw his eyes widen in fear. A shot rang out and the man ran into the bush.

The police officer sprinted into view and stopped at the second man who was writhing in pain in the fetal position, clutching his balls with both hands. The officer put a knee on his neck and twisted one arm behind his back; he grabbed a handful of hair, pulled him to his feet, and frog-marched him to the cruiser.

Moving back to the front window, Danny watched the officer stuff the man into what appeared to be a rather full back seat. He literally pushed him in with his foot. Then he leaned into the front seat and pulled out his radio transmitter. Danny decided this was as good a time as any to leave. He scrambled down the stairs and out through the kitchen. The barn door hung open to reveal a crimson and gold inferno. He staggered as close as the flames would allow, slack-jawed at the white heat consuming the wood, plastic, and plants. A beam crashed to the floor and he was slammed backward by a blast of hot air and sparks.

With the cop parked by the gate, leaving by car wasn't an option. He stumbled across to the three-wheeler and couldn't believe his luck when he found the keys hanging in the ignition. He jumped on the machine, cranked it, and drove away to the sound of gunfire. The satchel flapped in the wind and banged against his right knee.

Tears streamed down Perko's face. He choked back the sobs, but nothing could be done about the water pooling in his eyes.

He couldn't see much of anything from where he knelt in the brambles, convinced Hell could be no worse than this. His hands and face were scratched and bleeding from the blackberry bush he had thrown himself into when he could no longer clench his cheeks. His pants were bathed in jalapeno fire. Hotter still was the swirl of ganja-laced smoke as his glorious operation went up in flames.

He had no idea who had been caught and who had got away. All he knew was he faced death or worse when this disaster was laid out at the clubhouse.

Until a minute or so ago, Perko had clung to the hope he could make his way to his bush bike while the cops were distracted. But he'd just heard it drive away. Based on the gun shot that followed it, he knew the driver wouldn't be stopping for passengers.

Struggling in the dark, he'd only managed to further tighten the belts and straps around his belly, finding no relief from the gurgling mass of cheese and beans that burbled there like so much lava.

At the sound of more cars arriving, he finally made his move. He crept toward the back of the farmyard along the edge of the woodlot. The heavy undergrowth made the going slow. As more and more flashlights scanned the bushes, he kept having to hunch to the ground and freeze.

"Think I've got something here," he heard someone yell and a beam of light held its line right on him. He held his breath.

"No. Nope. Just some burlap or something," the cop called out and the light moved away.

Relieved, Perko gasped for air and then sounded a fart like the loudest butt trumpet in gangland. And he fell to his ass and cried some more.

In the back of the cop car with Terry, the two Latinos whispered in Spanish. The guy on the other end of the seat whimpered and swore nonstop in French. When his seatmates were finally hauled out and thrown into separate cop cars, Terry stretched his damp legs as well as he could in the cramped compartment, leaned his head in the corner, and wondered whether this mess was somehow his fault.

Officer Ainsley had left the front windows open to air out the squad car. Between squawks on the radio, Terry listened to the cops outside.

"Must have been one helluva factory in there."

"No kidding. This was no Nasty Nancies set-up. That French faggot we nabbed is going to have some stories to tell."

"That should be a cakewalk. The pussy was already crying for his *Maman*. Kept smoothing his damn hairdo like he was getting ready for his mug shot or something."

"Weird ass fruitcake. We've seen him before. Name's Bernie or something."

"What about them two Mexicans?"

"I thought they were Cubans?"

"Who the fuck can tell? All I know is no one's seen them before. Must be from Toronto."

"Hey, who broke this thing anyway? The narcos ain't even here yet."

"Ainsley, I think. Trying to play the hero, looks like. The call came out for backup at this location maybe ten minutes before the fireworks started. Sounded pretty routine."

"I think they were waiting for a judge on a search warrant. What a freak show."

Terry watched Officer Ainsley and another cop drag a flabby bearded man up the laneway. He was wearing funny-looking leather pants.

"Can you believe the fringes on that guy's chaps?" someone said.

"Who does he think he is? Fucking *Tonto*?"

"Hey, Ainsley, watch out he don't scalp you."

Officer Ainsley snapped back: "I'm more afraid he'll crap on me. He's a Libido, for sure, but that bulge in his jeans is something entirely different."

"You been checking out his package, Ainsley?"

"What I'm saying, gentlemen, is this poor slob just shit his pants worse than a two-year-old having a tantrum. I found him in the woods by smell alone. Thought something had died in there."

Terry stared at the biker's face, cut, bleeding, and contorted in black anger. He decided that whether or not he'd caused this circus, he'd best shut up from here on in.

TEN

The three-wheeler was perfect for a cross-country get-away. Skeritt's analysis had been pretty darn prescient, Danny thought. Not only had the police shown up, but it was an utter shit show. He'd been lucky to escape with his skin intact.

At the top of a rise just shy of Ernie's place, he stopped to think things through. The more he tried to think, the more confused he became. He had no idea who the three-wheeler belonged to, but stealing it had to be the least of his worries. Who were those toughs running helter skelter all over the barnyard, down the road, and off into the bush? Had anyone seen him? If he was on the run, he'd sure like to know who from. Cops? Bikers? The dude on the phone who left the envelope of cash every week? He couldn't even go to the police because he had no one to turn in. And then there was the small matter of Lester rotting in the woods.

Danny's dream life was a bust.

Gone was the ten thou bonus, his cool grand a week job, and limitless ganja. He pictured himself huddled in a lean-to with Skeritt, fighting over a jar of peanut butter.

He got off the ATV to pee at the side of the road. It was a cool clear August night, the sky brilliant with stars. He picked out The Big Dipper and followed the handle to Orion's Belt. His mother had taught him the easier constellations when they camped on their special island by the Indian Reserve. He'd lean back against her knees while she nursed a cup of tea spiked with Triple Sec. What he wouldn't give to be back there now. He snorted at the thought. To think he'd been afraid of being attacked by wild animals. "Oh, we'll make a big bright fire with lots of smoke," his mom would tell him. "That'll keep the animals away and then the guys on the Reserve will see it and come check it out. They know how to deal with bears and everything. Don't worry." And that had always been good enough, on the island. Tonight, though, he doubted the Indians or anyone else could deal with the angry cops and bikers sure to be on his tail.

There was nothing for it. He'd have to follow Skeritt's advice, boneheaded as it seemed.

He trudged back to the three-wheeler. For the first time, he took a good look at the satchel. It was heavy brown leather with thick handles. He unzipped it and looked inside. His sphincter tightened and for a moment he forgot to breathe. He was looking at more money than he'd ever seen: stacks and stacks of green twenties, red fifties, and brown hundreds.

He dropped the bag in fright. This was money like you'd see in the movies. He fell to his knees and stuck his head into the bag, breathing deep. Money you could smell—even through the humid stench of pot that permeated the leather.

Hands trembling, Danny started to pull stacks out of the satchel, digging underneath, unable to believe the whole bag was full of nothing but cash. He thumbed a stack of bills. There were fifty a bunch, making each stack of twenties a thousand, the fifties twenty-five hundred, and the hundreds five thousand each. He emptied the bag and sorted the piles. It took five minutes for him to do the math and then he did it again. No question. Danny Grant had run away with seven hundred and fifty thousand dollars. More exactly, he was stinking rich.

Giddy with fear, he crammed the bundles back into the bag and squatted on a rock ledge at the side of the road. From where he sat, he could almost see Ernie McCann's cabin. He was petrified and shaking with excitement at the same time. Ten minutes ago, he'd known he needed to disappear. Now he had the cash to do it. He desperately wanted to talk to Skeritt or his mom but Ernie would have to do. He wouldn't tell him about the satchel, though. Skeritt could say all he wanted about Ernie being like family: people got weird about money. And scattered though his mind was, Danny knew it was better if nobody but nobody knew he had this kind of cash—never mind where it had come from.

He drove the ATV down the hill to Ernie's place. There was no light inside the cabin but Ernie shouted a gruff "Who the hell is there?" as soon as Danny got within thirty feet of the door. "This shotgun is loaded and it's pointed right at you."

"Ernie, it's me. Danny."

"Danny? What the hell are you doin' skulkin' around in the middle of the night? Gonna get yourself shot. Best come inside."

Danny stumbled through the door into the pitch dark room. He felt Ernie's hand on his elbow, guiding him to a kitchen chair. He sat down but only one of his cheeks reached the seat and he would have fallen to the floor were it not for Ernie grabbing his arm with a chuckle.

"Never did understand how you sighted people survive without busting all your bones every time the electricity's out. Here, let me help you."

Danny listened to Ernie step firmly across the room, lift something off a shelf, rattle a box of matches, walk back, and slide something across the tabletop. Danny felt in the dark for the plunger on the Coleman lantern, unscrewed it, and pumped a bit. Then he grabbed a match, opened the lantern's valve so he could hear the gas hiss softly. He used the match to light the mantle. As the light grew, Ernie's face slowly appeared out of the darkness, grinning, big yellow teeth peering out from under eyes black as coal.

"Skeritt told me you might be along. Hardly expected to see you this soon. Want a beer?"

The lantern burned brightly now and Danny said he could get it himself but Ernie waved him back onto his foam-cushioned chair and ambled across to the fridge. Everything about the near barren room was comfortable as Kraft Dinner and about as inspired. Next to the fridge was a two-burner gas stove and a hand pump hung over the sink. There were six cupboards: three up, three down. The top ones had no doors and held a smattering of mismatched dishware and glasses. There were no books or magazines, no curtains on the windows. The shotgun with which he'd been threatened moments before leaned against the door frame. After handing him a beer, Ernie walked over and felt along the door until his fingers wrapped around the gun's barrel. He picked it up and hung it back in its place on the wall.

"How's your mom?"

"Mom's good, Ernie. But I'm in trouble. Deep shit. Real deep."

"Do tell, Daniel."

And he did. Danny brought Ernie right up to date, telling him everything about the grow op, but leaving out the bit about the satchel sitting outside.

"Just one cop car?" Ernie asked.

"Yeah, why?"

"Doesn't sound like much of a bust, does it?"

"How do I know? Maybe there were more on their way."

"Well, there sure as hell will be more now. That's no small operation you're talking about. Are you sure no one was following you?"

"Positive. I stopped a few times and turned off the motor. Silence every time."

"Good. They're going to be looking for that damn machine though. And they'll be using dogs, too, with all that pot on the loose. You won't exactly be hard to track. You reek."

Danny pulled his T-shirt to his nose and sniffed it. Ernie was right. He smelled like a bale of skunk weed.

"There's a bar of Sunlight soap by the sink. You can wash yourself in the lake. Throw your clothes in the fire pit. I'll burn them in the morning." Ernie stood and crossed into the bedroom, returning with a pair of coveralls. He handed them to Danny, saying, "Here, these don't fit me anymore. They're clean."

As he took them, Danny saw Ernie's name stitched on the left pocket, over a picture of a circular saw blade. The coveralls must have come from the sawmill. He started to ask Ernie a question, then caught himself. There'd be time to talk later.

Ernie said, "Go get your stink off." Then he told Danny where there was a cliff nearby. "Drive the bike over the edge, they'll never find it."

"I'll do that tomorrow."

"No, you're going to ditch that thing tonight. I don't want it around here. From what you told me, both the cops and the bikers are looking for it by now. This place is less than a ten-minute drive. You'll be able to walk back before dawn."

"Then what? Skeritt said you'd have a plan. Know where I can go until this blows over."

"Listen, Danny, this isn't exactly going to blow over. Tomorrow, we'll get you to the Reserve. Find someone to help you disappear for a while, get out of the country, or lost deep in the bush, whatever."

"Why the hell would anyone do that for me?"

"Because I'll ask them to. And Indian is Indian. Now haul your butt down to the lake and get scrubbing."

Danny did as he was told. The peaceful skinny dip in Pigeon Lake seemed surreal. Floating on his back on flat black water, surrounded by soap suds and staring up at the Milky Way, Danny could have been ten years old all over again. He could just as easily believe he was sixteen and there was a bonfire sparkling at the water's edge surrounded by friendly chatter and the sound of someone strumming a guitar. For a few minutes, he felt safe, more relaxed than he had been in months, worry-free, deeply tired, and free.

Naked and dripping wet, he made his way up the slope to the cabin. The cool night air snapped him back to reality. Ernie had said he'd get him to the Reserve and the Indians would help him disappear. Good enough, but how would he get money to his mom? So she could join him, assuming she'd want to.

He opened the satchel and took out six bundles of hundreds. Ripping the bands off, he ruffled the bills against one of the tires. He'd have to trust Ernie to give the money to his mother; he'd tell him it was his pay from the grow op. If he was lucky, the man wouldn't be able to see how much money it was. And if he did, well, he was family, right?

He still needed to figure out what to do with the satchel. There was no reason to expect that the cops would look for him here tonight. Still, Danny wasn't taking any chances. Enough shit had gone wrong the last few days. If Ernie was right and the cops used dogs, they'd be sure pick up on the pot smell that had soaked into the bag's leather. Scanning the yard, he found the perfect spot to hide it, then went in to get the coveralls and give Ernie the cash for his mom.

* * *

Ernie's directions were precise. Naturally, they were perfect for driving in the dark. Danny rode the ATV out the laneway and turned left. He followed that road until there were three bends in a row: left, right, then hard left again. About a minute later, after a steep rise, the road leveled off, veered right, and Danny felt a gust of humid air blowing off the lake. He slowed down and kept an eye out for the break in the fence Ernie said he would find on the left side of the road. He gunned the ATV through the ditch with ease and headed straight for the edge of the cliff, stopping just short.

He used duct tape Ernie had given him to tape the accelerator in place, giving the three-wheeler just enough gas to get moving. He threw it into gear and guided it the first few feet toward the cliff then stood back and watched it rumble off. There were a couple of loud crashes and then a muffled splash as it hit the water. In the dark, Danny didn't dare approach the edge.

"You can jump right in with it, if you like," Ernie had told him. "Some of the kids do that with old bikes sometimes. The cliff's only about twenty feet high, and the water's deeper than that pretty much right up to the edge. I used to jump it myself the first few years after I lost my sight. Thrill of a lifetime—like tumbling through space, not knowing which way is up. But you've got to give it a bit of a run to make sure you don't hit the granite slope underwater. Back then, I wouldn't have half minded if I busted my neck doing it. I was pretty angry, I guess. Nowadays, I just like heading over there once or twice a summer to listen to all the hooting and cheers when the young bucks make the leap."

Danny sat on a boulder, fished a baggie of weed from his pocket, and rolled a quick spliff. Lighting it, he marveled at how still the night air had become. Even next to the cliff, with water below, there was barely an updraft. The cloud of smoke hung about him like fog. He imagined leaping off the cliff into an abyss deep enough to protect him from facing reality.

He was an out-of-work dope farmer with nowhere to live. He had killed a man. Killed his dog, too. His accomplice after the fact had fewer active brain cells than the lizard who was his closest confidant.

He did have one thing going for him. A shitload of cash.

Danny grinned. He wondered what would make his mother more proud: all that money, or the fact he'd sent an ATV to its death? "Murder-cycles," she called them. Yeah, he'd done good.

Then he wondered what she'd call baseball bats if she knew about Lester.

Grinding the roach into the ground under his running shoe, he walked away from the cliff edge and began retracing the route to Ernie's cabin. He'd been on the road five minutes when he saw lights flicker over the next hill. He dashed into the ditch and scrambled over the ever-present rock pile. He rolled down the other side just as the cop car's headlights crested the rise and lit the road like daylight.

He held his breath and his heart pounded so loud he was sure the cops would hear it. A search light mounted next to the windshield swept back and forth across the stubble in the field behind him. Then, quick as they'd arrived, the police were gone. He got up and walked along the field, afraid that if he returned to the road, they'd show up faster next time and he wouldn't have time to escape to the shadows. Navigating the field made the going slow until he reached a footpath cutting through a woodlot. By the time he came out the other side, clouds had rolled in, threatening rain. Without starlight, Danny got disoriented. When the rain started, he crawled into a crumbling outbuilding next to an abandoned farmhouse and curled up in an old tarp to keep warm.

The tarp smelled of mouse shit. Bits of indeterminate fluff stuck to Danny's skin and made him itch. Exhausted, he dozed off for what felt like less than a minute before he was awakened by the sound of distant barking. Ernie had been right: the police had called out the dogs.

The pre-dawn chill gnawing at his bones, he crept out of the shack and peered into the dark. There was no visible movement and the dogs sounded like they were still a mile or more away. He started out at a jog, crossing the field toward a depression he hoped would lead toward a creek. It wasn't much more than a rivulet, it turned out, a muddy trickle ripe with fresh cow manure, but after a while it joined another trickle and grew stronger. The water had cut the ground deep enough that only his head and shoulders peeked above it. Problem was, the path taken by the water was anything but direct. It kept doubling back on itself, winding to and fro. Finally, Danny grew frustrated and climbed up to ground level to get his bearings.

As he drew himself up onto the field, he detected a rise in the excitement level of the barking dogs: he'd been spotted. Breaking into a run, he traversed the farmer's field as fast as he could. Three times he had to scramble down into and back up from the mini gorge cut by the brook. The dogs were gaining ground quickly.

Where the brook poured into a full-on creek, the rain had raised the water to a foot deep in spots. Bent double, he ran down its center for a few hundred feet before spotting salvation.

In the next field, a tractor trailer sat at an angle to the road. The field abutted a secondary highway and the trailer had been wrapped with a billboard advertising Timbits. Sanctuary. What's more, the barking had ceased. The dogs must have reached the creek. He vaulted over the farmer's fence and stumbled across the plough furrows to the trailer. The sliding door was unlocked but rusty. He pulled himself up onto the lip and kicked at the door to loosen it. The banging of his foot on metal sounded like a massive out-of-tune gong, but after just two or three kicks, he managed to screech the door open about a foot—enough to squeeze under. Inside, he did his best to pull the door closed again, getting it to within four inches of the trailer floor. Sweating in spite of the cold, he sat down and pressed his back to the wall, breathing deeply.

After what seemed like hours but could hardly have been ten minutes, Danny heard the dogs approaching through the field. At least two cop cars made their way slowly along the gravel road, tracking them. The dogs came right up to the trailer. He held his breath, listening to them snuffling along the door until a shout drew them away and he breathed a deep sigh of relief.

He'd come within inches of getting caught, but somehow luck was with him. Trampling through the creek must have dampened his smell. He was glad as hell he had bathed in the lake and changed into Ernie's clothes so he no longer reeked of pot.

He breathed deep. He was going to make it. Collect his money and make his way out of the country. Live on some distant shore, in a grass hut maybe. Eat well, drink well. Roaring bonfires every night on the beach. This called for a celebration!

Danny pulled the baggie of skunk weed from his pocket and rolled an extra fat doobie. Firing it up, he toked deeply and held the smoke long in his chest. When he exhaled, the cloud hung thick about his head and the smoke curled around his body, some of it swirling out under the trailer door. By the time Danny realized what he had done, it was too late. The dogs were back and this time they were *really* excited.

ELEVEN

The municipal jail cell was dank and dimly lit. Jersey "Hawk" Hawkins ignored the perfunctory shove the cop gave him as he squeezed past the full metal door. The grimy eight-inch window was laced with half-inch wire to prevent shattering. Hawk pulled his sweatshirt over his head and used his sock-covered foot to jam it tight into the crack along the bottom of the door.

The Nancy's Nasty named Bernard hadn't moved from his fetal position on the bottom bunk. Hawk put his foot on the man's hip and pressed until he heard a whimper.

"Roll over, dipshit."

"What you want, asshole de merde?"

"Let me see your pretty little face."

"Fuck you."

Hawk reached down and grabbed a fistful of Bernard's afro. He used it like a handle, lifting the man to his feet and turning him so they were breathing each other's air real close. Hawk's long grey hair was tied in a ponytail, knotted every couple inches with leather strips. The last couple knots ran through one-inch square nuts. With a quick jerk of his neck, he flicked the pony tail around and slapped the chunks of stainless steel into the side of Bernard's head. He was well-practiced, and managed to land the hits where he was holding the other man's curls out of the way.

Bernard flinched, but didn't make a sound.

"Tell me what the fuck went down out there. Give it to me straight first time and maybe I won't make you eat your kneecap."

"How the hell I know? Frederick and me, we just do what Mr. Ratwick he tell us. Me, I drives a car and next thing I know the cops they come and bang wham into jail." He squirmed a bit then stopped when Hawk pressed his shoulders into the top bunk and twisted his neck backward.

"The money," said the Libido. "Where the fuck's the Skeleton's payday? They take it with 'em?"

"No way, man. That's Frederick. For sure no shit he take the money."

Hawk glared at him, one eyeball at a time, saying nothing.

Bernard's lips curved into a half smile, eyes shifting back and forth. He said, "Yeah, that's it. Frederick, he's your man for sure. Me, I tried to save it for you, eh? I kick him good, down der you know? Still, he run away."

Hawk threw the man to the ground and told him to take off his pants and underwear. Bernard looked confused and maybe a little hopeful. Until Hawk scooped his shorts, balled them tight, and rammed them into the Nancy's Nasty's mouth. The scrawny wannabe was no match for the Libido; he grabbed for Hawk's pony tail and tried to pull him down. Hawk yanked it free and batted him about the face with the steel nuts. Then he wrapped one pant leg tight around his neck and pulled hard on the other.

When his victim had stopped kicking, Hawk tied the loose pant leg around the light bulb cage above the door. Bending over, he picked up his sweatshirt, rolled it into a loose pillow, and lay down on the bottom bunk to sleep, Bernard's feet dangling in front of his face.

Two days later, Perko sat at the kitchen table in the Libidos clubhouse. That morning, the gang's attorney had finally arranged for his release on bail. The day and a half in jail would have been routine had it not been for the constant ribbing Perko took on account of his shit-soaked chaps.

"So you lost the whole mess." Mongoose barely stifled a snicker.

"Fuck you, too," Perko said.

"Hey, don't you go getting all antsy on me, Mister I'll-run-my-own-show-like-it-or-not. This was your call and I's gonna make sure you pay for it."

"I'll sort it out."

"Right. You's got a major grow burned to a crisp and some joker in custody with every reason to talk. Even the money is gone, Perks."

"The money's not gone. It's missing."

"For alls you know, your big payday went up in smoke with the rest of the operation. What I hear, that's what the cops are betting."

"Not a chance," Perko said. "You see any one o' those lowlifes leaving a bag of cash behind just because the building's on fire?"

"Ha! They'd more'n likely fry fightin' over it."

"Exactly," Perko said. "They grab it and run. And I'm gonna find the dough and break the neck of the sonofabitch who took it."

"And that would be...?"

"Like I said, it's gotta be either Frederick or my shithead farmer. They're the only two people got away. Frederick's too smart to steal from me, so my money's on the punk."

"What about the Skeletons?" Mongoose asked. "Maybe they took off with the dope *and* the money."

"Not a chance. I'm telling you, the cops showed up *after* the Skeletons loaded the trucks. Money woulda been in our control."

"Alright, but why'd they leave the Nicaraguans?"

"'Cause the first fucking pig showed up just as they finished loading. I'm pretty sure Frederick was still inside the barn."

"Which shoulda been you, if you hadn't been busy shitting your pants. Scared shitless, you was."

"Laugh all you want, asshole. I had a fucking Pepto-Bismol moment and my chaps got in the way. Could happen to anyone."

"Hoo-hoo-hoooo! To anyone wearing diapers, maybe."

"Like I said, fuck you." Perko glared at Mongoose until the larger man stopped laughing. Then he said, "Ten minutes alone with Bernard and I'll learn where Frederick's run off to. Once I track him down, we'll know which of the two shitheads has our dough and we'll be done."

"Well, you're gonna have to be something pretty special to get ten minutes with Bernard. He hanged himself."

"Hanged himself?" Perko felt woozy. "Gimme a fucking break. You guys did it, didn't you?"

"Naw, it was suicide. Said so right in the newspaper."

"Right, like I'm gonna believe that. Who did it?"

Mongoose grinned. "Hawk. He got himself thrown in jail for brawling down at the City Lights. We paid off a guard to put him in the same cell as Bernard. Then, we pays a couple more because Bernard was eatin' his own shorts when they found him and that didn't square with the suicide line, but it's all taken care of."

"Taken care of."

"Yeah, you know. One for all and all that crap."

"How the hell am I supposed to beat information out of a corpse?"

"I feel for you, Perk, but, you know, we were all just a bit concerned about what that pussy was gonna tell the cops. As for who the hell absconded with our money, he says it was Frederick. Anyway, that's *your* problem, not the club's. You see, Perko, how the fuck do we know you didn't cook this whole thing up and maybe you're hiding the money for yourself?"

"Like I said..." Perko bit his tongue. Mongoose was flushing red and he was in deep enough shit as it was. He asked, "What about them two Nicaraguans?"

"We's trying to get a line on them. They's moved to another joint. Something to do with immigration status. Whatever the hell. Anyways, we'll get them soon enough. You should be more concerned about finding the money. Where did you say you found your farmer?"

"I told you. Frederick came up with him. Arm's length. He's not attached to no one."

"You better hope not."

FOUR YEARS LATER

TWELVE

Sweat streamed down Danny's face. Pinned in place, he could only move his head and arms. Excited barking drew closer as a pack chased its prey. He struggled to free himself from the pile of rocks piled right up to his armpits. He tossed stone after rounded stone as far as he could until he uncovered his chest. As he worked down past his stomach to his thighs, stones rolled from behind to fill the gap.

The barking pressed in on him. He struggled to shift his legs. His face, chest, arms, and hands slick with perspiration, he lifted one smooth rounded rock at a time. Every few stones, Lester's hate-filled eyes stared out at him, the apparition fading as soon as he dared touch it. Still, each gruesome illusion shook him as much as the first.

By the time he dug far enough to reveal his knees, the barking had reached the edge of the clearing. He felt his right leg free itself and tugged harder. That wedged his calf in place, giving him the sense of being off-balance yet unable to fall down. He sat, exhausted, and kept pushing stones from in front of his shins. The barking kept up, non-stop, louder and more frantic by the minute. Still the beasts did not appear. It was all he could do to drop the round rocks at arm's length. He built a ridge in front of himself and most of the way around either side. A couple of times, a stone he added to the top of the ridge careened back down the pile to smash a kneecap.

When he released his left foot, he found he could wriggle his right as well. Three more stones and he was free. The dogs were almost on him. He scrambled over the rock pile and saw his legs were unmarked—no scratches, no bleeding, just pain. He ran for the forest and got maybe twenty yards before he tripped on an exposed pine root and crashed to the ground. As he staggered to his feet, he looked over his shoulder to see the pack break out of the forest. He froze in place. The enraged animals swarmed him, lunged at his back, and clawed his thighs. Instead of snarling dogs, no fewer than thirty barking lizards were at him, each with Lester's stone cold crazy eyes. All with Shooter's razor sharp teeth.

Danny laughed until he started to sob. After maybe a minute, he took a deep breath and peeled his eyes open to stare at the grey concrete ceiling of his prison cell. His cooling perspiration made him shiver and he said out loud, "Ninety-nine"—the number of days until he would be eligible for full parole, four years into his seven-year sentence.

Every nightmare since his arrival in prison had involved dogs. Rocks, too. And Lester. Iggy was bound to show up every so often. Danny was glad his nightmares rarely involved his fellow prisoners or the place where he had spent the last four years of his life. He refused to accept it as reality, preferring to focus his *waking* dreams on some vague Caribbean paradise and his big bag of appropriated cash. He kept tourist brochures taped to the walls of his cell. He thought of his mother and how she'd forgive him. He imagined the girlfriend he would woo. He wondered whether she'd be blonde. He spent a lot of time on that.

Four years of prison life had been dreary as hell. Sheer boredom, the constant threat of violence, a sense of utter uselessness, and complete absence of self-esteem. It was soul destruction by design. Danny had withdrawn to games of checkers with his cellmate and kitchen duty. He appreciated the relative safety of the kitchen. Since it involved knives, the real wackos were excluded. Plus there were always at least two prison guards close by to reduce the likelihood of random violence. He kept his nose clean and rarely got involved in altercations with other inmates.

Day ninety-nine-and-counting, Danny made his way to the admin section for his day parole hearing. On the way, two thugs slammed him into the washroom.

"Must be getting excited," said the first, a pimple-faced crackhead. The second guy twisted Danny's arms behind him, back to the wall. The guy with the bad acne said, "Any day now you'll be outta here and then it's payday, ain't it?"

"Told you guys before," Danny said, "I don't know what you're talking about." After a few months of near daily beatings, the Libidos thugs had pretty much left him alone.

"You got a choice," said Waste Face, an improvised plastic knife cradled in his palm. "The guys are gonna turn your face to pulp once you're outside. You cough up the story now, maybe I don't cut you."

"You really oughta visit the infirmary, dude," Danny said. "Your face looks like a goddamn tumor fest." He spat in the guy's eyes and swung his hips hard right. Sure enough, the bastard thrust the knife hard toward where Danny's waist had been. It slipped past him, grazing the guy holding his arms and ran straight at the wall behind him. The Face bleated like a stuck piglet as his weapon pushed back, sliced into his palm, and sent blood spurting all over his pal who loosened his grip just enough. A little splattered on Danny's shoulder as he dodged and ran out.

At the end of the hallway, Danny banged on the wire mesh door and grinned. If they were still on him about the money, the Libidos hadn't found it yet.

THIRTEEN

Skeritt grabbed another slice of Wonder Bread from the pile on the kitchen table and folded it in half. Using it to scoop a mouthful of peanut butter from the gallon jar of Skippy on his lap, he munched the sandwich with gusto. A half-empty carton of milk sat on the table beside the bread. He drained it in one gulp and threw the empty carton at the dead body on the floor.

"Bastard."

He ate two more fistfuls of peanut butter, stood, and opened the fridge. There being no more milk, he took an apple, chomped it in three bites, and tossed the core at the corpse.

"Stupid bastard. I warned you more than once. You paid no heed. And now you're dead."

Skeritt ignored the beer in the fridge and took a slab of two-year-old cheddar from the deli drawer. He ripped the plastic off with blackened fingernails and gnawed at it. He sat at the table again, staring at the corpse for a long time, occasionally dipping the cheese in the peanut butter and chewing with a scowl.

He stuck out his foot and rolled the dead man onto his back. Ernie's eyes were open and the bottom half of his face was missing, a pulpy mess of bone and teeth where his mouth should have been.

Still eating the cheese, Skeritt scanned the interior of the cabin.

In the living room, which really wasn't a separate room at all, a square-backed couch and a striped brown La-Z-Boy faced a 50" plasma television. A short bookshelf under the window overflowed with Blu-rays, many more of which were strewn on the floor next to a big round coffee table.

He walked over to the table which was made from a four-inch slab of tree-trunk more than three feet across, supported by tree trunk legs with the bark still on. Carved into the table's top face in gouges half an inch deep were the letters S-K-E-R-I-T-T.

He pulled a hunting knife from where it hung on his belt and added three letters next to his name.

He went into the bedroom where the dresser drawers had been emptied onto the bed. Rummaging in the closet, he found a knapsack. He crammed in three sweaters, two plaid flannel shirts, and two pair of trousers. He tossed in every pair of socks from the bed and two more dirty pair from the floor, zipped the sack shut, and walked back into the living room.

Ernie's shotgun leaned against the wall by the front door, and two boxes of ammunition were on a shelf nearby. He put the ammunition in his trouser pockets, and walked over to the corpse. Looking down he said, "Guess you won't be needing the gun any more, will you? Load of good it did you anyway, huh? Bloody bastard."

Skeritt took a can of kerosene from the kitchen counter and poured its contents onto Ernie's dead body, soaking the man's clothes from head to toe. He threw the empty can at the living room window. It bounced off the glass and rolled under the couch. Snarling, Skeritt picked up the coffee table and heaved it at the window as though it were nothing more than a Frisbee. It smashed through the glass and tumbled into the brush outside. Striking a safety match from his shirt pocket, he tossed it at the corpse. It lit up like a bonfire.

"Bastard," he said again as he stomped out of the cabin, stopping only to grab one more slice of bread and peanut butter.

Skeritt walked the short distance to the outhouse. He opened the door, dropped his trousers, and sat down. It faced the cabin and he left the door hang open. As he did his business, Skeritt watched the fire intently. The oxygen from the smashed window fed the flames and they spread rapidly through the main room. When the stove's propane tank exploded with a crash loud as August thunder, Skeritt grinned like a little boy.

He wiped his hands on the leaves of a young maple tree, put the knapsack on his back, slung the shotgun over his shoulder, and walked away. He said, "Goodbye, you stupid bastard. Thanks for letting me use the shitter."

* * *

Danny's lawyer motioned to the purple plastic chair next to her. In the hallway outside the meeting room, the chairs were bolted to the cement wall.

"We've got a few *minutes* until they call us in," she said. Linette Paquin had a way of placing undue emphasis on seemingly random words when she spoke—a tic that only got worse the more nervous or excited she became. Danny figured it had something to do with having spent too many years studying the equally random Criminal Code.

The first day he'd met her, Linette told him she never really focused on defense work. "Real estate, wills, a little *corporate* is what I prefer, but we all have to pay our dues in this business. Social responsibility and all." Danny didn't much like having a disinterested twit as defense lawyer but the alternates proposed by Legal Services had been no better.

She was less dangerous than the dweeb who only wanted to compare notes on keeping lizards as pets because he had three geckos in a terrarium—*"I'm telling you, every day I come home and my kitty is laying on the lid, soaking up the heat from the light, and tap-tap-tapping the glass with her paw. One of these days, she's going to get at them, I'm sure of it. What did you feed your lizard?"*—or the greasy gray-haired guy who reeked of gin before lunch—*"Trust me, pal, I know how to deal with these gangster types. What we have to do is convince the coppers that you'll wear a wire, see, and then you get all on the low-down and whatever and get them talking about where the money may have gotten to—you don't have to tell me if you don't want to—and then they'll get some real long time and you'll get packaged off on witness protection—I know a guy, you'll see, you'll meet him soon—now, about that bag of money..."*

So, he had stuck with Linette Paquin and prayed a lot.

They had worked out a deal on Lester. Manslaughter, arguing that the burial effort with Terry had been an act of public decency. They got lucky, catching a judge who was a serious cat-person. "Son," he said. "I'm giving you a three-to-one credit for your pre-sentencing time because I think those fools on Peterborough council need to outlaw those darn Pit

Bulls." Shooter was a Rottweiler, but who was he to argue with a judge?

And now his time was nearly done.

"You can expect three months of day parole," Linette told him. "Should have been six, but, well, you know, scheduling this meeting was hell. They'll move you to Frontenac first. Have to be in minimum security for unescorted daily."

Danny grunted.

"Do you have anyone on the outside that can help you find a job?"

"I'm kind of short on references."

"What about *your* mother?"

"I haven't heard from her in nearly a year." Danny recalled Skeritt's words scrawled on a birthday card: "Life's a beach. Your mother's fine." She hadn't paid him a goodbye visit. He prayed she was okay.

The door clanged open and some guy in a suit waved them in. Danny shuffled through, trailed by his professional help.

FOURTEEN

"What's up, Wort?" Judy Jackman jiggled the empty leash. Normally her tawny Lhasa Apso would scamper to her side as soon as he heard the silver chain rattle. Instead, he barked in a voice much larger than his body and ran ahead.

"Wort. Heel. Heel, boy." Judy was flabbergasted. Top of his class in obedience school, her dog was extremely well-behaved and never caused her the least bit of trouble. She didn't mind his barking at all, and resented it when her more opinionated friends said Wort was yappy.

Maybe someone's at our house, she thought. But that couldn't be. The Big Bald Lake Environmental Action Committee meeting wasn't until tomorrow and she hadn't ordered anything from L.L. Bean in weeks. For a moment, she worried her dog might have heard hunters in the bush; there had been blasts on and off all afternoon, a couple of which had been far too close for comfort. "Wort. Come. Heel. Sit. Oh, damn." Judy shuddered and looked nervously around as if there might actually be someone nearby to hear her swear. "Oops," she said, giggling at herself, and ran after the tiny yapping dog.

At the corner, Judy expected Wort to cut across the light brush and head up the hill to her log cabin. When he passed the dirt path which served as her driveway, she started to worry. Then she smelled smoke and worried more.

Wort was running toward Ernie McCann's. It wasn't hard to tell this was more than a barbeque. Could Ernie be burning leaves again? The smoke didn't smell right.

"You heel, boy. Wait up!" She came over the rise and saw smoke pouring out of Ernie's cottage. Wort had stopped fifty feet short and stood there barking at the flames. As Judy stumbled past him, his bark changed to a growl, then a whine, but he would go no further.

Twenty feet of garden hose lay coiled next to the vegetable garden. It was connected to a pair of rain barrels raised six feet off the ground. She turned on the spigot and aimed the weak stream at the smashed living room window.

"Ernie, are you in there? Ernie McCann! Can you hear me?" she shouted. She choked as rancid steam engulfed her. She moved around to the door where the air was clearer. But when she pulled the door open, a hot humid blast sent her sprawling backward.

Wort barked louder. He sniffed her leg as she struggled to her feet and retreated from the burning cottage. She pulled her mobile phone from a vest pocket.

"911 Emergency," said a woman's voice. "Do you need Police, Fire, or Ambulance?"

"Ernie's place is on fire and I don't know where he is."

"Where are you now, Ma'am? Have you left the building?"

"But I don't know if Ernie's inside."

"Are you inside the burning building, Ma'am?"

"No. I'm outside. I have a hose." Wort barked. "And I can't see Ernie. He won't answer when I call."

"You can't see? Get out of the building."

"I *am* outside the building." Wort barked loudly. Whenever Judy got excited, he joined right in.

"Ma'am. I can't hear you over that yapping dog. Is the dog on fire?"

"MY DOG DOES NOT YAP." Judy would have slammed down the phone if it had a cradle to slam into.

"I'm sorry, Ma'am. Can you move away from the dog so I can hear you?"

"Wort. Good doggie. Shhh...Nice doggie-woggie." Wort sat down, whining, and thumped his tail in agitation.

"Please tell me where you are located."

"Outside. I told you. I'm outside Ernie McCann's and it's BURNING."

"And where is Ernie McCann's, Ma'am?"

"In Lakehurst. Well, it's Buckhorn really but more Lakehurst on the map."

"I'll need you to be a little more specific. The Fire department is being dispatched now—to Lakehurst. Do you have an address?"

"Uh, yeah. It's—well it's right across the road from 2311 Century Lane. That's my house."

"Thank you. Are you safe where you are now?"

"IT'S ERNIE WHO'S NOT SAFE. AREN'T YOU LISTENING?"

"The fire department is on its way. Please don't try to be a hero, Ma'am. Just move back from the fire and wait for help."

Judy aimed the water at the living room window again. She called out, "Ernie. Are you in there? Can you hear me? ERNIE?"

Ernst McCann was silent.

Wort whined. Just a bit.

The pager buzzed softly. Terry reached out and managed to turn it off with his left big toe before his hump buddy noticed. She panted something about him putting out her fire. Terry didn't want to disappoint.

The pager was standard issue for volunteer firemen and was the one piece of official equipment Terry was allowed to carry with him all the time.

"Ooh, Terry, bang down my door. Ooh, yeah. Ooh, yeah, I'm burning up, baby."

He couldn't believe this one. Since becoming a volunteer fireman, Terry had been milking the sex appeal that came with the job as much as he could, but this bombshell from New Jersey was as hot as they came.

The idea of joining the volunteer fire department had come up when Terry had discussed life options with a social worker three years before. He'd just been released after being held about five months for his part in the burial of Lester Freeden. The charges had eventually been dropped—something to do with all the beans he spilled in those long conversations with Officer Ainsley and his pals. At the detention center, Terry had learned CPR, the highest certification he'd ever received for anything. It was hardly enough to get a job as a doctor, but he wasn't about to put it to waste. He remembered the night he got arrested; the firemen looked to be having way more fun than the cops. As it turned out, Terry had been more than a little underwhelmed by the level of appreciation he received for his part in that particular event, but it inspired him to serve society. The fringe benefits were pretty darn good, too.

The pager buzzed a second time and Terry punched it again with his foot. It stopped, but it slid a couple of feet across the floor of the cabin cruiser in which Terry was busily banging another man's wife.

The other thing Terry had schooled in while at the detention center was a little line of thievery that had become quite lucrative since his release. His cellmate had described it to him as they lay in their bunks at night.

"Tourists."

"What about 'em?" Terry had asked.

"Endless supply. They keep coming. They keep moving. They've got cash. They're distracted. Fish in a barrel."

"You mug tourists for a living?"

"Mug them? Too much work. I go through their suitcases 'n stuff, lighten their load."

"You break into hotel rooms?"

"Too risky. Cameras in the hallways. Besides, anything of value is usually in the safe." He leaned his head down from the top bunk, the vinyl-covered mattress squeaking as he did. "I do boats."

"Boats?"

"Uh huh. People moor them along canals and stuff, get drunk, wander out for dinner in town. Lotsa time they party on each other's yachts. It's pretty easy to slip into most cuddies."

"What do you get from boats?"

"Not much. Fancy electronics, fishing gear, booze. Every so often, I get lucky and hit some jewelry or a stash of cash. The trick is not to take too much. Just pick up a couple of things and most of the time, people won't even notice they're missing anything until they've moved upstream. Then, maybe they think it fell overboard or they can't figure out which town they were in when it disappeared. Let's face it. Who's gonna spoil their vacation by turning around and boating back to file a police report."

"Still, you got busted. You're here."

"Yeah, this is the third time I've been pinched. I gotta do about four months. Only drag is I'm missing the heavy season right now. I been running the scam up and down the Rideau Canal for near on five years. Maybe it's time to look for different digs. I'm thinking maybe Europe, except I gotta be careful—some of those places make you do real time, even for stealing and stuff."

Terry's fundamental laziness being stubbornly hard to shake, he had borrowed the scheme upon release. The locks along the Trent-Severn meant a steady supply of summer tourist income. They also created a transient atmosphere that extended into most of the local towns, with the rental cottages, summer residents, and no shortage of seasonal trailer parks. It was a heyday for a single man with every intention of staying that way. As long as he wasn't overly fussy about how unattached the women were, Terry could get laid on a regular basis, especially in the days following a forest fire, while the patina of being a fireman made him smell rather like a hero.

So it was that when Terry Miner's pager buzzed even more loudly to announce the fire at Ernie McCann's shack, the volunteer fireman was wrapped up in the sheets below deck on a thirty-three-foot Sea Ray. The Sea Ray, the sheets, the open bottle of champagne, and even the Stan Getz CD playing in the background all belonged to man named George Meade. At the precise moment the pager buzzed, however, Mr. Meade's third wife, Cindy, belonged one hundred percent to Terry Miner—or at least that's how it looked to him.

"What's...that...noise," Cindy managed to puff out. Terry didn't stop.

"Fire," he said.

"Huh? Uh...fire...oh, so...Terry!"

Without leaving the bed, Terry tried to reach the pager again, but he had kicked it too far. On the fourth buzz, it changed pitch and screeched loudly. That was enough for Cindy.

"Get—off—ME." She shoved him hard and panted as he slid to the floor.

Terry rolled over and grabbed the pager, turning it off and swearing. The address on the pager was 2311 Century Lane, Lakehurst: less than two kilometers from the locks and a good deal further from the fire station. He figured he'd better go straight there.

"Shit. Gotta go. Someone's on fire and I gotta snuff 'em out. Catch you tonight, okay?" He pulled on his jeans and, not finding his own T-shirt, grabbed one of George Meade's from where it hung on a peg near the captain's bed.

"Can't, Sweetie. George'll be back to the boat tonight. How about next Tuesday? He's going fishing at his buddy's cottage for a couple or three days."

"Nearly a week without you?" Terry made puppy dog eyes.

Cindy pulled him back to bed. "I'm so lucky to have my very own fireman," she cooed.

"Mmmmm, my li'l sex machine. See ya Tuesday." Terry kissed George Meade's third wife goodbye.

His car was parked at the side of the road at the top of the hill next to the locks. He strode up the hill with pride and purpose, doing his best to look heroic in an everyday sort of way. Then he jumped in his somewhat dented baby blue Ford Fiesta, cranked the FM stereo to max volume, and drove away in a shower of dust. He honked at everyone he passed, flashing stern looks and his volunteer fireman's salute.

Buckhorn boasted a population of eighteen hundred in summer but that fell to just four hundred twenty during winter. When he first joined the volunteer fire brigade, Terry figured it would let him get to know some local folk a little better, give him a good reputation—especially with the ladies—and maybe earn him a free beer now and then at the Legion. Besides, how many fires could happen in a town of four hundred twenty people? Plenty, it turned out.

Winters in Buckhorn were cold and there wasn't a whole lot to do except snowmobile. Cold and boredom are a lethal combination, he learned. People tended to stay inside and drink by the woodstove. The drunker they got, the more likely they were to shove just about anything burnable into their stoves rather than head outside to split logs. And if they did venture out into the minus thirty cold, they were prone to grab oversized logs and cram them in, with every intention of shoving them the rest of the way just as soon as they burned down to size.

When an alarm sounded in January, Terry and the rest of the crew could pretty much count on arriving at the scene to find a half-crazed yokel in long johns, running around in the snow shouting, "Damn thing just exploded, eh! Right in front of my eyes. Kaboom! Burning coals all over the floor. Darn good thing I was awake, eh?"

Spring and fall fires, on the other hand, were often false alarms—the result of neighbors ratting each other out for unannounced drum fires used to burn leaves and branches. City folk up for the weekend got especially twisted out of shape when decent people used a little fire to clean up their properties. Those calls were just plain irritating for Terry—busting up a perfectly good day—typically a Saturday or a Sunday—and hardly worth the effort of suiting up.

In summer, there were mostly two kinds of fires. The ones Terry preferred were the campfires out of control down by the locks. A big bonfire in a Hibachi meant someone was having one helluva party. Once the fire was brought in line, there was no rule that said volunteer firemen couldn't stay behind for a few brewskies. Terry had woken up more than one morning on the roof of a houseboat, bleary-eyed, head pounding from the hot morning sun, still wearing his regulation rubber boots.

The other kind of summer fires were the worst fires of all: forest fires. As a volunteer fireman, Terry would never get the glory jobs like trekking into the forest to cut a new fire line, never mind flying the water bomber. Instead, he spent days slogging along the edge of the fire, running errands for the real firemen who worked for the province, and missing whole weeks of hanging out by the locks ripping off tourists.

Fortunately, Terry had felt under the weather the couple of times he had been called to fight a forest fire. As a volunteer fireman, there was no sick pay to collect, but nothing's perfect.

This particular fire could be for real, he figured. The barrel burns were mostly done for the season, and it was a waterfront address, so it was even less likely to be a forest fire. Pulling up to 2311 Century Lane, he was far from disappointed. Not only was this a real live cabin fire. To boot, a good-looking lady was spraying it down with a garden hose. Bonus.

At first Judy mistook the young man in the bright green "A Knotter Yot" T-shirt for the pizza delivery boy. The one who still owed her ten dollars for gas money borrowed three months earlier. When he swaggered over and asked, "Where's the fire, ma'am?" she stared at him blankly. Wort had barked at his arrival and now he followed the man closely, barking non-stop.

"Hey, down boy. I'm a fireman," Yot Boy said. He bent over and extended his hand to pat the dog's head. Wort snapped. He pulled back and flashed Judy a smile full of teeth. "My name is Terry."

She looked him up and down. "*You're* a fireman?" Terry nodded. She asked, "Where's your truck?"

"I'm the advance crew. Survey the scene. Identify the plan, er, choose an approach...y'know...complicated stuff this fire business."

"We have to *do something*." Judy struggled to keep her voice steady. "I think there's someone inside. Ernie. My neighbor."

"Well, now, ma'am why on earth would someone go inside a burning building. Unless he's a fireman, I mean."

"He didn't *go* inside. I just think he's in there. In the FIRE."

Terry's eyes squinted, lids protecting eyeballs from the intense heat and blowing smoke. He pulled a package of Export A cigarettes from under his shirt sleeve. "Wanna smoke?" Judy looked at him, frowned, and said nothing.

"Calms my nerves," Terry said after lighting his cigarette. He kicked a stone toward the cabin and said, "Think I'll go around the other side and see if it's burning hot over there, too. Just keep that hose on the house there, lady. And, uh, maybe soak the ground a bit now and then. The truck will be here real soon. Just let me go check if maybe I can see your friend on the other side."

Judy watched him walk away, glanced over to where her dog lay panting in the shadow of his car and said, "Wort, I never want to see you smoke. Understand?"

She turned her full attention back to the blazing living room window. A strong offshore breeze carried the thick black smoke up the slope and across the road to where her own cabin stood. She moved a few steps in the direction of the lake to breathe easier. She clung to her prayer that Ernie wasn't inside his cabin, after all.

When two fire trucks pulled up, lights flashing, sirens off, she was surprised Wort didn't bark. "Wort, baby, where are you? WORT."

The firemen leapt from their perches and began unraveling their much bigger hoses. Two men dragged them toward the cabin while three more began unraveling a feeder hose down toward the lake. One of the firemen, the only one with a white helmet, strode over and asked, "Are you the lady who called this in?"

Ignoring him, Judy screamed for her dog, "WORT. WHERE ARE YOU? WORT." Fearful he might have somehow ended up in the cabin, she started flailing her dribbling hose back and forth wildly. She stepped toward the cabin. It felt like the flames would crackle her skin.

"Ma'am, step back from the fire. Drop the hose and come over here. Lady, can you hear me?"

Tears streaming, she gagged on the black smoke. The wind shifted direction again and she was engulfed. She gasped as heat filled her lungs. Choking, she fell to her knees and pointed the hose to her face. The cold splash gave her an immediate relief from the heat but then her mouth filled with water; she coughed, soot, mucus, and bile gushing from her nose and mouth. An enormous rush of adrenaline coursed through her body and her thighs wobbled jelly-like. She collapsed in a heap on the ground. The last thing she felt was a pair of strong hands grabbing her, rolling her onto her back; then she felt herself rise up, up, up into a sky full of smoke and into the glorious fresh air beyond.

* * *

When Judy came to, she was lying in the shade well-back from the fire. The fireman fanned her face with his white helmet.

"Lady, wake up. That's it. Open your eyes. No, DON'T MOVE. Just lay there. You blacked out."

What with the thump-thump-thump of the blood in her head, the roar of the fire, and the all the shouting of instructions back and forth among the firemen, Judy couldn't make out what the fire chief was saying to her. Her mind raced back to Wort and she struggled onto her elbows.

"WORT."

He came running from the other side of the cabin, yapping wildly, his long hair in flames. He ran straight to where Judy lay on the ground and the fireman immediately grabbed him and rolled him over twice, putting out the flames.

Yot Boy stumbled out from behind the cabin seconds later and drew up short when he saw Judy, Wort, and the chief.

"Uh, your pup's safe. Good thing. Whew, I was sure worried there for a minute," he panted. Looking at the truck, he said, "Alright. The gang's all here. Hey, boss, let's get that pumper going. We got a real barn-burner."

Mongoose slammed his ham-sized palm onto the painted plywood countertop that served as a bar in the Libidos' Liquid Lounge. Perko, Hawk, and several other bikers ranged around the room.

"Guys, alls I know is Perko's dopey farmer's startin' day parole. We gotta be tailing him if we want him to lead us to his money."

"*Our* money," said Hawk.

"Right you are. Our money."

Perko winced. *My money.* He knew he'd be lucky to get an extra bill or two out of the haul if the gang ever did get their paws on it. He'd been busted to shit duty for the last four years. If it hadn't been for Hawk, he would have been hung out to dry—literally—the day his grow op burned to the ground.

"Why the hell do we have to waste our time following the little shit?" asked Hawk. "I vote we just beat the crap out of him. He'll talk."

"Tried that, Hawk," said Mongoose. "You knows our guys beat him regular his first six months in the can. Promised him all kinds of goodness when he got out. Even offered him his pick of fresh ass 'case he wanted a girlfriend on the inside, but nothin'. Either he don't know where our cash is or he's one stone-faced motherfucker who ain't gonna give up a goddam thing."

Mongoose had turned his back on Perko in disrespect, shutting him out of the conversation. Perko stared at the back of his head, wondering how in hell the man managed to cut it almost square like that. Did he have to hang himself upside down with the shears?

Hawk said, "He's tougher than anyone figured. Holding out like that? I say he's gonna go for the cash first good chance he gets."

"'Xactly," said Mongoose. "We gotta be watching the little pecker."

Hawk nodded. He looked at Perko over Mongoose's shoulder and said, "Perko, you tail him from the drop. And don't wear your colors neither. Comb your hair and put on your Monday-go-to-court suit."

Perko scowled, held Hawk's stare as long as he dared, then headed to the kitchen to empty the garbage.

FIFTEEN

It was five days after Ernie McCann's charbroiled finale that Danny Grant awoke extra early for day parole. At Frontenac, he'd been bunked with a guy named Carson who took more of a shine to him than he cared for. Carson was so flabby he had full-on tits. He kept them shaved and let guys suck them for the price of extra dessert. As Danny swung his legs off the top bunk, Carson grabbed hold of his ankle and held on tight.

"Don't *gooooo*," he whined. "It'll be lonely here without you."

Danny snorted. "Actually, I was planning to use day parole to do something stupid. See if I could get sent back to Collins Bay for few extra years. Just to get away from you."

"Have it your way." Carson rolled over to face the wall.

The guard unlocked the cell door and disappeared as Danny walked down the hall to the showers. Security was a lot looser in minimum security. Inmates could often move around at will and many got some kind of unescorted temporary absence privileges. Of course, the guards used that fact as one more bargaining chip in the never ending tug-of-war of inmate discipline. Carson didn't get day parole, but he used what pull he had to get a fresh guy bunked with him every few weeks.

Ninety-four days and counting, Danny told himself as he lathered up. He'd survived the darkness of prison life without becoming an animal. With day parole, the few remaining months would be easy. He'd watched other inmates panic approaching full release—wondering how they'd survive on the outside. But he wasn't like them. For him, prison had been a waiting game, nothing more. When he got out, he'd have all the cash he'd ever need to lead a decent life, as long as he didn't splash around too much too soon.

He closed his eyes to rinse the shampoo from his head. No sooner had he shut them than an all-too-familiar stench burned his nostrils. Carson. The bastard smelled so bad it permeated even the acrid chemical fog of the shower stall—a mix of industrial-strength soap and that body odor particular to hyper-stressed men. The one good thing about Carson's distinctive reek was the warning it delivered when he crept up behind you.

Danny twisted on the balls of his feet only to find himself pinned at the wrists, his arms stretched wide, a fat knee wedged between his thighs.

"Shit, Carson, gimme a break. This here's my big day. I'm going downtown!"

"Hee-hee-hee." The freakishly young voice twittered in his ear. Carson's breath replaced his body odor as the three hundred pound con licked Danny's earlobe and pressed his belly into his back. "I'm a-goin' to *take* you downtown, show you aroun', and make it *my* big day, now ain't I, Danny-girl."

Danny relaxed, giving his best impression of submission under the circumstances and when he felt Carson's penis start to slide between his cheeks, he kicked like a mule and caught the lovelorn man high enough on the thigh to make him jump back. He felt the grip on his wrists loosen just enough for him to wriggle free. Ducking under a flabby arm, he made a dash for the outer room and called for the guard.

Three hours later, Danny sat grinding his breakfast into the second hour at the Minute Diner in downtown Kingston, Ontario. The prison shuttle had let him out right across the street. He'd walked all of sixty feet with his first taste of freedom. All day breakfast for $5.99 and a waitress who kept him coffeed for a fifty cent tip. Danny was in heaven. He stirred three sugars and two creams into his sixth cup, then smeared a full packet of orange marmalade onto a half slice of toast and wolfed it down. He drained his cup in one gulp and signaled the waitress for a refill. As she poured, Danny asked if he could buy a cigarette.

"Here, just take one," she said and handed him her pack of smokes. "How long were you away?"

Danny felt himself shrink. How could she tell? Then he looked down at the Woody Woodpecker sweatshirt he'd stolen from Carson's hook on the way, and the pale green trousers beneath them. Who the hell else would dress like this?

"Too long. But I'll be out soon enough. Thirteen more weeks."

"Oh, so you're on day parole, eh? What're you in for?"

"For being stupid," Danny said, ending the conversation. "Hey, can I read that paper over there if you're finished with it?"

"Sure, pal. I'll bring it right over. It isn't today's though. It's from last Saturday. I'm just working on the crossword, about halfway done. Don't go throw it out on me."

Watching her ass as she went to retrieve the newspaper, Danny felt his heart pump a little harder and then grow heavy again. He was sure he'd seen her smirk at the ridiculous sweatshirt.

When he got out, first thing he'd do is buy some new clothes. He'd be rich and dressed right and able to ask a good-looking waitress what time she got off work. But would he still be a fuck-up? Would he still make bad choices? Or, would he finally dial it all in and make a real life for himself? Whatever that meant.

Danny certainly had no illusions about working for a living. Nope, he was headed straight for retirement. For four years, he'd lain on his bunk staring at the dirty yellow concrete ceiling, listening to his cellmate mumble and moan on the bunk below. The guy spent the day "singing" along with Def Leppard, playing the same silent tunes over and over on his iPod. By now, Danny could recite the lyrics to *Hello America*, and he'd never even heard the song. Another three months and he'd pick his own damn radio station. Still, he knew there would be complications.

As a paroled convict, he couldn't up and leave the country, fly off to Jamaica, and chill. And if he hung around Peterborough spending the dough, he'd get noticed for sure. Then there was the question of his mother. Would she get in touch with him once he was released? Was she so pissed that she'd disappeared for good? Skeritt would know how to reach her, but would he tell Danny? And would Danny tell *him* about the money?

The money.

The thought of having it, spending it, counting it, and knowing it was his had kept Danny going all these years. It was how he had dealt with the sham of pleading guilty to manslaughter, how he had kept from bawling his eyes out when he said goodbye to his mom in the courtroom, how he had watched weeks turn into months in prison without losing his mind.

He drained the last of his coffee and got up to take a leak. On his way to the men's room, he noticed this guy in a booth near the back of the restaurant who seemed to be grinding away the morning just like him. The man had walked in as Danny was digging into his own plate of eggs and bacon nearly an hour and a half earlier. All two hundred fifty pounds of him were stuffed into a cheap polyester suit, brown with blue stitching. It was the kind of suit Danny imagined some do-good might give him the day he got out of prison. "A little something to get you started on the right foot," his parole officer would tell him.

The men's room had one urinal, one stall, and one sink. In theory, it could be used by two people at a time, but it was barely large enough for one. Danny had to lean uncomfortably close to the urinal when the guy in the bad suit followed him into the tight space just as he unzipped himself. He listened to the man piss into the toilet with a throaty sigh. A relieved moan followed a robust fart. Then the man coughed, cleared his throat, spat, and walked straight out. He neither flushed the toilet nor washed his hands.

Danny still hadn't peed.

Beads of sweat popped out on his forehead. Three years in the slammer hadn't made him particularly fond of shared washroom facilities. Not every con had a telltale scent like Carson.

On his way back to his booth, he threw a scowl at the beefy guy once again seated at the back of the diner. In his own mind, when Danny pulled his eyebrows low and squinted, he looked like the meanest convicted criminal imaginable and not at all like some kid on a high school quiz show about to get eliminated by a simple question. The bulky target of his best attempt at an evil eye picked his teeth and ignored him.

Waving the waitress over, Danny ordered a slice of raisin pie. "Oh, and maybe a little more coffee to wash it down, while you're at it."

Despite his apparent indifference, Perko Ratwick had indeed been paying very close attention to the day-paroled convict, tailing him from the moment he stepped out of the prison van. The seemingly coincidental trip to the men's room had allowed him to confirm the window was too small for Danny Grant— and certainly himself—to crawl through.

As he watched the punk dig into raisin pie and slurp back yet more coffee, Perko's stomach tied another knot. The brown polyester suit he had outgrown five years earlier did little to make him feel like a fully-patched member of the Libidos Motorcycle Club. Despite never having met Danny Grant face-to-face, he'd had plenty of time to dream up ways to kill him, and that went a long way toward making their relationship intimate. His preferred method would be to stuff the puke's head in a toilet and flush repeatedly, but he knew he'd settle for strangulation, suffocation, just about anything that involved using his bare hands. As long as he could watch him die and be certain Danny knew exactly who did the killing. Unfortunately for Perko, snuffing Danny Grant was off limits. The Libidos wanted him alive. Besides, since his screw up at the grow op, Perko's own chip stack around the clubhouse had been pretty darn short.

The humiliation was acute. For the first year, he'd been barred from even the clubhouse couch, forced to spend every night offsite at Shelley's whether he wanted to or not. Eventually, Hawk had managed to convince Mongoose to lay off his protégé, saying he was less of a risk held close than far, and that he was their best chance of finding the stolen money. Nonetheless, Perko was tagged with responsibility for bullshit clean-up jobs. He was fed up with busting chops when street-level dealers tried to fuck with the count or delivering baggies to those upright members of society whose reputation didn't allow them to buy their drugs from the local riffraff. He hated that gig the most because it involved wearing street clothes not unlike this stupid brown suit.

For his part, Mongoose razzed Perko non-stop. About the fire, about the money, about the humiliation dealt to him in front of the cops, the Skeletons, the Nancy's Nasties, and those spic extras. Every couple of months, Mongoose would get take-out from Aunt Helena's kitchen. And every time, he'd order a double helping of her newest dish: *Perko's Paella.* "Guaran-fucking-teed to flush you clean," he'd announce.

There'd be a time and a place to deal with Mongoose.

For now, though, his anger focused on the shithead farmer. Seeing him up close for the first time, Perko could barely contain himself. What was with the fucking Woody Woodpecker sweatshirt? Was the runt bastard laughing at him? *Ha-ha-ha-HA-haaaa! Ha-ha-ha-HA-haaaa! Heh-heh-heh-heh-heh-heh-HEH!*

When the jerk started reading the newspaper again, Perko groaned and had another wet dream about murder.

Danny was thinking he should take in a movie or maybe browse the used CDs in the music shop down the street. He found it hard to relate to the newspaper. Stories about business confused him and since he hadn't voted in the last election—or any election, for that matter—he found politics a bore. There was a paragraph on page five about Indian Summer accompanied by a four-column picture of two girls sunbathing; he read that until his pie was done. The bikinis duly committed to memory, he turned the page and coughed up a noseful of coffee.

Two pictures ran under the headline: "Volunteer hero saves much-loved doggie."

On the left, a woman with an exceptionally dirty face clutched what appeared to be a white fur hat to her chest. In the picture, the hat was licking the woman's chin. Upon closer inspection, Danny decided it looked like a Pekinese whose face hadn't been smushed quite all the way in. He wasn't interested in the dog, though, nor the woman for that matter, although she *was* pretty. It was the smoking hulk of a cabin in the background that caught his attention.

The article described how "a local volunteer fireman saved a beloved pet Lhasa Apso from certain death in a fatal fire that took the life of longtime Lakehurst resident, Ernst McCann."

That, in itself, would have been enough to freak Danny out of his gourd. What really blew his mind, though, was the picture of the beaming volunteer firefighter. None other than Terry Miner. The dog lady was quoted as saying "I couldn't see what he did because he went around to the other side of the cabin and the smoke was so thick, I thought he might have got caught in the fire himself." Danny couldn't tell whether she was talking about Terry or her dog. The article went on to say "Miner's actions were nothing short of heroic." The reporter practically suggested Ernst McCann might still be alive if only the local hero had arrived on scene sooner.

Terry Miner. *A hero?* Maybe in some sick and twisted dream. Even with four character-building years behind bars, Danny wasn't prepared for this. He knew the universe had a dark, brutal, often nasty sense of humor. He could handle that. And Terry's ability to slither through life unscathed was aggravating, for sure, but ultimately irrelevant. Now, however, the fucker was messing with Danny's future, his retirement fund, and his mother's health plan.

He tore the article from the paper and stared at the photo of Ernst McCann's cabin, smoke rising from its twisted beams. He conjured up his own twisted headline: *"Here is where Danny Grant hid $750,000 of biker money that nobody knows about."* He wondered how true that still was.

SIXTEEN

Judy Jackman spent the first couple of days after the fire trying to make the best of a sooty situation. From her four-room bungalow across the road, she could smell the sodden ash. Twice, she had noticed fresh smoke and scurried over with a bucket to put out small fires smoldering in the woods near the cabin. At night, she slept fitfully, leaping to the window whenever Wort snuffled or she heard a twig crack outside her open window.

By day, she attacked the ashen mess with a pitchfork and a long-handled spade. Ernie's yard was, after all, her view, a once romantic tableau anchored by a well-worn log cabin with a rusted red roof perched on the side of a hill overlooking Pigeon Lake. Blue water peeked between the mixed pine and maple trees that surrounded the cabin. With the cabin destroyed, she could see a little more of the lake, but mostly what she saw was a twisted pile of scorched metal and charred logs.

Next spring, she could toss wildflower seeds to create a meadow, a colorful new vista in Ernie's memory. In the meantime, the raking was cathartic and helped her feel close to him.

In the year or so she had lived there, Ernie had always been kind to her. His gratitude for small favors was immense. If Judy picked up fallen branches from his laneway or the path which led down to the water so Ernie wouldn't trip on them, he'd bring her a pie from the local pastry shop. Once, when she offered to sweep the pine needles off his roof so their acid wouldn't ruin his shingles, he had called up the hardware store and had them deliver a safety ladder and a leaf blower to her home. Judy protested, but Ernie waved it off: "It's for me, not for you, okay? I just don't want to be worried you'll fall and break your neck on my account." And sometimes, when Judy would read him his mail, he'd try to pay her cash for her time.

At that, she drew the line. He would shrug as if accepting her refusal, and then she'd find a twenty dollar bill stuck in her mailbox the next day.

With what remained of his eyesight, Ernie could make out large shapes and colors, but reading was out of the question. Perhaps because of that, he always knew when there was going to be a particularly spectacular sunset after a warm summer day. He'd call out for Judy to bring Wort down to his dock. There they would sit and watch the day slide into the evening until the mosquitoes drove them back inside, Judy giving the colors whimsical names and Ernie describing how the sun's final heat chased the cool lake air across his cheeks.

Thinking about those evenings now as she raked, Judy paused and looked down the sloped yard to the dock. Tears filled her eyes but she forced a smile: she was grateful to have known Ernie. And her somewhat warped Buddhist bent suggested he might come back as an osprey. Judy wasn't convinced human incarnation was all it was cracked up to be. Ernie, she felt sure, would rather spend summers soaring high above the lake able to see fish flash under the surface where others saw only the reflection of a blue sky.

Positive renewal was vital to Judy. Without it, she believed the world was headed to Hell in a hurry. She'd grown up with a fear of acid rain that gave way to hatred of PCBs only to be overcome by a deep conviction that the world's ozone layer would scarcely outlast her thirtieth birthday. When that event had come and gone and Judy found she could still walk outside without spontaneously combusting, she mellowed a bit. She decided her contribution to the planet's health would be more local in nature. With nothing in particular to keep her in the city, she packed her bags and rented a cabin in the country.

Wort made the transition easily enough, although the burrs and twigs and smellier forest detritus turned his long white coat into a matted mess that Judy had to clip off every few months in an evening of yelps and whining complaint. After the scissors, the doggie soap, and the dunking in ice cold water, the dog's reward was getting snuggled extra close and not relegated to the foot of Judy's bed.

It didn't escape her attention that Wort was the only man in her life. It hadn't been for lack of trying: she'd had at least a dozen relationships that could be termed "serious" and not one had been blessed with an anniversary dinner. Over the years, different men had told Judy she was too uptight about the planet's ills, too easygoing about finances, a clean freak, a sloppy green enviro-leftist, clingy, overly independent, intimidating, and fragile. Wort alone offered Judy the two things she felt important in a relationship: consistency and forgiveness.

When her girlfriends in the city told Judy that her relationship with Wort stood in the way of her ever getting a good man to stick around, Judy's only response had been to grow even closer to her dog. At least Wort didn't constantly remind her of his superiority between bouts of emotional ineptitude. Until she moved to the country, it had been easy enough to hook up with one flame or another for an occasional evening out, or in. She'd even invited an old boyfriend out to her cabin once when she craved male attention shortly after moving up to the lake. After spending the weekend dabbing him with calamine lotion and listening to him moan about the lack of television, she decided it just wasn't worth it. It'd be her and Wort until she was good and ready for a guy.

And then she'd met Ernie. A man who didn't mind needing her help from time to time and who actually listened to her describe the difference between store bought kibble and the potato turnip meals she lovingly prepared for Wort. A man who wasn't forever telling her what to think while showing no interest in what she *did* think. A man whose only disqualifying trait was that he was older than her father.

Standing now next to the soggy char that had claimed the life of the only really good man Judy had known in years, she leaned over and gently scratched the top of Wort's head.

"You know, Wort, once they haul away all the metal to a scrapper, and we clean up the rest of the garbage, this place won't look half bad, will it?" Wort barked in reply, stood up, and wagged his tail. "I'm even sort of glad Ernie's outhouse didn't burn down. All grey and worn and with those ferns growing around it, it looks kind of pretty, don't you think?"

The Lhasa Apso snuffled, as if to say he wasn't convinced Ernie's shitter—or any shitter, for that matter—could be called pretty. The dog underlined his point by strolling over to the four-foot-wide structure and lifting his leg.

"Tsk, tsk," Judy said. Over the past two days, Wort had followed her even more closely than normal whenever she went outside. She could tell he was as shaken up by things as she was. It wasn't surprising: he had nearly died in the fire, after all.

She kept replaying the events from the day of the fire over and over in her mind. Calling 911, battling the flames with the garden hose, calling out to Ernie over and over and praying all the while that he had slipped into town without her noticing. And then that local yokel fireboy. Two days later, Judy still wasn't quite sure what to make of Terry Miner. Once he had pulled on the regulation jacket, pants, and big rubber boots, he looked just as handsome, purposeful, and downright virile as the rest of the volunteer firemen. When she tried to ask him what had happened with Wort, he appeared bashful. Almost humble, she thought. And he seemed to work every bit as hard as the other firemen to control the inferno that eventually consumed the log cabin. In fact, Terry seemed positively passionate about fighting the fire. Twice, Judy overheard him asking the chief if he could get called on "real fires like this one" more often. Later, when a pretty blond reporter showed up from the local newspaper, she overheard Terry decline to accept the accolades the woman tried to heap on him; though she did notice he was the only fireman who stopped his work to chat with the reporter at all.

All in all, he seemed like a somewhat goofy guy who had failed to grow up properly; Judy had known plenty of those. With his dirty blond hair, longish eyelashes, and crooked grin, he was certainly good looking—in a Bad Boy kind of way— though he looked like he'd go to seed pretty bad before too long; he already had a bit of a donut roll above his waistline. What turned Judy's stomach, though, was what Terry had asked her when the fire was nearly out and the other firemen were venturing carefully among the still smoking timbers with their pike poles, trying to determine whether Ernst McCann's corpse was among the rubble.

Terry had sauntered over to where she leaned against a tree, Wort on her lap. She was still being observed by a pair of paramedics. Terry pulled a cigarette from his pack and raised his eyebrows at Judy in question: "What are you doing for dinner tonight?"

Creep, Judy had thought at the time.

Low-life creep, she thought again now as she raked the cold coals around the edges of the collapsed cabin. "Guys like him are why we live alone, Wort. There's creeps and then there's guys whose friends are creeps. Show me a guy who is creep-free and I'll show you a...a...an anomaly. That's what I'll show you, Wort! And then, well, we'll just see, won't we?"

Wort snuffled. He was licking a large disc of wood that had somehow escaped the fire. Judy recognized it as Ernie's coffee table.

"You like that, Wort? The tree it was cut from must have been over a hundred years old. Should we roll it home, Wort? Something to remember Ernie by? He was no creep, was he, Wort? He was a kind man. And old. And alone. That's right, Wort. Ernie was alone because he wasn't a creep and he had no creep friends, which meant he had no friends at all, eh Wort? See what I mean?"

She'd got the table up on edge when a bright yellow Jeep pulled up at the side of the road. The driver's hiking boots were a strange match for her crisp blue suit, but they made sense in the ashen muck. She had black hair pulled back in a bun so tight it stretched her eyes up at the corners. Her lips were as thin as the rest of her and they barely moved when she spoke.

"What are you *do*ing? You can't be here! This is a *fire* scene! It's *priv*ate property!"

Wort squared his front haunches, glared at the intruder, and growled.

"Good afternoon to you, too, Linette. So nice of you to drop by." Judy felt her chest tighten involuntarily in anger. There was nothing pleasant, nice, or good about Linette Paquin.

"*You* simply cannot be here." The lawyer was bleating. Actually bleating. Like a goat. "You...you...this is com*plete*ly inappropriate. There was a *fire* here, you know, and, well, there has to be an investigation, and, just what are you doing with that *rake*, anyway?"

"Trying to clean up a little," Judy said. "It's what Ernie would want. What are *you* doing here?" She snapped the rake away as Linette lunged for it. Wort barked in protest.

"You...you...you cannot *possibly* be serious about cleaning up the scene of a fire. I *mean*, a man died here. Show some respect. What if *there* is an investigation that has to happen? What caused the fire? *What* if it was arson? You could be destroying evidence."

Judy knew lawyers could obsess about "the rules," carry logic to extremes, and make rationality seem positively irrational, but this woman was way off the deep end.

"Linette, I really don't see how this fire is any of your concern. I'm Ernie's neighbor, and *I* am cleaning up, which is more than *you'll* ever do here. Don't think just because Ernie's dead you can get your claws into his property. He told me he would sooner see his land slide into the lake than let you build some monster home on it and block out the sky."

She had seen Linette's yellow Jeep parked in front of Ernie's cabin at least half a dozen times since moving in. Once, she went outside and heard shouts drift across the way. When she asked, Ernie said the lawyer was hounding him, trying to buy his land. "She's relentless," he told Judy. "And nasty. The crazy bat accuses me of hogging the best view on the lake when I can't enjoy it myself."

Watching Linette sputter, Judy said, "I think maybe you should leave. Ernie wouldn't want you here."

"Well he isn't here to tell me himself now, is he?" Linette stomped through the ashes, kicking at remnants of the old man's furniture. Wort darted back and forth around the edges of the fire heap. He snorted, growled, and barked in his lowest voice.

Linette picked up a twisted piece of metal that looked like it might have been part of the screen door and used it to poke among the ashes. Judy asked what she was looking for.

"Nothing! I'm not looking for anything. I'm poking, that's what I'm doing. I'm poking to see that this here fire is good and out. You never *know* with these *volunteer* firemen. I'll make sure this fire is absolutely extinguished and then I...that is...yes...I am going to buy this place and build my dream home right here. Yes, right on this very spot. Or over there."

She stabbed the ash some more. Judy tried to go back to her raking, but her anger was making her arms shake.

"Linette," she said as calmly as she could, her voice pinched and tight and an octave higher than normal. "I really think this is rude and inappropriate of you and I just think that..."

Judy never finished her sentence. As she spoke, Linette, wild-eyed, had started toward her, still clutching her metal spear. Wort held back just long enough and then leapt straight at Linette, jaws open as she reached the former cabin's perimeter. His teeth grabbed hold of Linette's blazer and he flapped wildly through the air as she shrieked and spun around in a vain effort to dislodge him. Wort hung on. She threw down the hunk of metal and bolted for her Jeep.

Judy ran behind, waving her rake. Wort sprang from the car window as Linette peeled away in a shower of dirt.

"That woman is nasty, Wort," Judy said, dropping the rake to scoop him up. "We'll never let her live here. That woman is a...you know what, Wort? I think that woman is a creep in lawyer's clothing."

The dog, momentarily silent, licked her face.

Danny left the diner hell-bent on doing something. Exactly what, he had no idea

Ernie's cabin had been torched; he was sure of it. Somehow, the Libidos had connected Ernie to Danny to the cash. The newspaper article suggested foul play wasn't being ruled out, and only a particularly foul kind of person could ever do anything nasty to someone as harmless as Ernie McCann. Like a Libidos lieutenant keen on extracting information. He felt chill. It hit him like a baseball bat between the eyes that his window of opportunity would run out sooner than the three months he had left until full parole.

Even if he was wrong about the Libidos, Ernie's cabin was on a primo location on Pigeon Lake. It would take no time at all for whoever inherited the land to sell it. Some fat cat from the city would buy the two acres with three hundred pointed feet of pristine waterfront and bulldoze the hell out of it. Either some lucky sap on a backend loader would find the satchel full of cash or it would wind up buried under a concrete basement floor.

Danny considered his options, none too good. He could wait and hope that by some miracle Ernie McCann's cabin property would remain undisturbed until the Correctional Service of Canada decided in its wisdom that Danny was ready to return to society. He could try to scramble to and from Pigeon Lake during his next eight hours of day parole—but where would he hide the bag of cash once he retrieved it? He couldn't exactly take it back to his room at the Handcuff Hilton.

Or, he could run.

After all, wasn't that what day parole was about? To find out whether a convict would run? You couldn't really call it escaping. "Escape" conjured up images of desperate criminals prepared to dig tunnels with spoons and fingernails. Or hide in putrid laundry bags. Or perform strange sex acts on prison guards for a chance to get outside the wall. Walking away from day parole required nothing more than not showing up at the station at the end of your afternoon at the movies.

Since Danny had no job, his next day parole excursion might not happen for another two weeks. Waiting that long would be, well, unnecessary. He made up his mind and strolled over to the Kingston Bus Station.

Someone else could bunk with Carson tonight.

SEVENTEEN

Buzz Meckler, Ticket Counter Associate for Kingston Greyhound, tidied his stack of ticket blanks, moved his stapler from the left side of his ticket wicket to the right hand side and then back left. He considered moving it to the right again but instead turned it around so that the end with the teeth faced him. He reached across with his right hand and tapped it lightly, satisfied that he had determined the right position. Letting out a small sigh of accomplishment, he tapped it again, a little harder this time, and flinched when the stapler spat out a crushed and spoiled staple.

Glancing to his right to make sure Aldwyn Bright, Senior Ticket Counter Associate, had not noticed, Buzz scooped the wasted staple off the counter and tossed it into the trash can at his feet.

This was Buzz Meckler's first day on the job.

Before being allowed to man the ticket counter, he had undergone no less than two weeks of intensive training. There, he learned why the simple act of purchasing a ticket from Kingston to Toronto could take up to five minutes. Turns out it had nothing to do with a level of basic incompetence shared by all ticket sellers. Instead, the complex set of procedures that ticket counter associates had to follow formed the basis of Week One training. It was heady stuff, even for a guy whose previous job had the impressive title of Entertainment Selection Coordinator. Buzz's most recent retail stint had been at the eighth largest video store in Kingston.

Getting paid to go to bus ticket school meant Buzz had hit the big times. Gee, he thought, if they'd paid me to go to high school back when, I might have finished grade nine. What Buzz did not know was that the two-week training program qualified Kingston Greyhound Bus Station for federal Job Skills Improvement funding which covered thirty-five percent of

Buzz's wages for his first six months on the job. To make up the second week, Kingston Greyhound had crafted two new learning platforms.

The first centered on customer service. Students role-played being polite to customers and they learned how to stop using swear words in casual conversation. Buzz had wanted to know whether it was okay to swear at a customer if the customer swore first. That had been one of his favorite parts of working at the video store. In fact, he had found cussing at belligerent customers was often the most effective way of cutting short otherwise bothersome arguments over late fees. Buzz was big as a barn and looked every bit as sturdy. Some customers would take twisted pleasure mouthing off at a guy who looked like a professional wrestler stuffed into a ridiculous blue and orange striped uniform—complete with a jaunty little baseball cap, two sizes too small, with a googly-eyed owl mascot on the brim. They'd get angry, raise their voices, and swear at him like he was some kind of gutter trash. Rare, however, were the customers who stood their ground and argued about six dollars in late fees once Buzz pulled off the baseball cap to reveal his punked-out hair and let loose his tongue. Faced with a wild-eyed, bad-acned, spittle-spewing country boy who swore an R-rated blue streak and kept his nervous hands hidden beneath the counter, people paid up their late fees and got the hell out of the store.

Shrugging off his dismay at not being allowed to exercise what he considered to be one of his most employable attributes, Buzz worked harder than most of his co-trainees at being extra polite. He found that he could actually affect a special kind of intimidation by being cucumber cool. He would refuse simple requests with icy tones that tended to frustrate the role-playing customer across the counter. Once frustration set in, Buzz was adept at raising its level to the point that his co-working co-trainee would often start swearing. That gave Buzz the opportunity to prove he could counter froth-mouthed anger with frigid reserve.

The final piece of training was a two-day course on the identification of likely prison escapees. Kingston was home to no less than seven prisons, with a couple more just outside of town. It wasn't that the local population was particularly prone to criminal activity—at least not before the families of inmates started moving to the region to be close to their loved ones—it was just deemed to be geo-effective by the bureaucrats in Ottawa who'd located new prison facilities over time.

Kingston Greyhound felt no particular civic duty to identify possible prison escapees. Rather, the course in possible escaped prisoner identification was designed to take advantage of another federal grant, intended to offset the negative economic impact of locating a high concentration of prisons in a specific geographic location—of which Kingston was the only one in Canada.

Whatever he thought of the limitations placed on his use of foul language, Buzz Meckler felt positively empowered by his perceived authority to apprehend prison escapees. As Entertainment Selection Coordinator, Buzz had watched many unwatchable movies and not a few of them involved stories about people who had been to prison—or would be going there soon. Whenever he watched films featuring criminals—which was often—he rooted for the police. Even where the men in blue were set up as a force of evil, Buzz liked to see criminals handcuffed or shot by the end of the show. His pathological self-righteousness, which had driven him to refuse to forgive even the most abusive video rental late fees, boiled over at the idea of prisoners not serving full sentences.

Any escape from justice stuck in his craw.

Already this first morning behind the real counter at the bus station, Buzz had refused to sell a student ticket to a fourteen-year-old when the kid failed to produce student identification. Then he'd forced a mother and two toddlers to wait three hours for the next bus to Montreal, rather than radio the bus driver to wait one extra minute for three final passengers.

No question. Buzz's new gig offered lots of opportunity to flex his authoritative muscle. He served with pride.

Danny walked through the automatic sliding doors and took a half step back when confronted with two men in matching blue Kingston Greyhound Bus Station uniforms. They were both young and neither looked terribly intelligent. The one on the left was a beanpole and looked bored. The one on the right was built like a hockey player. He stood erect, had an intimidating fire in his eyes, and was fidgeting with something on the counter. Both his hands were out of sight. After years in the Collins Bay Medium Security Correctional Center, Danny could be forgiven for imagining he was standing in front of a pair of prison guards.

So when the automatic sliding doors started to close on Danny and the door to his left touched his shoulder, Danny jumped backward, out of the bus station, and watched the doors slide shut in front of him.

Still stepping backward, he moved away from the door. In prison, you learned to keep your eyes on the guards, and Danny had no reason to think anyone was behind him. Until he felt a considerable beer gut press into his back. Danny flashed back to Carson's belly flattening him against the concrete wall in the showers that very morning.

Without pausing to wonder whose hand gripped his shoulder, he spun one hundred and eighty degrees on his right leg and brought his left knee arcing upward with as much centrifugal force as he could muster. His knee bone connected squarely with all the soft fleshy parts between the legs of the man in the bad brown suit. The man's groan went on and on. Had he simply stood and listened, Danny might have marveled at just how long that groan lasted.

But Danny wasn't sticking around. Even in prison, you ran toward the screws when you had to. He caught a glimpse of an incredibly red face as the heavy set man doubled over clutching his balls with both hands. It was the same tough-looking character from the Minute Diner.

Danny raced inside to the ticket wicket staffed by the guy with the over-caffeinated eyes and the bad Mohawk haircut. Breathless, he said, "I need a one-way ticket to Peterborough."

"One-way?"

"And fast."

"That fat man giving you a hard time?"

"Yeah. Step on it, will you?"

"Of course, sir. One way to Peterborough. Are you looking for the Express or the regular bus."

"I don't care. Just gimme the ticket."

"Well, they cost the same, but the Express won't stop for coffee or other refreshments, sir. Just straight on through it goes."

"It's a two-hour drive. I'll survive."

"Well, like I said, there's no difference in price, so it's really up to you."

"The ticket..."

"Of course, the Express doesn't leave until two o'clock, sir, whereas the regular bus leaves in just about a minute and it will get to Peterborough a little before one o'clock."

"I'll take it."

"Bit of a criminal element, is he?"

"Who? Oh, him."

"Leave him to me, sir. I know just how to handle his type. We receive training on this sort of thing here at the Greyhound."

"I'm happy for you."

"Ticket coming right up," said the clerk. "The bus is just about to leave. Give me just a moment while I radio the driver to wait for you." While he called up the driver, he used his free hand to type the destination code into the terminal in front of him. "$34.70," he announced, beaming. Danny fished two crumpled ten dollar bills from his pants and rummaged through his other pockets, piling their contents on the counter. Besides the torn article about the fire from the diner, a half pack of gum, and a handful of dimes and nickels, he had nothing. His heart sank.

Mohawk dude locked Danny's gaze and winked. "Or just $19.50 for the student rate. You are a student, right? 'Course you are," he said with a self-satisfied smile as he slipped two quarters and a ticket across the counter toward Danny.

Danny nodded his thanks and turned to go.

"Hey, you want this other stuff?" the guy called out at him as he ran toward the bus platform.

"It's all yours," Danny said over his shoulder.

In less than forty-five seconds, Danny Grant, escaped convict, had purchased a discounted bus ticket on the Kingston Greyhound bound for the Kawarthas. One minute after that, he was in his seat, watching his would-be attacker roll on the ground, still clutching his balls, now moaning more than groaning, as the bus rumbled out of the parking lot and down the road toward Highway 401.

As soon as the clean cut customer had left the counter, Buzz dialed the police hotline to report the assault he had witnessed and to tell the police the rough-looking perpetrator was still at the bus station. While he watched the burly guy in the bad suit lie on his back in front of the entrance, Buzz scanned the newspaper article left behind when the guy ran for the bus: something about a fire and some little dog that got rescued. Firemen got to be heroes a lot, he mused. Well, now he wore a uniform, too—that was something at least. For three whole minutes, he leveraged all his training in minor crisis management, maintaining a business as usual stance behind his ticket counter, waiting for the police to arrive.

Aldwyn Bright, meanwhile, apparently relying more on instinct and experience than on training and procedure, logged off his computer and announced he was going on break, pausing only to say, "You're in charge, Buzz."

Brimful of pride and determination, Buzz kept his eyes on the thug outside. With a grimace, the man rolled himself onto his knees and pulled himself up in stages, first one leg, then the other, then finally struggling to unbend his waist. His chest heaving, he tugged at his shirt collar, ripping off two buttons. Barely upright, he shuffled through the door, very nearly dragging his knuckles on the ground.

Buzz Meckler glared at him, one hand fidgeting with the stapler, half his brain imagining it was a side arm, and his mind still racing with a hero's adrenalin at having aided the escape of the young man being chased by this obvious thug.

"You see that guy who jumped me?" the thug's voice was a cross between a grunt and a squeal.

Buzz just stared at him, doing his best impression of a cold hard cop. The tough guy took a deep breath and leaned across the counter. He puffed out his words, clutching his winded gut as he did. This had the effect of sending a rush of morning-after-too-much-tequila breath directly into Buzz's face.

"Where did that little puke go?"

Buzz was, at that moment, every tough cop in every B movie he had ever watched. His uniform was a source of pride. He was all that stood between a raving lunatic with murder on the brain and the innocent defenseless citizenry who counted on the men in blue to keep them safe. His Kingston Greyhound identification tag was a shiny brass badge. And the stapler by his right hand was a weapon of peace.

From the moment he stumbled into the bus station, Perko's blurred vision started playing tricks on him. He knew the mammoth asshole behind the ticket counter couldn't be Mongoose, but his square shoulders and the five extra inches he had on Perko felt like a physical putdown which was all too familiar. Even his Mohawk hairdo was reminiscent of Mongoose's oddball buzz cut, although this guy wasn't a redhead.

"I'm sorry, sir," the clerk said in a voice that was way too cheerful. "I am not at liberty to discuss the travel habits of our Greyhound guests. Is there something else I can do for you today?"

"Listen, you pimple-headed fart," Perko snapped, "I'm not here to chat about your fucking rule book. Answer the question, and I won't pound your face to silly putty."

The ticket clerk swallowed hard and blinked repeatedly with little nods as if counting to ten in his head. "Now, now, dear sir. There really is no need to get nasty, is there? Perhaps you would like to sit down and I can get you a fresh glass of cool water before..."

Perko snarled and bared his yellow teeth. "How about I give you a fresh glass of your snot pressed out through your ears, shit-for-brains." The biker's arms, bent, shook at his sides, taut like an animal straining against its leash.

Apparently the time for polite dialogue had passed and the clerk began visibly frothing at the mouth. He said, "Sir, you must—"

"I *must* nothing, shithead." Perko couldn't believe this guy was standing up to him. Then he remembered he was wearing the ridiculous brown suit. Laying in a little extra snarl, he said, "Tell me where the fucker went."

The clerk began to tremble. His mouth opened and closed twice, like a fish, with no sound coming out. Then he closed his eyes tight for a count of three and reopened them wide, a half inch of white visible round each iris. He said, "You mouth-breathing fuck-for-breakfast horse's asshole-licking piece of ignorant SHIT." The dude's eyes no longer blinked at all; they rolled back in his head. "Think you can raise your scrotum-stinking pie-hole squeaker of a voice at ME?"

He snatched up something shiny from behind the counter and thrust it hard into Perko's exposed neck.

As the weapon flashed across the counter and the first staple pierced his skin, Perko screamed, "Fucking Taser ME?"

The clerk tried to step back, but he wasn't fast enough, and the fleshy pile of fury that was Perko Ratwick lunged across the counter, yanked him by the lapels, and sunk his teeth into *his* neck. The bigger man grabbed Perko's hair and started swinging.

Perko pushed his face into his assailant's neck, closed his eyes, bit down as hard as he could, and waited for the charge.

The shithead bus ticket clerk kept slamming the damn thing into his chest, his arm, anywhere the punk could reach. Tears streamed down his face as Perko hung on for dear life. Everything Hawk had told him was true. The Taser was hitting him over and over, but all he could feel was little pin pricks. He knew the charge must be passing through him and back into the fool in the uniform because Perko could feel the fire pouring out the top of his head, as if someone was pulling his hair. The blood he could taste in his mouth was not his own and he knew as long as he kept the juices flowing, they would carry the charge away.

With the counter between them, Perko's feet dangling off the ground, the clerk's fingers buried in Perko's hair, and Perko's teeth deep into the other guy's neck, the two men looked like shivering rag dolls tossed over the back of a chair. Neither one could stop the dance.

That was how the police found Buzz and Perko when they finally showed up. Their clutch had weakened by then and they were more trembling than shaking, but neither one would let go. Even after the men were handcuffed, Perko's teeth had not left Buzz's neck.

The cops did the only thing they could. They Tasered Perko Ratwick. And the charge traveled through him into Buzz Merkel. It worked like a charm.

EIGHTEEN

Linette Paquin pulled her canary yellow Jeep into the parking lot at the township office. She changed her ash-covered boots for more lawyerly pumps, checked her mascara in the rearview mirror and wiped a smear of lipstick from her teeth. It never hurt to look her best when she had to deal with the records clerk.

Located halfway between Bobcaygeon and Buckhorn, the low-slung municipal building was a model of patient efficiency. She went straight to the records office and drummed her manicured fingernails on the service counter.

"Can I help you?" A fresh-faced young man sprang from his desk to greet her. A cheap white polo shirt and uncomfortable-looking trousers did little to hide his farm-boy physique.

"Hello, Steven," said Linette, leaning on the counter just so. "I wonder if you could help me *pull* the municipal rolls for a piece of property."

From the back of the room, an older woman barked, "There's a form for that."

Ignoring her, Linette said, "Only if you've *got* the time, Steven."

"Sure thing, Ms. Paquin," said Steven. "Which lot are you interested in?"

"Ernst McCann's."

"That's a little quick, even for you, isn't it?" The woman somehow managed to look even more disapproving. "Old Ernie isn't even cold in the ground."

"His ashes looked pretty scattered to me, Mrs. Montgomery," said Linette. "I just want to know whether any other names are listed."

"That's easy," said Steven. "You see, we practically own it."

125

"It's not 'we,' Steven," said Mrs. Montgomery. "The Township isn't 'we.' I've explained that to you. 'We' work for The Township."

"Right. Sorry, Aunt Maude...I mean, Mrs. Montgomery. Anyways, like I was saying..."

"What *were* you saying?" asked Linette. She leaned a little closer to make sure he could smell her perfume. Record clerks could be useful in her line of work.

"What Steven was referring to," said his aunt, "is that Ernie McCann has not paid one dollar of taxes in twenty-six years. The township will take possession once the matter of his estate is settled."

"Oh, I see," said Linette, trying hard to refrain from licking her lips. "If that's the case, why wasn't anything done sooner?"

"Something to do with an explosion way back when," Auntie said. "Some people still feel bad for what happened to Ernie. Other folks just didn't want to look heartless kicking a blind man out of his home. He had no family."

"*No* family at all?"

"Nope. He was a foster kid. Grew up in Peterborough. Never married. Just a lonely old man. Nice enough to meet him, he was, but he pretty much kept to himself out by the lake."

Linette asked as nonchalantly as she could, "Do you know whether the township will auction the property immediately?"

"There's no bank involved, far as I know, so no one's going to rush things."

"Be sure to let me know if anything changes." Linette slid a business card across the counter toward Steven's sweating hand and tapped it with her index finger. "Call me right away."

She gave him one last smile and headed out the door.

It was almost too easy sometimes. A teensy part of Linette Paquin felt it was wrong to leverage her sexuality as freely as she did. But it paid off so often, it was darned hard to shut it down. The very fact she was interested in Ernie's property had its roots in her booty business.

A little more than a year before, she had purchased a high-end home theatre from Eyes and Ears Entertainment in downtown Peterborough. She wasn't overly interested in audiovisual extravaganzas, but she liked it when Joseph

Gordon-Levitt's chiseled features filled her screen. And it would be nice to freeze frame on Benjamin McKenzie's buttocks in the right pair of jeans.

Hooking up all those cables might have been downright nasty. The store charged seventy-five bucks an hour for a service call, but Linette knew a six-pack of beer and the right nudge would get her the same result. Besides, the sales guy was kind of cute.

With her gear properly mounted, they did a quick sound check and wound up testing more than her electronics.

Later, when she said, "Tell me that isn't the sexiest *installation* you've ever done," her conquest misunderstood. With the ashtray rising and falling on his sweaty chest, he started gushing about an *even better* set-up he'd done the week before.

"You wouldn't believe it," he said. "The dude can't hardly see, so he shells out for this massive screen and loads up on like a hundred Blu-rays to boot." He went on and on about how the guy bought a generator because he had no electricity.

Linette was not impressed. When he started reciting the names of the guy's audio components, she tuned out. She stared at the ceiling, wondering what Gabriel Macht would look like *out* of his suit. She was about to kick the techno-weenie out of her bed when he said, "Ernie McCann. Because of him, I made salesman of the month. Got a certificate and everything."

McCann. Wasn't that the old coot whose clothing Danny Grant had stolen the night he was caught running from a cannabis inferno? Grant had told the cops—and her—he stole the pants and shirt from some random clothes line, but he'd never given a good explanation for why he needed the wardrobe change. And they'd never recovered the duffel bag full of drug money. She didn't buy the rumor her Legal Aid client had run with the dough. If he had access to that kind of money, surely he would have hired himself a better defense attorney.

Unless it was all part of some diabolical plan.

What if Danny Grant had stashed the money with the old geezer and then used Linette to run a quick plea bargain? After all, an out-of-work wannabe forklift operator couldn't afford a real criminal defense lawyer. Coughing up the fee would have been as good as admitting he had the money. Instead, he was doing short time on the manslaughter charge, soon to get out of jail. And then what? Come collect a treasure? How was that fair?

For a country real estate lawyer like her, penny ante Legal Aid work had been a crummy community obligation. Getting taken for a ride wasn't part of the deal.

And so, she'd gone for the prize, confronting Ernie McCann about his spending habits. The conversation on the old man's doorstep started poorly and then fell off a cliff. "You want a piece of what?" He threatened to pump her full of buckshot if she didn't clear the hell out.

Linette Paquin was nothing if not persistent. No matter how many times he denied knowing about the money, she kept dropping in on him whenever business brought her near Century Lane. But her come-ons got her nowhere, and it turned out she wasn't particularly adept at threats or blackmail.

It became an obsession. One that lasted until the old man perished. Dead and cremated in his cabin by the lake. Gone. Along with whatever he knew about her client's loot.

Danny's cheek lay flat against the window of the Greyhound bus. Every few minutes he shifted to find a fresh patch of cool air-conditioned glass. Out the window, farm fields were cut by woodlots, two hundred-year-old grey barns, beef cattle, sheep, and, every so often, a horse or two. It was good to be out.

It was only two o'clock. He wouldn't be an escaped convict for another three hours. Technically, he was still on day parole, though riding a bus out of town breached the conditions of that parole. If caught, he'd be arrested, re-processed, and returned to Collins Bay, or worse. On the other hand, if he got off the bus and hightailed it back to town by five o'clock, he could be home at Frontenac in time for roll call, dinner, and free time in The Zoo. It kind of creeped him out to be thinking of his shared cell with Carson as "home."

Not that the thug from the diner was any more pleasant. The guy had biker written all over him, brown suit or not. Whoever he was, he now had a rather personal reason to be angry with Danny.

The crackle of the bus driver's two-way radio broke Danny's reverie. The engine hum and the white noise from the bus's air conditioner made it impossible to eavesdrop. Still, Danny convinced himself it was bad news. He watched the driver's face in the cabin view mirror. The driver caught his eye and held his gaze for a moment, sending a shiver down his spine.

Were they onto him? Maybe someone had spotted him getting onto the bus in Kingston. Or maybe the biker thug had squawked to the cops. Or the guy at the ticket counter might have picked up on his nervousness. Whatever it was, he needed off the bus. Nothing would be worse than getting caught by the cops like some runaway sheep. Besides the extra time added to his sentence, the guards and the other cons would make his life hell for screwing up the escape.

When the bus stopped to pick up passengers in Norbold, Danny made his getaway. The driver shot him a friendly smile and waved as he shut the door and drove off.

Norbold resembled any number of small Ontario towns whose heyday had passed. The train yard in the middle of town had seen busier times. A few stray flat cars were covered in heavy chains that once held loads of lumber in place. Empty barrels stood in a corner and a stack of tarred railroad ties lay next to the one-room station house. In the days when the lumber mill still operated, there would have been two trains a day. Now the freight train only made special deliveries. Passenger trains had given up on the town entirely.

Across from the rail yard, the hotel had stopped renting rooms in the eighties. A sign in the tavern window encouraged locals to drink Molson Ex and watch sports on the "NEW Widescreen TV!" Danny's mouth watered but fifty cents wouldn't buy him a taste, even here. He felt someone staring at him and looked up the street to where a man loaded cans of paint into the back of a pickup. The fellow grinned and squinted as if trying to place Danny. Then he waved and went back about his business. Danny gave a half wave back and strode down a side street like he knew where he was going.

Away from the main street, the town was even quieter. Kids would be getting out of school soon enough but in the meantime the only people he saw were a couple of old timers sitting on a broken porch in front of a senior's home. They stopped chatting to watch him walk by. He felt exposed.

By the third block, the houses thinned out to half-acre lots and he moved quickly down one driveway then across the unfenced backyard to the house next door. It only took four tries for him to find a bungalow with the back door unlocked and a grey Volvo parked outside. He stepped in and shouted, "Anybody home?" Silence.

The keys to the Volvo hung on a peg by the back door which opened directly into the kitchen. Empty cereal bowls filled the sink and three pots with smallish houseplants crowded the counter by the window. One looked like the Swedish Ivy his mom used to grow. He helped himself to a stale tuna sandwich from the fridge and packed a bag with apples, beer, rye bread, and salami.

Danny walked out the kitchen and down a short hall to the bedrooms. In the master bedroom, he found a spare change bowl with over fifty dollars in loonies and toonies. His pockets jangling with the coins, he checked out the second bedroom. Above a child's bed and a crib, someone had painted an amateurish mural: a barnyard with a cow that looked rather like a zeppelin, a reasonably good scarecrow, and a windmill. Danny's gut clenched when he spotted the shelf full of Dr. Seuss books. The same ones he'd grown up with.

He felt light-headed walking back down the hall, through the kitchen and out the backdoor. He took the child seats from the Volvo and leaned them up against the house. By the time the last house on the edge of town was in the rearview mirror, his heart no longer raced. He marveled at his calm.

He'd become a bona fide crook.

For all his forty-four months in the slammer, Danny had felt wronged and out of place. Sure, he had killed Lester, but that was self-defense. And his job at the grow op had been, well, a job. It wasn't as if the pot was really *his*. He never sold it to anyone. He hadn't even really stolen the $750,000. He hadn't *meant* to take it, after all. And, besides, how wrong could it be to abscond with the proceeds of crime from a bunch of bikers? Hell, the government did that all the time, didn't they? By comparison, the low-lifes Danny had lived with in prison were serious criminals. They were put there for all sorts of reasons, and everyone he met inside had been there at least once before. It seemed most of them had been introduced to the system as juvies and spent the rest of their lives rotating between prison and the world outside.

Danny could relate to none of them. Not the lifers. Not the gangbangers. Not the petty criminals on the rise. He certainly wasn't the only person in jail to claim he didn't belong there, but in his case, he really believed it.

Until now, he thought, driving out of Norbold in the stolen Volvo. *Now I'm a car thief, a home burglar, an escaped convict.* Part of him was excited by the distinction, part of him afraid. And a big part of Danny Grant was ashamed.

Soon, the Volvo's owner would arrive home from work and find it stolen. Danny doubted the "Sorry" he had scratched on the notepad by the kitchen phone would earn him much forgiveness. When word of the theft got into the system, how long would it take for them to connect it to his no-show at the end of day parole?

He could drive most of the way to Buckhorn before then, but the gas tank was less than a quarter full, so he'd better fill up sooner than later. The first service station he came across after leaving Norbold had a pair of pumps out front of a two-bay garage. There was no self-service sign but Danny figured if he waited for a mechanic to wander out from the bay, he could be there all afternoon.

He pumped twenty dollars' worth of regular and walked in to pay. The mechanic who took Danny's handful of coins had a lazy left eye which looked at him incredulously. "Only twenty bucks?" He snorted in disbelief. "Lemme check." They walked side-by-side back to the gas pump. "Ain't goin' too far today, are ya?"

Danny tried to appear nonchalant while he did his best to look the mechanic in the face while avoiding his laggard left eye.

"A short ride is all. Pay day isn't until next week."

"Uh huh. Turn it on, would ya."

Danny got back in the car and turned the ignition. When the man stuck his head in the window to look at the gas gauge, he breathed stale beer in Danny's face.

Straightening, he said, "Well, then, have a nice *short* ride."

"Yeah, bye," Danny said and gunned the accelerator, cursing himself for kicking up gravel as he drove off the lot and back onto the road.

The mechanic wandered back into the garage bay in no particular hurry. "That dude just ripped off Todd Porter's Volvo," he said to his workmate.

"Oh yeah?"

"Yep. Sure as sugar."

"So you gonna call the cops?"

"Nope."

"Nope?"

"Nope."

"Why not? Todd's a good customer. We oughtta look out for him, don't you think?"

"Yep," Lazy Eye spat on the floor, "but that guy said he ain't goin' for but a *short* ride."

"Oh yeah?"

"Yep. Besides, Todd's Volvo has a diesel engine...and that moron just put sixteen liters of gasoline into a near empty tank."

"Oh."

"It'll be a real short ride."

"For sure. And Todd'll be back. And his insurance will pay for it."

"Yep. That's about it. Turn up the radio would ya? That's Guns 'n Roses."

NINETEEN

A little after lunch on the day of Linette's visit, Judy made her way to the local grocer's in Buckhorn. Too small to be a true supermarket, the owner stocked it with more than the bare necessities, especially during the summer and shoulder seasons when urban cottagers could be counted on to buy seven dollar jars of salsa and over-priced tomatoes with the vines still attached. He brought in fruits and veggies every two days during cottage season, as opposed to once a week the rest of the year.

Judy missed the organic products you could buy in the city, but a local cooperative of farmers' wives supplied fresh pies. Most were of the canned variety, but the thought was nice.

Judy was deciding between broccoli and rapini to accompany her whole wheat penne al olio when a woman in a worn Toronto Raptors jersey sidled up and said, "Too bad about your neighbor, eh?"

"Oh, hi, Brenda. Yeah, it was pretty horrible. I only hope Ernie didn't suffer. I just can't figure why he didn't up and leave."

"They said there would have been a pretty good blow-up from the propane tanks. Guess that would have done him in. I mean, it's not like he would have had a hard time finding his way out or nothing, 'cause of the smoke, I mean, him being blind as a bat and all."

"Uh huh."

"I read in the paper where there was some hero saved your dog? Terry someone?"

"Wort was pretty shook up. He won't let me leave him alone for more than a few minutes at a time since the fire. He's tied up outside the store right now, and hating it."

Across the vegetable stand, a woman wearing a hot pink tummy top two sizes too small compared tomatoes. The straw basket over her arm, her turquoise flip flops with a spray of plastic daisy on each toe, and her bum hanging out of her short shorts in spite of it being late October all screamed "Tourist— Just Passing Through." Judy could tell she was half-listening to their conversation so she looked over and smiled a friendly hello.

"Beautiful day for a boat ride, isn't it?"

"Huh? It certainly is. You live in a wonderful part of the world, you do." The tomatoes were so big and juicy, they overflowed the petite woman's palm. She was practically fondling them, running her pink-nailed finger tips back and forth across their paper thin skin.

"Local," said Brenda. "They're like as not McKendrie's from down Fifteenth Sideroad. Best darn tomatoes you're likely to find anywhere. Hothouse now, but you should see 'em in July. Positively gushing with flavor."

"They do look fine," said the tourist. "Hey, pardon me for snooping. I just couldn't help over-hearing about the fire. My...er...that is, a friend of mine, well, this fellow I know, is a fireman and, well, I guess maybe he was there, too."

"Who's your friend?"

"His name is Terry Miner."

"Really? He's the one who saved my dog," said Judy. "Is he a good friend of yours?"

"Oh, no, just a guy I ran into barbequing down by the locks. My husband and I are mooring here and over in Bobcaygeon for a week before taking Miss U2—that's my husband's boat— back home for the winter." The woman had chosen the plumpest tomato she could find and put it into her basket, her fingers lingering on it just a little bit too long.

"Well, that fireman friend of yours—not sure what exactly he did to save my dog—but he somehow got it in his mind that I'd be grateful enough to let him put his big rubber boots under my bed. He tried to come on to me with some line about being Mr. February in the Buckhorn Fire Fighter's Calendar." Judy blushed, without knowing why.

"Ooh!" The woman's hand squeezed the tomato hard, two of her fingers piercing the skin. Juice and seeds spurted across the aisle. "Oh my."

"Told ya they were somethin' special," Brenda said, selecting an English cucumber and putting it in her basket. "Tell ya what, though. Sooty or not, a fireman comes knocking on my door, he'd better be ready for something hot, I tell ya," she threw her head back and exposed a mouthful of fillings. "My Jerry's been pretty much useless at putting out *my* fire ever since he retired. Hard to tell just what he's good for besides cutting the grass, these days."

Judy suppressed a giggle, took a plastic bag from her purse and started to fill it with baby spinach. "Where is home for Miss U2?" she asked.

"New Jersey," said the tourist, her face nearly as red as the tomato she had just skewered, and clashing badly with her pink halter. "We came up earlier this summer. Ran all the way up to Georgian Bay. It's kind of like a late honeymoon. We got married two years ago—my second, George's third—and we waited 'til he semi-retired—he has a car dealership—his son's going to run it now—so we could have a nice long time together. Most of the time, though, he's gone fishing or golfing or playing poker with buddies he meets along the way. He's friendly that way. Makes friends in an instant. We always have people over in the backyard at home, too. Not that I mind, I mean, it makes it like a party with the pool and all, but they're all like fifteen years older than me, and...oh my, am I rambling again? I'm sorry. I guess I don't get to talk to folks much...kind of lonely on a boat...except for the barbeques and stuff...everyone's so friendly, you know. Do you boat much?"

Judy focused on her bag of spinach, selecting the yellow leaves and picking them out with the tongs. Brenda stood stock still staring at the tourist lady, one eyebrow cocked in disbelief. She said, "Judy don't boat much. Her dog is liable to get yappy on the water. I'm kind of a landlubber myself."

"Oh, but you live in such a wonderful land of lakes."

"It's nice to look at," said Brenda, "and plenty of folk fish. Me, I like my water in the bathtub—hot and full of bubbles. Preferably with candles, good white wine, and a fireman to soap my back."

Judy thought she saw the woman blush, or maybe it was just the light reflecting off her pink top. "I'd better get moving. Wort will be getting antsy."

Walking away, she wondered if Brenda had it right about men—that the good ones all smelled of hard work, yet still had hands soft enough to give a good sponge bath.

Terry had been called to a grass fire again, this one next to a bridge where day-fishers liked to cook their catch. He was back on the trench-digging crew which left him covered in mud and smelling decidedly unlike a hero. He headed straight to his rendezvous with Cindy on George Meade's cruiser. She hadn't arrived, so Terry stripped to his underwear and dove in to splash off the worst of the crud. He figured he could handle the cold water, having swum at least once every day right from the May long weekend to Thanksgiving. Even for him, though, today's water was frigid. He felt his lungs contract and barely got half a breath before grabbing the boat's ladder and hauling himself back aboard.

Cold water swimming was the kind of achievement Terry figured would impress the right kind of girl on the right kind of bar stool in the middle of winter when the pickings were slim around town. After all, the line about "I been inside, y'know" had worn kind of thin kind of quickly. The women who hung around country bars after tourist season took it for granted most locals had spent a few nights in a cage for one reason or another.

Terry's brief fling with the justice system had been pretty run of the mill. The night of the big bust, he had wound up in a holding cell at the OPP station in Peterborough. Early next day, after questioning, the cops determined he knew nothing at all about the grow op and set him free.

It wasn't until a week later that Officer Ainsley showed up at his trailer, with three other policemen, and arrested Terry for the murder of Lester Freeden. Not about to take a rap like that, he told them everything they wanted to know. By the time Danny pled guilty to manslaughter, he'd been in provincial holding a few months. He was surprised how many of his old high school buddies he ran into at the detention center in Brockville. The potheads seemed to like it well enough. Dope was more expensive than on the outside but at least the supply never dried up.

Real time like what Danny was doing, now, *that* was a badge of honor. Chicks were bound to be impressed when he got out. Terry might almost have felt jealous were he not so damn comfortable lounging on George Meade's Sea Ray. Cindy found him there, stretched across the bow soaking up the three o'clock sun, when she showed up with her arms full of groceries.

"What are you doing here so early?" she said. "Someone could see you. George is already suspicious. He can't believe how fast we're going through beer and Doritos."

"Tell him you've made a new friend in town. Lots of ladies around here can pound 'em back pretty good."

"Funny you should say that. I just ran into a couple of women over at the grocery store. One of them says she knows you. Says you saved her dog the other day at that fire you ran off to. You really are a hero, aren't you?"

Terry puffed out his chest and said, "Part of the job. Doing my bit for the community and all."

"How'd you save her dog?"

"I, well I, er, it was all on fire, like, and I...well, I chased it over to the hose and we sort of put out the fire together. It had long hair. Guess that's why firemen always have Dalmatians, eh? Their hair is short and they already kinda look burned up a bit with all them black patches and stuff."

Cindy struggled with the key in the latch on the door to the boat's cabin. "And then, she says you made a pass at her?"

"A what? Who? Me? No way, doll. I mean, you're my babe. Some ladies just can't see a man in a uniform without getting all hot and bothered." He grinned his shiniest grin. "Here, doll, let me carry those groceries below decks for you."

Later that afternoon, while Cindy slept in the afterglow of fireman sex, Terry borrowed the keys to George Meade's boat and slipped over to the hardware store to make a spare set for himself. No sense getting Cindy in trouble by hanging around outside on the boat the next time he showed up early. Always thinking of others, he was.

* * *

Danny slumped forward, his forehead pressed into the steering wheel which he gripped white-knuckled. The horn blared non-stop, its ear-splitting shriek washing in through the Volvo's open windows. The dead Volvo. He'd realized he'd screwed up the fuel as soon as the engine coughed, sputtered, and seized. As the fumes cleared, he could smell the fallen leaves, wet wood, and damp earth that meant autumn was well advanced and night would be cold. He sucked the musky air deep into his lungs and fought off the sobs that threatened to tear his chest apart.

The horn raged on.

He sniffled, felt tears stream down his cheeks, and began banging his head onto the steering wheel over and over. Snot splattered from his nose and mixed with his tears until Danny's face was smeared with slippery goo that stuck to his eyelashes and pasted his hair to his forehead. With each bang of his head, the horn sounded another piercing yelp but Danny's ears had gone numb with the rest of him. How could he have been so stupid?

Finally, he threw his head back onto the headrest, let his arms drop to his sides and wailed. The anguish pouring from his chest and throat was perversely soothing. When he gulped for air, his wail changed to a sob, and Danny's shoulders began to shake. He hummed to himself loudly, like he had never done since he was a kid, like he'd wanted to night after night in prison but never did, like all little boys do when they want their crying to be heard by their mother, or by someone, anyone, who'll go tell her her baby needs her.

A car drove past, startling his stupefied brain back into gear.

He grabbed the bag of food and beer from the passenger seat, wiped his face on Woody's, and set out on foot. The third car to pass him was a bright orange dune buggy with pink and purple blossoms painted all over the bulbous body. A minute later, it came back the other way, did a U-turn behind him and headed back again. It pulled up alongside him and stopped.

"Gorgeous day for a walk, isn't it?" the driver asked, all bright white teeth and surprisingly well-coiffed silver hair for all its blowing in the wind. The hair looked like a helmet.

"Yep," Danny said, pasting on his criminal frown.

"How's about a ride?" Silver Mane said.

Danny hadn't spent all those years inside without learning how to spot a come-on. This dude couldn't have found a tighter pair of white Capris if he shopped in the children's department. Which is exactly where the dune buggy looked to come from, right down to the "Flower Power" stenciled in bulging pillow-shaped lettering on the oversized rear fender.

"Nice car," Danny said. "I had a Tonka toy just like it."

The man looked him up and down through burgundy sunglasses. The soft amber lenses barely concealed the eyes of a wolf.

"Hop on. Rides smooth as silk."

The tuft of hair peeking out of the man's turquoise polo shirt was too close a match to the hair on his head not to have come out of the same bottle.

"Ride sounds good," Danny said. He jumped in thigh-to-thigh with Silver Mane, half expecting to feel the older man's hand land in his lap right away. The car's manual gear shift was on the steering column, allowing for a puffy single bench seat. The engine popped out of a cutaway in the rear hood, and exhaust fumes swirled around them while the car stood still. The wind blew all that away as soon as the dune buggy roared back onto the road. It was too loud to talk, so Danny settled into what felt like a boat ride on a windy day, mouth open, eyes squinting, heart racing like a dog's.

The heavy-duty seat springs came in handy when Silver Mane pulled off the road and the car bounced across terrain best suited to a Hummer. The oversized tires, shocks, and extra-high independent suspension did their trick. Danny bounced up, down, and sideways. He grabbed hold of the mini roll-bar where the windshield otherwise would have been.

"Where the hell we going?"

"Gonna show you what this baby can do." With a glance at Danny's billowing sweatshirt, Silver Mane added, "Hang on to Woody's Pecker."

Danny cursed. He'd been ready to fend off the advances he knew would come soon enough and didn't doubt he could deal with Silver Mane in a more determined struggle off in the woods if it came to that, but this little detour did nothing to put distance between him and the stolen Volvo. He seriously considered leaping into the tangle of poplar saplings and underbrush at the side of the trail. Before he could make up his mind to jump, the dune buggy emerged from the forest into a wide-open sand pit flooded with sunshine. Three more dune buggies were busily chasing each other up and over piles of sand and rock in a grown-up version of a sandbox.

In spite of himself, Danny felt the exhilaration of a ten-year-old. Right about now, he should have been boarding the caged minivan for transport back to the penitentiary, smelling the stale sweat of anxious men. Instead, he was bucking through the air on a jalopy straight out of the sixties, surrounded by the carefree hoots and hollers of men with time to burn and gas to go with it. He shot a glance at Silver Mane, teeth bared to the wind, sunglasses glinting in the late afternoon light. Pride, passion, and appetite rolled into a tight column of power fueled by the dune buggy's deep-throated throttle.

And it was over as soon as it started. Without a word or a sign, Silver Mane steered his beast out of the off-road park and back down the trail to the highway. Halfway there, he made his move. Danny let him grab his thigh, even parted his legs a little. Once the guy was good and distracted, Danny reached across and twisted the steering wheel hard right. The underbrush at the side of the trail caught the undercarriage and they came to a hard stop. Silver Mane was tossed up onto the forward roll bar, winded.

Danny used his feet to push the man to the ground. He said, "When you hear tomorrow's news, you're going to realize you got off easy. Do yourself a favor and come up with some kinky story about how you lost your ride in the woods. I find out you gave me up, I'm liable to come back for your nut sack. And not the way you'd want me to."

The dune buggy had enough gas to carry him about an hour closer to Buckhorn. He managed to run it down an embankment into a woodlot before the engine coughed its way to silence. By then it was dark, the temperature dropping fast. He wolfed down the stolen sandwiches and beer and crept under the engine for warmth. Commuter traffic had picked up with dusk and he didn't like his odds as a hitchhiking fugitive. Better to wait an hour or two, then see if he couldn't find another car to steal.

He fell asleep trying to convince himself the authorities wouldn't be all that pissed. It couldn't be all that big a deal to skip out on barely three months of easy time.

TWENTY

Perko Ratwick sat in the holding cell with no laces in his running shoes and no belt. It was what he hated most about getting arrested. Giving up his belt. When he paced in his eight by ten foot cell, he had to keep tugging up the brown slacks like some overweight teenager wearing low-rider jeans. Handcuffed and walked through the corridors to interrogation rooms, he'd clutch and tug at the back of his pants every few steps. Frequent arrest was part of the job and it got so this humiliation almost made him try to lose weight. But not quite. His beer belly was too much a badge of biker honor.

He'd always assumed they painted cell walls puke green so real vomit would blend in. But they were actually quite clean, hosed down and squeegeed on a regular basis. The combination toilet and sink was seatless and made of stainless steel. It was in the back corner, visible to anyone walking past the bars at the front of the cell. The classic barred door had three-quarter inch vertical bars on two-inch spacing. Perko could stick his hand between two bars, but his forearm would jam well short of his elbow.

Two metal cots protruded from the wall one above the other, each two feet wide with no mattress. He had a thin blanket in case he wanted to sleep. Since his jacket had been taken from him, he could either roll up the blanket to use as a pillow, or cover himself and lie pillowless on the metal slab. Past experience told him to expect a stale ham sandwich and a half-pint of warm milk if he stayed more than ten hours.

On this particular visit, the cops hadn't asked Perko much on the way in other than who it was he had roughed up at the bus station. They dismissed his version: that he'd been the victim of two random attacks, one outside by a stranger and one inside from the ticket agent. Instead, they assumed it was a simple collection exercise gone wrong. That Perko had followed a bad debtor to the bus station and roughed him up before he ran out of town. They spent most of their interrogation razzing him for letting the punk get away, for getting plonked in the nuts for good measure. They had a good guffaw imagining the reception Perko would get on his return to the Libido's club house. Then they threw him into the holding cell to wait for a morning arraignment on two charges of assault.

Sitting there, he heard the door to the second holding cell clang open and shut.

"You two had better keep cool now," he heard a cop say. "Or one of you is gonna go next door...and that dude doesn't like company."

Perko figured himself to be "that dude."

"Well ain't this jes' one somnabitch mess. Good for nuthin' little crapper." The crackling voice sounded like it had been soaked in bourbon and roasted over a smokey fire. "I knew I shoulda creamed ya but good when I had the chance. Dumbhead."

"Like it's all my fault." The second voice was much younger, just a boy's. A whiney twang that Perko could feel in his teeth. "Couldn't a kept it in your goddamn pants, could ya? I done told you she didn't want you no more. Jes' who the hell d'ya think you are? Casa-fuckin-nova?"

"She was my damn girlfriend afore she was yours and you shoulda shown her respect. She was practically yer STEP-MA."

"Step-ma? She's only three years older'n me, Pa. You're too damn old for her. Look in the mirror when you brush your damn tooth and face the facts! She'll be warmin' my bed from now on."

"Not under my damn roof she won't. You're the one shoulda gone lookin' for someone else to cuddle your bones at night. I been kissin' and huggin' and havin' her and I ain't gonna stop on your say-so."

"We're gonna be together, Pa. We'll jes' move the hell outta the house. You can kiss both our damn social security checks goodbye is what you can kiss. Mama and Cousin Billie gonna give us a room."

"You try that, Jonah, and I'll break every bone in yer body, startin' with the one in yer head and ending with the one 'tween yer goddamn legs."

"Try me, old man."

The next thing Perko heard sounded like a bag of flour landing with a thud against the floor. Then a groan, and the younger voice saying, "Oh shit..." and then, "GUARD."

Perko heard the duty cop step back into the corridor. He grabbed his waistband and crossed to the bars to watch as the guard peered into the cell next to his.

"How the hell did you do that?" the cop asked.

"He's gonna need a doctor or something," said the kid. "Whole lotta blood coming out from his head...and he ain't none too smart to begin with."

"Next door, punk. In with Mr. Ratwick. I can't have you killing your father on my shift. The paperwork will keep me here all weekend."

A moment later, Perko was joined in his cell by a scrawny wretch with peach fuzz on his chin. Blood, both fresh and dried, smeared the front of his Slipknot T-shirt. He looked like he hadn't bathed in a month and Perko figured that was being generous. The kid smelled worse than beached sunfish.

"Stay on that side of the cell, over near the bars," Perko told him.

"But there ain't no bunk here. I'm supposed to get one of the bunks. Top or bottom, longs there's just two of us in here."

"Good for you, shit-for-brains. But you see, that's my invisible friend, the jolly green incest machine, lyin' up there on that top bunk. And he don't like sharin' it with people who have a different last name. I'm sure you can relate. Stay in the corner and I may not give you a toilet bath."

The boy named Jonah hesitated for a moment. He looked at the top bunk and back at Perko as if to confirm that anyone lying up there was invisible for sure. He looked ready to argue the point, but Perko watched him glance at his biceps and then down at his own thighs, which were considerably thinner. It took a moment or two to sink in, but ultimately the boy seemed to accept that sitting on the floor in the corner up against the bars was his most comfortable option.

"Jes' you wait," he grumbled.

"Shakin' in my boots," said Perko. He gave his pants a tug and lay down on the bottom bunk, feet toward the toilet, the top of his head confidently pointed at the river rat by the cell door.

The boy sniffled and pulled his knees to his chest. For a while, the only sound came from the cell next door. Two cops swore under their breath as they prepared to drag the old man out of the cell and down the hall to where he could wait for paramedics.

"Fifty bucks says he won't make it," said one cop.

"This old coot? He's seen worse," came the answer. "I been here long enough to know this skunk'll be round again. Tell ya what, I'll match your fifty and double or nothing says he'll be back here on some other charge before New Year's."

"You're on. Grab his legs."

After the lights were turned down, Perko asked, "Why the hell do you screw your father's girlfriend?"

"What's it to you?"

"It ain't nothing. Just can't figure it out, is all. There's lotsa women. No need to do the nasty at home, is there?"

"Ain't so many women where I'm from. We live way up, more'n ten miles off of Buckshot Lake Road. Town named Wex Corner but they ain't even a store no more. Closed two years ago. Apart from us and my cousin there's only one other family within a day's walk. Only girl there looks like she's half horse. Smells like a stable."

"Still don't get it."

"I don't gotta explain nothing to you. My honey chose me over my pa, and I ain't gonna let her down is all."

"So how'd you end up in here?"

"Fightin' with my pa. We hitched a ride down to Madoc, pick up our checks, drop in the hotel for a drink. Could a just had our beers and gone home. 'Stead, my pa gets right pissed. Decides to rip off a pickup from the parking lot out back. All 'cause he saw boxes marked 'Splosives.' He loves that stuff. We was always blowing shit up out back o' the house...ever since I was a kid. Fact is, Pa moved us on up to this frigid country o' yours ten years back thinkin' he could get into Fleming College, get all learned an' git *paid* to blow things up."

"No shit. Your old man's got a college degree?"

"Naw. Seems ya need your letters 'n all afore they'll even let ya into 'splosives school."

"Smart enough to steal a truck though."

"Weren't that complicated. My pa just snatched the keys off the table while some greasy bugger was trying to get close with the waitress. Pa grabs my arm and hauls me outside. Next thing you know we were rolling outta town and on our way to home. That's my pa. He's always doing shit like that when he's on a tear. Can't handle his alcohol."

"So then the cops came after you and caught you and brought you in here."

"Nope."

"Guy with the truck follow you with his buddies and a shot gun?"

"Nope. Good thing, too. Dude looked mean as dirt. Fact is, we'd a got the truck home if we didn't crash."

"Crashed the truck?"

"Yeah."

"The one you just stole."

"Yeah."

"Your pop was too pissed to drive."

"Nope."

"Then, what the—"

"It was me driving. Not my pa. He was pissed, alright, and besides, I can drive faster, so he gave me the wheel. Then he starts into me about how he wants me to lay offa his woman. Go find my own girl. And he grabs my ear and starts whacking my nose over and over. I elbowed him but good and shoulda left it alone. But when he called me a no-good loser who couldn't get his own girl if I was the last man alive? I grabbed his throat and punched him one good left to the head. And that's when the truck ran off the road and smashed right into a parked FedEx van."

"Oh." Perko couldn't fathom the stupidity. He'd spent his entire adult life in the company of bikers and had no illusions about his own particular smarts, but raw moronic behavior was beyond him. "Lucky you didn't blow sky high. What with the 'Splosives,' I mean."

"Naw, it couldn't blow. Weren't wired up or nothing."

Perko wasn't convinced it was a good thing Jonah knew so much about dynamite.

"FedEx van weren't so lucky. Busted the back end wide open. For a minute there, I figured we struck it rich. Maybe find some 'spensive stuff like a big ol' TV like that poor slob burned to death over by Lakehurst there."

"Someone get toasted?" Perko was finally starting to drift to sleep.

"Yeah, some old dude in a cabin with a honkin' big TV. My pa said he heard tell they think someone offed him. 'Tweren't just a fire, maybe."

Kind of like a bed time story, Perko let the runt drone on.

"Some kind of a recluse or something. Place burned to the ground, him inside it. Can't figure out why he stayed put. Seems he was blind and all, but the bugger could walk. Why not jes' walk right on out?"

Perko marveled at how a stunted yokel who likely couldn't spell his own name would know details about every backwoods crime that happened within a hundred miles.

"Who was this guy?" he asked.

"Just some guy. My pa says any time a guy fries least he's gonna be ready for Hell."

"Your pa is one sick bastard."

"Yeah, well, he knows what he says is all. And he says this guy knew somethin' for sure. Says bikers and cops and everyone been all over him for a coon's age, him just tryin' to be a hermit and all, and then suddenly a year or so ago he starts having all this cash, buys a big TV and everything, and the bugger can't even see worth a damn. Blind as a bat, says pa. Helluva waste of a TV set."

Perko rolled onto his side and looked at the crumpled kid in the corner. "What'd you say his name was, this guy with the TV?"

"How the hell am I supposed to know his name? He's just some guy is all. My pa told me about it."

Lying on the hard bunk fighting sleep, Perko wondered if there could be two blind guys living in Lakehurst that *bikers and cops* had taken an interest in? And if this Jonah jerk was, indeed, talking about Ernie McCann, how had the old man suddenly come into a bunch of money? The more Perko thought about it, the less he liked the answer.

Danny awoke shivering. He sat up and whacked his head against the dune buggy's oil pan. Stiff and aching, he shimmied out from under the car and made his way to the side of the road. He wished he knew how to read the stars well enough to tell what time it was. From the lack of cars on the road, he knew it had to be late. Each time one did come along, he threw himself in the ditch and waited breathlessly for it to pass.

By the time dawn came, he was exhausted and chilled to the bone. In a daze, he barely made it to the ditch at the sound of an approaching engine. An RV slowed for a look. The driver honked its horn and three kids plastered their noses against the window, waving.

Around the next bend, civilization appeared in the form of a low-slung building with fake log siding and a pink neon sign on its roof: "All-day Country Breakfast $6.99." The RV that had just passed him was parked at the far end of the building.

Danny had little trouble jimmying open its side door.

He found the spare set of keys right where he thought he would. In the arm rest console, in a plastic envelope along with copies of the ownership and insurance and the waste water instruction manual.

The driver's seat was still warm and for a moment, he sat there, drowsy, soaking it in. Then he fired up the engine and pulled the camper out onto the highway. Driving it was easier than he'd imagined, and surely he'd have at least an hour before those kids would be done scarfing breakfast.

The eastern sun bathed the road in front of him with sharp autumn light. Within minutes, he thawed out enough to day dream about road tripping with his mom. They'd often talked about trekking west in a halfway decent car with a real good tent. The dream had never involved driving an RV. Now he could afford one.

"You're the guy from the radio, aren't you?"

The voice startled Danny so badly he swerved across the road and nearly rolled the camper. He shot a glance to his right and looked straight into the most piercing blue eyes he had ever encountered. The eyes were set in a wrinkled prune of a face and the little old lady to whom the face belonged looked ready to rumble.

"You're him," she croaked.

"Who...?"

"Him. From the radio."

Danny's knuckles whitened.

"I don't know what you're talking about. I'm stealing your bus, Granny. And you're getting off at the next stop. Oh look! Here it comes now."

"I've been listening to it all morning on the police band: you're the murderer who ran from the prison. You're him, aren't you?"

"What the fuck?" Danny couldn't believe it.

"Saw you back there in the ditch. Kind of a giveaway."

"Okay, lady, you're getting off here," Danny scanned the road for a rest stop or a gas station. Nothing but tree-lined road ahead and a soft shoulder to boot. A pickup screeched by, the driver leaning on the horn. It gave Danny such a jolt he nearly sideswiped the guy. "Just as soon as I find a place to stop this thing."

TWENTY-ONE

Linette's Jeep was parked outside The Boathouse in a lot full of pickups. A small circle of people with coffee cups in one hand and cigarettes in the other huddled around two rickety picnic tables at one end of the ramshackle building.

Inside, the music was country and loud, despite it being breakfast hour. Linette shared a darkened corner with a square-shouldered man piling into three eggs over easy. She nibbled a piece of his toast and said, "You think I should give up? Get chased away by enviro-barbie and her scrawny dog?"

"I'm telling you there's nothing *to* give up, Linette," said Officer Maxwell Ainsley. "We scoured that place four years ago. You of all people should know that. You were Grant's lawyer, for God's sake. If there was something there—drugs, money, anything at all—we would have found it."

"Keep your voice down, Max," she said, hushing her own and leaning close to him. "I could get disbarred for talking to you about his case."

"What do you think the squad room would do if they found out I'm sleeping with a defense attorney?"

"*Former* defense attorney," Linette corrected. "I did my stint at Legal Aid. Much happier doing what I do now." *Making money*, she thought. "Besides, if your pals haven't figured us out yet, there's not one of them gonna make detective. It's not as if we're hiding things." She clinked her coffee mug to his.

"We're not exactly a couple, either. All we do is shack up and talk about *The Case of the Missing I Don't Know What.*" Linette rolled her eyes as the police officer went on: "You know, Linette, sometimes I get the impression you're only banging me because I arrested Danny Grant." He squinted at her.

She drew her skinny lips into her best fake pout. "I recall you *chasing* my skirt around the court house. You were still married."

The cop frowned. "Barely. While I was out risking my life chasing bad guys, my ex was busy boffing some long-hair audio tech."

"I hear they get around."

Officer Ainsley drained his coffee and signaled the waitress for more.

"Don't look so glum," Linette said. "You'll make me think you miss your wife."

"It's not that," he said. "Just thinking about that old man."

"And?"

"I dunno. Strange him dying in a fire, I guess."

She said, "Bad way to go."

"My uncle burned to death," he said. "Died in Patterson's sawmill fire. Thirty years ago."

Linette struggled to keep from rolling her eyes at the history lesson. She kicked off her shoe and her toes found Maxwell Ainsley's calf under the table.

He said, "He and Ernie McCann worked together. Ernie may have been blinded, but he still got off easy. He survived."

She stroked him until his breathing took on a different rhythm before saying, "Maybe he buried it. Or *hid* it up a tree."

Max gave her a confused look.

"The money, Max, the *loot.*" Linette didn't want to talk about fires, new or old, or the men who died in them. This time, her pout was genuine, even if her skinny lip resembled the tip of a tongue depressor. "What if it was Ernie who hid it somewhere?" she said. "It took you guys three or four days to figure out the coveralls Danny Grant was wearing belonged to Ernie McCann."

"One of my finer investigative moments," Max said, sitting back in his chair.

"Maybe Ernie *hid* it for Danny. Maybe they were in cahoots! Could be that's why he's dead now. Burned to a crisp by the Libidos 'cause they found out! What about that?"

"Linette, Ernie was a whacked-out loner freak, for God's sake. What the hell would a punk like Danny have to do with him? We found no connection and no money. We must have searched twenty acres around his place with the dogs. Far as I'm concerned, if it didn't go up in smoke with that barn, then the Skeleton crew took the money *and* the dope back with them across the border."

"You said yourself, the Libidos have been doing deals with the Skeletons for years both before and after that bust. There's no way they would've kept the traffic open if they had any doubt about the New York crew."

"What about that other fairy—the one who got away?" said Max. "Bernard said the runner was a Nancy's Nasty. Wish to hell I'd got a name out of him before he hanged."

"No way some gangbanger disappears with that kind of money and leaves no trail. Everyone was watching—especially the Libidos." She pushed her toes a little higher on his leg. "What say we sneak over, look around a little together, Max."

"I've got a better idea. How 'bout I swing by your place when my shift ends? I've got three days off. Cook a couple meals for you?"

She dug her big toe into the soft flesh behind his knee. "Why wait for your shift to end? I can peel out of the parking lot in my Jeep. Let you chase me down in your patrol car, try to give me a great big *fine.*"

"Again?"

It wasn't hard for Granny to convince Danny he couldn't ditch her. The longer it took for the family to miss their RV— not to mention their grandmother—the longer it would be for the cops to get their next pointer. She told Danny being kidnapped by a fugitive was one experience she'd never had, and confessed to finding it rather exhilarating. Besides, how much worse could it possibly be than spending the next three days with her infernal son-in-law?

"'Dickhead.' That's what I call him. The darned fool can't drive this bus worth a dang. My husband, bless his soul, should never have willed it to him. Thought he was doing me a favor, not having to deal with selling the thing. Now that blowhard my daughter married thinks it's his destiny to haul me all over Hell's half acre until I keel over from sheer boredom!"

Cars passed Danny every few moments. Most honked.

"You sure drive slow for a young buck, don't you?" The old lady shot him another brilliant blue glance.

"Trying not to attract attention," he said.

"Ha! Kidnapping an old lady in a forty-foot RV. Yeah, that's laying low alright. Why don't you try tossing a string of firecrackers out the window while you're at it? Call it camouflage." When Danny said nothing, she added, "I've got a pack of Lady Fingers in the back."

Danny leaned on the brake hard as they came up on a bridge.

"You'll fit," said Granny. "Thirteen-foot five. We're twelve nine."

Danny sped back up.

The blue-eyed old lady smoothed her dress with her palms. "I'm curious. What did your mother say, when she found out you killed a man?"

"What do you mean?"

"Children do all manner of things their mothers don't expect. I know my kids did. My youngest son became an interior designer. Against his father's wishes. Put him in his grave, I'm sure of it. And then my daughter marries Dickhead who thinks driving an RV across the country is some kind of royal outing. Like we should all kiss his boots for it. With a figure like hers, she could have married anyone—a doctor, a lawyer—not some fish tackle salesman who can't give her a vacation that doesn't involve schlepping through campsites." She sighed. "Kids disappoint. It's what they do. But murder? Can't say I've dealt with that. So I just wonder what your mother thought about it."

"Manslaughter."

"What?"

"Manslaughter. That's what I pleaded to, and that's what it was. Accidental death. Probably would have gotten away with something even lighter if I'd had a real lawyer."

"Lawyer-schmoyer. What I want to know is, *What did your mother think?*"

Danny gripped the steering wheel tightly. They were driving down a stretch of highway with solid bush on both sides of the road. There was no one immediately ahead or behind. He desperately wanted to stop the RV and throw the old lady out the door. She waited in silence for an answer to her question. It was obvious she had all day.

"My mother believed me," he said. "She knew I would never knowingly kill a man. Don't think I could even have done it in self-defense. Just not wired that way."

"So she forgave you."

"Didn't even have to. Nothing needed forgiving. One of those wrong time wrong place kind of things."

"So she's stood by you? All this time? Visits you, takes care of you from the outside? I've always wondered how people do that. How they don't break down themselves, with loved ones in jail, I mean."

"Yeah, she took care of me. For a while anyway. She had to go away, though. For her health." Danny couldn't figure how the old lady was getting him talking. He wondered whether he could tie her up without hurting her. "Maybe you should get off at the next Timmy's," he said. "I'm sure your family must be worried about you."

"Phfffttt," spat Old Blue Eyes. "Don't be stupid."

"I know, I know. If I kick you out, I might as well just call the cops myself," he said. He couldn't very well bop her on the head. In the movies, that made people sleep for a while; Danny figured Granny was like as not to die no matter how carefully he whacked her noggin. "Like Lester," he said under his breath.

"Like *who?*"

Danny looked over at her, stunned that she had heard him.

She pointed at her ear. "Hearing aid. Best money can buy. I have a pocket remote. I turn it off when Dickhead talks too much."

"Oh."

"So you were saying?"

"Huh?"

"Like *who? Lester?*"

"Lester is the man I killed."

"How'd you do it?"

"With a baseball bat." Danny hoped in vain that would shut her up.

"Gruesome," was all she said. "Why?"

"Look, it was an accident."

"That what you said to the cops, too? When they arrested you for murder, I mean? 'I didn't count on the gentleman dying when I beat on him with a baseball bat, officer.' Hunh?"

Danny sighed.

Not skipping a beat, his captive asked, "So where'd your mother come up with enough money to go away? I mean, leaving your son to rot in jail while you run away 'for your health' isn't an everyday kind of bingo jackpot."

Danny's chest tightened and he got a pain behind his eyes. Was the old lady in his head? What if something bad *had* happened to his mother? What if the Libidos really *had* gotten to Ernie and found his stashed cash and that's why they burned him and his shack?

"Listen, lady," he said finally. "Where my mother got hold of her travel cash is none of your damn business."

"I was just asking..."

"Maybe you should stop asking. Maybe you should sit quiet and keep a look-out for cops or something. Just...just be useful, okay?" Danny couldn't believe he felt intimidated by the pint-sized crone, but she had got under his skin. Deep.

After a mile of silence, the old lady looked over at him and winked. "Kind of like Bitch Cassidy and the Some Chance Kid, eh?"

Danny stared straight ahead. "Why don't you turn on the radio?"

"Thought you'd never ask." She reached across and pressed a switch. The cabin filled with John Denver singing *Take Me Home, Country Road*.

"My son-in-law," she said. "Dickhead pays for XM radio just so he can make us listen to commercial-free schmaltz. Here, let me find us a better channel."

"I mean the cop radio. You said you have a cop radio."

"Oh that? It's set up in the back. I listen to it in my bunk. Brings back memories of riding with my husband, rest his soul. I could have left it connected up here for Dickhead but he wouldn't know how to use the darn thing. Want me to go get an update?"

"Yeah."

"They've pretty much figured out you're headed to Peterborough, you know. You're hardly an enigma. Leaving a bit of a trail, you might say."

Danny grimaced. "Just go check it out for me, would you?"

"Back in a jiffy."

Danny changed the XM station. After about ten minutes, Old Blue Eyes returned.

"I'd say your goose is cooked."

"Why, they know I'm in the RV?"

"Yep. Found out maybe five minutes ago from the sound of things. They know you must be in this county, except a little bit further west, on account of how slow you're going."

"Shit."

"Sorry our little adventure has to come to such an early end. I was just getting to like you. Thinking maybe you'd be better for my daughter than old butter-for-brains."

"So, they're setting road blocks ahead?"

"Sort of, but they're talking about how they have to be careful about how exactly they stop you."

"Really? Why?"

"Because of the cargo you're carrying."

"What cargo?"

"Me!" and she flashed him the bluest blast he'd seen yet.

Danny said, "Y'know, maybe there is one thing you could do for me."

The roadside sex scene had become a role play staple. The best part was Linette and Max could play themselves. They had originally hooked up during an innocent traffic stop when the cop pulled the lawyer over in her spanking new Jeep.

"Oh this is embarrassing," she had said, recognizing him immediately as the police officer who'd arrested her once-upon-a-time pot-growing murderer.

"You're telling me. License and registration please."

"Oh, officer, they really ought to be here," she'd said, rustling through her purse.

"If you can't find them, ma'am," he told her playfully, "I'll have no choice but to take you in, lock you up."

Linette had protested and insisted he help her search the vehicle for her paperwork. Somewhere between the glove compartment and the armrest, their groping changed focus and they wound up in a tangle on the stiff leather back seat.

Officer Ainsley was freshly divorced. Linette Paquin was only too happy to make time with the one man who might know more than her about Danny Grant's case.

Since that first time, they repeated the scene every week or so, occasionally changing things up a bit for excitement. Today, Officer Ainsley ordered Linette into the back of the cop car.

"Oooh, officer, it's so cramped in there. I'm afraid I'll bang my knees."

As he prepared to follow her, the radio crackled. "*Squad three-two-nine, hasn't the suspect hit the roadblock yet?*"

"*Negative, base. Think he might have turned off?*"

"*Not if he was headed to Peterborough. You go north off Seven there, he would have ended up on the wrong side of Stony Lake. Maybe he headed south, or maybe we'll squeeze him in. We've got two units headed west behind him.*"

"*Roger, base. We'll hold tight for further instructions.*"

Linette did her best pout.

"Hon, can you turn that stupid thing off? This damn plastic in my back is bad enough."

Twenty minutes later, sitting on the passenger seat with his feet out the door and smoking a cigarette, Officer Ainsley radioed the cop shop that he wasn't feeling so good and he was going to book out.

"Mind if I keep the car?" he asked the dispatcher. "Bring it by tomorrow morning? I'm off until Saturday."

"*No biggie, Max. Light day, anyhow. There was some escaped con headed this way but he seems to have headed in a different direction.*"

"Oh really? Anyone special?"

"*Naw, some guy took a walk on day parole.*"

"Morons."

"Go figure, eh? See you tomorrow."
"Roger, out."

TWENTY-TWO

Perko Ratwick sat dead center in the main room at the Libidos' clubhouse, still wearing the brown suit he'd put on thirty-six hours before. He knew he should have changed before showing up to take his lumps, but he'd had errands to run. Life-altering shit, in the face of which gang protocol seemed downright petty.

"Alright, Perkoset. Tell us again how that scrawny little ferret hoofed you in the berries and disappeared into thin air before you got your fat ass off the ground."

Perko wiped sweat from his forehead. Four ceiling-mounted spotlights pointed straight at him, bathing him in light and pretty much blinding him to anything more than ten feet away. He'd been on the other side of the lights often enough. He knew this was hardly a real interrogation. If it was, there'd be at most three or four bikers in the room with him, not the fifteen or so he could hear snickering in the shadows. That his humiliation served as evening entertainment for his peers made the experience all the more degrading.

He balanced on a bar stool which had two of its four legs sawn off short, one by an inch, the other half an inch. Since the stool was four feet tall, he couldn't rest a foot on the floor while seated. The net effect was to make it very difficult to sit still without constantly teetering back and forth. Perko weighed just over two hundred and fifty pounds, a fact driven home each time he crashed to the floor. It had happened twice already.

"Danny Grant didn't disappear, Mongoose. The turd got on a bus. Cops showed up before I could follow him."

"Follow him where?"

"Who the fuck knows? He's running from prison. Had enough. On the lam. Whatever the fuck, *Mongoloid.*"

159

Mongoose lurched forward into the ring of light and had his collar grabbed by the biker next to him at the bar. Perko did his best to glare in his general direction.

"Take a pill, Perko. Just tell us what the cops were after." It was Hawk who spoke to break the tension.

"It was the weirdest thing, Hawk. Like they didn't have a clue who Danny Grant was. They just figured I was doing a little collection that got out of hand. I played along and told them it was some grinder who got in over his head at one of our Texas Hold 'em outfits. Gave them the name of Bartholomew, no last name. Told them I forgot it."

"They bought it?"

"No question. Who the fuck'd make up a name like Bartholomew?" Perko pulled himself up straight. The sudden change in weight distribution sent him rocking back. He crashed flat on his ass as the stool shot out from under him and flew across the room.

"Sumnabitch!" yelled Mongoose, the stool bouncing off his shin. He took a step toward Perko and was held back a second time.

Perko decided to keep his mouth shut about the piece of shit yokel with whom he'd spent the night at the cop shop. He was still digesting what the lowlife had said about Ernie McCann's final bonfire.

"Keep your cool," Hawk snarled. Perko knew the gaunt biker would be sprawled on a couch nursing a beer, commanding respect without moving a muscle. "We didn't wait the last four years to get our dough back just so you could mess it up now, Monny. There'll be plenty of time to crack Perko's skull when this is all over."

"Damn right," Mongoose said, shaking off the hands holding his arms. "How are we gonna find this guy?"

"We tossed that Buzz jerkoff from the bus station," said a voice Perko recognized as belonging to a gorilla who still wasn't full patch. "Got him on his way home from work a couple hours ago. He said the fucktard bought a ticket to Peterborough."

"He's going home," Perko said. He hadn't moved from the floor, hoping no one would order him back onto the rickety stool. "The money can't be far from there."

"Home? He's got no home," Mongoose said. "Ain't got no family. Even his mother abandoned him after he went in. Guys in the joint say she quit visiting ages ago."

"He's gotta have a girl somewhere," Perko said. "Something. Punks like that always have a couch or two to crash on."

"After all this time?"

"Shit, I don't know," Perko said. "But where exactly don't matter. He's gonna go to the cash and it's gotta be somewhere nearby. Somewhere between the farm and where they busted him in the Timmy's trailer the next morning."

Perko grimaced in silence. After spending the night locked in the cell with the backwoods lowlife, he had waited for him outside the courthouse. They'd both been arraigned by noon. The Libidos' lawyer put up two grand bail for Perko, while Jonah was released on his own recognizance; Perko was pretty sure the dumbfuck had no idea what "recognizance" meant. He'd told the kid to get hold of a motorcycle and meet him at Shelley's later that night, figuring he'd be useful as long as he didn't know exactly what was expected of him.

"I still say it was that faggot Frederick," Hawk drawled from where he lay on the couch. "Nancy's Nasties never saw him again. You ask me, he split with the money."

"He'd never cross me like that," Perko said. "He knows I'd fry his ass."

"Last thing Bernard told me before I hanged him," Hawk said, "was he fought Frederick for the money. Says he took off with the bag."

"I don't buy it," Perko said.

"You was shittin' your pants in the bushes," Mongoose said. "What do you know?"

"I'm telling you guys, when that runt stole my bike—"

"Trike," hissed Mongoose.

"—he stole the dough, too."

"You better hope you're right," said Hawk. "We've waited four years for you to make good on this debt. Patch or no patch, you either wring it out of this Grant puke's hide or we wring it out of yours."

Mongoose said, "Why don't do it now, Hawk? How do we know this fucker didn't let the Grant prick disappear on purpose. They worked together before. Why not now?"

Perko sensed the room's mood shifting. Snickers had become grunts of agreement. He heard Hawk rake his fingers back and forth on his cheek. The rasping sound made the hair stand up on his neck.

He said, "I wonder if it matters someone barbequed Ernie McCann."

"What?" Mongoose asked.

"Something I heard in jail last night. Didn't think about it 'til now."

"Happened last week," Hawk said.

"What are you talking about?" Mongoose was getting agitated again.

Hawk said, "Ernst McCann's house burned to the ground and him with it. Looked like an accident."

"But why would it matter?" Perko asked, sweating now. He should have known someone in the gang would have heard about the fire. Hearing Hawk say it *looked like* an accident made him wonder whether the fire was a Libidos job he'd been shut out of. How far outside the circle of trust was he operating?

"I remembers," said Mongoose. "Got blisters from those two cords of firewood you made us deliver for the old man's troubles. The mess we made tossing his place. But the money wasn't there."

"Could be connected, though," said Hawk. "We gotta start looking somewhere."

Perko breathed deep and hauled himself to his feet. "So, that settles it. Find the turd and follow him to the stash." He shot what he hoped was an authoritative look into the glare. "I'm on it."

Mongoose snorted, "You's gonna screw it up again." He took a step toward Perko and this time no one held him back.

"Fuck you, Mongoose. I'm done listening to you bitch and complain. You want a piece? Come get it." Perko hunched his shoulders.

"Chill, boys," Hawk commanded. "If you're gonna do each other, it ain't gonna be today. We've got work to do." The lights came on as he swung his feet to the floor. He let his empty beer bottle roll under the couch. "Perko, you'd better hope we can find this sucker before he makes it out of town with our prize. Mongoose, you come along for the ride. We ride in an hour."

Perko tugged on his sweat-stained brown lapels.

"I'm gonna change my suit."

"You're looking a little worn out, Perkie," Shelley commented when he walked through the door to her apartment.

"How perceptive," he grumbled. Between getting Tasered—*twice!*—being stuck in the cage with the village vermin, and getting the bullets sweated out of him in the Libidos' limelight, he'd lost a couple pounds easy. Maybe his chaps would be easier to get into.

"You been a bad boy again? A little tough stuff with the lads? Nothing a lady has to be worried about, I hope?"

As if to assert her claim on him in case he'd been doing the nasty with some biker tramp, she ordered him to strip, shower, and screw her. Preoccupied as he was, Perko had to work hard to deliver the wall-banging work-out Shelley demanded. When they were done, she lit two cigarettes and asked him where he'd been.

"Getting fucked over by everyone and his cousin," he said.

"Rough couple of days in gangland?"

Perko sighed. As accustomed as he was to Shelley's refusal to take his vocation seriously, he was in no mood to be mocked. He said, "This time they've gone too far."

"Who's *they?*"

"Everyone. Mongoose and the rest. The cops who think they can bust my chops whenever they want. And especially that shithead who ripped me off and fucked up my lifestyle."

"Oh, please tell me you're not going to start whining about that punk again. You'll bore me to tears with that old rag."

"Well, you won't have to hear it much longer. I'm gonna do something about it."

"Spoken like a real he-man."

Perko felt his already limp dick shrivel a little further. "You watch," he said. "I've got a line on this thing. Met a guy in the mayor's motel. He's gonna help me deal with this mess once and for all, let me keep all the dough for myself. Just you wait and see."

"You've got a new partner in crime?"

"An assistant, more like."

"An *assistant*." She stifled a giggle. "Aren't we important?"

Perko scowled and stabbed his cigarette into the ashtray that lay on Shelley's belly. He started to get dressed. As he pulled on his chaps, there was a knock at the door.

"Shit. I told the little runt to meet me downstairs," he said.

When he opened the door, Jonah stood there looking from Perko's chaps to his hairy gut and back again. "Izzat a cowboy costume?" he asked.

Shelley stuck her head and one bare shoulder around the door jamb. She took in Jonah's droopy moustache and guffawed. "Shave Perko's stomach and you'd look like Sonny and pregnant Cher!" She disappeared back around the corner, giving both men a good look at her bare ass as she moved away.

Jonah's eyes were wide at the sight and he looked like he was trying to keep from licking his lips. Perko cuffed him and sent him to the parking lot. Then he followed Shelley into the bedroom to finish dressing.

"So that's your new team?" she asked with a sneer.

"Shut up," said Perko. "He's more like a temp."

"Well, I hope you know what you're doing. I sure would hate to imagine he's the one who's got your back in a brawl."

"There ain't gonna be no fightin'. A little fireworks is all."

"Be back in time for breakfast," Shelley said, chuckling again.

Perko grabbed a satchel he'd left by the front door and headed outside to find Jonah sitting on a dirty yellow 180cc rice burner. One of the cheapest Korean-made pieces of trail-bike trash the biker had ever seen.

"You can't be serious," Perko said, hands on his hips. "Thought you and your old man were in the wheel stealing business."

"I had but no time to get hold o' this sucker. You said git a motorcycle and that's what I did."

"If you want to call it that." Perko shook his head in disgust. "Never mind. It's not like we're gonna be in a fucking parade."

"Right. No parade. What *are* we doing?"

Perko answered by handing the kid the satchel. Inside was a bundle the size of a cigar box, wrapped in meat paper.

"What's this?"

"Dynamite."

Jonah fondled the package, grinning.

"The fuse and instructions are in there," said Perko, pointing at the satchel. "You can read, can't you?"

"'Course I can."

"Good. Watch out for the black and green wires. They're the ones you can't afford to get messed up. Everything else is pretty straightforward."

"Jes' what is it you want me to blow up with this here dy-no-mite?"

"Not what. Who."

"Who? What? You want I should kill some-un fer ya? What are ya, nuts?"

"You get all coochie-cooed with them chicks I sent to your room?" Perko had set him up at Aunt Helena's Mexican Restaurant and Motel.

"Uh-huh." Jonah drooled.

"You want to see them again someday?"

"Ooohhh yeah."

"Then read the damn instructions. Make sure you know the drill. Especially the remote. Then wait till I let you know where and when to plant 'em. You pull it off, I can promise you a lot more of what you had today."

Jonah gulped and nodded like a child. He took the satchel Perko handed him and put the package back in it before tying it to the back of the yellow bike with a bungee cord.

"Go back to the hotel. The Pay TV's all taken care of. Wait for my call." Perko handed Jonah a prepaid mobile phone.

"What about if I git hungry?"

"Room service. Just don't order Mount Saint Helena's Nachos."

"Why not?"

"Trust me."

TWENTY-THREE

Well past midnight, Danny pedaled to the rise above Ernie's cabin. He had taken the bicycle from the back of the RV and said good-bye to Granny. She'd agreed to drive due south—and *fast*—to lead the cops away from his true destination.

"Heck, maybe they won't catch me," she'd said before waving and speeding off. "Imagine Dickhead's face if I stole this rig for real."

It had taken all day and all night for Danny to cover the remaining ground. Although he'd bulked up behind bars, prison was the very definition of a sedentary lifestyle. At least the bike had one of those cool water bottles. He kept it refilled at Tim Hortons outlets along the way.

Granny had insisted he put on a pair of Dickhead's racing pants but he drew the line at the neon blue and yellow spandex top. He'd stuck with the ever dirtier Woody Woodpecker. No one gave him so much as a second look. One cop had even flashed his lights, friendly-like, when he passed Danny on a bridge.

Coasting down the final hill, he stretched his legs out to either side as if flying. *It's all been worth it*, he thought. He could have whooped like a victorious child, but the last thing he needed now was to wake one of Ernie's neighbors. He rolled silently onto the wooded lot and leaned the bike against a tree trunk.

Staring at the charred remnants of Ernie's former home, Danny felt a stab of sadness for the old man; somehow, he knew, he was responsible for his death. He shrugged it off as soon as he spotted a long-handled spade leaning against a tree. Things were going his way. Lighting a Marlboro from Dickhead's pack—a parting gift from Granny—he looked around the once-familiar lot.

That fateful night, before running the three-wheeler off the cliff, Danny's options had been few. His first thought had been to conceal the bag of cash in the woodpile, but he would have made one hell of a ruckus restacking enough logs to cover it, and Ernie would have been sure to hear. The garden shed which was joined to the main cabin by a breezeway had been padlocked, so that was out. The fact the shed was locked also meant he couldn't even get his hands on a shovel to do a rough temporary burial. Never mind that it had been just a day and a half since he and Terry had buried Lester; digging another hole in the stone-infested Kawartha ground was the last thing Danny felt like doing that night.

Then he had noticed the outhouse. It stood between the cabin and the road, nestled among three maple saplings for shade and screening. Although nearly three feet long, the satchel was less than twelve inches square at either end—small enough to squeeze down the toilet. He lifted the seat and stuffed the bag through the hole, listening to it drop with a thud onto the pile of shit below. The bag was brown, the hole was dark, and the outhouse smelled pretty much like any other. Danny scooped a couple of trowels full of lime from Ernie's barrel and sprinkled them over the bag. His stash would be safe from cops and dogs alike until morning, he had told himself. He was right about that, as it turned out. And had he not sparked up that fateful joint in the donut-hole bedecked Timmies trailer, sending smoke signals out to the pack of police dogs, he would never have been caught and thrown in jail.

This time, Danny vowed, no more stupid mistakes. All he had to do was dig up the money and disappear. He gave the outhouse a little shove; it wouldn't budge. Ramming the head of the shovel beneath the two-by-four foundation, he leaned on the handle with all his weight to pry it loose from the ground. The damp two-by-four structure creaked as he put his shoulder into it. He pushed the tiny building back on its heels until it was propped up against a poplar tree that stood behind it for that very purpose.

Immediately, the shit pit stench rose up to greet him and made him grateful for the darkness. If he didn't breathe too deeply, he could pretend it wasn't night soil he was digging. He piled the mess onto the ferns that grew next to the outhouse and marveled at how much shit one man could produce. Lucky thing Ernie had lived alone.

It took half an hour of digging for Danny's shovel to strike the first stone. The hole was more than three feet deep. His back muscles knotted and he still hadn't unearthed the bag. He figured the satchel must have shifted to one side or the other, so he squared off his digging to the full perimeter of the pit. He went at it for another twenty minutes, telling himself shovelful by painful shovelful that the next one would hit pay-dirt. But when Danny had reached bottom from edge to edge to edge, and there was still no sign of treasure, he hurled the shovel at a tree and stumbled across the yard to where he had left the stolen bicycle.

Trembling from exertion, he flopped down in front of an oak trunk and lit a cigarette. The smoke curling around his face and hair wasn't near strong enough to mask the smell of composting excrement.

He didn't realize he was crying until he wiped his face with a grimy hand and felt fresh tears mix with the sticky sweat on his cheeks. His shoulders started to shake, setting off a full body tremor as the perspiration on his back evaporated into the cool autumn night. The shivering made the cigarette heater dance where he held it propped on his right knee—a blurry red smear that lurched with every sob.

He'd blown it. Again. Instead of collecting his payday and celebrating his self-determined early release, Danny was now an escaped con with no cash and nowhere to go. His chest ached and he gagged on a drag from the cigarette, smoke burning his nostrils even as the warm nicotine rush rubbed the edge off his shakes.

What the hell had happened?

Could Ernie have discovered the satchel? *Impossible!* The man's vision was so weak, he couldn't even make out his own hand in front of his face unless it was wearing a bright orange glove. And there was no way the cops had found his loot. For the past four years Danny had lived in fear of them pulling him into a prison interrogation room to tell him they had found the cash and were going to use it to link him to the grow op and keep him locked up for an extra few years. They never did.

He stubbed out one cigarette and mindlessly lit another. *What now?* His grand plan, his permanent freedom, his ticket to Margaritaville—dashed and destroyed, leaving him with nothing but one big pile of crap. A spandex-clad fugitive on a ten-speed. Or a thirty-six speed, or whatever the fuck.

A screen door slam across the road jerked him out of his pity party. He heard a woman's voice call out, "You stay close, Wort. Just do your business and back on inside to bed."

Danny rolled to the ground beside the oak tree and pressed himself flat. He listened as a dog snuffled toward him, kicking up leaves along the way. After years of nightmares involving canine predators, Danny was in no mood to face a real dog in the dark. Belly to the ground, he tried to slither into the underbrush, praying the poison ivy wouldn't be active this late in the fall.

When he heard the dog growl and let out a single low bark, he realized how close it had come; he pushed himself to his knees, wondering if he could outrun it on the bike. Remembering how Shooter had once chased him in his car, he decided to stand and fight. He bent to the ground and felt around for a stick, coming up with nothing better than a fallen branch with leaves still attached. Where was a good baseball bat when you needed one?

He clenched the branch in his shaking fist as he more sensed than saw the dog continue toward him. The mutt growled steadily.

"Get lost," Danny hissed, hoping like hell he could frighten the dog without raising his voice. He backed away slowly, waving the branch in front of him. He still couldn't see the damn dog.

"Wort, baby," the woman's voice called out again. "Where you going, Wort? Yoo-hoo. Wortie-boy. Home, Wort. C'mon back to bed. Wort?"

Danny listened, feet rooted to the ground, and stopped waving the branch. The dog paused, too, snuffled as if tormented, then began to growl again. To Danny, it sounded angrier than before.

Without warning, the dog leapt at the extended branch, barking madly. By the time Danny realized the fluff ball was small enough to strangle with his bare hands, the woman from across the street was charging over with one of those 100-watt flashlights.

The dog had latched onto the branch and wasn't letting go. Danny held his arm fully extended, the dog dangling like a fish, jerking itself back and forth as it tried to wrest the prize from his grasp.

"I'm sorry, mister. He just loves to play. He's a Leo. Lotsa Lhasas are. Wort, you let go now."

Danny dropped the branch and stared dumbfounded into the harsh glare of the flashlight.

Upon hitting the ground, the dog stood up and gave its head a good shake. It whimpered a bit and pulled the branch over to where the woman had stopped a few steps short of Danny.

"Do you mind pointing that thing somewhere else?" he asked, shielding his eyes with his hand.

"Sure. I mean...No. What's going on here, anyway?" She kept the flashlight pointed straight at him.

"I...uh...I'm just..." Danny wiped his nose on his sleeve, his mind racing to come up with a plausible lie. He said, "This is Ernie's place, right?"

"Uh-huh. So?"

"Well, I, uh, see, I heard there was a fire here. Thought I should see if he's alright."

"The fire was last Tuesday," the woman said. She kept flashing the light from side to side then bringing it back to Danny, as though she was trying to make sure he was alone. "Ernie is dead."

"Okay. Geez, that's too bad. Well, I guess I should be..."

She cut him off. "What on earth is that god-awful smell?"

"That what? Oh..."

Danny realized his nostrils had gone numb. Glancing down at himself, he saw his shit-smeared outfit was covered in bits of leaves and twigs. He looked as though he'd been dipped in molasses and rolled in All-Bran. "Uh, sorry. I think that's me you smell."

"What is it? Manure? If it is, I think your cow might be sick or something."

"It's uh...it's from..."

"Wait! You're with that creepy lawyer, aren't you? She sent you, didn't she?"

"What? Who? What lawyer?"

"Don't you play games with me, MISTER," the woman said. The dog named Wort said *grrrrrr* and sneezed. "What the hell are you people looking for?"

"Listen, lady. I don't know what you're talking about. I just need to get my stuff. Something that belongs to me. What's it to you, anyway? This ain't your property, is it?" Danny shifted a little to the left, hoping her flashlight wouldn't illuminate the upended outhouse forty feet away.

"What's it to me? What is it to *me?* It's the middle of the night—THAT'S WHAT IT IS. I don't know who you think you are, mucking around in the ashes where a wonderful man burned to death. People poking around here every day and now you and—"

Wort growled, a snout full of tiny teeth bared in Danny's direction.

"Even my dog is upset. That's what's it to *ME*, MISTER."

The flashlight danced as the woman shook with anger.

"I'm just a guy who lost some stuff. No big deal," Danny wheedled. "And Ernie—the guy who lived here—he was my friend, too."

"Oh, so now you're a friend of Ernie's? You expect me to believe that?"

"We go way back."

"Then how come I've never seen you before. It's not like Ernie had a lot of visitors, you know."

"It's been a while. I've been sort of tied up." He needed to calm this woman down, get her to leave him alone, let him figure out what to do next. The shit-bedecked spandex was starting to get itchy. He scratched his thigh. He said, "I know Terry, too."

"Terry who?"

"Terry Miner. The fireman. I read in the newspaper how he helped put out this fire here. Saved someone's dog, I think.

Yeah, that's it. He's a hero or something. Good friend of mine."
The flashlight was getting steadier.

"The fireman Terry?"

"Yeah. Good ol' Terry the fireman."

"He's your friend?"

"Yeah. That's right," Danny said. "We go way back."

"Oh, you go way back?"

"Yeah."

"Like you go way back with Ernie."

"Yeah."

For a moment, the woman was silent, her dog's huff-and-puff breathing the only sound punctuating the dark forest air. Finally, her voice stronger now, the woman said, "Terry is an asshole. A real creep."

Danny swallowed. "Oh...it's not like we're pals or nothing. I just know him is all."

"Uh-huh. And so, what? You come here in the middle of the night looking for *some guy* you know who's a fireman? Or, no, let's see, you're here to pay your respects to Ernie? I'm sorry, but you're going to have to do better than that. This is private property, and I've had just about enough of weirdoes hanging around here all hours of the day. I think maybe I'm just going to call the police."

"No no! Don't do that," Danny said, immediately wishing he hadn't.

"Why not? Maybe they'd like to talk to you. You and that creepy lawyer, too. Maybe they'd like to know whether you had something to do with the fire."

"I couldn't have."

"You can tell that to them." She started to turn away, then stopped. "Ernie was a good man. A harmless man who burned to death for no reason. And I'm just sick to my stomach thinking—"

"My mother took care of Ernie sometimes," Danny blurted. "Ernie McCann was my friend, too." He couldn't believe he felt tears welling in his eyes again.

"Your mother? What are you talking about? Some other someone I never saw?"

"She helped him go shopping. We'd come over for lasagna after. He was my friend. He even helped me when—"

"What?" said the woman, cocking her head and taking a step back toward him. She shone the flashlight straight in his face. The harsh glare made him squint, but Danny kept looking at her, holding her gaze even as every bone in his body told him to jump on his bike and ride away. Finally she spoke. "Where did your mother work?"

"Mostly at The Boathouse. In Buckhorn. By the locks."

"No way. You're not Danny, are you?"

Danny gulped. Did she know he was a fugitive? Was she going to turn him in? Before his mind could leap to nastier conclusions, she said, "You *are* Danny. You're the one Ernie told me about. He had your picture. Couldn't see it himself, but he had a picture of you in his wallet. A real fan of yours, you know. Said you got in some kind of trouble, though, and had to go away."

"That's putting it mildly."

The breeze picked up, and the woman coughed as she caught wind of Danny's sweat de toilette.

"You know, you *really* stink."

"I think you mentioned that already."

"I can smell you from here."

"Well, the winds kind of—"

She cut him off again. "Listen, you still haven't told me what the hell you're doing here, but I know one thing for certain. If Ernie were alive, he'd be helping you. Maybe you should come over and get cleaned off. "

Danny couldn't believe his ears. He said, "Get cleaned off?"

"Yeah. I've got a shower you can use. I'll put on some soup."

A shower and hot soup? His instincts for danger had been honed in prison, and he felt none here. This woman was for real; it made no sense to him but he was in no position to argue. Besides, where the hell else was he going to go? "Sounds about perfect," he said. "What's your name anyway?"

"Judy. Judy Jackman. This here is my dog, Wort."

"Oh yeah? Wort? Nice dog."

Wort barked.

Danny followed Judy Jackman across the street and out behind her cabin to where she pointed at a hose hanging over a tree branch. The hose ended in a simple flat head shower nozzle.

"It's really not all that cold," Judy said. "It's fed from a big black bag on top of my roof. In the summer, when it's sunny, the water can actually get uncomfortably hot. I just filled it this afternoon, though, so it's probably a little bit chilly. Well, sort of. Maybe in between."

"Do you have some soap?"

"Of course. Best there is. See that big old bar of Sunlight in the crook of the branch there?" Judy pointed her flashlight at the tree trunk. "It's what I use on Wort when he chases a skunk or brings me home a fish."

"Great," he said.

No shower could ever be less pleasant than the one in prison, but this one came close. The stall, if one could call it that, had no sides. It was positioned behind the cabin so its occupant would be invisible from the road. Brushing by the ferns and long grasses on their way over, he and Judy had awoken a cloud of mosquitoes who were surprisingly hungry for autumn. Danny did his best to keep most of his body splashed by the trickle of cold water while he lathered himself up with the rough bar of yellow soap. Judy had given him a wicker basket for his dirty clothes, saying she'd wash them in the morning.

"There's a towel hanging off the tree there," she called out through the screen door. "I used it on Wort yesterday, so it should be dry by now. I'll heat up the soup. It's beet. Homemade. I had quite a good crop this year."

Danny washed himself three times head to toe. The soap made his hair stiff but he really didn't want to call out and ask Judy for shampoo. The shrinkage brought on by the cold water was not something he wanted to share.

A few minutes later, wrapped in the dog towel, Danny sat on a log upwind from the fire pit. Judy had lit it while he showered and it was burning strong by the time she came outside carrying two bowls of soup. Instead of joining him on the log, she pulled up a stump and sat where she could keep an eye on him. As she watched him eat, half-naked, Danny caught her checking out his abs. He flexed just a bit.

"Good soup," he lied. The sweet sticky broth warmed his belly nicely, but it was all he could do to force the thick red goo past his tongue. After years of bland prison food where the strongest flavor of any kind was ketchup, this frothy concoction made him want to retch.

"Thanks. It's a Moosewood recipe. Well, sort of. I didn't have most of the ingredients but there were tons of beets and I threw in a little potato to starch it up. If you like, I can get you some hot sauce."

"No, that's fine. Could I maybe borrow a T-shirt, though? And maybe some sweat pants? Something I could fit into? The mosquitoes are starting to find me again."

"Sure. I've got a couple of pair of Ernie's pants. I was patching them for him. He did all his gardening on his hands and knees. Pretty much by feel. Wore out the knees in no time." She disappeared inside and was back in an instant with sweatpants and a T-shirt two sizes too big.

"You were a big help to him, I take it," Danny said.

"I just did what anyone would do. He was such a sweet man. Other than the social services that helped out now and then, Ernie was pretty much alone. Especially since your mother went away. I think she must have been sending money, though. Ernie said she was like that. Every so often, out of the blue, he'd have a few hundred dollars—one time, more than a thousand—and he'd insist I spend it fast. On something he needed or something I could use or just on a great bottle of scotch that we'd polish off over a couple of evenings."

Holy shit, Danny thought. Unless Ernie had kept a bunch of the cash he'd intended for his mom, he must have found the stash after all. It still didn't add up, though. The man wasn't exactly the save and savor type. He'd have been the first to fly off to an extended Caribbean beach holiday if he'd found that much dough in his shitter.

"What'd he tell you about my mom?" he asked Judy.

"You mean about how she'd help him?"

"No. About where she went. When she left."

"Oh, that. That was some kind of mystery. I don't even think he knew. He just said one day she took off. Indefinite vacation, the way he put it. I figured maybe she needed a break, what with you being in jail."

"You knew I was busted?"

"Ernie told me all about it. Well, enough to know that you got caught growing a whole bunch of dope and you landed a teetotaling judge who decided to make an example of you and sent you off for a bunch of years. Real bum rap, it sounds like."

"You're not kidding." Danny saw no percentage in telling Judy what he had actually pled guilty to.

"Most people just get a slap on the wrist for growing pot. I figured you must have had some big crop or something. Even then, it's a drag. Marijuana should be legalized. Get the gangs out of it, I say. Tax it like alcohol and use it to pay for homeopathy."

"Yeah," Danny said.

"So the first thing you do when you get out is come nosing around Ernie's place in the middle of the night looking for some creepo volunteer fire-stud."

"Did he really rescue your dog?"

"I rather doubt it. From what I hear around town, it's not dogs he chases."

"Huh?"

"Seems he slips in and out of any cuddy offering a warm bed and free booze."

"Sounds like Terry."

The soup and the fire had worked and Danny was feeling warm all over. Even the mosquitoes had retired for the night. In the glow of the flames, Danny could see that Judy was even more attractive in person than she had appeared in the newspaper photo. He stood up to add a log to the fire, hoping her earlier peeks at his jailhouse physique, honed by countless hours killing time in the gym, would convince his hostess to invite him inside.

As though she could read his mind, Judy said, "There's a Mexican hammock just over there." She flicked on the flashlight and pointed to a clearing in front of the cabin. "I'll get you a sleeping bag that zips up over your head. You'll be comfy enough."

Ten minutes later, wearing Ernie's clothes for the second time in his life, Danny was shut out of the cabin and left hanging between two maple trees. Wort's on-and-off growling ensured dogs would feature prominently in his dreams.

Grabbing a tuft of long grass so he could swing the hammock, he slowly rocked himself to sleep. His heart ached and he wanted to cry like a baby, but no tears came. He felt robbed. Wronged. He had been patient, and kept his mouth shut. He had done his time—well, most of it, anyway. He had endured threats and beatings and countless hours locked in small rooms with beefy police officers who breathed stale coffee in his face and drilled him with the same questions over and over, trying to trip him up. He had spent half his young adult life in a tiny cell convincing himself that it would all be worth it; that his personal pot of gold was assured even if his life's road was anything but a rainbow. And here he was, ready to claim it, about to ride off into the proverbial sunset. And now this?

If what Judy had said was true and Ernie was blowing cash he oughtn't have had, the old man must have found it. He decided that made the most sense. But then what of the fire? Danny remembered Ernie fetching him the lantern in the dark. How the guy could whip his shotgun off the wall and use it to challenge unwanted visitors. Not the kind of guy who'd start a fire in his cabin. Much less hang around and burn to death. Someone else must have done it. Someone with a reason to want Ernie dead. It had to be connected to the loot.

Where in hell was his stinking bag of money?

TWENTY-FOUR

Danny woke when something nibbled his fingertips. It had to be five in the morning. Half-dreaming, he wondered where the dogs had come from this time. His arm hung from the hammock and his first waking thought was he was still in his cell, Carson getting frisky from the bottom bunk. "Get your goddamn tongue back in your mouth before I shove it there with my foot, asshole," he snarled before remembering where he was. Panic quickly replaced relief when he realized whatever was gnawing his hand was neither human nor canine but some unidentified nocturnal beast.

Danny pulled his hand away and, failing to realize the dynamics of a hammock, rolled over to face his nighttime lover. The hammock rolled with him and dumped him out. As he tumbled to the ground, he made out a thick white stripe against inky blackness before the body of the oversized skunk collapsed under his chest. For a moment, he felt the animal squirm—a death rattle—and then he was enveloped in the rankest fumes he had ever experienced. The stench scalded his nostrils as he gasped, trying to clear his lungs, succeeding only in filling them deeper with the mist from the skunk's flattened sack.

He made a mad dash down the lane, across the road, and down Ernie's lot to the lake. He plunged his head into the frigid water and pulled out gasping. He gulped and dunked repeatedly until his brain pounded from the cold.

Stumbling back up the hill, he stopped short of the hole he'd just dug. He stared at the tilted-back shitter, then the pile of soot, and back again. Something was wrong. Something had changed. *The outhouse had been moved.* Instead of standing between the road and the cabin, Ernie's shit shack was to the lakeside of the cabin. It must have got full up and been relocated. Danny had dug the *wrong hole.*

He paced up and down, kicking at the earth, trying to remember just exactly where Ernie's outhouse had stood. The underbrush had grown too high to find the spot in the dark, but the stash would be easy to find by daylight. He retrieved the dead skunk and dropped it in the empty shithole. Then he climbed back in the hammock and rocked himself to sleep.

Morning came quickly. The hammock was hung where it would catch late afternoon sun but was well shaded before noon. Danny slept soundly until he was shaken awake by Judy, leaning over him and whispering in his ear.

"Danny. Wake up. There's men at Ernie's. I'm surprised their motorcycles didn't wake you."

Instantly alert, he looked across the road to see three Harley-Davidsons on their kickstands.

"You smell even worse than last night," Judy said. "Did you run into our skunk?"

"You might say that."

Through the trees, he watched the men poke around the far side of Ernie's burnt out cabin. One of them was checking out the bike he'd stolen from the RV. It looked like the guy from the bus station except he was wearing some kind of centipede pants. Wort stood next to Judy, growling steadily.

"Why would they push Ernie's outhouse back like that?" Judy asked.

"It's me they're after."

She stared at him blankly. "They've no right to be mucking around his place."

"You're so right. Why don't you go set them straight."

Judy bit her lower lip and Danny could tell she was considering how involved she was willing to get.

"They're *your* friends," she said. "You go talk to them."

"Those guys aren't friends."

She looked back and forth between him and the bikers, as if trying to decide who stank worse.

"Distract them," he said. "Chat them up. Let me disappear into the woods. And you'll never see me again."

She frowned. "Get yourself gone. Quick. And I'm doing this for Ernie—not you." With that, she marched across the road, Wort at her heels, whispering back over her shoulder, "Jeepers, you stink."

Perko stared down the hole, one hand splayed across his mouth and nose. "Jesus H. Christ. Never thought I'd be this close to a skunk and not able to smell the damn thing. What kind of a twisted mind drops a skunk in a pile of shit?"

"Same kind of weird fuck who kills his friend and feeds him to his dog, I figure," said Mongoose.

"But what's it mean? Is he trying to tell us something?" Perko asked. "Throw us off the scent?"

"Looks like we got company," said Hawk. He jerked his head toward the road where a woman wearing sandals and a tie-dyed wrap-around skirt stomped toward the clutch of bikers. She was followed by a tiny white mutt.

"Good morning, gentlemen," the chick called out when she got close.

"Mornin', ma'am," said Perko, giving her an approving once-over.

"Can I help you with something?" she asked.

"This here your place?"

"No, it belongs to Ernie McCann. Or, at least, it did. I'm his neighbor." Her dog sniffed Perko's leg.

"Well, neighbor lady, we won't be but a moment or two," Perko said. "My friend Mongoose here is a bit of a firebug, see. Likes to burn things and stuff. We heard about the fire and thought we'd swing on by for a little peek."

"Musta been quite the blaze," said Mongoose. "You see it?"

"A man died here," she said. "I'm not sure I like the idea of you treating it like a tourist attraction."

"We're not tourists," Perko said. "More like business people." He jerked his knee, but the dog was intrigued by his Centiagues.

"Business people?"

"Yeah, kinda like insurance adjusters," said Mongoose.

"Only freelance," Hawk added.

"So if you saw the fire," Perko said, "then you would know if anyone was hanging around. Looking suspicious and stuff."

"What are you? Detectives?" she asked. She snapped her fingers at her dog; he ignored her.

"We don't really represent anyone," Perko said.

"Independent," said Hawk.

"So?" Mongoose stared at her hard.

"So what?" she asked.

"So, did you see anyone not from around here or what?"

"Either at the fire or maybe pokin' around after," said Hawk.

"Like you, you mean?" To her dog she said, "Wort, stop that."

This cookie is tough, Perko thought. He said, "Maybe someone else, sweetheart?"

The woman hesitated, looking from one biker to the other.

"Just one," she said, "besides the police and such."

"Who's that?"

"A lady lawyer. All uptight and curious. Her name's Linette Paquin. That's who."

"A lawyer, eh?" Perko looked over at Mongoose. "Much obliged, ma'am. Why don't you run along now and we'll be out of your way in no time."

"Run...what?" Little Miss Tie-Dye flushed bright red. Perko thought she was about to slap him. She lunged for him, hand open, and he stepped back, but not quick enough. He felt the dog's pee splash over the top of his boot and trickle down inside.

"Oh, I'm so sorry, mister," the woman said. She scooped up the dog in her arms and clutched him to her. She did her best to cover the grin that crept up her cheeks. "I'll be going now," she said.

"One more thing." Hawk pointed at a road race bicycle leaning against a tree not far from the outhouse. "That your bike?"

She looked at it, shook her head then nodded. "It must have belonged to the man who lived here," she said and walked away.

"You believe that?" Hawk said once she was out earshot.

Rob Brunet

"Woulda snapped that runt dog in half if she hadn't snatched him away," Perko said, bent over wiping his boot with dried leaves.

"About the bike, I mean," said Hawk.

"It's too new?" said Mongoose. "That it?"

"The fucking guy was blind. You ever seen a blind man on a bicycle?" said Hawk.

"Oh, yeah, man is *she* stupid," said Mongoose.

Perko said, "Far as I'm concerned, if Grant found what he came for in that shitter, there ain't no way he's sticking around to find a dead skunk and toss it down the hole."

"And if he rode up on that bike, why'd he leave on foot?" said Hawk.

"Unless he's still here," said Perko.

Mongoose looked from the burnt out cabin to the upturned outhouse. "Where?" he asked. He watched the lady and her dog cross the street to her cabin. "Think he's with her? Let's go check."

Hawk said, "Hang on a minute. If Perko's right, we head over there and the guy sees us coming? He knows we're onto him. He disappears into the forest, and we're shit out of luck."

"What's we gonna do then? Wait here?"

"Something like that," Hawk said.

Danny crouched in a tangle of dry undergrowth a few hundred feet away, far enough into the trees so the bikers wouldn't see him. He was sure the guy with the weird ass pants was the same one he had kicked in the gonads two days before. He didn't think for a second that the posse was after him for that particular infraction, but he had no doubt it would influence the dude's mood.

Being prey felt familiar, and he didn't like it one bit. Worse, if the bikers had put two and two together, the police wouldn't be far behind. His only way out was to locate the old outhouse hole and dig it up fast. Without his ticket to paradise, he was just another loser on the run, ripping off convenience stores whenever he got hungry.

183

The Harleys roared to life. He ducked into the bushes and watched them speed by—one, two...where was the third? He waited until the sound of their engines had disappeared over the horizon and swore under his breath: three bikers, two bikes—the meathead from the diner had stayed behind.

He darted across the road and crept back toward Ernie's. There was no sign of the chunkster. No big surprise. The biker was hiding. He made his way back to Judy's cottage by a circuitous bush route. Wort was on him the instant he slipped in the back door, snapping at his ankles and barking ferociously.

Judy stormed into the kitchen. "Sit, Wort. Sit and be quiet." Then she looked at Danny. "I thought you said I'd never see you again."

"I lied."

"Why am I not surprised?" She walked over to the counter and poured herself a cup of coffee. She was wearing a cut-off T-shirt and he noticed hair sticking out from her armpits. She said, "I think maybe it's about time you tell me what's going on."

"Alright," he said, "but that coffee sure smells good. Mind if I have a cup?" What kind of woman didn't shave her pits? Danny stifled a Carson flashback.

"Frankly," Judy said, "I don't even know how you *can* smell coffee, reeking the way you do. That stench is unbearable. I'll bring the pot outside—right after you shower. With this." She handed him a large bottle of hydrogen peroxide and a box of baking soda. "It works on Wort. Scrub hard."

In daylight, Judy's shower set up wasn't half bad. Danny alternated the frothy skunk bath with the coarse yellow soap and splashes of cold water until he shone like a baby.

Judy reappeared with two cups and the coffee pot on a hand-painted wooden tray as he dried himself off. He couldn't help but notice her watching him, and flexed a bit for her benefit. *Hairy armpits aren't all bad,* he thought. *Isn't that a tree-hugger thing? Free love and all that?* He sat at the picnic table, a towel wrapped around his waist.

"Okay, shoot," she said. "Start with why you dug up Ernie's outhouse."

"I...er...that is...what do you mean?"

"This isn't starting so well, Danny." Her eyes drifted down his neck to his shoulders and chest. "The thing was dug up and there was a dead skunk in it. What kind of weirdness were you up to in the middle of the night?"

He sipped the coffee. It was the best he'd tasted in years, even without half a handful of sugar in it. He said, "I was looking for something."

"What on God's Green Earth would you expect to find in Ernie's toilet?"

"I'd rather not say."

"Listen, buster. A good man is dead, his home burned to the ground, and this quiet little backwoods lane is being overrun by cops, lawyers, bikers, and strangers who show up in the middle of the night to shovel shit!" Judy's eyes bulged and her cheeks flushed red. He couldn't tell whether she was blushing at her language, or the fact he'd started popping his pectorals. Judy locked her eyes on his. Danny did his best to stare her down, then gave up and averted his gaze.

"I stuffed a bag of cash down Ernie's crapper," he said.

It didn't seem possible, but Judy's eyes pushed even further out of their sockets. She asked, "Is that where you normally hide your money?"

"I was in a hurry."

Judy stared. Danny suddenly wished he was wearing a shirt.

"I was scared," he said. "Being chased."

"By who?"

"By the cops. And those bikers, I guess."

"Why were they chasing you?"

He gulped more coffee. Man, it was good. He said, "It was their money."

Judy squinted. "So, you stole money from a motorcycle gang and stuffed it down Ernie's toilet."

"I *accidentally* stole it." He tried a glare, then mumbled, "But yeah, I stole it. Sounds crazy, don't it?"

"Sounds dangerous is what it sounds."

"That, too."

"So then you got sent to jail?"

"Well, not exactly."

"Huh?"

"Well, not for stealing the money anyway."

"Then why?"

Danny stood up and said, "Maybe I should be going now..."

Judy reached across and grabbed the front of the towel, holding tight. For a split second, Danny considered twisting to leave, towel be damned. In that brief moment he felt blood rush to where Judy's hand was grazing his abdomen and he froze. They stared at each other, neither moving. Danny wondered what it would be like to get it on with Judy in the hammock. And whether her legs would be furry.

He sat back down, clutching the towel and pressing himself into his seat. He felt like a small boy who'd been caught in his mother's underwear drawer. Judy's face was crimson.

She said, "So why then? Why did you go to prison?"

Danny drained the last of his coffee and lit a cigarette before saying, "They sent me to jail for killing a man."

Judy blanched, going from red to white so fast Danny thought she might faint. Her voice weak, she said, "I am sitting in my backyard on a sunny fall morning drinking coffee with a murderer."

"More like a manslaughterer." And Danny told her all about Lester and his nasty dog. Acutely aware of Wort's presence near his right ankle, he left out the part about poisoning Shooter with Lester's left foot.

"You killed a man," said Judy when he was done.

"It was an accident."

"Like stealing the bikers' money was an accident."

Danny nodded.

"Sounds like a lot of accidents happen to you," she said. "Shouldn't you have got off on self-defense or something?"

"I might have," Danny said, "if I'd had a real lawyer. Still, the Libidos would likely have killed me outright if I'd been on the outside. Dragged me around by my toenails until I gave up the dough. Buried me alive."

"So why are you still here? I gave you a chance to get away. Distracted them, like you said." Judy started to look nervous again.

"Because the money is still in the ground."

"What do you mean? You dug up the outhouse. I saw the hole."

"That's not where Ernie's outhouse was when I stuffed the money down."

"What?"

"He must have moved it. All I gotta do is find the old spot. The money will be there for sure." He put out his cigarette. "There's just one problem."

"What?"

"One of the bikers stayed behind. To watch for me, I figure."

"You mean there's a biker watching you now?"

"I don't think he saw me come here. I was real careful."

"You *think*? What about me? What if they saw you come here?" Judy's hands trembled to the point she spilled her coffee.

"That sort of occurred to me, too," he said.

"So now what? I'm just supposed to wait here, hoping some thugs don't show up looking for you?"

"Or, you could help me."

"Again?"

"I need to sneak out of here. And I need to borrow a few hundred bucks. I was thinking maybe you could drive me into Buckhorn."

"What? You just said the money is here."

"Yeah, but there's someone in Buckhorn who can help me out."

"Who's that?"

"Terry Miner."

Buzz Meckler had spent the night and the day and the night again replaying the events. After the cops had Tasered both him and the goon who attacked him, they'd arrested the biker and hauled him off. Then they spent nearly two hours interviewing Buzz without even once commending him on his fearless intervention. After that, in spite of his protests, his boss had insisted he leave work early. So much for being a hero.

Trudging home, he was yanked into an alley and beaten with rubber piping. His attackers made him reveal the destination of some guy named Danny who he quickly understood had been the target of their cohort's brutal attack.

As he nursed his wounds with bags of frozen peas in his two-room apartment, the phone rang. It was his boss, informing him that instead of receiving a medal, a promotion, or even a raise, Buzz would be sent for more training. First, he was ordered to take a week off. "Stress leave," his boss told him.

Buzz sensed his role as lone protector of the bus-traveling public of Eastern Ontario was in jeopardy. He foresaw a future of drinking cheap beer in a Kingston tavern reminiscing about the hero he might once have been.

He decided to take destiny into his own hands.

The poor schmoe he had saved two days before had been headed to Peterborough. The toughs who'd tossed him made a big deal of wanting to know that. Then there was that article about the dog rescuer. Clearly, Peterborough was where the action was and Buzz wanted in on it. Heroes are all about action. It wasn't much to go on, but things always worked themselves out in the movies.

TWENTY-FIVE

The Boathouse served the best greasiest breakfast in Buckhorn. The Libidos were known to close down the bar at three a.m. and suck back a few warm ones outside. A huge slab of Canadian Shield granite served as a parking lot. They'd pass out next to their bikes and stumble back in for breakfast once they'd slept it off.

This morning, Hawk and Mongoose were clear-eyed as they packed into plates piled high with scrambled eggs, bacon, homefries, pancakes, sausage, and toast. Mongoose ordered them orange juice for the health of it and used his winning smile to convince the waitress to add double shots of vodka.

"Whaddya figure," Mongoose asked, "were we too late? If he's been and gone, what are the chances he'll come back?"

"Hard to know," Hawk spewed, his lips shiny with back bacon grease, "but Perko was right. We had to make it look like we cleared out or Grant would have disappeared. He's waited four years. What's another few days?"

"I think you's trusting Perks more'n ya should. He's losing it. Like he's mind-melding with this punk or something. 'Obsessing.' I saw it on Dr. Phil."

"What bothers me most is why pick up a damn skunk and throw it down the hole?" said Hawk. "I mean, let roadkill alone. This guy's got fucked in the head while he was in the joint."

"They's somethin' weird about that chick, too," said Mongoose. He squirted ketchup on a forkful of eggs and bacon. "Pushy. For a scrawny bitch, I mean."

"She was lying. No doubt."

"What about that lawyer she talked about?" Mongoose said. "Wasn't that the same shyster who did the plea bargain for Grant when this whole thing went down?"

"One and only," Hawk answered. "Pass the syrup. These pancakes are amazin'."

"Didn't you shake her down after the punk pleaded guilty on that baseball bat rap?"

"'Course I did. Me and Perko did her good. She didn't know a thing. Dumb-as-fuck Public Pretender. Caught Peterborough's first murder in three years and then went back to doing real estate deals. I don't buy she was there."

"More lies?"

Hawk nodded.

"You's sure?"

"Here's what I'm sure of, Mongoose." Hawk stabbed his fork into the table. "This ends today. Time to cut our losses."

"You wants to forget about the money?"

"Never," said Hawk, "but Perko's got 'til nightfall to find it."

"Tonight?"

"No cash. No leads. No Perko."

"Hawk, if it weren't for you, you know I'd a done him a hundred years ago. Something's off about him. Not one of us."

Hawk waved at the waitress for a new fork. "I'll take the next watch and send Perko over here. You'll finish the day. Play it cool. Don't let on what's gonna happen. There's still a chance this punk will show up and we don't want two bodies on our hands at the same time."

"Sure as shit," said Mongoose. "You gonna eat that sausage?"

It was drop dead easy for Perko to let himself through Judy's front door. It had the kind of forty-dollar knob lock he'd learned to punch open doing teenage B-and-E's. Had he bothered to check, he would have found the chick had left her back door unlocked anyway. This was friendly country, and people only locked up when they went "away." When Perko had been a practicing thief, the targets for break and enter were invariably the cottages belonging to rich folk from the city. It wasn't so much that you didn't steal from your neighbors; more like you stole from people who had better stuff than you did.

That was the point, wasn't it? And Perko liked to tell himself he only stole from folks who could afford it, people with insurance, people who'd be grateful he gave them an excuse to go buy the latest piece of electronica.

Today wasn't about stealing, though. Perko had watched from the bushes as the chick drove off in the aging hatchback, dog yapping out the window. He'd decided he wanted to know more about Ernie McCann's neighbor. Something felt off about her. Even if Hawk was right that applying pressure could scare their prey away, it couldn't hurt to be ready in case things changed. Besides, he had gotten bored waiting for the punk to show up.

The cottage was sparsely furnished, yet cluttered. Potted ivies, cacti, and an assortment of flowering plants grew on tables and shelves everywhere. Books were interspersed with a collection of antique bottles and a few odds and sods of old-time farm life—a set of bellows by the fireplace, an oil lantern, and a couple of cowbells. Little stained glass birds, butterflies, and flowers hung in almost every window. *Utne Readers* were stacked on a round rough-hewn coffee table, one bent open as though half-read.

In the kitchen, a long wooden shelf sagged under the weight of mason jars stuffed with spices, nuts, seeds, beans, and a half dozen flours. The narrow kitchen table was covered with a gingham-checked oil cloth the likes of which Perko hadn't seen since he was a kid. A black school slate mounted on the wall beside the fridge was crammed with notes in pink chalk. The curly handwriting was reminiscent of a grade school teacher. It listed, "Bake 3 pies for Church social. B'day card to Miriam. Plant garlic before frost!!!"

Was this woman for real? He shrugged off a twinge of guilt and headed to the bedroom.

No surprises there. An overstuffed quilt piled on a simple double bed with a painted metal headboard. Chest of drawers and closet full of natural fibers and soft colors. Then, the first extravagance he had seen in the cottage: a pair of serious stereo speakers mounted in the corners facing the bed and a subwoofer in the corner. Before Perko could ask himself why these weren't in the living room, he spotted the stack of CDs near a simple

TEAC player: *Blissful Rest; Tangerine Dream; The Ocean is My Pillow; Oxygene* by Michel Jarre.

In the bathroom, he found a parade of natural sponges and glass jars with hand-scripted labels rhyming off body butters and ointments. Even the toothpaste was by somebody named Tom. Tiger Balm was the only product he recognized apart from the deluxe brand of toilet paper. Stacked in a corner was a mini washer drier combination, the kind that used almost no water.

He was turning to leave when his eyes fell on the wicker laundry basket by the door. Neatly folded on top was a grey sweatshirt with a picture of Woody Woodpecker emblazoned on the front. He grinned, his left lip curling up almost to his nostril. "Gotcha," he growled.

Danny Grant was within reach. Perko didn't care how the shithead was connected to the girl. It didn't matter. She was leverage. It was time to get Mongoose out of the picture, collect his prize, and get his good ol' life back. Even patch things up with Hawk and wangle a promotion out of this somehow.

He pulled his phone from his pocket and punched in the number for Aunt Helena's Mexican Restaurant and Motel.

"Get your ass to Century Lane. Number two-three-one-one," Perko said when Jonah answered the phone.

"Where the hell is that?"

"By the lake. Pigeon Lake. Just past the bridge at Gannon's Narrows. Be here in an hour." He hung up.

When Terry arrived at George Meade's boat, ashes still clinging to his boots from a barbeque gone awry, someone was there waiting for him in the darkened cabin.

"Welcome aboard, loser," the man sneered.

Terry jumped backward and banged his head on the cabin hatch.

"What the hell?" Terry's mind raced as he ran the back of his hand across his eyes, trying to focus in the half-light; instead, he only filled them with more grime. He reached for the knife in his belt but before he could pull it out, he was slammed to the floor and felt a foot land on the back of his neck.

"I'll go. I'm outta here, George. She's your wife, uh, your boat, I mean. She told me it was hers. Honest. And—"

"Shut your beer-soaked beak, Terry," the man hissed, pulling the knife away and landing a quick kick to his ribs. He stepped back, out of Terry's reach. "It's me. Danny. I could care less whose boat this is. It's you I'm here for."

"Danny?" Terry's eyes darted back and forth. They had adjusted to the dark and he was looking for anything he could use as a weapon. "Danny *Who?*"

He caught sight of the man's foot aimed at his head just in time and rolled away from the kick. "Danny Grant? Is that you? How the...? When did...? I mean, like, what the hell are you doin' here? I heard you got day parole, but you ain't supposed to be out for another three or four months! Wow, I mean, like, good to see you..."

"You lying piece of crap. 'Good to see you?' How stupid do you think I am? D'ya figure they fed me moron pills for breakfast in the joint? Maybe some hairy-assed gangbanger screwed my brains right outta my head?"

"C'mon, man, I'm your pal, right? You know I'd never..."

"Pal?" Danny spat on the cabin floor. "Kinda of pal squeals first chance he gets and lies his ass off to the cops instead of doing his own time fair and square?"

"I..."

"Shut it, Terry. You keep digging your hole, you're gonna strike water. You know damn well why I went to prison. They couldn't pin the dope charges on me, no thanks to you. And the only way they connected me to Lester was you had to go steal his damn car."

"It wasn't my fault, Danny. The cop, he nearly beat me to a pulp before I told him about the grow op. I coulda died, you know. The torture was somethin' else, I tell ya."

"Close your yap. 'Less you want a *real* beating."

"Aw, c'mon, Danny. Lemme help you out. You must be needin' cash right about now, eh? Maybe I could cut you in on this scam, I got goin'. Kinda money-for-nothing and chicks-for-free if you know what I mean. I can make it up to you, Danny. Honest, I can."

"Yes, you can."

Danny pulled open the curtain, letting the afternoon sunlight flood the small space. With the window behind him, he was still a silhouette to Terry. He flopped down on the bench, lit a cigarette, and tossed the pack over to where Terry cringed on the floor.

"How'd you find me, Danny?"

"Wasn't all that hard, dick-for-brains. How hard do you think it is to find a volunteer fireman can't keep from unfurling his hose?"

Terry beamed.

"I need you to help me do something." Danny spoke slowly, watching Terry's face as if to make sure he was following. "You're a smart guy. Real smart. And I need someone with a lot on the ball to help me pull something off."

Terry had put a cigarette in his mouth and was trying to light it with a shaky hand. Danny leaned over and steadied the lighter while Terry took a haul. Terry sniffled and leaned back against the ladder to the deck. He drew his knees to his chest, then winced at the pain in his ribs where Danny had kicked him.

"Sure I can help ya, Dan. Do whatever it takes. Hell, you're fresh outta jail and all. Someone's gotta help, right? I mean, what are friends for?"

Danny tossed a small bundle of bills at Terry's feet. "I want you to blow five hundred bucks on a little party."

Terry said, "I think I can handle that."

The sound of his tortured breathing drowned out the soft slap of wavelets against the boat's hull. In. Out. In. Sputter, cough. Inhale. Wheeze. And out. From where he huddled on the floor of George Meade's boat, he could see the jumble of sheets spilling off the bed behind Danny. A fleeting image of Cindy Meade getting dressed before darting off to play tennis that morning flashed through his mind. Thinking of Cindy made him grin.

"You think this is a joke, Terry?" Danny hissed.

"Well, you are kidding me, right?" Terry paused to take a drag on his cigarette. "I mean, are you messed up or what? I'll take your money, Dan, but you gotta tell me what this is all about."

Terry reached for the handful of fifties and winced as Danny's heel landed on the back of his hand, pinning it to the floor.

"Not so fast," Danny said. "You're going to take a little stroll over to The Boathouse. Some of the Libidos are there. And they're looking for me."

"Ya, so? Why don't you head over there yourself?"

Danny kicked Terry's shin.

"Shut up and listen." He gave Terry precise instructions and made Terry repeat them back to him three times:

"I flash some cash and tell 'em how you gave me a wad to drive you over to Bobcaygeon." Terry's face crumpled to a contorted frown. "Shit, Danny, but that's a load a cash. Why'n't ya just take a taxi?"

"I'm a fugitive, shit-for-brains, remember?"

"I just don't get why want me to go tellin' lies to the Libidos. They're gonna beat the shit out of me."

"Maybe they will. Maybe they won't. One thing for sure, you don't help me, I'm coming after you with a bat and a dog. You remember how that goes?"

Terry said, "No offense, Danny, but I'm thinkin' I like my odds with you more'n a bunch of bikers."

Danny looked out the porthole toward The Boathouse. His breath was shallow and his lips were white with dried spittle. When he leaned over Terry, his breath reeked of stress. Terry tried to turn his face away but Danny grabbed his chin and pressed in even closer. Terry's back was hard against the hull.

"How about I give you another thousand bucks."

"What am I? A human punching bag? Pay me enough I can take a few shots to the head?"

"Five thousand."

"Gimme a break. Why don't you promise me a hundred thousand, Danny? It'd be just as easy to believe as five." Terry chortled. "Like you could ever come up with five thousand bucks, fresh out of prison and all."

Danny stood up and paced up and down the cramped cabin. With his back to Terry, he said, "I haven't told you everything."

Terry sat still and stared at Danny's back.

"I need you to get the Libidos off my tail. Send them in the wrong direction. I need them distracted, looking at something else. For a couple hours is all."

"I got that part, Danny. But why?"

Danny turned back toward him, licking his lips. "Because I know where the money is. The money from the buy. The night of the bust. It's right where I stashed it. And I need time to go get it."

"*You* took the Libidos' cash?"

"Uh huh."

"You mean to say you stole my job running the greenhouse, and then you stole the money from the Libidos?"

Danny nodded.

"And now you want me to get my head cracked by that bunch of thugs, send them on a wild goose chase looking for you *and* their money? And you ride away in the sunset with a bag full of dough?"

Danny shrugged.

"Boy, you musta gone to school in prison or somethin', come up with a winner like that. I may not be bright as you but that's insulting, is all. Think I'm stupid enough for a plan like that..."

"Ten thousand bucks."

"No way..."

"Fifteen."

"Geez..."

"Twenty-five."

"I...uh...fifty?"

"Thirty thousand, Terry. Tops."

Terry frowned, scratched his ear.

"What is it you want me to say to them again?"

Buzz dunked the honey cruller in his large double-double and took a bite. This was the third Tim Hortons he'd stopped at since arriving in Peterborough in the car he had borrowed from his father. It wasn't much like a cop car, but Buzz fashioned himself more of a detective, anyway, undercover like.

The thing was, nobody in the donut shops took him all that seriously. He'd stormed out of the last place in red-faced humiliation. A bunch of high school kids taunted him for asking about "Terry the fireman." They suggested he go buy a fire stud calendar if that's what he was into. Or maybe google "men with hoses."

He struggled to recall how cops got strangers talking in the movies and decided there must be a Detecting for Dummies book he could pick up. When an older couple sat down at the table attached to his, he laid the newspaper article between their soup and sandwich platters.

"Excuse me, folks," he said. "I'm trying to find this place. There was a fire about a week ago? Guy died in it and everything. You wouldn't happen to know where that happened, would you? I think that dog in the picture was mine. He ran away from our campsite when a groundhog showed up, and..."

"Lakehurst," said the old man without so much as a glance at the article. "Fifteen miles out of town. Straight up number 26 and across the Gannon's Narrows. Ask up there. Everyone's bound to know it. Biggest thing that's happened out that way in a coon's age."

"What a pretty pooch," said the man's wife. Buzz thanked the couple and had to tug a bit to take the article away from her. He grabbed his coffee and headed back to his car. He still had the hero's touch after all.

TWENTY-SIX

Perko fumed. The Grant bastard still hadn't shown up. The more he thought about it, the more he wished they'd leaned on Little Miss Tie-Dye when they had the chance. Whatever. It made no difference to this part of his plan. He waited in the bushes until Jonah showed up on the crotch rocket.

As Jonah got off his bike, Perko hiked up his chaps and strutted through the undergrowth to Ernie's clearing.

"Wow, big fire," Jonah said. "Izzat the one my pa was on about?"

"You got it."

"Roast in Hell." Jonah glanced around. "Where's your wheels at?"

"Camouflaged. We gotta move fast. You bring the explosives?"

Jonah pointed to the satchel strapped to the back of the trail bike.

"You straight with the instructions?"

"Yep. Old hat."

"Then wire the dynamite to the underside of that there outhouse."

Jonah gagged at the skunk in the shithole. He fished it out and pitched a few shovelfuls of composting crap over top of it before strapping the sticks of explosive to the cavity under the shitter.

"Man this thing is built but good. They's like an oil drum or somethin' under here on the inside. Prob'ly hardly smells at all when she's set right."

Perko stood at a distance and picked his teeth. With his luck, Hawk or Mongoose would show up early and his plan would be foiled. He needn't have worried. Jonah worked fast.

"That'll do her!" the yokel called out, beaming like a proud puppy.

"Good. Now, give me a hand righting the damn thing."

The two men groaned and strained and pushed the heavy structure back upright.

"Built like a rocket," Jonah said.

"Guess the old fucker had time on his hands." Perko wiped the sweat from his forehead as he walked away, putting distance between himself and the outhouse. "I scouted a location by the shoreline. It'll put you a couple hundred feet away. That bunch of brambles will keep anyone from wandering over."

"And you want I should run my ignition wire from here to there?"

"Yeah, get at it."

Jonah did as he was told. Perko helped, covering bits of exposed wire with loose leaves. The fire mess made concealment easy. When the job was done, Perko showed Jonah where to hide his bike.

"Sit tight on the shore," he told him. "The guy you're waiting for is big as a brick shithouse. He'll be wearing a black leather jacket, bright red hair standing up on top like a rooster; he spits a lot. Thing is, there's another guy may come first. He's skinny, my height, has a pony tail. He is *not* your target. Got that?"

"Blow the fuck out of the rooster." Jonah spat for emphasis.

He was well-hidden by the time Hawk showed up for his turn on the stake-out. Perko was pissed. It would have been so much simpler had Mongoose taken the second shift. His demolition expert was at the ready; he felt in his bones that Danny Grant *and the money* were nearby; and he desperately wanted to see Mongoose blown to smithereens. He'd even planned to stick around and watch. Now, he had no choice but to drag his ass back to The Boathouse and practice patience one more time.

"Punk-ass farmer is hooked up with granola girl from across the street," Perko told the senior Libido. "Saw his shirt in her laundry. He'll be back."

"You'd better hope so," Hawk said. "Thing is, Perko, I'm not so sure Mongoose won't want to beat your head in, regardless, after all the grief you've caused us."

Perko watched Hawk, waiting for a smile, a wink, anything. Hawk was stone-faced. Without so much as a sneer, he said, "Just sayin'." He spun around, whipping Perko's cheek with his steel-nutted pony tail, and walked to the bushes.

Perko took his sweet time getting back to The Boathouse. He rode up and down every county road on the way into Buckhorn, breathing in the crisp autumn air. He knew it was a long shot he'd see the car belonging to the neighbor chick, but anything was better than chilling with Mongoose.

When he arrived, he immediately asked the waitress to deliver an extra-wide slice of raisin pie to the other biker where he sat by the window. It paid to know a man's weaknesses. Then he went to the can and shoved three rolls of paper down the toilet, causing a minor flood and putting the washroom out of order. He called Jonah on the burner to give him the green light. "Remember. He's a big motherfucker with a Mohawk 'do. Not the guy you just saw me with. Can't miss him. He should be there in an hour or so." With a gut full of breakfast grease, the raisin pie was bound to push Mongoose to the outhouse when he arrived at the cabin for his watch.

While Perko was on the phone, some scrawny guy with long blond hair perched himself at the bar. He made a production of ordering one bourbon, one scotch, and one beer. Perko watched the newcomer throw back the shot of bourbon and smack his lips. He dipped his tongue into the scotch, then downed it with the same elaborate arm movement, elbow high, banging the shot glass so hard Perko half-expected it to shatter. Hardly skipping a beat, the guy picked up the mug of beer and blew the head of foam across the wooden bar. He chugged about half, then slammed it down with the same force as the shot glasses before it.

"Here's to Mr. Thorogood!" he said, flashing Perko a toothy grin.

"Big fan, are you?" Perko didn't think he'd ever seen anyone act out the famous blues song before.

"Closest I ever came to seeing Hendrix on stage."

Perko said, "Huh?"

"You know, the whole *Johnny B. Goode* thing. Damn good cover."

"Right."

"Just thought I needed a special kind of toast today. Hey, Barmaid! How about a round for my friend here?"

The waitress glanced at Perko. He nodded. Shooting the shit with this joker would be a welcome relief from Mongoose's incessant bitching. "What's the occasion?" he asked.

The new guy said, "Buddy o' mine got out of jail, is all."

"Lucky him," said Perko, doing a quick mental check to make sure no one he cared about was due for release.

"Yep sirree," the blowhard went on. "My good ol' buddy ol' pal just got free and gave me a nice wad o' cash for looking after his cat while he was inside." He pulled a roll of bills from his jacket pocket and thumbed it with pride. "Nice cat. Shed a little much. Hated changing the litter." He raised a finger signaling another shot.

Perko thought even Mongoose's moaning might be better than listening to this bullshit.

The stranger raised his shot glass and said, "Here's to Danny Grant."

Perko had his mouth full of bourbon when the name reached his brain. He snorted. Eighty-proof alcohol flooded his sinus cavity, making his eyes water and sending a hot shot up his nostrils.

"You say 'Grant?'" he managed to sputter.

"Yep. Good ol' Danny. Known him my whole life. He went away for better part of four years. Just got out this week."

"Really. What was he in for?" Perko struggled to keep his hand from shaking, the shot glass clattering against the top of the bar. He let it go and watched it roll into the glass rail.

"Oh, this and that," the long-haired dork seemed to relish the attention. "A little trouble with a baseball bat, but really, he was into like growing pot and stuff. Serious bad guy. Anyway, he called me up this morning said he wanted to give me five hundred dollars for taking care of his cat, and asked if I'd drive him over to Bobcaygeon. He said he had some banking to do. Helluva nice guy. You know him?"

"Never met him. Thanks for the drink."

Perko got off the barstool and ambled over to where Mongoose was busily stuffing the last of the pie into his mouth, wiping up the plate with his index finger. Perko gave his chair a little kick from behind and said, "Caught a break. Text Hawk and tell him to get his ass back over here. We've got work to do."

Hunched down in the back of Judy's car, racing back to her place, Danny looked up at the back of her head and marveled at how nice she was being to him. He thanked her for about the hundredth time for loaning him the five hundred bucks. Without it, he doubted he'd have been able to convince Terry to risk his life with the bikers.

"Least I can do," Judy said. "Ernie would be helping you if he were alive. It's kind of in his memory, I guess, that I'm doing this."

Danny couldn't help but think the ten grand he'd promised her for her troubles held some sway in the "least I can do" department.

As they pulled into her driveway, a volley of backfires erupted from the bushes a couple hundred feet up the road. Danny peeked out the window to watch a Harley speed away. The rider was tall and thin with a scraggly grey pony tail that hung limp over the unmistakable Libidos patch on his black leather jacket. Danny was surprised it wasn't the chunkster, but it didn't matter: Terry had done his thing.

TWENTY-SEVEN

Perko tightened the bungee cord around Terry Miner's chest and said, "This'll keep you from falling in the water." Then he climbed back up the ladder on the side of the lock, grinding his boots onto the guy's shoulders and head for good measure.

Mongoose stared over the edge and nodded with a half-smile. "Gots to hand it to ya, Perks. Not a bad idea."

They had strapped Terry to the ladder that descended into the concrete-walled channel between two enormous wooden gates. The channel was wide enough for two large boats side by side and over a hundred feet long. In peak season, as many as ten boats would be tied off in the lock. Water was alternately flowed in or drained, moving boats between Buckhorn Lake and Lower Buckhorn Lake, whose levels were about six feet different depending on the season.

Since he was tied to a ladder on the lock wall, only Terry's feet were wet for the moment. Once the lock filled, however, he would find himself under water up to his forehead.

The lock master just happened to enjoy the kind of favors the Libidos were known to dispense among locals. They were friendly to those who helped move guns, drugs, and assorted chattel around the neighborhood by whichever means were most convenient. Perko gave him a thumbs up and called over the side, "You know how this works, Terry—if that's your real name. It'll take all of seven minutes for the water to rise to the level of your chin. If you're done talking by then, I'll let Billy-Bob over there know he can close the valves while I untie you. If, on the other hand, I'm not happy with what you've told us, well, you'll be done talking anyway. Way I see it, you've got, oh, I dunno, six and half minutes to convince me I should let you live." The biker lit a cigarette, his hand cupped to protect the match from the wind.

"I don't get it," Terry whined. "I told you where to find the dude who stole your money and now you want to drown me?"

"Kind of. Yeah."

"But why? I can, like, you know, be useful to the gang and all. Hey, you guys want a boat? Real nice Sea Ray—thirty-three footer. I got a key and everything."

Perko spat into the water. "Focus, punk. Listen to the questions." Terry jerked his head up and down. Perko said, "You just finished lying to me about some fucking cat. We were all over that punk's life when he disappeared into prison. He never had a cat."

"Alls we want is to make sure you tell us the truth, the holy truth, and no butts," added Mongoose. "You do that, we cut the cords and you swim on outta here."

Perko looked across the water. The motel was closed for the season and there was just one car parked outside the hardware store—likely the owner's. If the dude started screaming, there would be no one to hear except the lock master and maybe the waitress in The Boathouse. He said, "Mongoose, maybe you should go keep our waitress friend busy until Hawk shows up. I got this under control."

The bigger biker snorted and shuffled off to the bar. Perko saw the water had reached Terry's knees. The man whimpered and squirmed, saying, "What do you want from me?"

"Tell me again how you know Danny Grant. And where it was you saw him."

"I told you, man. I dropped him off just outside of Bobcaygeon. At the, uh, at the bowling place."

"So a guy escapes from prison and the first thing on his mind is to go bowling."

"Escape? Danny didn't escape. He was done. On parole now."

"Parole, yes. Done, no. Danny ran away from day parole day before yesterday. We been chasing him ever since."

"No shit! Danny's an escaped con? Holy fuck is that cool."

Perko rolled his eyes and asked, "And the cat?"

"What cat?"

"Danny's cat you said you babysat for him."

"Aw, shit, so there was no cat. I just didn't think you'd believe me that Danny gave me five hundred bucks."

"So you see why maybe I don't believe you about the bowling."

Terry looked confused.

Perko said, "Listen. I don't know where the fuck you get your crazy ideas, but you'd better have a good one right about now or I'm out of here and you're fish food. When I cut the bungee cords, you're just one more moron who drowned swimming in the canal."

"Alright, alright! I'll tell you what I know. But, first, you gotta know this wasn't my idea."

Perko took a drag of his cigarette, sat down on the top rung of the ladder and rested a foot on Terry's head. He said, "Spill it."

"You know how Danny ran your grow op?"

"Uh huh."

"Well, that was supposed to be me."

Perko remained silent.

"And my buddy-ol'-pal, Danny Grant, well, didn't he just go steal my rightful job. Right out from under me, like."

"Go on."

"So, then he, like, he stole your money from you. See I would never have done that. I would never have got the place busted and I would never have taken your money. It shoulda been me running that scene and then everything would have been cool."

"What's this bullshit about Danny giving you five hundred bucks?"

"That part's true."

"And the bowling alley?"

"I made that up."

"Like the part about the cat."

"Shit, Danny told me to tell you that I left him in Bobcaygeon. Like twenty minutes ago. Hey, have him stop the water, man. It's freezing my balls off!"

Perko dropped his cigarette into the water and lit another one. "It's always a bit chilly this time of year, don't you find?"

Terry sputtered. "And...and...and Danny said he'd pay me thirty thousand dollars just for talking to you. Hey, maybe I could, like, split the thirty thou with you?"

Perko dropped his feet so they dangled to the right and left of Terry's head. He swung them out and let them flop back down, boxing his victim's ears with a thud. "WHERE DID YOU LEAVE HIM?!"

Terry's head bobbled and flopped and came to rest with his chin on his chest. Perko swung himself around and used one leg to splash ice cold water on his face. "I SAID WHERE?!"

"I...uh...oh shit. I dunno. He just...he said...he wanted me to send you away from the fire scene. Place where I saved a pooch last week. Said he'd give me thirty thousand bucks. Just needed an hour or so."

"Son of a bitch." Perko pulled himself up and looked over toward where his bike was parked. If he split now, he could just make it onto a side road before Hawk passed him coming the other way. He could still recover the money on his own, and decide later whether he wanted to be a big shot Libido or just a loaded biker on the run.

"Hey, tell him to turn off the water," Terry said.

Perko stepped back from the edge, saying nothing.

"Aw, c'mon," Terry said. "Listen, can I still get the thirty thou? Maybe a little finder's fee bonus or something?" The water had made it to Terry's chest. "How about ten grand? You'd never notice ten off the top, would you? Hey! Hey, you still there?"

Perko took one last glance at Terry Miner, struggling in vain against the straps around his chest and wrists. A small mouth bass swam up and nibbled his neck. If it tickled, he didn't show it.

Officer Max Ainsley offered Linette Paquin a cigarette across the front seat of his cruiser.

"Thank you, Officer," Linette cooed. They were driving back to her car after having carried their shared fantasy back to her apartment. Linette had insisted Max pretend it was the county jail. They'd been creative with handcuffs all night long and slept until well past noon.

"You're wilder by the day," he said.

"Play your cards right, I know a little clearing where you can tie me up. And interrogate me. Woodsy-like."

He growled his best bear imitation and said, "Hang on a sec while I check in with dispatch." He switched on his radio. "Nine fourteen. Check-in. You there, dispatch?"

After a pause, the radio crackled: "*Base to Nine Fourteen. Afternoon, Max. That was quite the tummy ache, I guess.*"

"What do you mean, Chuck?"

"*Been trying to raise you since last night. That escaped con yesterday? Turns out it was Danny Grant. You know, that punk you, uh, nearly busted for only the biggest pot shop this county has ever seen.*"

Max scowled at the mention of the grow op gardener's name. "No shit. Have we picked him up yet?" He looked at Linette.

"*Naw, it seems he made it all the way to the States in some RV he'd stolen. Kidnapped an old lady and everything. Forced her to do the border crossing. Apparently, he threatened to expose her son-in-law as a witch or some damn thing. Then he drives her all the way south of Rochester. Lucky for her, they ran out of gas before he could get wherever he was headed. Left her stranded at the side of the road. She flagged down a radio car for help. They've got a massive search on in northern New York. That's why I was radioing you.*"

"What can I do about it?"

"*They want to know why he would have taken off that direction. Any connections you know of?*"

"The Skeletons. They're the ones bought the dope."

"*Yeah, they thought of that. Seems strange he would go running there, though. I mean, unless he was somehow connected. You know, the whole thing some scam against the Libidos all along.*"

"Huh. Never thought of that." Officer Ainsley wrinkled his brow. Linette was waving her arms at him to get off the radio. "Guess we're lucky he left our jurisdiction. Would have hated to miss my long weekend."

"Perfect fishing weather. Sure wish I was off. See you in a bit, Max"

He turned off the radio. Linette's jaw was working hard but the words barely made it out of her mouth: "...ugh...I...there...I mean...something's messed...go straight to ERNIE'S."

"What the hell are you on about, Linette?"

She took several deep breathes before speaking again.

"Don't you *see*? If Danny splits from prison right after Ernie's place burns, it's got to be related."

"Could be, yeah. So what?"

"So Ernie's place is burned, right? If Danny runs from prison, it must mean he knows the cash isn't in the cabin, right?"

"Right, because he figures the Skeletons have it and they burned Ernie once they got their bony hands on it. *They're looking for him in New York, Linette.* Why go to the cabin?"

"Because...because...because there was no need to burn down the cabin. The money has to be outside. Don't ask me how I know, Max." Officer Ainsley looked at her as though he didn't recognize her.

"This isn't your M.O., Linette," he said.

"Just take me there. *Please?*"

In no time at all, Danny discovered what had to be the remnants of Ernie's previous outhouse. The ground was mounded up a bit and it was covered with exceptionally healthy poison ivy. What really gave it away, though, was the evidence of non-stop human traffic leading to what had once been the back door to Ernie's cabin. Even after a couple years of disuse, the telltale packed earth and exposed ground stone was clear as day.

He started digging.

Compared to the hole he had dug the night before, this one was somewhat harder going. He was happy for the strong cold wind blowing off the north end of Pigeon Lake. The first few inches were cover soil. That was followed by heavily compacted human waste filled with worms and other creepy crawlies busily returning dust to dust.

Danny had only gotten about twelve inches into the ground when the sound of a footstep from the forest behind him made him stop what he was doing and spin around. The wind was so loud, the dude from the diner had made it within a few feet of him before Danny heard anything.

"Arh, matey. Digging for gold, are we?" the biker said, looking even nastier than he remembered him.

Danny stood frozen to his spot. Even without the distortion, his gut instantly reacted to the voice from the telephone from four years before: his boss, the bastard biker whose plants he'd tended.

The man said, "The chores they gave you on the inside weren't shitty enough? You had to break out and dig dirt?" It was the disdain. The way he made Danny feel worthless. His knuckles turned white, wrapped tight around the handle of the shovel as the biker stepped toward him.

"Whatcha gonna do? Dig up a whole Kawartha acre until you find *my stash?*"

Danny swung. The thug was ready for it. He threw up his arm and blocked the shot, sending the shovel spinning out of Danny's hands. He lurched forward and grabbed Danny by the hair, yanking his head down toward the ground so that he was bent double at the waist. As he went down, Danny saw the biker pull a gun from a holster under his armpit. A second later, he felt it jam into the base of his skull.

"Now, you little prick, you've got two options. One, you pick up that shovel and start digging again for Captain Perko. Two, I bury you headfirst in the old man's shit—'cept we'll use the fresher hole over there. What's it gonna be, punk?"

Danny grimaced. "I'll do what you say."

"'I'll do what you say, *Captain.*'"

"Yes, Captain. Whatever you say, Captain."

The biker stepped back from the hole and kept the gun pointed at Danny.

"Dig, motherfucker."

As Danny dug, he wondered why the hell Judy hadn't given him a warning signal. She mustn't have seen the meathead approach, but surely she could see him now, pointing the gun at him. He stole a couple glances across the road when he pitched shovelfuls of dirt that direction, enough to determine she wasn't outside. But he didn't want to send the biker's attention in that direction either, so he focused his energy on digging up the cash. Now he knew the guy's name and face, Danny had no illusions. His reward for unearthing the bag would be to get shot in the head.

It took twenty minutes to empty Ernie's Shitter Number One. The two men looked down at the exposed roots and raw rock. Everything coated in muck. No bag, no money, just heavy brown compost with a noxious smell.

Danny felt faint. Four years of waiting, two piles of stinking dirt, and now all he had to look forward to was getting shot and buried in Ernie's shithole.

"What now?" he asked. Turning to face Captain Perko, he saw Judy sneaking toward them; it was all he could do to stare unblinking into the man's eyes while she crept up behind.

"Here's what now. You tell me who the hell knew where you buried my money," the biker growled loudly. Danny took a half step backward away from the hole, drawing the chaps-clad chunkster with him. Judy's normally yappy dog was all hunkered down, belly to the ground, creeping along behind her.

"Nobody knew anything," Danny said. "This is where I left it, and I never told no one. Shit, I don't know. Maybe the cops found it?" Judy had made it right up behind Perko and crouched down between him and the outhouse hole.

"Gimme a break, punk, I'm gonna—"

As he started to take a step toward Danny, Judy ploughed into his knees from behind and Danny lunged at him. It was enough to table-top the much heavier man into the hole, headfirst. Wort jumped forward, snapping and snarling as loud as a dog three times his size, coming close to sliding into the hole.

"RUN. Get your car," Danny said. He whacked the biker's squirming body with the shovel before piling several shovels full of composted crap onto his head.

As they started up the laneway, a cop car came over the rise, traveling fast.

"Shit. Now what?" said Danny.

"To the water. Ernie's got a canoe." Judy took off toward the lake, Danny half-running, half-sliding down the hill behind her. Wort paused to kick a little extra dirt into the hole.

By the time Perko managed to pull himself out of the shithole, he found himself face-to-face with a cop. Not just any cop. It was the same damn cop who had frog-marched him out of the forest four years before.

"Jesus, Mr. Ratwick. Do you *always* smell like shit?" Officer Ainsley grinned.

"Fuck to see you, too, Officer."

A familiar-looking woman stumbled up behind, struggling in high heels on the soft ground. When she got close enough, Perko made her for the punk farmer's lawyer.

"What are you doing here?" Linette Paquin hissed. "Are you *stealing* my money?"

"What money? Your money? Who said anything about money?" Perko stammered. "I'm just out for a ride, noticed this here cookout and came in for a look-see. I don't know a thing about no money."

"You mind telling me how you ended up with your head in that there hole," Officer Ainsley asked, visibly stifling a chuckle.

"And, and, and what was in that hole?" asked Linette, clearly failing to find any humor in the situation. "And *what's* that over there?" She had just noticed the pile of dirt over by the outhouse and hurried over to take a look, breaking a heel on the way.

Ainsley glowered at Perko and said, "Spill it. Unless you want to ride back to the station with me. Frankly, I don't want you in my car, covered in shit and all, but I *will* run you in if you don't start talking."

Perko spat, wiped his lip on the cleaner of his two hands, and cringed. "Asshole punk farmer brat bastard pushed me in the fucking hole."

"Who?" asked Officer Ainsley.

"That fucker Danny Grant." Perko saw no percentage in lying. Whatever went down next, by now the cops would know Danny had run and it wouldn't take them long to connect his own Kingston arrest to the shithead's escape. The last thing he needed was to be tossed back in a cell for questioning, while Grant ran around on the outside. "I trailed him to the Greyhound day before yesterday and figured this was where he was headed. Then the fucker dumps me in the hole. Someone helped him do it. Tripped me. Who the fuck, I don't know."

"Where are they now?"

"Headed toward the water."

The two men walked past the remains of the cabin to a spot where they could see the lake. Perko's heart pounded. Danny and that chick from across the road were paddling a red canoe five hundred feet off shore. He was sorely tempted to pull out his gun and take a shot, but he figured he'd miss. Never mind that he didn't imagine the cop would be all that impressed. That, and the barrel was undoubtedly clogged full of shit.

A shriek cut through the air and both men turned to where Linette had found the dead skunk beside the outhouse—Jonah hadn't done a particularly good job of burying it. One hand clasped to her mouth, she staggered away from the outhouse and sank to the ground, sobbing hysterically.

Ainsley got down on one knee beside her and put his arm around her shoulder. Perko stared down at the two of them. It sunk in that the cop and the lawyer shared more than a business relationship. He said, "Mind if I ask why you two are here?"

"Linette?" Ainsley prodded. "Could tell me that now? How did you know Danny would be here? You were in such a rush to come..."

"I didn't know he was here," she coughed. "I just knew the money had to be."

"I don't get it. How did you know?"

"Because it wasn't in the cabin!" she croaked, and then broke into gut-wrenching sobs. Ainsley held her, rubbing her shoulders as they heaved and shook with her crying. Perko looked on, dumbfounded.

"Maybe you should explain that to us, lady," said the biker.

She looked up at him with her mascara-streamed face and blubbered, "I knew the money wasn't in the cabin because I searched it."

"Yeah, the lady from across the road told me you were here the day before yesterday."

"But the cabin had already burned by then," Ainsley interrupted.

Linette looked from one to the other, her eyes ringed like a raccoon.

"I searched it...before...before the fire," she stammered.

"What? You never told me that. How'd you manage that?" He glanced at the pile of ashes. "Ernie hated you. Did you break in, Linette?"

"No break. Just enter. I had come by to talk to him. Persuade *him*. He was down at the dock. The wind was blowing heavy off the lake so I knew he hadn't heard me. I snuck in to have a look."

Both men continued to stare. Ainsley stood up and took a step back.

"I searched the place. Top to *bottom*. I kept looking out the window to make sure he wasn't coming back. He was fishing. I had time. I looked everywhere. In the closets, under his bed, the sink. Everywhere. The money wasn't there."

Ainsley shook his head.

"Oh, he had the money alright," Linette said. "He had a TV worth five thousand dollars and he had crates of stuff—a full box of single malt scotch, a ton of *peanut* butter, and other stuff...stuff people don't have when they're on social assistance. Things he had no right to afford.

"I crawled up into the rafters when I heard him putting his gear in the shed." She looked from one man to the other, quickly. "He came back in the cabin. Right away, there was a scuffle, Ernie shouting, and then a gun blast. And another. I didn't move for maybe half an hour. Whoever shot him just left."

"So then what?" asked Ainsley.

"When it had been quiet *for a while*, I crept down from the rafters and there he was. Dead." She looked at the ground, breathed deep, then turned her eyes back to Ainsley. "I didn't kill him, Max. Really. I just..."

She pointed at the charred ruins of what had once been Ernie's home. "Lying there in the doorway to his home...the gun that killed him at his side. It was horrible...I think I threw up..."

Officer Ainsley shot a glance at Perko and moved his hand to his hip, reflexively, seemingly stunned to find no holster there. Linette breathed deeply, trying to regain a little composure. Perko was impressed. "So then you torched the cabin?" he asked. "Why?"

"No, I didn't do that, either. I was freaked out, for sure, but I figured there was no way anyone could tie me to his death. I had *parked* down around the corner. I wanted to sneak up without that little busybody from across the street coming over to stick her nose in my business with Ernie. Besides, I'm still an officer of the *court*. No one's going to blame me. Good riddance, I thought, and I just needed to get away from this place."

"Linette, this is a real problem," said Ainsley. "The man was burned to a crisp. The fire marshal's report was inconclusive. With all the empty bottles lying around, everyone figured he'd gone on a tear and burned the place down himself. If someone killed him because of the money—"

He leaned back against the trunk of a massive sugar maple. "You just confessed to something. Knowledge of something at least. Accomplice, I don't know."

"I didn't do anything, Max. Trespass, maybe, but the door was open, and—"

"Uh, and then the door had a dead man lying in it," said Perko.

"You had motive. Opportunity," the cop counted out on his fingertips.

"Max..."

"Seems you two have plenty to talk about. I guess I'll be on my way," Perko said. "And, Officer Ainsley—"

The cop made no move to stop him.

"—I reckon you owe me one," Perko said.

He turned his back and marched over the hill to where he'd left his Harley. He had parked the other side of the rise, so Danny wouldn't hear him approach. Fuck of a lot of good that had done him.

He really didn't give a shit *who* had killed Ernst McCann. Except that the killer was probably the same person who had his money. Danny Grant had come here for the stash and Perko believed the thieving bastard really was as surprised as he was that the dough was gone. Still, he didn't have a clue where to look next. All he could do was hope the punk had more ideas than he did. By now, Danny and the girl had a decent head start in the canoe. He needed to get his hands on a boat and fast.

And he still had Mongoose to worry about. He needed a new excuse to send him back here to the burnt-out cabin and the outhouse. (Jonah could freeze his ass off waiting, as far as Perko was concerned.) And how could he tell Hawk he had let Danny get away? Without the cash. One thing he knew: if the punk didn't lead him to his money, he'd make damn sure the fucker died trying.

He climbed back on his Harley for the ride back to The Boathouse, hoping Mongoose would have relieved Terry Miner of the keys to the Sea Ray before the loudmouth drowned. He cranked the accelerator wide open and took air coming over a rise half a mile from the cabin.

And he said a prayer.

TWENTY-EIGHT

Buzz Meckler was freaked. Rounding a blind corner less than a mile from the place in the photo, he nearly creamed some guy on a chopper. The guy's bike slid out from under him, showering Buzz's windshield with gravel. Like it was a normal everyday thing, the rider stood up, brushed his leather chaps and strode toward the car, stopping cold ten feet away.

"What the—" the man said.

In spite of the dramatic costume change, there was no question: Buzz was face-to-face with the dude in the bad brown suit who'd attacked him at the bus station. He started to open the car door, aching for revenge, then thought better of it when the man pulled a gun from under his leather jacket.

Buzz slammed his foot on the gas, peeling out, his door flapping shut. A crash behind him showered him in glass from the rear window.

For a second, he considered pulling a one-eighty and confronting the guy. Wasn't that what a real hero would do? But the biker had a gun, so short of running him over, Buzz was at a loss how to deal with him. Besides, the guy was racing *away from* the cabin fire's location. Who knew what dastardly deeds the outlaw might have committed? His latest victim might need Buzz's help. There *had* to be a victim at the fire scene. Didn't every scoundrel leave a trail of victims? That's how it always worked.

Less than a minute later, Buzz narrowly missed a second head-on collision, this time with a cop car that fishtailed around a bend. His tires churned the soft shoulder. As the car blew past, he had time to see a woman in the passenger seat. She seemed to be yelling at the policeman driving. *Hot pursuit!* thought Buzz. *We all have our roles to play.*

He was shaken when he arrived at the scorched scene. He sat there wondering what to do next. His latest extra-large double-

double cup of coffee had gone cold, but he drained it anyway. He got out and scanned the lot. No victims. He decided a little investigative stroll might give him some ideas. He looked at the freshly dug hole and then noticed the outhouse on the other side of the burned-out cabin. He wandered over and opened the door.

It looked clean enough.

Jonah was fit to be tied. What started out as a simple game of *blow-up* had become one of the longest afternoons of his life. Why the hell hadn't Perko warned him this was going to be a bloody circus?

No sooner had he got comfortable by the shore than some scrawny bugger with a pony tail had shown up and started blabbing with Perko. Then the new guy hid himself, too, which kind of stuck in Jonah's craw. But what did he know about professional hit men. Maybe they always worked in pairs. Besides, it wasn't long before the guy ran from the bushes and hightailed it away on his motorbike.

Soon as the longhair disappeared, some dickwad showed up and started digging a hole in the ground. Jonah was tempted to blow *him* up just for practice, but he never went near the outhouse.

When Perko himself showed up again, Jonah watched in frustration as Perko held a gun on the dirt digger while the guy shoveled deeper and deeper into the ground. As impressed as Jonah was that the biker was getting the guy to dig what was starting to look like his own grave, he was pissed with being hung out to dry with the damn detonator. He crept halfway up the hill with a view to giving Perko a piece of his mind. He was almost within shouting distance when some girl came out of nowhere and the biker ended up tossed into the hole the other dude dug.

Jonah's head was spinning. Should he give chase? Run and help Perko? Before he could make up his mind, some cop rushed in with a lady who looked like she was on her way to a wedding or something, all dressed up and such—and Jonah'd had quite enough of cops of late. He skulked back to his hidey hole, spitting curses, and watched dickwad shovel guy and the other chick make off in a canoe.

Ten minutes later Perko, the cop, and the fancy lady were all gone, too. The sun was low in the sky and it was getting darn cold.

This was not the deal he had struck.

Perko had promised it'd be quick, simple, and back to the motel for booty call. Instead, he was likely to end up with a bad case of poison ivy and a runny nose. He was about to leave when another car pulled in. At first, Jonah dismissed the new arrival as yet another clown, but then the guy stepped out of the car. He wasn't riding a Harley and his clothes looked like they'd been picked out by his mother, but he was big enough to fit the bill and his hair, while brown, all stood up on top of his head. Besides, after barely a minute, he headed straight for the outhouse.

Jonah licked his fingers and pulled the detonator onto his lap. He stroked the wire that ran from it and watched as his target stepped into the shitter. He waited, salivating, savoring the moment, and then pressed the red button firmly.

And it blew.

Man, did it blow.

The shitter really was built like a rocket. Watching it lift off was like nothing Jonah had ever experienced. His chest filled with pride, and he wished his Pa were there to see it with him.

The outhouse sailed straight up and over the bushes where Jonah was hiding. It splashed down into the lake behind him and a small part of him wanted to go have a look at the damage he'd done. A far bigger part of him, however, urged him to hightail it back to Aunt Helena's Mexican Restaurant and Motel, which is exactly what he did.

Stephanie Silver was easily the spunkiest gal Rick Stevens had met since graduating top of his class in finance and administration. She was also the hottest, by a long shot, to accept one of his oft-declined invitations to a weekend in the country. Rick had concocted an image of the perfect romantic weekend. It involved a roaring fire, hard-to-pronounce wine, and soft acoustic jazz recorded someplace warm and Latin. Unfortunately, he was woefully unprepared when Stephanie Silver said, "Sure, I'll go. How about this Thursday?"

Since Rick had only ever *dreamed* about sweet romance in the boonies, and since his budget precluded either of the four-star inns still open late October in the Kawarthas, he'd done the next best thing. He'd rented a houseboat.

The last houseboat, actually, according to the grizzled rental guy who'd taken a good long look at Stephanie's ass as she climbed aboard. The guy had chortled about being careful "not to make too many waves at anchor." Then he'd wandered back to the marina parking lot, bouncing the keys to Rick's freshly-leased BMW in the palm of his hand.

Stephanie told Rick overnighting in a floating trailer park special was not exactly what she called luxury *or* romantic.

"You heard the guy," Rick protested. "Everything else is dry-docked. The season's almost over. We were lucky they still had this baby on the water. Hey look, pumpkin, it's got a space heater and everything!"

Turned out the forty-foot floater handled a little differently than your average cigarette boat. It had taken nearly two hours to fight their way four miles up the lake into the wind. At first, Rick hugged the shore for fear of open water. Twice, he crunched the pontoons onto barely submerged boulders. The sickening groan they produced was only slightly more discouraging than Stephanie's non-stop muttering about freezing her tush off on this fisherman's yacht.

She paced back and forth, hugging a bright purple fleece tightly around herself. Rick wore an identical jacket, having bought the pair at Walmart in a fit of ardor that morning. He hoped the fact she was still wearing hers meant they might yet cuddle by the electric fireplace when the sun went down.

He was fumbling with his iPod, looking for a little Spanish guitar, when a thunderous crash sucked the air out of the houseboat cabin.

Together, Rick and Stephanie rushed out the door to see an outhouse sail through the sky. It flew over top of them, and splashed down a few hundred feet away. As the shack fell toward the water, they listened to a non-stop stream of obscenities so blue Rick cupped his hands over Stephanie's ears. Soft brown pellets drifted to the water, not a few of them splattering on the houseboat deck. Clods stuck to their spanking new purple fleeces.

It took a moment for Rick to comprehend he and his intended had been showered in shit.

In a bright red canoe approaching the houseboat's stern, Danny and Judy watched the same explosion.

Judy stopped paddling, her head shaking with short jerky movements. "Paddle hard," Danny said in a low voice. Wort cowered in the bottom of the boat.

Within a minute, they had reached the houseboat and pulled up alongside just as the motor restarted. Danny clambered onto one of the pontoons. Judy threw the bow rope around a strut.

Danny marched through the houseboat's rear bedroom and surprised the couple huddled by the steering wheel. "Gonna make a trade," was all he said.

"What the...? Who the hell are you?" the man said.

"*I'm* the guy stealing your boat. *You're* the guy not putting up a fight."

The man started to protest, but Danny grabbed his wrist and pulled one well-manicured hand behind his back. "Okay! Okay!" the guy said. "You can have the boat. Just take us to shore and—"

"You get off here," Danny snapped.

"But, but, but I can't swim!" the wiener whined.

"Shut it. Take your lady friend out the back. There's a canoe there."

The man didn't move. He actually smiled as the woman buried her face in his chest.

"NOW. Or I'll throw you off the damn boat and you can learn to swim on your way to shore."

"But there was an explosion..."

"We heard screaming." The woman started to blubber.

Danny grabbed the man's elbow and ushered him along with the weepy woman to the back of the houseboat. Judy had already climbed on deck with Wort. She wore an apologetic half smile and shrugged a little as Danny squeezed past her with his charges. The canoe rocked and nearly overturned as he thrust them aboard. As they drifted away, facing each other, Danny heard them argue about which end of the canoe was the front. He hustled back to the captain's chair and gave the boat full throttle. The motor roared but the craft moved near as slow as the canoe. He was pretty damn sure he could swim faster.

"Run that one by me again?" Hawk growled. "You say you had the guy in your hands and you let him run?"

Perko stood in front of the table in The Boathouse with his hands in his pockets. "Like I said, the cops showed up. Must've put two and two together. There was about ten of them. Lights, sirens, everything. I couldn't very well let them take him in, could I? Haul his ass back to prison for who knows how long? Then how'd we get the money back?"

"So you let him go?"

"Uh huh."

"*With* our money."

"Well, I, uh, I didn't...that is, he didn't exactly *have* it while I was holding him."

"What?"

"He...I was shaking him. Like this." Perko pulled his hands from his pockets and made like he was strangling someone with his bare hands. "And then I let him go 'cause the cops came, and then, when he was running away toward the water, I saw him pick up a duffel bag. Must've dug it up before I got there. He had it hiding behind a tree, I guess. Took it with him in the canoe." Perko looked at his feet.

So far, neither had said a word about Mongoose. Perko had dialed Jonah from The Boathouse parking lot before coming in, intending to tell him the deal was off, he could go play at Auntie Helena's. Instead, Jonah told him he was already back at the hotel, and that Mongoose was splattered across the lake. "Blowed up somethin' fierce" were his exact words. Perko had been struggling to contain his glee while Hawk interrogated him. He was so giddy he was afraid he'd mix his lies up with his exaggerations.

Hawk was saying, "No matter how the bastard got away, fact is, he's got our money; he's on the water; we go get it."

"What about Mongoose?" Perko asked, figuring it was the thing to do.

"He took off back to the cabin when I showed up. Looking for *you*," Hawk said. "Far as I could tell, he was on his way to crack your skull. Pissed you'd left him alone with the boat thief."

Perko fought back a grin. "We'll see who cracks who," he said, trying not to sound glib. "So you gave him the green light on me?"

Hawk ignored the question.

Perko said, "The other rat. Miner what's-his-name. Drowned?"

"Nope," said Hawk. "Thought he might come in handy. He knows Grant. He's tied up outside, behind the garbage bins."

"He was bragging about some boat he could get us."

Hawk nodded. "If the cops are swarming, we're going to need some lead. I'll call our guy in Bobcaygeon while you get the boat. And Perko?"

"Yeah?"

"You smell like shit.'"

TWENTY-NINE

"Now what?" Judy asked.

Danny looked at her, sitting with Wort on her lap. The late afternoon sun barely lit the houseboat's cabin but still her hair kind of glowed. He felt terrible he'd dragged her into his mess.

As if she could read his mind, she said, "I'm okay with this, you know. I mean, I could do without running from the police and being chased by a biker gang. But I'm okay about stealing this boat."

"Really?" Danny said.

"Do you have any idea how much garbage these houseboat partiers leave in the water? They're worse than fishermen. And I swear one of their bonfires is going to burn down a forest."

Danny nodded. Most island parties he'd been to were a potent mix of beer, sun, and motorized amusement.

"Still," Judy said, "I wouldn't mind knowing where we're headed."

"I wish to hell I could tell you," Danny answered. He'd been scanning the shoreline for evidence of a faster boat he could steal. Even a fourteen-footer with a nine horse motor would be an improvement on this tug, but each time he spotted one, it was docked at one of the few cottages with smoke pouring out the chimney. Everywhere else he looked, the docks had been lifted, made ready for winter.

Judy set Wort on the cabin floor and came over to stand beside him at the wheel. She asked, "If you don't know where we're headed, then where are we going?"

He ignored her question and breathed deeply. With the window open, fresh water sprayed him each time the pontoon splashed across a big wave. He knew it should feel liberating, but all thoughts of freedom were crowded out by the fear of getting caught. Any minute now, his sorry ass could get hauled back to his prison cell. Or stuck in some less pleasant hole.

"I haven't got a fucking clue," he said. He shut the motor off, stepped away from the window, and slumped onto the bench. Judy followed him and draped her arm over his shoulder. It was the first friendly human touch Danny had felt since his mother had disappeared. He trembled as Judy caressed his shoulder. She gripped his bicep and gave it a little squeeze before she gently pushed him to face her.

"Danny, the world doesn't end if you go back. You could call your lawyer."

He snorted.

"What's the deal for skipping out on day parole? It's not like you actually broke out of prison. You could go back. Finish up your sentence. Start over when you get out."

"You don't get it," he said, his voice cracking. "The money's gone. They know I had it and now they know it's gone. There's nothing to keep the Libidos from killing me—in or out of prison. I'm done." Danny leaned back and let the tears flow. He felt Judy brush them from his cheeks with her finger tip. He pushed her hand away, embarrassed. Next thing he felt was her lips on his wet cheek and this time he didn't resist. He popped one eye open and got a blurry look at her nose. He shut it quickly before she noticed and willed his tears to continue even though his mind was rushing in a totally different direction. He could practically feel the blood pump from his head and accompany the adrenaline rush to elsewhere.

He tilted his head back just a touch to bring his lips into contact with hers and felt her tongue slide to meet his own. He gulped and a shudder ran through his chest and arms as he wrapped her and pulled her close.

Judy straddled him and helped him pull her fleece over her head, dropping her bra to the ground before he even started to fumble with it. She tugged at his shirt and their hands tangled together on each other's belts. Together, they tumbled to the floor. After a minute or two, Judy suggested, "I think the room in back is more comfortable."

Danny followed her to the bed. He forgot everything he ever knew about prison, about running, and about boneheaded plans for life ever after on a desert isle with his mom.

For five minutes.

Lying on his back, with Judy's head lolling on his sweaty chest, Danny breathed deep and stared out at the twilit sky. Judy smelled wonderful head to toe, hairy armpits and all. He struggled to maintain the bliss, but it was swiftly crowded out by more mundane thoughts. Like how he was going to survive. And whether he'd get to have sex with Judy again before he got caught.

"I've got a friend I've got to find," he said.

Without stirring, Judy murmured, "Who's that?"

"Friend of my mom's. Bit of a wacko, lives in the bush and stuff, but he's pretty smart. Maybe I could go off the grid with him for a while. Figure things out."

"Hmmm..." She used her finger to trace lines back and forth around his belly button. "You're an outie," she said. Danny felt the blood head back to his groin, not entirely surprised Judy could bring him to attention so quickly.

"I just don't know where to find him," Danny said. "It was always the other way around. He'd find me. Or us. He showed up a lot when we went camping. And he told me Ernie could always get hold of him, if I needed it, but now..."

Judy had started nibbling Danny's nipple. She paused to say, "It's not like Ernie had a lot of friends. What's his name?" She gave him a playful bite.

"Skeritt."

"Hunh?" Judy lifted her head and looked straight at him.

"Skeritt. That's his name. I don't know if it's his last name or—"

"'Skeritt', like S-K-E-R-I-T-T?"

"How the hell do I know how he spells it? It's a weird name is all."

Judy looked confused. "Danny, I think, I mean I don't know what it means, but, there's this table Ernie had." She drew herself up on one elbow. "I took it so I'd have something to remember him by. It's in my living room now."

"Yeah, so?" Danny liked the way the sheet had fallen away from Judy's shoulder when she propped herself up. His mind began to wander.

"Well, it had that name carved into the top of it," Judy said.

"What do you mean?"

"It's this big old round table. Rough looking, like it was built from a tree trunk. It has your friend's name carved into the top."

Danny smiled. How typical of the old man. "They were close, them two. Skeritt saved Ernie's life. From a fire of all things. Weird he should end up dying in one."

Judy thought about that for a moment. "Who's Bif?" she asked.

"Bif?"

"Yeah. Bif. Right next to 'Skeritt,' someone carved the name Bif into the table. It's new, rougher than 'Skeritt,' like whoever carved it was in a hurry."

"I dunno. Never heard of anyone called that. Must be another friend of Ernie's. There was a gang of 'em worked together." He sighed and pushed a strand of Judy's hair out of her eyes. She smiled, kissed him lightly on the lips and went back to stroking his chest and stomach.

She hadn't asked how the hell he intended to find Skeritt. Good thing because he had no idea. They were adrift in the middle of Lower Buckhorn Lake. Heading north overland would be the right direction, but as to northeast or northwest? Who knew which forests the old man chose to roam?

Before he could wrap his head around the question, Judy stepped up the pace of her nibbling and shifted against him. That's when it struck him. Bif wasn't Bif. It was BFI.

Danny struggled to sit up but Judy elbowed him firmly back onto the bed. He looked down her back to where the curve of her hips pulled the sheet taut and decided they had time to spare.

Terry had pretty much abandoned hope this was just some intense outlaw initiation ritual. The bikers had bungee-corded him to the Sea Ray's foredeck and they were running the boat across the water at fifty miles an hour. Perko had returned barely ten minutes before and informed Terry they would take him up on the offer of George Meade's cabin cruiser.

Still soaking wet from his dunk in the locks, he tried to remember his winter water rescue training. Something about how all snowmobilers who went through the ice would appear stone drunk, but some weren't—they just needed a little thawing out. For Terry though, the nasty cold autumn air failed to induce peaceful hypothermic sleep. He tried to conjure up an image of sailing away with Cindy and wound up in a feverish prayer for survival.

The skinny one named Hawk was driving the boat. He throttled back and pushed the window open, calling out to Terry, "That where the cabin is? On that shore over there?"

Terry nodded and twisted his head around so he was facing the bikers. He said, "That's it. That's where your money was. That's where old Ernie was burned to a crisp! How about you untie me now, bring me inside?"

Both bikers were drinking brandy-spiked coffee from Styrofoam cups. They looked past Terry and down the lake.

"Think they'll still be up that way? I don't see nuthin'," Hawk said to the nasty guy named Perko.

"They're in a canoe. There's only so far they could get in twenty-five minutes."

"Let's just hope we find him before the cops do," Hawk said.

Before Perko could reply, a red canoe drifted into view from behind a small island. There were two people on the canoe, one of whom started waving her arms.

Perko grinned and wiped his forehead with the palm of his hand. Hawk revved the engine. It took less than a minute for them to plough across the lake.

Terry wondered how Danny would react to seeing him again. But as they got closer, he could see the man in the canoe had blond hair. And he was wearing some kind of purple fleece jacket that was color-coordinated with the lady's.

"Not them," Perko groaned.

"What?" Hawk said, clearly exasperated.

"That's not Danny Grant. It's a red canoe, alright, but that's not the shithead."

"There's no one else on the lake," Hawk said. "These two had must've seen them, at least."

When they got close enough to shout, Hawk cut the engine and called over. "You all see another couple people in a canoe?"

"Help! We've been kidnapped!" the woman yelled. "And...and...they stole our houseboat."

"I CAN'T SWIM," said the man.

Perko raised an eyebrow at Hawk then asked, "Which way did they take your boat?"

The man in the purple fleece pointed up the next branch of the lake. Then his eyes grew wide as he noticed the massive bow wave from the cabin cruiser headed his way. He dropped his paddle and grabbed both sides of the canoe. The woman shrieked.

"Hang on, tight! It'll pass," Hawk called out. The canoe bobbed up and down a couple of times before the water leveled out. Only then did Hawk fire the engine and head in the direction the man had pointed. "Houseboat," he said. "We'll catch that in no time."

Terry wheezed. He didn't know what to hope for anymore. For ten altruistic seconds, he worried about Danny and what they'd do to him. Then he went back to freezing to death.

"Max, you've got to believe me," Linette said. "I did not kill Ernie McCann."

They sat in the cruiser, parked in front of Officer Ainsley's house on the water.

"You know me better than that," she said. "It was a horrifying experience, him dead like that. As much as I hated the man, it was a terrible, terrible thing."

"Linette, I spent the last twenty-four hours screwing my brains out with a woman cold-blooded enough to step over a corpse after ransacking his house. I know you didn't kill him, but, man, that's cold."

Linette pouted. "Okay, so I'm a little ambivalent about the bastard. But he had no right to that money. What are you going to do? Arrest me?" She batted her eyelashes.

Max stared down at the water before answering. Linette followed his gaze. The lake was grey and choppy.

"That Grant kid made a fool of me once before. I'm not going to let it happen again," he said. "He's in a canoe. The sun's setting and it's going to get damn cold. He'll be looking for shelter, somewhere quiet, where there's mostly cottages. Something he can break into easily, no alarms, not draw attention. It would take days to run up and down all the fire lanes around these lakes. Nope. If we have any chance of finding him, it'll be from the water."

"We? You mean 'us?' Shouldn't you be calling this in to headquarters or something?"

"I'll bring him in myself. My collar. Solo." Stepping out of the car, he added, "We'll take my boat."

Drifting in the dark in a flat bottom canoe sounded romantic when Rick Stevens read about it in Cottage Life, but Stephanie was clearly unimpressed. The two of them had gone from arguing to crying to stone cold silence as they realized they were bobbing in the middle of a lake with only one paddle and neither of them particularly adept at using it. Stephanie huddled in a fetal position in the hull and hadn't moved for the past twenty minutes. It seemed no matter how hard he paddled, the wind and waves kept pushing them further from shore. He spent most of the time trying to point the damn canoe in the right direction.

Out of nowhere, the roar of an outboard motor gave him hope. A few minutes later, he was staring into a floodlight. An authoritative voice barked over some kind of megaphone: *"This is the police. Hold your hands above your head."*

Rick did as he was told and didn't even mind when he dropped the second paddle and watched it drift away from the canoe.

"Danny Grant, you are under arrest." The voice waited for some kind of an answer, but Rick didn't know what to say. *"Again,"* the voice added.

Rick was relieved to see Stephanie start to sit up but she collapsed again to the bottom of the canoe as a gunshot blasted over their heads.

"LINETTE, put that thing down," said the voice.

"What kind of cops are you?" shouted Rick. "I don't know who you're after but it isn't me. My name is Rick Stevens. We need your help."

The speaker amplified an otherwise hushed conversation between a man and a woman on the boat. From what he heard, Rick surmised the cops were after the hoodlum who'd stolen their rented houseboat. He told them as much and pointed in the same direction he'd sent the cabin cruiser.

"Now can you rescue us, please?" he called out.

"We're on official business here, sir. I strongly recommend you head for shore. And put on a life jacket while you're at it. It's dangerous out here at night with no lights. Not to mention the cold. You should know better."

With that, the boat roared off, splashing more than a little water into the canoe.

"'Let's spend a weekend in the country, *pumpkin*,'" Stephanie mocked from the bottom of the canoe. She went on, her voice's pitch rising, "'The people are nice there, *dearest*. And it's *safe, SWEETIE-PIE.*'"

She rolled onto her knees and turned to face him, her sudden movement rocking the canoe back and forth violently. With no paddle to slap at the water, Rick grabbed the gunwales with frozen white fingers and sucked air deep into his lungs. Before he could scream at Stephanie to calm down, something cold and wet grabbed his right wrist and tugged hard. He pulled back, yelling, "Mother of GAWD." Whatever had grabbed him let go and his momentum carried him over the opposite side of the canoe and into the lake.

He landed in the water upside down, arms and legs kicking in every direction as his mouth and nose filled with frigid water. With no light in the sky, he had no idea which way was up. Finally, his knee connected with the canoe, orienting him toward the surface and he flopped his arms in a desperate attempt to push his head out of the water. As soon as he did, he felt a hand grab him by the hair and pull his face clear.

"Breathe," a man's voice told him. "Here. Grab onto the canoe and *DON'T LET GO.*" He felt the owner of the voice propel him toward the boat. Then the man disappeared under the water, only to reappear on the other side of the upturned canoe and reach across to grab one of Rick's arms.

It was only then that Rick saw Stephanie's head bob up next to him. The man yelled the same instruction at her and grabbed her arm with his free hand. Even in the dark, Rick could see the man's face was a blackened smear.

"You're going to be alright," he told them both. "Canoes don't sink. We can kick our way to shore. It's not far."

Stephanie started to blubber and Rick said, "What the hell are you doing out here? Why did you throw us in the water?"

"Technically, you're the one who tipped the canoe," said the man. "I guess I frightened you."

"Frightened me?" Rick spat. "You popped up out of nowhere in the middle of a lake and grabbed my freaking arm."

"Sorry about that. I was reaching for the canoe."

"Who the hell are you?"

"My name is Buzz," the man said. "Consider yourselves rescued."

THIRTY

Overhanging trees shrouded the womblike cove. Detecting a break in the forest from a distance was impossible. Along the rocky shore, a stand of massive pines intermingled with squat cedars which dipped their boughs to the water's surface. Once the houseboat rounded the corner, it was completely concealed from anywhere on the lake. Danny felt the tension drain from his shoulders.

Not officially part of the Great Horned Owl Reserve, the island stood as a kind of no-man's land. The Indians claimed it as an ancient burial ground and the province pretty much left them alone with what was officially Crown Land. It only seemed fair. After all, much of the surrounding Ojibwa territory had been flooded to create the waterway well over a hundred years ago.

"I've camped here since I was a kid," Danny told Judy. "Always thought of it as my secret place. C'mon, I'll show you."

The sun had set without much of a show, the night cloudy, inky black, without a moon to light the sky. He threw a rope from the houseboat around a pine tree and gave Judy a hand stepping onto the rock ledge. He led her up a well-worn path through dense cedar. After a three minute climb, the orange glow of fire appeared ahead of them.

"Someone's there," Judy whispered. Wort snuffled beside her.

"I know," he said. "Don't worry. Pretty sure I know who it is."

Moments later, they stepped into a clearing where two men sat around a campfire. The nearer one had his back turned to them and looked about as big as a moose. The one across from him had a long matted beard and a craggy weathered face.

"It's about time," said Skeritt.

"Welcome," said the Big Fucking Indian from the Casino. "Skeritt said you'd come. Good to see you again. Pull up a chair." He gestured toward a couple of sixteen-inch logs which Danny rolled over for Judy and himself.

"Judy, this here is Skeritt," said Danny.

Judy shook his hand and turned to the other man. "And, I take it you're Bif?"

The big man chortled. "I think that spells Big Indian Fucker. True enough. Call me what you like."

Skeritt lobbed a piece of driftwood onto the fire, sending up a shower of sparks. "Want some rabbit?" He ladled a reddish mess onto paper plates. "Bif here was kind enough to bring along a quart of Swiss Chalet barbeque sauce. Delicious."

Bif stood off to the side and sliced green cedar boughs from trees encroaching on the fire circle. He tossed them onto a pile that was already quite large.

"Why don't you put those straight on the fire?" Judy asked.

"Too smoky," Bif answered. "It's cedar. Makes a nice bright flame, but it'll choke us out. We use it for celebrations and stuff. Watch this." He threw a clutch of branches onto the bonfire. After a bit of fizzling and a dense white puff, bright orange flames leapt up, carrying greasy black smoke with them. In a flash, the crackling inferno died down to nothing. Bif grinned ear to ear.

"You know, I might not have made the connection," Danny said, watching the Indian do his thing with the cedar, "but whenever we camped here, Skeritt drilled it in to be respectful 'cause this was Indian burial ground. Made sure I kept my fire in the pit."

"There's something cleansing about a fire," Skeritt said, poking at the glowing red coals in the pit until the log he had just added broke into flame. "Birth and destruction all mixed up into one."

"I get the destruction bit," Danny said after a moment's silence. "Where's the birth?"

Skeritt spat. His spittle sizzled on a flat stone. When the last of it had evaporated into nothingness, he said, "Freedom."

"Based on the last couple of days," said Danny, "I'd say freedom ain't all it's cracked up to be."

"That's because you're not really free," said Skeritt. "How much longer were you supposed to have inside?"

"Ninety-four days."

"Three months left and you decide to run."

"I had my reasons."

"Yeah, I'll bet you do. Seven hundred fifty thousand reasons."

Danny lifted his head and held Skeritt's gaze from across the fire. "How'd you know about that?"

Skeritt stared back, unblinking, and picked at something in his teeth with a short stick he plucked from the ground.

"I been your banker, Danny," he said finally. "Took a little interest here and there. Big Fucker and I had a couple parties. I peeled off an extra twenty thou to make sure your mom was set up on a beach down south, but most of it's still here."

"My mom? She's south?"

"Like you always wanted. Waiting for you. Nearly died laughing when I told her where you hid your pile of money."

"It was supposed to be temporary. Not like I had time to make a plan or nothing. But, SHIT, Skeritt. You had my money and didn't tell me about it?"

"I guess I was waiting 'til I saw you. No sense you knowing something you could do nothing about, far as I could tell. Then, with Ernie dead, well, things all happened kind of fast, didn't they?"

Danny frowned. "So you find it taking a dump?"

Skeritt grinned. "Sort of."

Bif, finished with the cedar, said, "I've heard this before. Anyone for a cold one?" Without waiting for an answer, he turned and walked back down the path toward the water.

Judy shivered and leaned a little closer to Danny. He had his arm around her, protectively. Exhausted, she hadn't touched her plate of rabbit stew. Skeritt stood and pulled a heavy wool blanket from a lean-to on the edge of the clearing. He draped the blanket over her shoulders and sat back down on his log.

Judy put the stew on the ground beside her and pulled the blanket tight. Wort seemed to like the barbeque sauce just fine.

"Must have been, oh, about two years ago," Skeritt said. "Dropped in on Ernie for the first time in months. Figured I'd use the outhouse on my way in, except the darned thing wasn't there anymore. It was dark out, no moon. I walked back and forth a couple of times, thinking I was maybe disoriented, but the thing just wasn't there. I gave up and headed to the cabin to ask Ernie what was up with the shitter. On my way there, I tripped on an exposed root. Fell flat on my face. Nearly busted my nose.

"So, anyway, Ernie tells me the shitter was full up and he pointed to where he had dug a new one. Said he got one of them helpers from the Social Assistance to help him drag the outhouse over after he dug the hole.

"Next day, I decided I better go chop out that root before Ernie tripped on it himself. Turns out it wasn't a root at all, but some kind of leather handle." Skeritt smiled and spat in the fire again. "And that handle was attached to one stinkin' pile of cash."

"Son of a bitch," said Danny. "So my money was safe all along."

"Yep."

"Where is it?"

"It's in the lean-to—"

Danny leapt to his feet and strode across the clearing. Skeritt watched him and shook his lion-sized head as if Danny were a small child misbehaving.

"Sit down, boy. Relax," he said. "It's not going anywhere."

Danny ignored him and rummaged among the sleeping bags in the earthy shelter. The money was in a newish red duffel bag and it looked like Skeritt had been using it as a pillow. He brought the bag out and laid it on the ground in front of his log. The others watched him in silence as he unzipped the bag to reveal a jumbled mess of bills, some still in neat stacks, more loose, mixed with a few candy bar wrappers.

"Guess I'm not the tidiest guy," Skeritt said.

Danny ran his fingers through the treasure, grabbing at it, squeezing it, feeling his breath come short and fast. He looked at Judy who stared back at him, eyes wide and unblinking. She looked more scared than happy.

"Ninety-fucking-four days," Skeritt spat. "You were so close to the end, Danny."

"C'mon, Skeritt. I heard about the fire and I figured someone was going to find it. I dunno, excavate the place, put in a septic system, anything. Or maybe somehow Ernie had found it already and now someone had killed him for it. Skeritt, my brain is hurting."

"Not surprised. Here," he said, reaching into an inside pocket and fishing out a leather pouch. "Roll us up a number, would you?"

For a moment, Danny was torn between fondling the stack of bills and rolling a celebratory spliff. But only for a moment. As he pulled twigs, crushed, and crumpled the pot in the palm of his hand, he asked, "What do you figure happened to Ernie? Was he lonely? Did he kill himself?"

Skeritt growled, "Don't you *ever* think that. Ernie would never have hurt a soul, never mind himself. More than once, I know for a fact he took shots at people, folks messing with him, trying to take advantage. But he made damn sure he fired in the wrong direction." Skeritt guffawed. "Imagine a blind man firing a shot gun in your general direction but missing by just a bit. Scare the bejeezus out of most people."

"I heard his gun go off late one night," Judy said, stirring at Ernie's mention. "He told me he thought it was a bear in his compost...that he fired into the sky."

"Sounds about right, and maybe it was a bear. I do know that Ernie would never have let you worry your pretty little head about the assholes who were on him."

Danny took a haul on the joint and passed it to Judy who shook her head. He got up and walked it over to Skeritt. He asked, "Who was hassling Ernie?"

"The Libidos, mostly, right after you got busted," said Skeritt. "Then the cops. Tore his place apart looking for 'evidence' they said..."

"And that stupid lawyer lady," piped in Judy. "She was on him non-stop to sell his place."

"Yeah, something like that," Skeritt breathed deep and puffed out a thick cloud of smoke. "She came looking for a cut of the money after I bought him the damn TV set out of your...ahhh...winnings. Seems she heard about it from Eyes and Ears Entertainment—biggest freaking screen they ever sold, so they couldn't shut up about it, I guess. It's my damn fault. I just figured since all Ernie could see was big bright things that moved, he might as well be able to enjoy a roomful of them."

"I always wondered how he could afford that huge thing," Judy said. "'Rich uncle' was all he'd say. He was private about a lot of things."

"More private than you can imagine," said Skeritt, gesturing to Danny to come get the joint again.

"Sometimes, we'd watch a movie together," Judy said. "I'd massage his shoulders. He liked that. First couple of times, I was afraid he'd think I was making a pass at him, but he never made a move. Nothing like that."

"That was Ernie, alright. A real gentleman."

Danny paced back and forth around the fire. "So what happened to him? Something's not adding up. You had the money, not him. Next thing you know he's burned in a fire. And you're sitting here waiting for me on this fucking island. What the hell is going on?"

Skeritt looked at Judy and grinned: "He's always been a little quick to the heat, this one." She gave a little smile back and tugged the blanket tighter around herself. To Danny, Skeritt said, "Sit down, would you? You're making me dizzy."

Danny handed him the joint and sat back down on his log.

"A couple of weeks ago," Skeritt said, "I dropped in to place an order for more peanut butter and kerosene. Ernie told me Linette Paquin had been putting on the pressure. Coming around more often. Just like a lawyer to feel they've got a right to a cut of anything goes by. He knew you were due out of the pen and he figured she was getting nervous that if she didn't find the money before you got out, you'd come get it and be gone."

"Were the Libidos onto him, too?"

"Oh, they'd drop in once in a blue moon. Or one of them would come up to him in the grocery store in town and make nice in the frozen food aisle. But they'd searched the place years ago, like I said. I'm sure they've got other ways of applying pressure—maybe a little more directly on you."

"They were on me like glue," Danny said. "Literally couldn't piss without one of them being up my ass. Sorry, Judy."

She shook her head.

"Anyhow, I told Ernie to be real careful," Skeritt said. "He laughed it off and pointed at this sucker..." He tossed the roach into the fire and reached behind himself, pulling a shotgun from the shadows. "Recognize this?"

"It's a shotgun," Danny said. "So what?"

"It's Ernie's gun, is what."

"Okay. So?"

"It's what killed him."

"Wait a sec, how'd you get Ernie's gun?" Judy asked, raising her voice and stiffening against Danny.

"Took from him right before I set his place on fire."

"YOU?" Judy jumped up, the blanket crumpling to the ground behind her. She lunged as if to round the fire and attack Skeritt. Before she could reach him, Bif reappeared; he stepped into the circle of firelight and snatched her, one-armed. He was carrying a six-pack of beer, dripping wet. Wort snapped at his heels then stopped abruptly and sat still when the Indian said something to him in a language Danny couldn't understand.

"Hate to break up your little party, but we've got company," Bif said. "Fishing boat. Seems they spotted our fire and are headed this way."

Judy struggled in his grip, spewing at Skeritt. "You killed Ernie McCann!"

"Calm down, little lady. It wasn't like that," Skeritt said, softening his voice. Then, to Bif, "Friendly?"

"Somehow I doubt it. Nobody knew we'd be out here, and the boat's not coming from the Reserve. Damn strange for there to be anyone on the water after dark this time of year. Never mind that they shut off their lights and throttled the engine back to near silent when they were half a mile away." He let Judy go and she stumbled back into Danny's open arms.

"So, what do we do now?" Skeritt asked.

"Might as well meet them at the shore. Try to stop them from getting on the island. They won't be able to see us in the shadows on land. But we'll be able see them pretty well on the water."

"Good point," said Skeritt.

"Besides, we have the advantage of knowing where they'll be headed."

"How's that?" Danny asked, tightening his arms around Judy who was trembling against him.

"Assuming its them Libidos jerks, they'll know the island, what with all the trade we do with them. They'll head straight for the cove. Every other approach is too full of rocks."

"Shouldn't we get out of here?" Judy asked.

"Not until we drive them off. Scare 'em a bit. Otherwise, they'd just come after us on the water."

"And exactly how do you propose we scare a bunch of mean-as-shit bikers?" Danny asked.

Skeritt rolled the shotgun in the palms of his hands and grinned. Then he jerked his head toward Bif who somehow made a rifle materialize over his shoulder.

"You're going to shoot them," said Judy.

"More like shoot near 'em," Bif answered. "I only shoot *at* things I intend to eat. But if Skeritt and me each take shots over the boat from opposite corners of the cove as they make their way in, it'll seem like there's more of us. They'll back off. Give us time to figure out how to get you out of here." He arched his eyebrows and looked straight at Judy. "My people have used this island for a long time. We haven't always outnumbered our enemies, but we've almost always outsmarted them."

Judy broke his gaze and her eyes scanned Danny's from six inches away. Her body seemed to weaken in his arms, the fight draining out of her. Danny looked from Skeritt to Bif and back again. He said, "Do as they say, Judy. If Skeritt trusts Bif, then so do I."

"Now you're talking sense, Danny," Skeritt said. "And you tell your friend here, I did not kill Ernie. Found him dead on the floor. I may have torched his cabin with him in it. But I did not kill him. Someone else did."

"Why? Why did you burn his place down and him in it? What kind of sick man are you?" Judy sobbed into Danny's chest.

"It's what he would have wanted," said the old man. "Purifying. Birth and destruction and all that shit."

When George Meade's cabin cruiser arrived at the locks at Bobcaygeon, Mongoose was there to meet it. With him, he brought a ski-sized duffle bag crammed with enough guns and ammunition to take down a herd of bison. From all appearances, Mongoose was very much alive. Perko nearly shit his pants.

"You is *distinctly* pissing me off, right about now," growled the burly biker. "First, you takes off on your own and then when I get back to the cabin they's this huge motherfucking crater where the shitter used to be. No Perko, no money, no nothing."

"How did...where did..." Fighting to control a sudden onset of the shakes, Perko stared out the boat's windscreen. Hawk shot him a dark glance and nosed the Sea Ray into the channel before the lock gate had quite finished its deathly slow swing open. Terry was still tied to the foredeck. Perko visualized tying Jonah and Mongoose and Danny Grant up there alongside him and then sinking the whole fucking mess to the bottom of the lake.

Mongoose said, "All's I know is I'm getting pretty much tired of this here stupid wild goose chase. I like my hogs on dry land."

"Shut up, Mongoose," Hawk told him. "Perko says the kid's got the money. We run him down and we're done here. He gets away and we're nowhere."

"Yeah, well, alls I know is how come he let the jerk-off get away again? After we're done with the punk, I says we kill Perks under pain of aggravation."

Perko's brow furrowed until his eyes were dark slits. He turned his back on the ape. If Hawk had called Mongoose without telling him, his hours were numbered. It was his own damn fault for trusting a bomb-happy backwoods dumbfuck like Jonah.

George Meade's floating home was littered with the trappings of biker glory. Bottles of brandy, tequila, and Southern Comfort taken from The Boathouse were tucked into cup holders; a couple of empties rolled around on the floor. Mongoose dug right in. No sooner had Hawk navigated the boat from the lock than the bigger biker staggered out of the cabin and leaned over the starboard railing. He spray-puked a brown stream of improvised Irish coffee to the wind, shouting how he was going to make Perko pay for dragging him out on the water.

Inside the cabin, Hawk killed all the boat's lights and spoke to Perko in an abnormally soft voice. "Tell me again why the hell you let the little shit get away from you."

Perko fumed. "Like I said, the cops showed up. I couldn't very well let them arrest him and haul his ass back to the joint, could I? I mean, he'd never get out and then what'd we do about finding my...ahhh...*our* money. I figured if I distracted the cops, sort of, for a couple minutes—"

"And then we'd follow him."

"Get the money. Yeah, that was my plan."

"Did your plan involve swimming?"

"Hey, how was I to know he'd go out on the lake?"

Hawk scratched his cheek against his shoulder and stared at Perko. "And if he'd run into the bush, what would you have done? Tracked him, maybe? Like a moose or something?" He paused, his eyes cold, unblinking. "After you were done entertaining the cops, I mean?"

Perko held the glare as long as he dared and then looked down and spat on the indoor-outdoor carpeting. When he looked back up, Hawk was still staring him down.

"So how'd you get all covered in shit?" Hawk asked.

Perko scowled. He'd done his best to rub off the composted crap with some bull rushes and more had scraped off when he skid out on his bike, but there was still crud stuck in his hair and in the fringes on his chaps. "He, uh, he threw some at me. That's why I throttled the fucker."

"Uh huh," Hawk looked back out the windscreen. "And then you saw him grab the money."

"I saw him grab a bag, yeah. What else would it be? It's not like he'd be carrying fucking luggage on the run."

After a long pause, the elder biker said, "See, Perko, I think you're shitting us. And I think I've given you about as much rope as anyone is due." He nodded at Mongoose bent double outside the window. "That man has been fixin' to kill you for the better part of four years and he's got half the clubhouse convinced he's right."

Perko winced. "Okay, so he got away from me again. Fucker had help. Someone came up behind me and knocked me down. Must've hit me with a log or something. Would've knocked just about anyone out cold. By the time I got straight, the cops had pulled up. Three cruisers full. I jumped on my ride and did a couple of donuts to kick up a little dirt before taking off and dragging their asses after me. Then I, uh, I took off southwards first, eh, to shake 'em off, like, and, uh, well then I came back," he held Hawk's gaze, feeling him warming, he thought, "to The Boathouse, I mean. Where I found you. And this Terry guy. Remember?"

Hawk sighed, clenching and unclenching his fist. Perko was about to start embellishing his story a little more when, seemingly out of nowhere, a fishing boat roared up behind them and streaked by, skipping across the choppy water. Hawk immediately floored the twin engines, but there was no way for them to keep up. When the driver of the fishing boat killed its own lights, Hawk throttled back.

Mongoose staggered into the cabin, his face green. "I thought we was 'sposed to be looking for a houseboat. That was a fishing boat went by."

"You see any other boats on the water?" Hawk asked. "Maybe the punk traded up."

"Or maybe it's the cops," said Mongoose.

"Cops wouldn't kill their lights like that. Plus, they would've checked us out," Hawk said.

"Only one way to find out," Mongoose said, pulling a rifle from the duffel bag on the floor of the cabin.

"Put that down," snarled Perko. "You can't see the damn thing anymore. What're you gonna shoot at anyway?"

Mongoose frowned, appearing to consider the question, and turned the gun in Perko's direction. Hawk reached over and pushed the barrel away with his open palm. "Go get that punk," he told Perko, waving his hand at Terry.

Chaps flapping in the wind, Perko crawled out onto the foredeck, pulled a knife out of his boot, and used it to cut the bungee cords that held Terry in place. He half-dragged him inside where Hawk handed him a cup of brandy with a splash of coffee in it. "Drink this," the biker said.

Terry slurped at it like a dog, the lukewarm liquid running down his chin. Perko stood next to Hawk, scanning the water with eyes blacker than hell. Mongoose slouched on the bench at the back of the cabin, his massive gut stretching Ozzy's face on his T-shirt into shapes more unnatural than even the singer could dream up.

"Okay, punk," Hawk said. "Here's your chance. Make yourself useful. Maybe even get off this boat alive."

Mongoose made a noise like the air being squished out of a wet balloon. Hawk shot him a look before going on. "Seems your pal has run off with our money. Again. When we find him, it ain't going to be pretty. The thing I'm wondering is whether you're gonna make yourself useful or just jump off the boat now and swim ashore."

"It's t-t-too fucking c-c-c-cold to swim."

"Kinda my thinking."

"B-b-b-but I d-d-don't know anything. D-D-D-Danny just sh-sh-showed up this morning and..."

"Drink." Hawk refilled the cup with brandy and Terry downed whatever didn't spill out as he grasped it with two shaking hands. He coughed, his red eyes filling with tears.

Perko turned to face him, leaned in close, and spat his words. "*Think*, shit-for-brains. *Where* would Danny go on the water? *Who* does he know? *Where* would he feel safe?"

Terry crumpled the Styrofoam cup and pulled his legs up onto the chair, wrapping his knees with his arms.

"TALK PUNK," Mongoose said, then let out a plaintive groan and grabbed his gut, his eyes rolling like marbles in his green face.

Terry took a deep breath and said, "D-D-Danny used to go to this island. 'S-s-s-s-not too far I think. I dunno. Maybe he went there."

"What island?" asked Hawk. Perko marveled at how he made his calm voice so much more unnerving than the anger he and Mongoose employed in interrogations.

"I never went to the island. Danny used to camp there with his mom. Near Burleigh Falls, he said. It belonged to the Indians, he said, but not like it was part of a reserve or nothing. Nobody lives on it. Just a place they'd go."

Hawk looked at the other two bikers and rolled his hands open, questioning. Mongoose spat on the floor. Perko looked out the window and back at Hawk.

"Perko?" Hawk looked at him, eyebrows arched.

The biker shrugged. "I'm thinking maybe one of them islands off of the Great Horned Owl Reserve. The ones no one can build on 'cause they're supposed to be burial grounds or something. We did a few deliveries out there couple years back." He nudged Hawk aside and opened the cabinet next to the captain's chair. He pulled out a sheaf of charts and started flipping through them.

"Here. Pike Lake. See, there's the reserve to the north," he said, pointing at a string of islands, some no larger than tennis courts. "These were all hilltops before they flooded the place to build the Trent-Severn. The reserve was still new enough and back then nobody cared much about island ownership, anyhow."

Hawk looked at the map. He said, "Must be fifty islands there. Could be any one of them. Or none."

Perko shrugged. "What else have we got to go on?"

Mongoose stifled a burp and said, "Just get a fucking move on. If I don't get onto dry land in the next fifteen minutes I's gonna break one of you's legs and I don't much care who's."

Max stopped the boat and let it drift in silence. He'd been doing that every five minutes or so the whole time he and Linette had been on the water. Stopping and listening for anything that could give them an idea of which way they should be heading. That, and sweeping the water with the heavy duty flashlight he had plugged into the boat's cigarette lighter.

"I expect they've gone ashore by now," he said. "They could have broken into any one of these cottages. Even if we only checked the ones with fires burning, we'd still be at it all night. If they got onto the next lake, there's another few hundred places they could hide. It'll be damn near impossible to find them until they decide to move again."

"Are you going to give up?" Linette asked. The damp chilled her to the bone.

"I hate to," Max said. "This is my chance to make it right. Silence all the yabos who've been busting my chops about the grow op fiasco." They both scanned the shoreline. Suddenly, Linette saw a puff of light at the top of an island, halfway to shore.

"What was that?" she asked.

"What?"

"Over there, on that island. There was *like* a sparkle or something."

"That's weird. There's no house on that island. Its Indian land," the cop said.

"It looked like a fire."

"Could be just a few guys from the Reserve, or..." He looked hard at the dense black outline where Linette was pointing. "You sure your eyes aren't playing tricks on you?"

"I'm sure."

"Let's check it out." He turned the engine back on but left it low and slow. Linette saw him unbuckle his holster.

Within minutes, they had reached the island and Max cut the engine again. He flipped on his fish finder and cursed. The six-inch screen showed him a bottom full of rocks off the bow of the boat and to either side. He trimmed the 225-horse motor out of the water and turned on the tiny electric bow motor. He'd been aiming toward what appeared to be a natural cove but now no matter which way he turned, the way was blocked by a ridge, a boulder, or four-inch deep water which wouldn't allow his boat to pass.

"Do you think maybe they walked ashore?" Linette whispered.

"I dunno, but if Danny came here with the houseboat, it's either very well hidden or moored around the other side. Whoever's here, I think we're better off sneaking up this side. In the dark."

"I thought you knew all the water around here. *Practically* know where the fish are depending what day of the week it is, is how I remember you saying it."

"They've drained the damn lake for winter. Must be down a good two feet." He stared at his fish finder's little blue screen. He spotted what looked like another opening and turned the boat into it.

They heard a hoot.

"What's that?" asked Linette, still whispering.

"Sounded like an owl." He pushed closer to the edge. They got to within fifty feet when suddenly they were surrounded by rocks. Some he could even see sticking up through the surface. He pushed the engine into reverse but in water this shallow, the steady wind pushed the boat sideways. Within seconds, they ran aground.

Max groaned as he felt the bottom of his fifteen thousand dollar hull drag across the granite outcropping. He heard the fiberglass screech in complaint, followed by a huge cracking sound as something somewhere gave out. He said, "So much for the element of surprise."

He dropped two anchors into the water, one bow, one stern. As he lifted a floor panel to check the boat's hull, there was a crash of light and the boom of a shotgun from shore. The pellets rained into the water behind them. Almost immediately, there were two sharper gun shots.

Max snarled, "We're not dealing with just Danny Grant, anymore."

"What do you mean? So, he's got a gun. He could have picked it up anywhere these past two days. Maybe even stole it from that RV."

"*Guns*, Linette. Not 'a gun.' Didn't you hear the different blasts? And we were fired on from two different directions. He's got help here. We're screwed."

"Can't we just take off?"

"You heard the hull scrape. We're wedged in. Even if I managed to get the boat back off the rocks, I'm pretty sure we're taking on water. Not that it matters: it's barely two feet deep here. We'll walk in."

Linette shut her eyes tight and wrapped herself in her arms, chin in her chest. "Fuck fuck fuck fuck fuck fuck FUCK!"

Max said, "The way I figure, they mustn't have been able to get a clean shot at us. Otherwise, they should have hit us, with the shotgun at least. See that huge boulder over there? They either have to climb over it or come into the water themselves. Either way, we've got at best three minutes to get ashore."

"Think again, Max. It's freaking October. I'm not getting in that water. Just maybe I *swim* the July long weekend. If I'm drunk enough. There's no way you're getting in me in that damn lake tonight."

Officer Ainsley shrugged and checked the clip on his service revolver. "Suit yourself," he said. "You can stay here on a leaky boat while a desperate escaped con and his nutbar buddy—or buddies, for all we know—take potshots at you. I'm going in."

He pulled a pair of hip-high gators from under one of the seats and struggled to pull them on over his pants. He lowered himself off the boat into the knee deep water and took a few steps. Linette saw him flinch as he lost his footing and slipped, his feet flying out from under him, allowing the frigid water to pour over his gators.

"Fuck it," he hissed. "I'm soaked now. Grab the flashlight and jump on my back. I'll carry you in. Come on!"

Linette wrapped first one leg then the other around his shoulders. She couldn't resist fluffing his hair, playfully. She cooed, "My *big strong* Officer Maximum."

THIRTY-ONE

Huddled together and using the canoe as a break against the cold off-shore breeze, Danny and Judy watched the low-slung fishing boat make its way across the water. Danny's blood pounded in his ears and his anxiety melded with a damp chill to cause a bad case of the shakes, only made worse by the rush brought on by Skeritt's killer weed.

"Shit," said Skeritt, "they're bypassing the cove."

Sure enough, the boat, which at first seemed to be pointed right at them, had veered off at the last instant. It headed east, where Bif was hidden. A distinct hoot, like an owl, cut through the air. Danny and Judy both looked at Skeritt.

"That's Big Fucker," said the old man. "I'm going to swing over that side. You two stay here. Spread out. No sense them catching us together if they make it ashore. If one of us gets taken, the rest will be able to regroup. Stay low and stay quiet."

A single shotgun blast freaked Danny right out of his gourd. Next came two cracks from what he hoped was Bif's rifle. From where he cowered inside a cedar bluff, he could make out the silhouette of the fishing boat. Someone clambered into the knee-deep water. The shadow disappeared for a moment and then seemed to grow larger before moving ashore. The pot Danny had just smoked was stronger than anything he'd had in prison. He was fried. He heard Bif's owl hoot again and another shotgun blast from the shore.

"All my fault. Every bit of this," he muttered.

So what are you going to do about it? Hide in the bushes and let everyone else clean it up?

Danny stiffened. That voice. It couldn't be. How the hell could the fucking iguana be out on this island in the middle of nowhere?

You didn't really think I'd just freeze my ass off in that farmhouse while you went gallivanting off to prison, did you?

"How the fuck did you get here?"

I've been hanging with Skeritt ever since he came round to tidy up your last mess.

"What're you talking about?"

The fire, numbnuts.

"Fuck off with the 'numbnuts' routine, scaleface. I didn't burn Ernie's cabin. That was Skeritt. He just told me he did."

No kidding. But I'm talking about the grow op. Didn't it strike you as a tad convenient the way that baby went up in smoke? Kept you from getting busted for the pot, didn't it? Made you stinking rich in the process, from the look of that duffel bag.

"And what? You think Skeritt did that?"

"Who are you talking to, Danny?" Judy whispered. The sound of her voice jolted Danny back to reality. He looked around and could have sworn he saw Iggy sitting on a boulder about fifteen feet away. Either that or it was a fallen branch.

"No one. Never mind. How the hell are we going to get out of here now?"

"Maybe we can make our way down to the water," she said, "get back on the houseboat, and take off."

"It's too damn slow," Danny said. "They'd catch us for sure. Like sitting ducks."

"Danny, I'm really scared."

She crept over, shivering. Danny wrapped his arms around her, pulling her into his coat. He asked, "You see that rock over there by the water? Is that a lizard on it?"

"I don't see anything," she said and leaned in tight.

Danny looked again, wiped his eyes, and saw that the branch—or the iguana—had disappeared.

Seconds later, Skeritt and Bif showed up from different directions, one just as silent as the other. Danny slipped one hand to Judy's head, cradling it into his shoulder. She didn't move a muscle—could have been asleep for all he could tell.

"We've got trouble," said the Indian, squatting behind a rock and lighting a cigarette.

"Ya think?" said Danny, his voice dripping sarcasm.

"Plenty." Bif showed no emotion whatsoever. He tossed the pack of smokes to Skeritt. The older man pulled a cigarette out of the pack, broke off the filter, and put the tight end between his blistered lips. He fired it up and offered the package to Danny.

Bif said, "There were at least two people on that boat. They came ashore."

"So much for scaring them off," Danny said.

"It should've worked," Bif said. "It's not like the Libidos to force a confrontation when they're outgunned. Especially when they have no way of knowing how many of us there are. They must be madder than hell."

"So, what now?" Danny asked. Judy remained deathly still by his side. "We all smokum peace pipe and trust in the Great Spirit to make things right?"

Bif squinted through the tobacco smoke swirling in front of his face. "You got any better ideas?" he asked.

"Like, maybe we get the hell outta here?"

"Uh huh," said the Indian. "White man gonna fly, or what? Last I looked, we've got a canoe and a houseboat. Your friends out there have two hundred and some horses on a fisherman's special. You haven't got a hope in hell of outrunning them." He took a deep drag of his cigarette and exhaled a cloud in Danny's direction. "I suggest you come up with a better plan."

"Can't we signal the Reserve? With a fire or something? My mom used to tell me—"

"No time," said Bif. "Like I said, they're on the island."

Danny glared at the Indian and pulled Judy closer to him. After thinking for a moment, Skeritt said, "I think we should split up. Danny and I will portage your canoe to the other side of the island. You take Judy on the houseboat and make a big show of running for it. By the time the bikers get back on the water and catch up with you, find out we're not there, we'll have ten minutes head start. In the dark, we may be able to make land before they figure things out."

"Not a chance!" Danny protested. "There's no telling what those bikers will do to Judy."

"They won't fuck with me, nor her if she's with me," said Bif. "We handle far too much border traffic for them to risk the fall-out. They'll be pissed off. But where I come from, there's nothing new about a bunch of angry white guys."

"He's right," said Skeritt. "Besides, look at her, Danny. She can hardly stay awake. Two of you in a canoe will be going so slow they'll catch you for sure."

"Listen to them, Danny," Judy mumbled. "I'll be alright. It's you they're after, not me."

Danny looked from one to the other and stood, helping Judy to her feet. She wrapped her arms around him, sighed deeply and said, "You're so strong, Danny. You'll be okay." She rubbed his back, running her fingers up and down, and murmured, "Your shoulders feel exactly like Ernie's." She must have sensed him stiffen, because she added, "From massaging him in front of the TV, like I told you. That's how I know his build. Silly."

Skeritt, shouldering his shotgun, muttered, "Of course."

"What's that, Skeritt?" Danny asked.

"Nothing. Say goodbye to your girlfriend here and give me a hand with the canoe."

Danny pushed Judy back a few inches and looked at her tear-smeared face. "Maybe one or two people ever been good to me besides my mom. I hardly know why you've helped me but someday I'll do you right. Promise."

Judy forced a weak smile and kissed him before turning to follow Bif back to the houseboat, Wort sniffing the path ahead of them.

Danny watched them go before slinging the duffel bag over his shoulder and lifting the canoe. Skeritt picked up the back end and shone a flashlight at Danny's feet from behind as they headed up the well-worn path.

When they were close enough to the island's crown to make out the glowing fire between the trees, Danny said, "Something I been wanting to ask you."

"What's that?"

"The night I got busted, you know, after you came to visit me at the farmhouse, there was this fire."

"Yeah, in the barn. So?"

"Did you start that? I mean, like the way you burned Ernie's place?"

"Horrible waste of pot that was. At the barn, I mean."

"So?"

Skeritt paused before saying, "Guilty. It's the only thing I could think of at the time."

"Thank you," Danny said.

"Pleasure."

The sound of the houseboat's motor echoed up the hill. As they stepped into the clearing, they set the canoe down next to the pile of cedar boughs to take a breather. Danny spoke again. "Something else you said back there that's buggin' me."

"What's that?"

"You weren't surprised about Judy giving Ernie massages. You made some comment."

"Wasn't that."

"What do you mean, 'wasn't that?' Do you know something I don't? Something I *should* know?"

"Maybe," Skeritt answered.

"Did Ernie tell you something? Was she—"

"Nothing like that. Not that I know, anyway."

"Then what?"

They could hear the pontoons creak across a couple of half-submerged logs as the houseboat struggled to exit the cove. Danny prayed the big Indian would keep Judy safe.

"Geez, Danny, haven't you ever wondered why Ernie would stick his neck out for you, the way he did? Did you really think he liked your mother's lasagna *that* much?"

"It crossed my mind, a couple times, yeah. But like you said, you were all such great friends, from way back at the sawmill and all."

Skeritt shook his head slowly. "Well, the stupid bastard's dead now, so I guess it's up to me. I never really agreed with the man, anyway, but it was his life, his story to tell. And your mother, well, I know she agrees with me, even if she doesn't have the courage to tell you herself."

"Tell me what?"

"Danny," Skeritt said, "Ernie was your father."

Perko spotted the fire first.

"That's got to be it," he said.

Hawk pointed the bow at the flickering smudge of orange light and pressed the throttle to full. No one spoke. With the engine noise and the wind whipping through the open vinyl flaps, conversation would have been impossible anyway.

A dark scowl settled on Perko's forehead and he flexed his knuckles, smelling blood. Justice. Money or not, the punk was dead meat. And his tool sidekick for good measure, he thought, shooting a glare at Terry. As for Mongoose, that was a bit trickier: if they didn't find the money with the punk on the island, Mongoose clearly had Hawk's support to deal with Perko. On the other hand, if the money *was* there—*and* if Mongoose should somehow have a little nautical accident before they arrived—Perko might still be able to talk Hawk into a little fifty-fifty split. Turning to where the not-so-jolly-green-biker was clenching his stomach, Perko grinned and said, "Here, buddy. Let me pour you another shot of Southern Comfort."

The cabin cruiser drew close to the island and Perko told Hawk to watch out for rocks. Hawk snorted. "Like it's the first time I drive a boat."

"Could've fooled me," Mongoose grumbled, his bulbous head hanging out the window.

"Don't look now," said Perko, "but there's the houseboat." Sure enough, the pontoon palace was putt-putting out of a cove on the north side of the island. It was less than half a mile away.

"Here we go," said Mongoose, pulling himself up straight, a rifle in his hands. He pointed the gun at Perko who made a move to push it away. "Ah-ah-aaahhhh," said Mongoose in a sing-song voice. "This is the end of the road for you, Mr. Ratwick."

"Wait a minute. We're almost done," Perko protested. "All we gotta do is get over to that boat, collect our money, and we're all square. Ain't that the truth, Hawk?" Hawk said nothing, staring straight ahead at the houseboat. He slowed the cabin cruiser's engines to a dull roar. Perko looked incredulous. "Hawk?" he said.

"Shut it, Perko. I gotta go with Mongoose on this one. We just spent the last hour and a half running around in this stolen boat, waiting for cops to pick us up, thinking we were chasing the money. But the way I figure it, there's a good chance the punk doesn't even have it."

Perko grimaced.

"Can I kill him now?" Mongoose asked. "Maybe play with him a little first? Beat his brains out?"

Perko backed away from Mongoose, eyes wide, starting to blubber. Hawk said, "By rights, we should be offing you. Mongoose ain't the only one wants you dead."

Reeking of stale puke, Mongoose leaned in real close and jammed Perko's belly with the rifle barrel. "Say the word, Hawk. I'se ready. I'll do it," he said.

"Instead," Hawk said, "we'll just let you off here, in the dinghy, with your new dipshit boat thief partner. I don't much care *where* you go or whether you *die* getting there, but show your face anywhere in the Kawarthas ever again, you're dog meat."

"Huh? What?" complained Mongoose. "But I wants to kill him. Him *and* his buddy."

"For what, Mongoose? Revenge? If I let every asshole who wants revenge kill every other asshole who deserves it, we'd have a hard time scaring up enough Libidos to put together a decent poker game. Frankly, I don't need the grief. We're gonna dump them here and we go collect our money from the jackass on the houseboat. If he doesn't have the money, *him* you can beat the shit out of."

"Can I kill *him*?"

"Whatever," Hawk said. "Just put these two into the dinghy and let's get this over with."

Faced with the gun barrel and Hawk's betrayal, Perko loosened the cords that held the dinghy in place at the boat's stern. Once it was in the water, he climbed aboard, followed by Terry, whose teeth were still chattering.

"Here, this'll keep you warm," Mongoose said, leaning over and handing Perko a full bottle of brandy. Then, in a flash, he pulled a knife from his boot. Without Hawk being able to see it, and before Perko could stop him, he poked a neat little gash in the boat's rubber skin.

* * *

"They're *getting* away." Linette's shrill whisper sliced under Max's skin like a paper cut. He was soaked to the chest, his water-filled gators warming slowly, uncomfortable as hell. Every step he took, lake water sloshed up between his legs like one of those fancy French toilets. He watched as the houseboat nosed out of the cove and then lurched as though caught up on something. He cursed himself for not having spotted the entrance earlier.

"What are you going to do?" Linette hissed.

Officer Ainsley pulled his pistol from its holster and fired a shot in the air.

"Stop!" he shouted. "Police! Danny Grant, you are UNDER ARREST!"

Linette said, "Like that's going to work."

"What do you expect me to do, swim after them?"

The houseboat motor strained against whatever had grounded it and Officer Ainsley took another shot, at the motor this time.

The gunshot snapped Danny back to reality, but it was Skeritt's words that echoed in his brain.

He had a father.

He had a father he knew, had known his whole life. Ernie had been there all along. His mind flashed images of fishing by the dock, Ernie showing him how to hook a worm, Danny wondering how the hell the old man did it, blind as a bat. Ernie patiently explaining that it *did* make a difference that lettuce seeds be planted in rows rather than helter skelter. And the choke in his voice when Danny showed up with his mom for Ernie's birthday dinner. And how he got pissed when he avoided the guy for six months after dropping out of high school the first time.

He had a father and his father was dead.

"Why, Skeritt? Why didn't she tell me?"

"Times were different, Danny. She was young. Single. Hurting from the friends she'd lost in the fire. Your mom and Ernie were friends, sometimes more, but they were never in love. They just needed each other, I guess. Patterson cast everyone away like so much trash, and we all helped each other through it."

"But he was my father..."

"And he always treated you right. Just didn't live with you. Intimacy wasn't his thing. Besides, it would have messed up his social assistance." Skeritt paused and looked Danny in the eye. "When you went to prison, he beat himself up for not having done a better job protecting you that night you ran to his cabin. Then the money and, well, we all figured we just needed to stay quiet until you got out."

A second shot rang out.

Danny said, "Skeritt, we're going back."

"What do you mean 'back?'"

"I mean one good person is already dead on my account. I'm not letting Judy—or Bif for that matter—get hurt or worse just so I can get away."

Skeritt shone the flashlight in his face. "You sure? I doubt that's the Libidos pretending to be police. You go back now, you're turning yourself in. The worst Judy could be charged with is helping you escape, assuming they could make it stick."

"It doesn't matter. I'm tired of running."

"It's your call."

Danny nodded.

"About face then."

Abandoning the canoe, the two men headed back toward the lake. Skeritt handed the flashlight to Danny, telling him, "I'll go in front. Take the flashlight and aim it at my feet. It works better that way, for both of us."

When they were nearly there, Danny shouted, "Don't shoot! I'm turning myself in!"

Briefly, the grind of the house boat motor went silent, and the only sound was the footfalls the men made on the forest path. Then a shout, maybe fifty feet away: "Danny Grant, is that you? This is Officer Max Ainsley. You're under arrest!"

Danny heard a familiar woman's voice carp, "You sure *say* that a lot."

* * *

Linette Paquin felt herself get aroused when Danny Grant emerged from the woods. Not by her former client's buff jailhouse physique. Nor by his companion's shaggy features, much as she dug mountain men. Instead, Linette's excitement had to do with the red canvas duffel bag Danny held at his side.

"Drop your weapon," Officer Ainsley told the hairy woodsman. Seemingly surprised by the request, the man leaned the shotgun against a tree and stepped away from it.

"What's in the bag?" Officer Ainsley asked. Without waiting for an answer, he said, "Throw it over here."

Linette's eyes traced the arc of the bag as Danny tossed it toward Max's feet.

Danny said, "It's what you couldn't find four years ago. It's cash from the grow op. But I ain't gonna testify. Gonna do my time and start over some day. I'm done running."

Max pulled handcuffs from behind his back, still keeping his pistol trained on Danny. He took a step toward him before the bushy fellow said, "Maybe there's another way we can do this."

Officer Ainsley looked at him, questioning.

"What if I could help you break some other crimes?"

"What if you told me your name?"

"Skeritt," the man said.

Sasquatch, Linette translated. Why the hell was Max indulging him? He smelled like day-old road kill even fifteen feet away. Beard or no, she preferred her men showered.

"I'm listening," Max said. Linette sighed.

The man named Skeritt said, "For starters, I torched Ernest McCann's cabin."

"You saying you killed Ernie McCann?" Max looked incredulous.

"No, I just handled his cremation."

"What are you doing?" Danny protested.

"Relax, Danny," said Skeritt, and to Max, "You know well as I do this boy never did anything evil. Dumb ass mistakes, more like."

"I don't see why I'd let him go just so I can arrest you for some bushwhacked pyromania."

"I also set the fire that burned down the grow op. That's destruction of evidence, isn't it? I can vouch for the provenance of that bag of money, if you like, tell a judge what I saw in the barn before I set it aflame."

"You big on burning things?" asked the cop.

"Fire's always been rather useful in my book."

"Then I guess I can arrest you right along with young Mr. Grant, can't I? With a lawyer here as witness to you confessing..."

"True," Skeritt answered, smiling, "but I imagine that might require some explaining. It's not as though I don't recognize Ms. Paquin." Giving her a nod, he said, "Finding her here with you, though, makes me wonder all kinds of things."

Linette looked back and forth from Max to Skeritt to the red bag at her lover's feet. She glanced at Danny, standing there eyes wide, his chest heaving with every breath. The Sasquatch shot her a toothy grin full of teeth too white for his face. He went on, "Besides, there's one heck of a difference between me turning myself in and you trying to arrest both me *and* Danny to haul our asses back to town."

Danny said, "Skeritt, just leave. You don't have to do this."

"I deserve to go to jail much as you, Danny. Difference is, you've got a life to lead, two women who love you, and maybe even half a bag of money if the kind officer agrees to take the other half. Me, I could use a state-sponsored holiday from all my years in the bush."

Linette said, "Max, don't listen to him. Arrest Danny. He can go back and finish his sentence. *Speaking* as a lawyer—his lawyer, I might add—I don't think there's any way to tie this particular money to a four-year-old *crime* with no other evidence. I can just, ah, I can store it for him. In my office, in a safe, I mean."

Danny looked at her for the first time. Max told her to shut up. In the momentary silence, Linette heard another boat engine start, somewhere out beyond the houseboat. The men paid it no attention.

"There's more," Skeritt said. "Remember the Patterson sawmill in seventy-eight?"

"What about it," Max asked, tensing.

"Fire that killed seven people?"

"I know the fire. What are you saying?"

Danny said, "Skeritt?"

"Guilty," Skeritt said. "But it wasn't supposed to go down that way." He paused and looked around for a stump to sit on, settling for a fallen log.

Now there was no mistaking the sound of the approaching boat. It sounded more like a ski-boat, and a big one at that. Not a houseboat at all.

"Max, someone's coming," Linette said. "Who cares about some fire from last century?"

"Linette, for the last time, shut your mouth," Max hissed. "Tell us your story, old man, before I shoot you." Linette and Danny stared at the officer in surprise, but his reaction left Skeritt unfazed.

"It was the Canada Day weekend. Everyone should have been gone. No-one was ever supposed to have been hurt. I just wanted Prick Patterson to get his come-uppance. Figured either he'd use the insurance money to rebuild or maybe some better mill would pick up the slack, hire us all on—someone who valued their workers more than a flatbed full of two-by-sixes."

Max interrupted, finishing Skeritt's story. "But instead, one crew had been held back, forced to work overtime, and half of those are the ones who died that night." His voice raised half an octave when he continued. "And my aunt held dinner until nine o'clock before finding out her husband wouldn't be coming home at all, that night or any other night."

"That's right," Skeritt said. "Brad Ainsley. Finest trimmer I ever worked with."

"You son of a bitch, you killed my uncle."

"I'm sorry, son. It wasn't meant to happen. But you see how maybe I should be the one behind bars, instead of this kid who never did anything you or I might have tried before we came of age. Shoot me if you like, but I think there's a better way."

Linette watched Max closely. He no longer held the pistol level. It hung limp at his side and his hand was shaking. He had moved over to lean on the tree where Skeritt had left the shotgun.

He said, "I'm taking you both in. Tonight." He slumped to the ground, his back against the tree, sending the shotgun tumbling to the ground beside him. He started mumbling,

"Show them all...bring in Grant...the Patterson fire...be a hero..."

Neither Max nor the others seemed to care that the houseboat had nearly reached the end of the cove. Linette looked beyond it and saw that the other boat was a cabin cruiser and it had come closer to shore as well. Finally, her eyes settled on the duffel bag, lying there where Danny had tossed it. Sensing her claim to a just reward evaporating, she turned off the flashlight, grabbed the bag by the handle, and made a run for the shore.

She hadn't gotten more than fifty feet when a burst of gunfire came from the second boat. She heard Skeritt shout behind her. "That's a machine gun!"

She was running across an exposed granite slab littered with pine needles when her feet slid in opposite directions. She dropped the flashlight and reached out to grab an overhanging branch to avoid tumbling to the water. As she swung across the rock face, still clutching the duffel bag in her other hand, she felt the double-punch of two bullets slamming into her ribs.

Linette Paquin did not hear her own scream as she face-planted onto the wet rocks below and felt nothing more.

"Put the fucking gun away!" Hawk spat at Mongoose. "We want that jerkoff alive. And even out here someone's gonna hear that goddamn gun and know it's not for hunting."

"Ain't no gun's for huntin' when it's dark out, Hawk. Don't see why you's gotta get so cross at me."

"Shut it and help me keep an eye on the depth finder here."

From the cabin cruiser, they could make out the houseboat deep in the cove. Mongoose, who had liberally sprayed the boat with fifty-caliber bullets, pointed and said, "See, it worked, Hawk. I done good."

"Look at the map. There's one way in and one way out. Problem is, the rocks make it hard for us to follow them in. I say we anchor here and wait here until morning. He's not gonna swim off the island with the money. And that pontoon plunker will be easy to catch whenever he moves."

* * *

"Paddle harder," Perko hissed. Terry struggled to maneuver the rubber lifeboat toward the island; the wind pushed hard the other way. Perko had wrapped three fingers of his left hand in a wet sock and stuffed them into the slit cut by Mongoose minutes before. With his other hand, he took a swig of the brandy Mongoose had given him as a going away present, the bottle already half empty. The dinghy's donut-shaped sides were getting spongy and no matter how hard Terry tried, the wind kept pushing them in the wrong direction.

Perko wished like hell he knew how to swim.

THIRTY-TWO

When Linette came to, she was staring into a wide brown face, creased more by weather than age. His head fringed with thick black hair, illuminated by a flashlight that kept flickering back and forth, the big fucking Indian looked positively spiritual.

"Am I dead?" asked Linette. She lay crumpled on her side on bright green indoor outdoor carpeting. The ground under the carpeting swelled gently up and down. She could make out several sets of legs. "Is this Hell? Am I on the River Styx?"

"You've been shot, Linette," said a familiar voice. "Stay calm."

"Shot? What?" she asked, her eyes rolling in her head. When they rolled, they hurt, so she closed them again. "Shot by who? Ernie? Did Ernie shoot me?"

"What's she babbling about?" another voice asked, older than the first one.

"Just relax and be quiet, Linette," said the familiar voice. She opened her eyes and scanned up the legs to the faces that towered above her and the Indian. They swam in and out of focus, but one of them was Officer Max.

"I think I'd like to hear what she has to say," said one of the faces, the one with the older voice. To Linette, the face's long grey hair and beard made it look a whole lot like an ancient Jesus. Maybe she was dead, after all. Was that a boat engine she could hear chugging nearby? Didn't they still use those long poles to push the death barges across the Styx?

Jesus Face said, "Why the hell do you think Ernie would want to shoot your ass?" Linette frowned, thinking Jesus had become more than a little rude in his old age. The bearded guy leaned in real close and breathed beer and barbeque sauce in her face. "You were there, weren't you?" he said. "Last week. When Ernie was killed."

"Yes, I mean, no, I mean...I was there. Max, tell them what I *told* you."

"Tell me yourself," said Jesus Face. She struggled to remember his name. Scary something. Wasn't Jesus supposed to be the good guy?

The Indian seemed a whole lot nicer. He leaned in close with a tuft of dried grass or something; it was burning flameless and he blew the smoke in her face. She closed her eyes again and listened to his smooth voice, chanting now.

"Nnnaaagitcha wooooo woooo haaaaa naaaaa weeeeooooh," it sounded like. Then she heard the Indian say, "She's going quick. Passage is going to be a thirsty one if she dies with lies on her tongue." He blew more smoke; it smelled sweet. But her throat was dry and cracking.

"Confession time," said Jesus Face.

"Don't say anything," said Max.

Linette felt as though she was passing out. She took a deep breath and choked on the pungent smoke before pushing the Indian's arm out of the way.

"I went by Ernie's cabin on the day of the fire," she said. "I was up in the attic when I heard him shout at someone to get lost. Next thing I heard was the gun blast. Twice. Then whoever shot him just walked away. No hurry. I didn't see who it was. And when I finally climbed down, Ernie was there, dead. There was a shot gun. On the floor. Beside him. I was so freaked out, I ran."

"You ran?" said Jesus Face. He was so close his long beard waggled on Linette's chin as he spoke. It tickled. Linette closed her eyes tight, as much to avoid staring into the old man's face as to lessen the pounding in her skull. Scary. Scary. Skeritt! That was it. She peeked with one eye. He asked, "Didn't you try to help him? Call an ambulance? Why did you run?"

"Hey, back off, buddy," Officer Max put a hand on Skeritt's shoulder and pulled him away. "The lady was freaked out, alright? You would be, too, finding a man lying in his doorway with his face blown off."

The old man wouldn't relent. "What were you doing there?"

"I was looking for the money," Linette said, expelling a lungful of charred air. At the end of it, she tasted blood. "The money Danny stole from the grow op. Ernie had it. I know he did! Max, can't you make this guy leave me alone?" She squeezed her eyes even more tightly shut and scrunched up her face as if she could shut out the world that way.

"Fucking hell!" she heard Danny Grant say. "You were supposed to be on *my* side!"

Linette peeled one eye open again and looked up to see him elbowing his way into the circle of men.

"You were my lawyer. If I couldn't trust you, who *could* I trust?"

"Never mind, Danny," Skeritt said to him. "There's something else here that's bothering me." He leaned in so close she could feel his acrid breath warm her cheeks. Spitting each word's into her face, he said: "I was there, too, lady. Right after you, I imagine, 'cause Ernie's body was still warm when I found him. Only he was face-down, not on his back like you're saying."

Linette used her open eye to scan his face. He was back down on one knee, his blackened eye sockets pressed close to hers. She said, "I didn't say he was on his back. He was face down, just like you said."

The Indian pulled Skeritt away and Danny followed them into the boat's cabin. Linette heard them murmuring to each other a few yards away. Max leaned down and took her pulse. Some kind of animal pushed a wet snout into her face. She tasted barbeque sauce on her lips, like she'd been kissing Jesus Face. She retched at the thought.

"You're going to survive this, Linette," Max said. "You're going to live and I think maybe you should just shut up, now."

"Why, Max? I didn't do anything wrong. Trespass, maybe. Not call the police? Who cares, the old coot was dead." The beastie had starting licking her ear. It nipped her when she shook her head. She swatted at it, connecting with a ball of fluff and ending up with a fist full of matted fur. The thing yelped and darted away, yapping.

Linette heard a woman call out, "Wort. Come back here, Wort. Oh, darn."

Skeritt and the Indian strode back across the boat deck. Linette saw Danny reach for the red duffel bag. "Max, stop them," she protested, pushing herself up on one elbow. "They're taking my MONEY." The bag banged against Danny's knee as he leapt onto the shore and disappeared into the woods followed by Ernie's nosy neighbor and her dog.

"STOP," Officer Max called out. "You two get back here." He put his hand on his holster, but the Indian stood in his way, arms crossed over his chest.

"I think we have a little more to talk about," Skeritt said.

Max looked from Skeritt to the Indian to Linette, who pushed her pout so hard her lip wrapped around her chin.

Skeritt said, "Start with how you knew Ernie's face was blown off."

"What are you talking about?" asked Max, standing there, staring.

"What's wrong, Max?" Linette said. "You're letting them get *AWAY*."

"See, when I got to Ernie's cabin, he was face down," Skeritt said. "Linette here says the same thing. Yet somehow you knew he had his face shot clean off."

The Indian added, "It was you, not her, said that about his face. A minute ago."

"The autopsy, they said—" Max started.

The old man cut him off. "I soaked Ernie but good before cremating him, and that place burned to the ground. You trying to tell me they found buck shot mixed in the ashes and somehow deduced it came from his cheeks?"

Max started to back away. The Indian stepped behind him and put a hand on his shoulder.

Skeritt said, "The only way you could have known he was killed by a close range head shot was if you were there when it happened." Turning to Linette, he asked, "Did you hear voices, arguing, anything?"

"Just Ernie...shouting...and the gun blast...twice..."

"What about after the gun? Between the blasts?"

"Nothing. Like I said. Max? What's he saying, Max?"

"Shut up, Linette."

"Tell us," said Skeritt.

Max's shoulders slumped. The old man shone the flashlight right in his face and she watched it twist with anger.

"Nothing but taunts and humiliations I got when Danny Grant got sent away. Biggest bust of my career it could have been. Wasn't my fault. Sure, I could have called for backup and maybe I didn't have a warrant for the farmhouse, but how was I to know what I was walking into?

"I got over it," he said. "Did the job well as anyone. Then you," turning to Linette, "you show up and start digging at me, asking all your questions, all that damn pillow talk, pumping me for information. I knew you were after the money long before you told me. And I figured if anyone had a right to it, why not me? It didn't belong to anybody. Just drug money. And ol' Ernie McCann, laughing at us all from the top of the world while my uncle died in a fire that...that you...YOU STARTED!"

"Sorry, pal," Skeritt said, "I never set that sawmill fire. I made that up to stall for time. Figure how to get Danny out of here."

"Bastard," said Max.

"I did know your uncle, though. Good man, that Brad. Rest his soul." Jesus Face smiled at him. "Can't say he'd be proud of you."

Pain rippled down Linette's back; she let herself lie back on her good side and shut her eyes tight.

She head Max say, "I went over that afternoon to try and strong arm him, tell him I'd oppose Danny's parole, try to make him tell me where the money was. But when I got there, he just laughed at me. Pointed the gun and told me to get off his property. I guess I lost it. I crouched low and charged him, figuring if he fired, he'd miss me. He aimed the gun high, fired a warning shot. I tripped on his step and we both went down. The gun fired again. I was on top of him, flat on his back, his face shot off. I couldn't stand to look at it. It was me rolled him over."

"And left him there to bleed out."

"If he wasn't dead from the blast, he would have wanted to be. You saw him. Saw his face. Doesn't matter the guy couldn't see himself in the mirror. That's no way to live. No matter how much money you have."

Max looked from Skeritt to the Indian and back. "So now what? Are *you* going to arrest *me?*"

"Not my line of work, but I believe we've got the makings of a pretty simple deal here," Skeritt said. "You're not going to say a word about finding Danny. For our part, we're going to forget what you just told us. Right, Big Fucker ?"

The Indian nodded, saying, "Besides, you don't need to be explaining to nobody how in hell you wound up out here in the middle of nowhere with a boatload of Libidos. Never mind your lawyer friend full of bullets."

Linette flashed back to images of the rocks rushing up to meet her and started to black out again. Maybe this was just a bad dream. Unless she was dying after all. She opened her eyes again. Everything was blurry and dark. "Do you have any more of that smoky medicine?" she asked.

"Made all that shit up," said the Indian. "Not bad, eh?"

To Max, Skeritt said, "Me and my pal are going to help you convince those biker buffoons they don't need no cop-killing on their rap sheets. But only after we're sure Danny has got away clean. Either that, or you can imagine what kind of fireworks we're all in for."

As if on cue, a shower of sparks and flame erupted into the air from the hilltop where the bonfire had been earlier. It was positively explosive, bright red and gold, shooting forty feet in the air, and crackling.

Linette said, "Fuck me. I've died and gone to *Hell*."

Chasing Judy chasing Wort up the path to the fire pit, Danny couldn't believe the energy she'd suddenly found. Gone was her stupor, replaced with an adrenalized strength that made it hard to keep up. By the time he reached the clearing, she had caught the dog and was holding him, shaking, on a stump by the fire.

"Help me load on these boughs," he told her.

"Why? This is no time for a bonfire."

"Just grab some. Throw them on the fire a few at a time." He'd already loaded an armful and, after appearing to smother the flames, the waxy green boughs were lighting up like a chemical blaze. He threw another armful and another. With each load the fire grew stronger and the fresh boughs caught faster until the flames raged as high as the trees ringing the clearing.

"Keep loading," he said, as Judy joined in. Wort dashed under the upturned canoe at the edge of the clearing and barked madly.

When all the cedar Bif had trimmed was loaded onto the pile, Danny scooped up Wort and motioned for Judy to help him carry the canoe.

"We'll go down the back side," he said. "This is supposed to be the best way to deal with bears. Let's see how it works against bikers."

By the time Terry's paddle hit rock, the water had started splashing over the dinghy's rubber walls.

"We can touch," Terry said, doing his level best to sound cheerful.

Perko launched himself over the side of the boat, splashing headfirst into the icy water. Sputtering, he pushed himself upright, seemingly oblivious to the cold. Terry saw that somehow he had managed to keep hold of the bottle of brandy though the bottom had broken off against the rocks underwater.

He heard some crackling from the island behind him and turned to see the sky lit red over the hill. It looked warm, Terry thought.

Hawk and Mongoose had the best view of the hilltop fire.

"Is that a volcano?" asked Mongoose. "I didn't know we had some around here."

"Gimme a break, Mongoose," Hawk answered. "It's a fire. A heck of a big one, too. Bet you could see that from the other end of the lake."

He told Mongoose to fire the machine gun in the air, telling him, "Let's make sure that punk and whoever's helping him know we're here, we're armed, and there's no getting away."

"What if they splits to the other side of the island?"

"And what, swim to safety? Do you have any idea how cold that water is? Naw, we just keep 'em busy until daylight and then figure out exactly what we're dealing with. Moron thinks this is a good night for a bonfire? A little something special, woodsy cuddling with his gal? Let him enjoy himself. We'll show him special."

Mongoose fired off a few more rounds and sat on the cabin bench. The fire on the island had already burned down.

"Hawk?" he asked after a few minutes. "What if them's got another boat? Like we had a dinghy on the cabin cruiser. Think maybe they could have somethin' like that on the houseboat? I'se just wonderin'."

Hawk took a long pull of bourbon and said, "I didn't see no dinghy."

"True," said Mongoose. "But it's dark out, ain't it? I just mean..."

Hawk looked at Mongoose, emptied the bottle and set it down on the cabin table. He stared without speaking.

Mongoose lit a smoke and lay back on the bench. "You know, a boat's not half bad when it ain't moving," he said. "Kinda rocks a bit, but if you pretends it's a waterbed..."

He never finished the thought. Out of nowhere, the sky erupted in a roar like ten Harleys. Hawk looked out the window to see a floatplane buzz the cabin cruiser. Mongoose leapt to his feet, cigarette dangling from his lip, and fired the machine gun into air after it.

The plane cut a wide circle behind the island and then reappeared, heading straight at them. This time, there was a blast of gunfire aimed at the cruiser. The plane dipped its wing nearly into the water and veered dangerously close to the boat before arcing back into the sky and disappearing again.

"I hit it, Hawk! I knows I did. You see that?" Mongoose was giddy.

"At least now we know what that fire was about. It was a signal." Hawk sniffed at the air. "You smell that?" he asked.

"What?"

"That. Gasoline." The smell was filling the cabin quickly. "They hit our gas tank," said Hawk. "Mongoose, put out your fucking smoke."

Obliging, Mongoose tossed the cigarette out the window and into the water. The slick surrounding the boat rippled into a bright orange dance covered by smoke darker than night. The fire on water appeared to mesmerize Mongoose until Hawk said, "Fucker's gonna BLOW."

The rail-thin biker kicked off his shoes, leapt out of the cabin, and did a long deep dive off the bow of the boat. By the time his head came back above water, beyond the ring of fire, Mongoose could be seen running back and forth across the foredeck, shouting, "I CAN'T SWIM. I CAN'T SWIM."

The boat was engulfed in flames. Hawk ducked under water when he heard the ammunition start exploding. He felt some shrapnel strike his body, its force blunted by traveling the last few feet under water. The cruiser's gas tank blew when his head was above water taking a breath. The heat dried his face in an instant and the last thing he saw was Mongoose, hair on fire, hurled through the sky lit up like a fireworks display. He screamed, "Ise gonna get you in Hell, PERKOOOOOO!!!"

THIRTY-THREE

The open water reflected what little light there was from the cloudy sky. It seemed dreadfully dark and gloomy after the bonfire. Danny hugged the island in the canoe, waiting until they were at its southwestern tip before making a dash for the mainland shore. There was less water to cross there and with any luck the wind would be lower and the waves a little smaller.

Judy huddled in the bow, shivering with Wort under a blanket Danny had grabbed from the lean-to. Danny told her to save her strength to help him paddle when they made the final dash.

They had gotten only a few hundred feet when the distant buzz of what could have been a cigarette boat grew to a thundering throttle as a float plane cleared the island directly above them. Danny thought he'd heard gunfire just before the sky filled with the engine's scream. Judy turned toward him, eyes bulged. Danny just grinned.

"Mom was right about the fire," he said. "Works like she said it would."

He stopped paddling and watched the plane dip its wings in a wave before turning back. When it disappeared behind the island, he shot Judy a puzzled look which became a frown when the gunfire erupted again, clearer this time, and more of it.

He listened as the sound of the plane receded and then started back again. The wind and waves had nearly pushed them onto the rocky shoreline while he'd been distracted. He took up the paddle to move them to deeper water. Explosions, one after the other, echoed around the lake. Danny leaned into the waves and shouted at Judy to paddle with him.

He never saw Perko until the soaking wet Libido lunged at him from his perch on a boulder just beyond the island's southernmost point. In his right hand, the crazed biker clutched a broken liquor bottle whose jagged bottom slashed Danny's arm. He tumbled backward into shallow water. Going under, Danny heard Judy shriek.

He jumped up and faced Perko. The biker teetered toward him, swinging the bottle like a windmill, around and around again. Danny reached out the paddle on the down-swing and Perko's own momentum plunged him into the lake. Danny was surprised at how strong the man became once his head was under water. The guy let go of the bottle and bear-hugged both of Danny's legs, wrapping his arms behind his knees and landing him ass-first in the lake. Danny tried to pry the larger man off with his legs but the cold sapped his own strength quickly and he felt himself slip under and breathe a lungful of icy Kawartha Klear. Perko clawed his way up his body, snarling like a dog.

"You punk piece of shit fuckhead farmer. Think I'd let you get away?" Danny felt Perko's shouts as much as heard them. The biker coughed and spat and shouted all at once. His fingers found Danny's throat and the two men tumbled together under the water, onto the jagged bottom. Danny choked and tasted blood. Then he felt himself drift weightlessly as he heard Judy scream from what seemed miles away.

His heels bounced along the rocks, waves splashing over his face. His lungs hammered water back up his throat. The sting inside his head brought on by the ice cold water coursing through his sinuses finally jarred Danny into a stunned reaction. He rolled to one side and felt his arm scrape a ridge of zebra mussels, slicing a hundred cuts. His hands and knees found bottom together and he pushed his back up out of the water, waiting for Perko's next attack.

The attack never came.

Instead, when Danny turned to face the biker, he saw Terry Miner, an oar clutched in both hands like a baseball bat, swinging while he shouted at a retreating Perko. The biker had blood streaming from his forehead and he kept collapsing into the water as he stumbled for the shore.

Judy held a paddle above her head like an ax, her arms shaking. "Leave him alone!" she screamed. She stepped toward Perko. "I'll kill you myself!"

The wind pushed the overturned canoe further from shore. Danny waded toward it and when the water reached his waist, he buried his face in the lake and swam for it as hard as he could. It was no more than forty strokes but by the time he reached it, it was all Danny could do to grasp hold and keep his chin above water so he could breathe. Following Terry and Judy's shouts, he kicked his legs and guided the vessel back toward shallow water.

The other two waded out to meet him. They tipped the canoe to drain the water, and struggled to lift Danny aboard. Before crumpling to the bottom, he peered over the edge and saw Perko stomping in anger, both arms waving in the air, but never coming further than knee-deep before retreating toward the safety of dry land.

It took only a couple of minutes for Terry and Judy to paddle the canoe with Danny in it over to the seaplane where it had landed during the fight with Perko.

Two stern-faced men with short black hair and leathery faces grabbed Danny under the armpits and hauled him onto the plane, clutching the duffel bag. He started to tell them who he was but they cut him off.

"You're with Big Fucker," one said, settling into the pilot's chair. "Where's he at?"

"We left him at the cove," said Danny. "The cops are there. Bikers, too."

The other man snorted, "I wouldn't worry about those bikers."

Danny sighed. "I need to get out of here."

"Something to do with that bag you're hugging?"

He held it tighter.

"Relax, kid," said the pilot, "we know all about your treasure. It may be a little light, actually. Placed a couple of big bets for you at roulette. Lost, I'm afraid."

"Think of it as 'Indian Tax,'" added the navigator.

"What happens now?" Danny asked.

"Figure maybe we can drop you in the States, northern New York, get you on your way."

"How the hell are you guys gonna get me across the border?"

274

"We fly in Indian airspace," the pilot answered.

"I didn't even know that existed," said Danny.

"Neither do the authorities, White Man."

Clutching Wort to her chest, Judy climbed into the plane and said, "I'm coming with you."

Danny pressed her against him, her arms curved across his back. His right arm was burning where the zebra mussels had scraped him. Bits and pieces of shell stuck in and under his skin. He knew he'd have better luck pulling the glass out of his other arm where Perko had jabbed him with the bottle.

To Judy, he said, "This is my road. You get caught with me, you're going to jail. You don't need that."

Terry looked up at them from the canoe, holding it against the plane's pontoon.

Judy dropped her arm from Danny's back and turned him toward her, shaking his shoulders. "You think I'm in this for kicks? Been helping you without knowing the risks? That gang isn't going to roll over and forget about you *or me.*"

Danny stared into her eyes, marveling. She was the first person to ever look back quite that way.

"Ernie was pretty much the only guy who remotely cared whether I even got up in the morning," she said, "and I told you from the start, I was in this for him. Now, you think you're going to leave me here while you go looking for your mother on some beach somewhere?"

"You'd run with me?" Danny asked her.

She kissed him and nodded.

The pilot started the plane's engine. It sputtered and died. He tried again, producing a whining sound that made him frown at the navigator.

"We got issues," he said.

The navigator stepped out onto the right side pontoon and clambered around to the front of the plane. Danny watched as he ran his hand along the engine cover.

"Shot all to hell and leaking big time," he said. "Lucky we landed when we did."

Terry said, "Whatever you two decide, make it quick. I'd kinda like to get a move on. Christmas on the island with Perko ain't my idea of fun."

Danny looked at Judy, took the red bag with him, and descended into the canoe. He reached up to help Judy follow him.

He said, "Terry, ol'-buddy-ol'-pal. Think maybe you could find us a boat?"

THIRTY-FOUR

Perko had scrambled up and over the island, finding his way to one of the trails that led to the Indian fire pit where he spent the night sleeping fitfully.

Now, morning, he stood on a granite ledge that gave him a clear view of the lake to the north, east, and south. His breath fogged around him. It smelled like it might snow. The cold air blown in from the north had settled on the trees, fringing everything with a dusting of frost that would have been spectacularly beautiful under different circumstances, even to the black-hearted biker.

He scanned the shoreline for any sign of life, but apart from two docks pulled high awaiting winter, this end of the lake was uninhabited, bordering as it did the Great Horned Owl First Nations Reserve.

To the northeast, in the morning water still as glass, he saw a small black dot with gentle ripples fanning out to either side. It seemed to take forever to approach the island, and Perko eventually realized it was neither an otter nor a muskrat. No, the only animal with a noggin that size was a bear. And, clearly, this bear knew where it was headed.

AUTHOR'S NOTE

The Kawarthas are a place not unlike most of rural Ontario, rugged in spots, genteel in others, rich in character throughout. You don't carve society out of rocks and trees in a couple hundred years of hard winters and mind-blowing summers without creating a few wackos along the way. I imagine the same can be said of dirt roads and bush wherever they be found. While I've done my best to capture the essence of the land, readers who know the Kawarthas will quickly see I have fabricated a little geography, bastardized some more, and retained a few parts intact. Thing is, if I'd left the map real, a few decent folk—and it is they who dominate the landscape, after all—could get mistaken for nut jobs. And a couple of these latter might get found.

ACKNOWLEDGMENTS

I didn't spend a decade crafting my debut novel without leaning on my friends along the way. I'd love to thank them all in print, but then my publisher would ask me to cut another 1,000 words or so.

Special thanks are due Les Edgerton, Chip MacGregor, Eric and Christy Campbell, and Elsa Franklin for believing in my work. And to Todd Robinson for being the first editor to pay cold hard cash for my fiction.

Thank you to Owen Laukkanen, DJ MacIntosh, Jill Edmondson, Melodie Campbell, Robert Rotenberg, and so many other accomplished Canadian crime fiction authors who gave feedback, answered boneheaded questions, and kept me plugging.

Tanis Mallow, how *can* I thank you enough?

And thanks to Dominique Racanelli, Dave Power, Laura Di Cesare, Mike and Saira Fitzgerald, Rosemarie, Bruce Saunders, Curtis and Rheo Brunet—all of whom slogged through a succession of drafts I dared call penultimate when *clearly* they were nothing of the kind.

I did my best to learn from the Imperial Literary Society (Dan Dowhal, Randal Heide, Brian Jantzi, Edward Lee, and Rob Crabtree), the Second Cup crew (Selena Cristo-Williams, Kristin Crawford, and Monica Pacheco), the Old Nick gang (Jann Everard, Kim Murray, and Scott Mathison), and a raft of other writers met under the auspices of the inimitably cranky—and *hilarious*—Cordelia Strube.

STINKING RICH simply would not exist were it not for the most meaningful, constant, daily dose of support from my wife Maria and our two children who grew up watching their old man write this thing: Alexandra and Jaeger.

ABOUT THE AUTHOR

Rob Brunet is the author of short stories appearing in Thuglit, Crimespree, Ellery Queen Mystery Magazine, Noir Nation, Shotgun Honey, and Out of the Gutter. He loves the bush, the beach, and bonfires. He lives in Toronto with his wife, son, and daughter.

Twitter @RRBrunet
http://www.robbrunet.com/

OTHER TITLES FROM DOWN AND OUT BOOKS

See www.DownAndOutBooks.com for complete list

By J.L. Abramo
Catching Water in a Net
Clutching at Straws
Counting to Infinity
Gravesend
Chasing Charlie Chan
Circling the Runway (*)

By Trey R. Barker
2,000 Miles to Open Road
Road Gig: A Novella
Exit Blood

By Richard Barre
The Innocents
Bearing Secrets
Christmas Stories
The Ghosts of Morning
Blackheart Highway
Burning Moon
Echo Bay
Lost

By Rob Brunet
Stinking Rich

By Milton T. Burton
Texas Noir

By Reed Farrel Coleman
The Brooklyn Rules

By Tom Crowley
Vipers Tail
Murder in the Slaughterhouse

By Frank De Blase
Pine Box for a Pin-Up
Busted Valentines and Other Dark Delights
The Cougar's Kiss (*)

By Les Edgerton
The Genuine, Imitation, Plastic Kidnapping

By A.C. Frieden
Tranquility Denied
The Serpent's Game

By Jack Getze
Big Numbers
Big Money
Big Mojo

By Keith Gilman
Bad Habits

(*)—Coming Soon